GODLY WARS

PROF CROFT 11

BRAD MAGNARELLA

THE PROF CROFT SERIES

1

"I need you to stay put," I told Tabitha.

"Do I look like I'm on the verge of springing into jumping jacks?"

I glanced over at the pet bed I'd brought down to my new basement-level lab. My cat not only filled out the bed, intended for dogs, but her stomach was slumping over the side. She stared at me with hooded lids.

"No," I said, "but I'm going to try to penetrate this thing—"

"Kinky."

"*And,*" I spoke over her, "it could produce some fireworks. This is for your safety as much as mine."

I circled the iron-topped island on which an elaborate casting circle had begun to glow. A tactical whip rested at the circle's center, a weapon I'd recovered from the shadow realm. It looked simple enough—a duct tape-wrapped handle and a two-foot length of steel cable—but it was infused with powerful magic. Magic a red-bearded biker had used to take me down and nearly finish me.

So far, my reveal spells had revealed only a robust layer of protection. If I wanted to see past it, I would need to up the risk factor.

Tabitha looked around with a sour face. "What am I even doing in this miserable cave?"

"Ricki needs her rest," I said, referring to my very pregnant wife, "and you weren't helping."

"I was just trying to be conversational."

"Asking if she's having triplets, when you already know the answer, is poor conversation."

"Well, you have to admit, she's looking appallingly large to be carrying a lone child."

I snorted. "'Appallingly large'? Coming from you?" Ricki looked fine—Tabitha had been goading her all morning, and now she was testing me. Before she could fire back, I said, "All right, shush now, shut up. This is serious."

Tabitha scowled, then made several attempts to flop onto her other side. "Darling?" she asked.

"*Vigore,*" I muttered, flicking my fingers. A small force invocation crossed the room and helped her complete the roll.

As she settled into place, I cracked my knuckles and lifted a scalpel-like instrument from beside the casting circle. Silvery light glistened along the blade's enchanted edge. After checking to ensure both my feet were inside my protective circle, I leaned over the whip's cable like a surgeon assessing a spine. I lowered the blade into position, poised to make a very fine, very subtle incision through the protection.

Thank God Bree-yark had completed the buildout of my basement space when he did. I wasn't sure I would have attempted this in our apartment. Tensing my jaw, I drew a short line with the blade.

Easy does it...

The tip passed between two of the whip's coiled strands, not quite touching steel. A crackle of magic on magic sounded and then a faint hiss, like escaping air.

It was working. The whip's protection was separating along the incision, coming open.

CRACK!

I squinted from a violent flash of light. The whip kicked upright, its cable branching into a terrifying tree of steel cords.

The cords began to writhe and snap like lightning, igniting a searing pain in my chest: an echo of the weapon's assault on me in the shadow realm. With the next flash, I caught the silhouette of a looming figure.

"Damn," I grunted.

Fist to my heart, I drew my cane from my belt. But the casting circle was working as designed. In a swirling column of copper, it climbed around the whip, shrouding the figure. More flashes and cracks erupted, but they were muted, like heat lightning in a dust storm.

Tapping into one of the casting circle's sigils, I called, "*Inspirare!*"

Magic coursed around the sigil's elaborate lines, and an oscillating hum took up. It rattled the books and spell implements on my shelves. And then everything collapsed back to the table, including the deafening sound.

I lowered my hands from my ears.

The whip lay inert, its protective layer intact again. The casting circle around it had gone dim, save for my special sigil which pulsed gently. Closer inspection showed a faint mist darting around the sigil's mazelike trap.

"Yes!" I'd captured a quantum of the magic powering the whip.

The next step was to prep it for examination, to discover the origin of the energy. I couldn't shake the feeling that whatever powered the whip was somehow connected to the absence of magic-users in the shadow realm, including me. Remembering the looming figure, I wondered if we were dealing with another god.

You're not supposed to exist, Red Beard had told me.

I buried the tactical whip in a bag of gray salt and placed it inside my warded safe. From a bin of bottles, I retrieved one with a dropper lid. The charged tip slid easily into the sigil's small opening. As the dropper inhaled the misty essence, my phone buzzed on a nearby shelf.

"You're gonna have to wait," I called, my voice tense as a guy-wire. I couldn't afford to lose focus now.

Upon drawing out the remaining essence, I squeezed it into the bottle and sealed the cap tightly. Only after placing the bottle beside the bag of salt in the warded safe did I release my breath.

When the phone buzzed again, I retrieved it, expecting to find Bree-yark's name on the display—he'd been coming over most days to add features to the hidden entertainment room —but it was Detective Hoffman.

"Hey," I answered. "Everything all right?"

"I should be asking you that," he growled. "You're late."

A quick perusal of my memory produced the forgotten deadline. "Crap. That's today, isn't it?"

"This morning."

We were talking about the release of Arimanius, a Greek god Hermes had delivered from the shadow realm and set loose in the city. During his time in New York, Arimanius had directed a host of wererats to kidnap civilians in an attempt to kickstart a comedy career—despite the god lacking a comedic bone in his body. Fortunately, we apprehended "Mr. Funny" before he could do more damage. Unfortunately, the amount of time the NYPD could hold him without charges had just expired.

"Nothing from Hermes?" Hoffman asked.

"No. Alec has been, well, Alec," I said, referring to the son of my shadow, who was under the influence of the Greek god.

"Great," Hoffman grumbled. "Know of any place we can stick this guy?"

Hermes had claimed to be holding the god as insurance, in the event he needed him for a war against Persephone. He didn't seem terribly worried about securing him, though. Did I mention I was sick of the Greek gods?

I peered around. "I suppose I can hold him down here."

"Fine. I've got the Sup Squad on standby for transport."

"Just give me a few minutes to prep the space and I'll head right over."

"You've grown on me, Croft, but if I have to song-and-dance the DA's office to buy us another couple hours, that might change."

"I'll work fast," I promised.

I ended the call and surveyed the basement again. Already warded, it just needed a couple modifications to hold the minor god. But first I needed to clear the space of all extraneous lifeforms. Across the room, Tabitha remained facing the wall. Miraculously, she'd slept through the entire ordeal with the whip.

"Good news, Tabs. You just pulled a 'get out of jail free' card."

Ricki wasn't going to be happy, but hopefully she'd

managed to get some rest. When Tabitha didn't stir, I took a second look at her. Something was off.

"Tabby?" I called, crossing the room. Her side wasn't heaving and sinking. No snores, either. When I touched her, fear bit the back of my throat. She was stiff. With some effort, I rolled her toward me.

"Tabitha!" I yelled.

2

_____

"What's going on?" Ricki asked, sitting up from the couch.

I shoved the apartment door closed with a foot and, teetering under the weight of my cat, carried her toward her divan. "Not sure exactly," I panted. "One minute she was the Tabitha we know and tolerate, and in the next, she was like this. Stiff as a board."

As I set her down on the cushion, my wife arrived beside me. She passed a hand in front of Tabitha's staring green eyes, then prodded her. Normally, her finger would have sunk to the knuckle, but it stopped cold. Ricki leaned an ear down to my cat's bared teeth and checked her neck for a pulse.

"I'm not feeling anything, Everson."

"I didn't either. But she's not dead," I hastened to add.

When Ricki lifted her eyes to mine, they were sympathetic but serious. "She's already in rigor mortis."

"I'll explain in a sec. Can you watch her while I grab something?"

I scrambled up the ladder to my loft and searched

around. Because I was still in the process of moving things to the basement, the space was in disarray. I hopped over a pile of spell books and began digging through a container of pre-made potions. There! I seized the smoky bottle and hurried back down to the main floor.

Ricki stepped aside, holding the pregnant swell of her belly.

"She's in a state of suspended animation," I said, shaking the bottle. "*Attivare.*" The charge that shot down my arm ignited a collection of tiny granules in the bottle, setting them off like fireflies. "It's a self-preservation technique. All of Tabitha's essence withdrew into a space at her core about the size of a charcoal briquette."

"A reaction to the work you were doing?"

"Most likely. When I opened the whip's defenses, the entire thing jumped to life with this wild, crackling energy. The casting circle should have contained it, but some must have leaked out. Tabitha's succubus nature reacted to it, I'm guessing." I eyed the raised bottle as I spoke, waiting for the potion to finish activating.

"Exactly how urgent is this?"

I looked over at her. "What do you mean?"

"If it's not life-threatening, can't she just... stay like this for a while?"

"If she were young and healthy, sure. I'd let her essence return in its own sweet time. I get it—we could all use the break, my wallet included. Her tastes aren't cheap. But that's the problem. Thanks to Tabitha's eating habits, and her resulting mass, she's at risk of crushing that briquette right out of existence."

Ricki raised a slender eyebrow in a way that asked, *Is that a problem?*

"We could lose her for good," I said, surprised by the emotion in my voice. Like a patched coat or a faulty appliance only I could operate, she'd become a habitual part of my life, oddly comforting. "Look, I know she's a forty-pound pain in the butt, but she's family. I mean, I tolerate your brother Carlos for the same reason."

Ricki smirked. "Fair enough. What's that going to do?"

The potion in my hand had begun to glow with silvery light.

"It's a stimulant. Though not specifically designed for cases like hers, it should excite her essence enough to return to her body."

I pulled a plastic syringe from a coat pocket, drew out half the potion, and rolled Tabitha's statuesque body over so her face was aimed toward the ceiling. Inserting the syringe into her mouth, I plunged the potion down her throat. "Hey, mind handing me those books beside my reading chair?"

When Ricki brought them over, I used the thick books to prop Tabitha in position so the potion wouldn't come back out.

"Okay," I breathed.

"How long will it take to act?"

"Not long once it seeps into her system. The problem is she's locked up so tight, the seeping-into-her-system part could be a while. She's going to need to stay positioned like this for the rest of the day."

"Well, a break's a break," Ricki sighed.

When my phone rang, I pulled it from my pocket and checked the display. "Crap, it's Hoffman. I'm overdue at IPP." I silenced the phone. "Would you mind checking on her now and again while I run downtown? Our time's up on holding the rat god, and I told Hoffman we could stick him in the downstairs unit."

"Here?"

"Just until I can come up with something better, or Hermes decides he doesn't need him." I peered past her at the closed door of our guest bedroom, where the son of my shadow had been staying for the past week. Having him here felt surreal and natural at the same time. Wonderful, in either case.

"Is Alec still sleeping?" I asked.

"He left about an hour ago, fully dressed and sporting his pack. I offered him breakfast, but he said there were some things he needed to do."

I nodded thoughtfully. He'd said the same thing to me a couple times that week. I suspected he was traveling to the shadow realm to check on his mother, which was dangerous enough. My greater concern, though, was that he was running errands for Hermes, who was in a standoff against a vindictive version of Persephone. Though Alec claimed Hermes hadn't visited lately, he really had no way of knowing. The disturbing reality was that no matter how much I trained Alec or how frequently Claudius or Mae loosened his bonds, the Tablet of Hermes had too powerful a hold over him.

Ricki's hand smoothed my brow, and she kissed my cheek.

"Go, babe," she said. "I've got everything covered here. Any special instructions for when Sleeping Beauty wakes up?"

"More like Queen Maleficent," I muttered. "Warm goat's milk would be good. A tuna steak, if she feels up to it—the fish oils will help lube out any remaining stiffness. She may just want to sleep, though."

"No, she'll want to eat."

I laughed. "You know her too well."

"She's not exactly an enigma." Ricki's smile straightened. "We'll get through this." She didn't mean Tabitha now. "We always do."

"I know."

But was it too much to ask for a clear board for our daughter's arrival? No more warring gods or shadow realms or threats to our existence? I rubbed the beautiful swell of Ricki's belly, kissed her softly, and drew my cane from my belt. The sooner I could straighten out this god mess, the better.

3

_____

"Sorry I'm late," I announced, arriving in a special holding area of NYPD headquarters known as the Basement.

"Yeah, what else is new?" Detective Hoffman grumbled, closing a folder and pushing himself up from a desk. The crinkly state of his polyester suit coupled with his messy wreath of tight brown curls suggested he'd been up late the night before on at least one homicide case, possibly several.

I produced a plastic-lidded cup. "Picked one up for you in the lobby."

He accepted the coffee with a grunt, took a sip, and gave a grudging nod. The coffee here tasted like water wrung from a dish rag, but it was good enough for Hoffman.

"The twerps from the DA's office haven't come sniffing yet," he said, "so you caught a break."

I nodded toward the nearer cell, one of two I'd prepped to hold supernatural beings. "How's our friend doing?"

Hoffman jerked his head. "Come see for yourself."

He ambled over, still in an orthopedic boot from driving

his foot into a filing cabinet three weeks earlier. I'd offered to heal the fracture several times, but though he'd come around to the idea of magic, subjecting himself to it remained a bridge too far.

He parked beside the cell door window, and I followed his scornful gaze through the reinforced glass.

Inside, the portly god with dark, greasy hair and a glum face was clutching a fistful of papers as he paced the cell. He read one and scribbled on it with a pencil stub. Then he shook his head and tossed it to the floor, where it joined other discarded pages. As Arimanius consulted the next one, Hoffman signaled to the desk to flip on the speaker.

Arimanius cleared his throat. "'My wife and I were happy for about twenty years,'" he read. "'Then we met.'"

That's actually pretty good, I thought before realizing it wasn't his joke. Arimanius repeated the punchline several times and appeared to underline it.

"Why is meeting his wife funny?" he complained in his high voice. "Why does that make people *laugh*? 'Then we met...' 'Then we met...'" He repeated it as though he were pondering a riddle, then let out a beleaguered cry. The piece of paper fell to the floor, joining the others, and he moved on to the next one. Each one must have held a joke or stand-up bit he'd heard, and now he was laboring to dissect them.

"Still trying to grasp comedy, huh?" I said to Hoffman.

"Yeah, and failing miserably. Is your space ready for him?"

"Pretty much," I said, thinking of the hasty additions I'd made to the basement's wards. "I can tweak as needed."

"Well, I hope your neighbors have earplugs." Hoffman rapped the door with a knuckle. "Time's up, buddy. We're moving you."

Arimanius looked over at us, the bags under his grave

eyes damp with frustration. His commitment to comedy remained a puzzle given that he was a god of darkness who commanded rats. Even more puzzling was why Hermes thought he'd be an asset in any upcoming war with Persephone.

"Set down everything you're holding," Hoffman continued, "and face the back wall."

Sighing heavily, Arimanius let the pencil and remaining papers fall to the floor as he lumbered around in a half circle. Members of the Sup Squad arrived and covered the door. Hoffman passed me a set of cuffs I'd designed for holding supernaturals.

"Can you handle him?"

"Sure," I said, taking the cuffs.

"Hey, Mr. Funny," I said, entering the warded space and stepping through the cast-off pieces of paper. "I don't know if you remember me, but I'm Everson Croft. We talked a couple weeks ago?"

"I remember," he said quietly.

"We're going to get you out of here. I'm taking you to my place, in fact."

"You don't need those," he said somberly as I placed the cuffs around his wrists. "I'm not going anywhere. I'm a hack, a worthless waste of space. I'll never cut it on a stage. I might as well not even exist."

Man, this guy was depressing.

"Well... give it time. Sometimes comedy just clicks."

It was tepid reassurance, and he moaned in response. I finished cuffing him, Hoffman patted him down, and we escorted him from the Basement into the back of a waiting transport van. We joined the driver in front. As the van pulled into traffic, Hoffman glanced over at me,

"Hey, I appreciate you taking this guy off our hands. Any idea when you're gonna hear from Hermes?"

I sighed. "I trust he'll deign to speak to me at some point."

But would he? It had already been a week, and he hadn't so much as cleared his throat.

"You're a wizard. Can't you just, I don't know, wiggle your fingers and make him talk?"

"I've been tempted, but it's not that easy."

According to Arianna, the leader of my Order, it was important that I let Hermes come to me. *You're dealing with a god essence,* she'd said, *and they're often capricious. Few more than Hermes.* He was also using Alec as a vessel, and I didn't want to attempt anything that might harm the boy.

"Well, for your sake, I hope it's soon." Hoffman gestured with his coffee toward a dashboard monitor. It showed Arimanius strapped into a seat in the van's warded hold. He was talking to himself and breaking down into sobs, still confounded by his utter inability to comprehend comedy.

As I nodded in agreement, the driver's radio crackled. "*All available Squad members requested to Twelfth and Fifty-second in Midtown. A major ten-fifty spilling out of a storage facility. Police on the scene, but it's beyond their control. I repeat, all available Squad members to Twelfth and Fifty-second.*"

Hoffman snickered. "Good thing we're not available."

"What's a ten-fifty again?" I asked.

"Catchall for a disturbance."

"If they're radioing the Squad, then it's supernatural in nature," I pointed out.

"Aw, c'mon, Croft. I just pulled an all-nighter. It's probably just a newly turned vamp going out of his head. The Squad can handle it."

I pulled up a mental map of the city. "Take us there," I told the driver.

Hoffman sputtered his next sip of coffee onto his lap. "What in the hell for?" he demanded, wiping his mouth with a jacket sleeve as he held out his dripping cup. "We've gotta deliver this joker to your place."

"I know what Hermes has been up to."

We arrived by way of Twelfth Avenue to find a police cordon rerouting traffic east down Forty-eighth Street. We'd received fragments of info regarding the incident en route, but it was scattered and inconsistent. The van pulled onto the sidewalk, and a police officer hustled up to Hoffman and me as we climbed down.

"What's going on?" Hoffman asked, showing his badge.

"Major brawl four blocks north of here," the large officer said in a New York accent. "Half-a-dozen participants. Wouldn't answer to police commands and shrugged off our attempts at crowd control. Gas, rubber bullets, sound—nothing fazed them. When officers started getting flung, we got orders to pull back and seal the area, wait for the Squad. I'm not sure those things are human." His official delivery was at odds with his anxious eyes. They bounced between me and Hoffman as if pleading for us to believe him.

"How do you wanna handle this?" Hoffman asked me.

"I'll check it out. When the Squad arrives, have them move in behind me. Salt rounds, but no shooting unless I say so."

Hoffman radioed the instructions, then said, "How are you so sure this is Hermes's doing?"

I finished cinching my coat to keep my potions and spell implements from jostling too much. "I'll be happy to explain it on the way, provided you can keep up."

"It's alright to leave Mr. Funny in there?" he asked.

"Even if the van wasn't warded, he's too depressed to make a break for it."

Hoffman hesitated, the prospect of exercise souring his face, but he handed off his coffee to the officer. I rounded the police cordon and broke into a fast walk. Four empty lanes stretched north. Far ahead, I could just make out an assortment of scuffling figures. Hoffman limped up beside me on his ortho boot, already wheezing.

"Hermes mentioned collecting gods for a possible war," I explained. "He's farther along than I thought."

"How do you know this is them?"

"Because the location is right across the street from Dewitt Clinton Park. Alec's been using the park to cross in and out of the shadow present, which means Hermes has, too. He's bringing gods here, to the actual present, to stash. I don't think it's any accident we're going to a storage facility."

"Where do these gods come from?" he panted. "Don't imagine they just show up at the Port Authority Bus Terminal."

"It goes back to the group that worshipped this version of Hermes. They were a thieves guild, and Hermes was a patron of thieves. Border crossings, too. Through worship of Hermes, and with the help of magic, the guild developed the ability to cross in and out of the shadow present. That's where they'd stash their loot. They eventually hid a powerful box there, one that held Hermes's essence. But then the group was wiped out, and the tablet got stuck over there. Over time, its power awakened other objects from the Greek world, drew them to the shadow city. That's where the gods are coming from."

A glance told me most of that had gone straight over Hoffman's head, but he grasped the important part.

"So it's Mr. Funny all over again?"

"Unfortunately," I said. "Only there are more this time."

He swore and hawked a loogie. "Just what I need."

4

The officer was right—the combatants weren't human. Hardly crack police work, though. Even from more than a block away, I could see that.

A giant woman traded impressive blows with a centaur, while a pair of what looked like girls grappled with a dwarfish man. Another man stumbled around in confusion, perhaps from too many shots to the head.

In a flash of light, the dwarf was flung into the front of a building, sending out a plume of dust. He reappeared a moment later, shook himself off, and waddled forward to rejoin the battle. The combatants were all screaming at one another, but amid the booms of colliding blows and magic I couldn't make out a word.

"Sweet Jesus," Hoffman panted.

I pointed to a light pole. "Wait here for the Sup Squad."

Heaving from exertion, he could only nod his sweat-soaked head. He staggered to a stop and leaned an arm against the pole.

After only three blocks? I thought in disbelief, but dropping him off lightened my load.

Drawing my cane into sword and staff, I sped into a run. The brawl was moving toward the border of Dewitt Clinton Park. A streetlight fell and the corner of a building crumbled in a cascade of masonry. Trees shook. The NYPD had blocked the roads, but had they bothered to clear the park?

Pushing power into my wizard's voice, I shouted, "Stop! Go back inside!"

Predictably, the combatants didn't so much as look over. It had been worth a shot.

Veering around debris and fresh troughs in the asphalt, I passed the building from which they'd reportedly emerged. Rizo's Storage featured a row of gaudy Greek columns rendered in cement, topped by a triangular pediment. The entrance itself, a set of steel doors, had been blown out. But the Greek theme removed any doubt for me that these were pawns in Hermes's plan and he'd stashed them inside.

Probably thought he was being clever.

I reached the park, hurdled a flattened section of iron fencing, and hurried up a flight of steps littered with torn vines. At the top, I teetered back. I'd arrived at the park's playground, and the Greek beings were a stone's toss away.

The giant woman, an Amazon with tied-back hair and wearing a green tracksuit, had entangled the centaur in the chains of a swing set and was treating him like a punching bag. Meanwhile, beyond the ruins of a jungle gym, the dwarf had one of the girls in a headlock. The other girl pounded his thick back. Though her fists were tiny, each blow sent out a flash of light followed by a shockwave that shook the potions in my pockets. The other being looked on slack-jawed, as though not sure who he was supposed to attack.

"Stop!" I shouted again, waving my arms overhead. "By order of Hermes!"

I needed to get them off the streets and back inside, ideally without entering the fray myself. I'd already faced a shadowy minotaur and a Cerberus, and they'd been hell to put down. Parts of my body still ached from those encounters. Plus, Hermes apparently had plans for these particular beings.

Sharing those plans would've been nice, I thought bitterly. *Controlling these guys, even nicer.*

In a burst of chains, the centaur kicked free from the swing set. His rear hooves met the Amazon's stomach and sent her over an eruption of boulders. She crashed through the fencing of a baseball diamond and tumbled to a stop near the pitcher's mound.

With a furious cry, she shook her head, sending her thick brunette hair tumbling to her waist. A group of teenage boys broke from the dugout.

Crap, the park wasn't clear.

"Hey!" I shouted. "This way!"

I waved them toward the ruined section of fencing—the shortest path to escape—but they were already scattering toward the outfield, where there were no gates. The Amazon tracked them with narrowed eyes as she thrust herself to her feet. Then, like a predator heeding its chase instinct, she launched after them.

Aiming my staff toward the shallow outfield, I shouted, "*Protezione!*"

The atmosphere crackled, and the air ahead of the Amazon hardened into a wall. She met it at full speed. The impact of mass on magic nearly knocked me to my knees, but I held the barrier. The Amazon rebounded a good five yards and released another savage cry. The boys reached the outfield fence and began scaling it.

Looks like they're going to make it.

The Amazon produced a massive spear.

Oh, c'mon. Thrusting my sword forward, I bellowed, "*Vigore!*"

But the spear was already out of her hand and hurtling toward the teens. I spread my force invocation into a broad cone. The edge caught enough of the spear to wobble it. The weapon cleaved the fence a foot from a boy's torso, dropping diamond links in its wake and clattering to the asphalt beyond.

"Thank God," I breathed.

But the relief was short-lived. Hoofbeats were approaching. I wheeled to find the centaur galloping in. I wasn't excited at the prospect of their brawl rolling like a wrecking ball through the rest of Midtown, but at least he would divert the Amazon from the boys until I could figure out what to do.

The centaur veered toward me.

"Hey, whoa!" I called. "I thought we were on the same side!"

I hit the turf and invoked a shield just as the centaur arrived in a thundering of hooves. "*Respingere!*" I cried.

The energy encasing me contracted, then detonated in a bright pulse. The force caught the centaur's muscular hindquarters as they trampled over me and sent him ass over end. The Amazon, who had produced another spear, turned toward us. Beyond her, the boys dropped over the outfield fence and ran away.

The Amazon sneered. "Who's this guy?"

"No idea," the centaur snorted, kicking himself upright. "But he's about to enter a world of hurt."

Great, I'd succeeded in aligning them against me.

The centaur took a messy swig from the wineskin hanging from his neck, then produced a long bow from seemingly nowhere. He nocked it and sent an arrow toward me. The projectile grazed my shield wide right.

"Listen," I said quickly. "I'm an associate of Hermes's. He just wants you guys to settle down and go back inside."

Shouldering his bow, the centaur brought his pinkies to the corners of his bearded mouth and whistled sharply. "Hey, did you hear that?" he called. "This little twit works for Hermes."

Back on the playground, the dwarf released the girl from her headlock. The other girl, who could have been the first one's twin, stopped beating the dwarf's back. They were nymphs, I realized. I couldn't place the dwarf or the slack-jawed man, but they were all looking at me in various degrees of contempt.

"You're the reason we're in this hellhole?" the white-haired nymph asked.

"No, no, it's not like that. I didn't even know you were here until just now. Hermes barely tells me anything."

The Amazon scoffed. "Sure, buddy."

"I'm serious. When did he bring you?"

But they were done listening to what I had to say.

"I've got an idea," the dwarf said. "Let's stomp him into jelly and spread him on toast."

I could think of few morning meals less appetizing, but he stalked toward me with a hungry grin. The nymphs, who just moments earlier had been intent on pulverizing him, moved into flanking positions. The slack-jawed man followed them like a confused dog, though even he was starting to look agitated.

Back on the field, the centaur and Amazon were advancing, too.

I turned in a circle. "Would it help to tell you I'm a big fan of your stories?"

Apparently not. I spoke into my blade's first rune, the one for banishment. Having already faced off against a few Greek beings, I'd discovered a weakness. Because they originated from the shadow present, they featured nether qualities. Banishment magic could hurt them, even destroy them.

If that scuttles Hermes's plans, so be it. It's not like the dipshit left me a choice.

As the blade's banishment rune glowed to life, I said, "Stay back if you value your existence."

That didn't stop them, either. I considered the challenge now of getting my blade into the six of them. As if in answer, Sup Squad personnel began arriving. They rushed into crouches around the playground's perimeter, rifles aimed. Their salt rounds would disorganize the beings enough to let me work.

I wet my dry lips, preparing to issue the "open fire" command, when a new voice sounded. "Well, isn't *this* a sight."

I turned to find Alec strolling toward me. He was dressed in a gray hoodie, black jeans, and a pair of Converse Chucks, but his jaunty steps coupled with the glimmering green light in his eyes told me Hermes was in control.

The closing ring of Greek beings slowed and looked on scornfully. I fully expected Hermes to assume command, to order them back to their holding area, but he only grinned as he arrived beside me. I signaled the Sup Squad to hold fire.

"We need to talk," I growled at him.

"Oh, absolutely. But in the meantime, I need a small favor."

"What favor?"

Hermes turned to his conscripts. "It's apparent I've lost your support, so I'll make you an offer. Pass a test and I'll release you, one and all. Fail, and you'll cease this internecine nonsense and pledge yourselves to the cause."

The Greek beings stopped advancing. "What's the test?" the dwarf shouted back.

Hermes squeezed my shoulder companionably. "Defeat Everson Croft in battle."

5

I wheeled on Hermes. "*What?*"

"Yes, you must best the wizard in battle," he repeated to the others. "But there is a condition. It will be a one-on-one contest, so choose a representative. Go on, talk amongst yourselves. You have five minutes."

"No," I said. "I'm not agreeing to this."

But the Greek beings were already congregating near the pitcher's mound.

Hermes sidled up to me and whispered, "Don't worry, my friend. I have faith in you."

"That's not the *point*." Blood rushed to my head. "This is your mess, not mine, and I've already cleaned up enough after you."

"I won't argue with you there. I've been tied up with other things. I should never have left them alone for as long as I did. It's made them unruly. But what's done is done. If I didn't offer them a way out, they'd undermine me at every turn."

"Then why don't *you* challenge them to a battle?"

"Because they'd stand no chance, and they know it."

"And if I don't fight?" I said.

"Well, since I've already issued the challenge, it would be considered a forfeit. I return them to the shadow present as agreed, and our situation vis-à-vis Persephone and the Cronus business becomes exceedingly dire."

Mythology used one name for gods like Persephone, but there were many variants of her, depending on the cult that worshipped her. This particular version of Persephone was a wronged god, a vengeful god. And having taken form in the shadow present, she was acting accordingly.

Her ambition was to free Cronus from Tartarus and refight the epic battle against the Olympic gods, payback for her abysmal treatment. If Cronus were to prevail in the Titanochamy 2.0, he would replace all of humankind with a mindless race of worshippers. And once that worship granted him sufficient power, the god of time would be able to transit from the shadow realm and wipe out humankind here.

Persephone had very nearly succeeded in calling him up at an old explorers club. I grimaced now as I recalled my battle with Eldred, who had severed his own neck with Cronus's scythe.

"But you will fight and you will win," Hermes continued, bringing me back to the park. "And then I have some information to share."

"So you've been using Alec this past week," I said.

"Why the sour tone, my friend? You knew the arrangement."

"From now on, I want you to tell me what you're doing with him."

"We can stand here debating the matter, or I can give you

a rundown of our friends so you'll be prepared for the one you may face." Hermes tapped his wrist. "The clock is ticking."

If he weren't using Alec's body as a vessel, I might have smacked the amused look from his face. I glanced at the six beings. They'd been arguing loudly, but their voices fell now, as if nearing agreement.

When I looked back at Hermes, I noted how his presence transformed Alec's face, from young and earnest to wily and knowing. I didn't like it, but I couldn't banish the god, not without jeopardizing Alec.

"You're taking care of him, right?" I said.

"How can I not? I'm utterly dependent on him."

I'd been counting on that dependence to protect Alec, and Hermes's confirmation helped a little.

I nodded at the Greek beings. "If I agree to this, what defines victory?"

"Your opponent being unable to continue, however that may come about. Short of death or annihilation, of course."

That took banishment off the table. I dispersed the final bit of power from my blade's first rune and sighed. "Go ahead. Tell me about them."

Hermes clapped his hands and rubbed them together. "That's the spirit! Given the constraints of time, the profiles will be brief. We'll start with that tall drink of water. I assume you've heard of Hippolyta?"

"Queen of the Amazons? That's her?"

I was about to be seriously impressed with Hermes's recruiting efforts.

"No, Madge," he said. "One of Hippolyta's daughters. The weakest, in fact, but an Amazon nonetheless, a warrior. Not nearly the stature of her mother, but she has the blood of Ares in her. She's their most likely choice. But listen, she wears a zoster, a special belt. Strip her of it, and her power diminishes."

I could make out a subtle bulge at the waist of the Amazon's tracksuit. Though I didn't relish the idea of ungirding her, it was good to know.

"What about the centaur?" I asked.

"Ahh, Phrixus. Powerful and skilled with a bow, but a bit of a drunkard. He did attempt to steal the wine of Pholos, after all, and was slain for his efforts. I doubt he'd be their unanimous choice." As Hermes said this, the centaur took a long pull from his wineskin.

"Hey!" The dwarf waved for our attention. "No potions or spells, all right?"

Hermes turned to me. "Are you comfortable with just invocations?"

"I don't know. Should I be?"

Hermes nodded back at the group as if the stipulation were fine. The dwarf flashed a cruel smile before rejoining the huddle.

"He looks like he's sporting for a fight," I remarked.

"Priapus? Yes, well, can you blame him?"

"Wait, Priapus the god?"

"A minor god, and one cursed with incredibly bad fortune. It's made him surly."

I remembered the story. Jealous of Priapus's mother, Hera cursed her son-to-be with trollish ugliness. And that wasn't the worst of it. As a god of fertility, Priapus sported a permanent erection. That no doubt explained his baggy pants and awkward walk.

"Wasn't he banned from Olympus for his looks?" I asked. "I can't imagine he'd side with them against Persephone."

"Yes, that might take some convincing, but I couldn't be choosy. While the power of my tablet attracted several objects to the city, only a few hold enough of the old worship to allow a being to take form. In the case of Priapus, that worship was contained in a phallic symbol made of copper—wonderful for storing energy. It's a part of his form, but his plums are his own. A well-placed shot will steal his thunder, if you follow. Be alert, though. He's known to use his phallus as a bludgeoning weapon."

I pictured what that would look like and wished I hadn't.

"I think I'd prefer fighting one of the nymphs," I muttered.

"Hmm, I'm not so sure. They wield considerable magic. The one with the white hair is a nymph of comets. And the green-haired one is a vine nymph. Their real names are hard for human tongues to wrap around, so let's just refer to them as Comet and Ivy, shall we?"

"We've made our choice!" Madge the Amazon announced.

"Ah, time's up, I'm afraid," Hermes said to me. "And whom have you chosen?" he called back.

"Koalemos!" she answered.

The slack-jawed man who had been wandering around while the others conferred stopped now and blinked dully.

I stared at Hermes. "The god of stupidity?"

"Like I said, I couldn't afford to be choosy."

"Yeah, no kidding." I looked over the motley collection of beings. "But why did *they* choose him?"

"I'm sorry, the contest has begun," he said. "I can no longer help you." He lowered his voice. "But remember, they're all born of artifacts from the Old World. Separate them from said artifacts, and you're halfway to victory." As he backed away, he jostled his backpack to indicate his own tablet.

The rest of the Greek beings followed Hermes from the baseball diamond until it was just me and Koalemos.

6

To that point I hadn't paid Koalemos much attention—he'd remained apart from the fighting, and Hermes hadn't placed him high in the pecking order of likely opponents.

I took a moment now to size up the god of stupidity. His scruffy sun-bleached surfer 'do framed a pair of puffy eyes and a jaw that hung slightly askew. There was nothing remotely imposing about the god. He looked like a stoner who mooched off his friends. Still, the group had selected him for a reason.

Pulling my cane into sword and staff, I began to circle him, cautiously.

He blinked slowly as he tracked me—or tried to. His eyes couldn't seem to keep up with my progress. I glanced at where the others had gathered beyond the fence. Was this some kind of joke? But they wore resolute expressions, no chuckles or knowing grins.

I spotted Hermes atop the outfield fence where he'd taken

a seat, legs kicking idly. He pointed at Koalemos as though telling me to keep my head in the game.

The god of stupidity had given up trying to track me and was scratching an armpit. I leveled my sword at him, but surprising him with a force blast felt dishonorable. More than that, it felt *dangerous*. Again, for reasons still beyond my grasp, the group was of the consensus that he was their best shot.

"You understand we're supposed to be fighting, right?" I asked him.

With considerable effort, Koalemos focused on me. "Fighting? Each other?" He released a lazy staccato laugh. "Gnarly."

Great, they pitted me against Jeff Spicoli.

I recalled Hermes's words, how these beings were all born of artifacts from the Old World. What would Koalemos's be? I struggled to recall where I'd read about him. It was a wonder the god had ever been worshipped given his scarce presence in the literature, not to mention what he represented. He wore no jewelry that I could see. No obvious bulges in the pockets of his Baja hoodie or knee-length shorts.

Need to get him in a position where I can pat him down.

From my satchel, I pulled out a polyethylene sheet, unfolded it, and spread it over the turf. A large copper casting circle glimmered at the sheet's center. If I could get him inside the circle, I could detain him long enough to perform a thorough search. I backed away until the circle lay between me and the god.

"Koalemos?" I called.

He'd begun to stare vacantly at the sun, but my voice brought him back. His slack mouth drew into a slow smile, as if I were someone he'd met before, but he couldn't quite remember who or where.

"Aloha, bud," he said. "What's up?"

"Would you mind stepping over here?"

"Sure, no problemo."

He sauntered up to the sheet's edge and looked down at the circle. "What the heck's this?"

"It's a, ah, magical scale. Your friends have been a little concerned about your recent weight loss."

I sucked at ad-libbing. When Koalemos remained staring down at the circle, not moving, I was sure I'd blown it. But he was only slow to process my explanation because a few seconds later he snuffed out a laugh, said, "Righteous," and shuffled his canvas slip-ons onto the sheet, bunching it all up.

"Now what?" he asked.

"Okay, wait a sec." I hustled over. "Can you lift this foot up? All right, now this one?"

Though I'd invoked a protective field around myself, I winced as I straightened the sheet beneath him, certain the god was going to surprise me with a prodigious blow to the back of the head. But he complied, if sloppily, until both shoes were squarely inside the circle.

I scooted back and uttered, "*Cerrare.*"

The circle glowed, and a column of gold-hued light grew around him. Koalemos laughed in surprise and peered from his enclosure with glittering eyes. "Whoa."

"Hold as still as you can."

All right, now I just need to... I hesitated. Needed to what?

The thought seemed to teeter at the edge of a cliff, almost within grasp, before plummeting from sight. I stared vacantly at the gold column holding Koalemos. What did I need to do?

I tried to haul the thought back up, but it was gone, lost in the abyss. I released a laugh, one that sounded sharp with disbelief in my mind but that emerged dull and stupid, much like Koalemos's.

Is that his power? I thought distantly. *Inflicting his stupidity on others?*

If so, he was using my magic as a conduit. I opened my mouth to disperse the circle, but my jaw hung slack. I couldn't recall the word.

"*Misfire,*" I tried. "No, no... *Dust bin.* Dammit, that's not it... *Dishwasher.*"

With each word, Koalemos chortled, but it wasn't malicious. In fact, he didn't appear to have the slightest clue of his effect on me. I made a few more attempts, each one more absurd than the last. For the life of me, I couldn't come up with the freaking word. I screwed up my face as if that might wring it from my brain.

Suddenly, it fell out of my mouth: "*Disfare.*"

Articulation was everything when it came to Words of Power, and this one emerged slurred. The resulting dispersion was a mess. The column wobbled and sagged, like a failing vase on a potter's wheel, then blew out. The brunt of the detonation lifted me from my feet. In the next moment, the outfield fence rattled violently against me, and I fell to the turf. Cheers erupted from the Greek beings.

"Stomp his ass!" the Amazon bellowed.

"*Psst,*" Hermes whispered from his perch above me. "Remember what I told you."

Back in the infield, Koalemos was stepping from the circle. Though my magic no longer surrounded him, my stupidity lingered.

I struggled to recall what Hermes had said earlier, but I could barely remember what we were even doing here. A plastic shopping bag tumbled across the outfield, distracting me. When it snagged on the fence, I thought, *Cool.*

Cool? What was cool about a fucking piece of garbage?

A shadow loomed over me, and a canvas shoe came down and planted itself firmly on my neck. "I'm just constricting your carotid until you pass out," Koalemos said, sounding oddly intelligent.

Right on, I mouthed.

"It shouldn't hurt," he added.

When I tried to nod, the pressure of his foot made the motion impossible. My smile warped into a grimace. But it wasn't until everything began to waver that my calm acceptance of the situation—an acceptance bordering on appreciation—turned to mild panic. And what was with all the cheering?

I angled my gaze to where Phrixus the centaur was clapping his hands and stomping his front hooves. Madge was pounding a fist into her palm in a form of applause, while Priapus waved the front of his tented pants back and forth. Even the sweet-looking nymphs were screaming for Koalemos to smite me.

From the fence, Hermes watched the action intently.

It suddenly occurred to me that I was supposed to be *fighting* this guy.

I swung my staff around only to discover my hands were empty. I'd lost my casting implements in the blast. Gripping Koalemos's ankle, I twisted one way then the other, but his foot held firm. He adjusted his stance until he was compressing what shielding remained around my throat into my larynx.

"Struggling will only expend your remaining oxygen," he said.

Damn, he's right, I thought as clouds began eddying through my vision.

But how was he right? He was supposed to be a god of stupidity, not sensible observations.

I stopped thrashing long enough to think. Like dragging an ill-formed object from the mud, a concept began to take shape. Transference. He'd induced stupidity in me, yes, but he'd also acquired my smarts. It was a two-way street. The insight didn't help, but it explained what was happening.

It also told me that if I didn't do something in the next few seconds, the contest was over.

From the ground I could see up the front of Koalemos's baggy shirt. Something dangled against his chest.

I instinctively stretched a hand for the beaded necklace but only got as far as his knee. My arm gave out, collapsing to my side. Beyond the hand, I could see where my sword and staff had fallen. Too distant to grasp.

Back at my fallen hand, my fingers jerked. I dimly recalled teaching myself to sign basic invocations, but I struggled for the specific configuration in this case. I relaxed, shut down my plodding mind, and let the muscle memory take over. As if by magic, my fingers signed a word independent of my thoughts.

Respingere.

What remained of the shielding around me drew in and detonated with a pop. Though short of maximum strength, it was enough to surprise Koalemos. He staggered back, his foot releasing my throat.

Air rushed into my lungs, and blood to my head. Brainpower too. I reached a hand toward my sword, snagging it with a shouted Word. The hilt met my outstretched hand as

Koalemos stepped back in. With his foot descending, I drove my blade up the front of his shirt.

"*Disfare!*" I shouted.

The blast scattered the necklace's energy, and Koalemos collapsed, bare-chested, to the ground. The Baja hoodie, along with the beaded necklace known as a chaplet, came off his head and hung from the end of my blade.

"Come, take a chaplet," the Greek playwright Aristophanes had written, "offer a libation to Koalemos, the god of stupidity, and take care to fight vigorously."

I removed the chaplet from the blade and held it up to the others—my declaration of victory.

Hermes clapped enthusiastically and leapt down from the fence, while the rest of the Greek beings skulked and pouted.

"Well done!" Hermes exclaimed, arriving beside me.

"Thanks," I said, pride inflating my chest despite my conflicted feelings about the contest.

Hermes turned to the others. "Come, come," he called. "Stop dragging your feet. Koalemos was a clever choice, but Mr. Croft won fair and square, and now we must all heed the agreement."

It *had* been a clever choice. It also explained why they had stipulated no spells or potions. The instant one of my raw invocations contacted Koalemos, I inherited his stupidity and he my intelligence.

Hermes took the chaplet from me and replaced it around Koalemos's neck. He then snapped his fingers in front of the god's face. The god of stupidity blinked his eyes open and squinted around.

"Whoa, what is this place?" he asked with a lazy smile.

"Home, for now," Hermes replied, then addressed himself

to the approaching beings. "Though you came up short, there is only one way to conclude a contest, and that is with feasting. Come, let's put these ill feelings behind us. Allow me to lavish you with New York's version of ambrosia and nectar."

Koalemos chuckled as he stood and knotted the sleeves of his hoodie around his waist. "I could totally go for that."

The prospect of food seemed to lift the others' moods, too.

"Hey, you promised me information," I reminded Hermes.

"Yes, yes, but let's get them settled first, hmm? Then I have much to tell you. So much to tell you." Mischievous light glimmered in his eyes.

"Can't wait," I muttered.

7

As we left the park, currents of Hermes's green-tinged magic swirled around us, cleaning up the debris and restoring fences, equipment, and buildings to their pre-brawl states. By the time we descended to the street, the block looked banged up but typical of the city. Detective Hoffman was leaning against one of the cement columns at Rizo's Storage. He pocketed his phone and limped forward to meet us.

"Everything cool?" he asked.

He eyed the mythic beings warily, which was only natural. How often did you see a centaur trotting alongside a seven-foot-tall woman? But his gaze lingered on Hermes, whom he'd only known to that point as Alec.

I knew the feeling. Same body, but clearly a different being.

"Yeah, it is now," I replied, deciding to spare Hoffman my doubts.

"Just so long as we don't have to deploy half the department again," he grumbled, then turned toward the transport van. "I had 'em drive up like you asked. Need any help transferring him?"

Adding Arimanius to the mix had been Hermes's idea, one I preferred to storing him in my basement, frankly. I just hoped his unhealthy obsession with comedy wouldn't trigger another knock-down, drag-out with the others.

"We're good," I said. "Go home and get some rest."

Hoffman nodded in obvious relief—not only for the break, but for the excuse to leave a scene that was well outside his comfort zone. "I'll tell the department they can release the traffic. Call me if you need anything." He stopped and reconsidered. "Better yet, give me a few hours, *then* call if you need anything."

I smiled. "Will do."

He clapped my shoulder, gave Madge the Amazon a final up and down, and signaled to the van driver to open the rear holding area.

Mr. Funny sat slumped in his seat, still muttering out comedic bits—and still without any sense of timing or understanding. I released him from the warded restraints and helped him down. He continued to mutter as I led him to where Hermes was surveying the blown-out metal doors to the storage building.

"And what happened here?" he was asking the others.

The beings glanced at one another guiltily before Madge spoke up. "Phrixus told Priapus that I was smelling up the joint, that I needed a bath. As if he's one to talk. Shouldn't he be in a stable?"

"I never said that!" Phrixus shouted.

"The nymphs are spreading rumors again," Priapus put in, adjusting his pants.

"No we aren't!" Comet cried. "We heard him!" Ivy added.

"Then you heard wrong!" the centaur thundered, balling up his fists.

Koalemos, who'd lost whatever intelligence he'd siphoned from me, could only watch with a gaping mouth. But before the argument spiraled out of control, Hermes sliced a hand through the air.

"You failed the test," he snapped. "All of you. As a result, you've agreed to put this silliness behind you." He stared each Greek into submission, even Arimanius, who ceased muttering and looked over at me worriedly.

"That's better," Hermes said, his taut expression relaxing out again. "You have a new roommate. Everyone, this is Arimanius, a god of darkness and vermin. Go on, introduce yourselves."

If the others were upset at having to share their space, they didn't dare show it. They greeted him in turn.

Mr. Funny regarded them somberly. "Do any of you do standup?"

"There will be time for that later," Hermes said. "Now we feast!"

He restored the ruined doors with the snap of his fingers and skipped his way up a ramp. The gods followed eagerly. Even Arimanius seemed to discover a small bounce in his step. The ramp led onto a corridor lined with large storage units.

No wonder they became unruly, I thought. *This place is grim.*

Hermes restored another damaged door and threw it open. It didn't give onto a cement cell, however, but an enormous penthouse fit for royalty. I followed the others into a common area with plush couches and chairs, fine rugs, a massive stone fireplace, and a sunken jacuzzi in the far corner.

With a sweep of his arm, Hermes gestured to a dining area, where a long table was already set. An array of platters held New York-style pizzas, thick pastrami sandwiches, and bagels heaped with smoked salmon and cheeses. Drinks lined the far end, sectioned into Manhattans, Cosmopolitans, New York Sours, and Long Island Ice Teas. The city's version of ambrosia and nectar, indeed.

"Go ahead," Hermes said. "Eat and drink!"

The Greeks wasted no time crowding the table. I was tempted to join them—I'd had nothing since breakfast and the pastrami looked especially tasty—but Hermes cocked his head at me.

I followed him into an adjoining library, where he set his pack beside a leather reading chair and sank into the seat. As a book junkie, I felt my browsing habit twitch, but now wasn't the time. Instead, I took the chair opposite Hermes. The library's oak door swung closed, muffling the sounds from the other room.

"Minor beings can be so exhausting," he sighed. "Brandy?"

He was already lifting two snifters of the reddish-brown liqueur from a table beside him. I accepted one, and he clicked his rim against mine.

"To a battle well fought," he said.

"To a battle I'll never fight again," I amended.

I matched his sip and immediately regretted it. *Holy hell!* I thought, grimacing and smacking my mouth.

"Something wrong?"

"A little sweet for my taste." Which was to say it had felt like drinking diabetes.

"My apologies." The drink softened to a light tannic color. "Try it now."

"Thanks, but I'm good." I set the snifter aside, not trusting that he'd tempered it down from god strength. "You have information for me?"

He chuckled. "You mortals always like to shoot straight to the point."

"Considering the circumstances, I don't think that's unreasonable."

He took another sip and cradled the snifter in his lap. "Very well. There have been some developments over there."

"The shadow realm?"

He smirked. "It seems our meeting with Persephone shook her up."

He was referring to our last visit to the shadow realm, when I'd helped the shadow Detective Vega and her husband escape the city. En route, we encountered Persephone's terrifying Iron Guard, a shadow version of Mayor "Budge" Lowder, who was under the goddess's control, and finally Persephone herself. I only glimpsed the goddess, but I hadn't been able to get her eyes out of my head. Eyes that balanced the darkness of the underworld, where Hades had forced her into queenhood, and the light and bounty of the living world, where she was allowed to return each spring.

Hermes must have caught something on my face because he said, "She's stunning, isn't she?"

"What? Not really." I felt my cheeks flush around the obvious lie. "Well, yes, but it's not every day that you look into a god's eyes. I mean, I think about yours, too—not in that way. Not in that way with her, either. My point is that gazing into a god's eyes—*any* god—isn't something one soon forgets."

My actual point was that my wife's eyes were the only ones I treasured, but with Hermes's face turning wistful, I doubted he'd caught most of my backpedaling.

"Ahh, yes, her eyes. My mind goes there often as well. It's a shame she wants me gone along with the Olympic order. Though her grievance is certainly justified. I never cared for Hades, the miserable sod." His expression soured before illuminating again. "But I can't describe to you the privilege of delivering Persephone from the underworld. It was like holding perfection herself. And to witness the light and joy on her face as I lifted her into the arms of her mother?" He pressed a hand to his heart and sighed.

Hermes's unrequited feelings for Persephone were well documented, but I didn't want this to devolve into a lovelorn confessional.

"Can we go back to the developments you mentioned?"

His eyes sharpened above a humorless grin. "Once again, straight to the point. Well, you asked earlier how I've been using Alec. If you allow me this small aside, I can tell you, because it relates to the developments."

"Go on," I said, becoming a concerned father.

"First, I had to relocate his mother. The last thing we need is for Persephone to leverage her against Alec, and let's face it, against you. We can't afford that disadvantage. I assure you, she's secure now."

I'd dated Jennifer DeFazio in this life, but I'd gone on to marry her in the shadow realm, where we'd had Alec. I had been nervous about her remaining in the city for the exact reasons Hermes just mentioned.

"Okay, good," I said cautiously.

"With that accomplished, I divided my time between seeking out more enlistees for our army and recruiting informants. I found the nymphs just the other day. Someone had buried bronze idols to them in a park." He chuckled. "Feisty little things. My informants have been busy as well. Their efforts are already paying dividends. It seems Persephone has drawn her forces tightly around City Hall."

"Why?"

"Isn't it obvious? She's working on another scheme to call up Cronus, and she can't risk us interfering this time. Using the explorers club and converting its members into raving devotees to Cronus—that was clever. But she didn't count on me calling to Alec, and in turn, to you. We stopped her, but only just. She's determined not to make the same mistake again." He drummed his fingers against the bottom of his snifter in thought. "And the fact she's being so obvious suggests she must be close."

"But the last time it took very specific organ offerings and a lot of worship to call up Cronus. How is she replicating that in City Hall?"

"You just answered your own question, my friend. Politics."

"I'm not following."

"Well, what is politics for many but religion by another name?"

I considered his rhetorical question with pursed lips. He had a point.

"The Society of Cronus claimed, what, a few hundred members?" he continued. "The city, even the shambles over there, boasts millions of inhabitants. If Persephone can channel their political allegiances into devotion to Cronus, even by proxy, it should be enough to open Tartarus and call him forth."

"That would explain her interest in Mayor Lowder."

He snapped his fingers and pointed at me. "Precisely. The mayor has already announced a referendum on his agenda.

Have a look-see." He reached into his pack, pulled out a flyer, and handed it to me.

The flyer featured a grinning image of Budge. Not the chubby-cheeked version with an unruly cowlick and "aw shucks" demeanor, but a slim power player with slicked-back hair. His hands grasped the lapels of a tailored jacket, showcasing his jeweled fingers as he beamed for all he was worth.

I read it aloud: "'Don't get left behind! Vote YES to support my "Full Steam Ahead" agenda! All aboard the Budge Train!'" I lowered the flyer with a grimace. "With a pitch like that he's sure to have at least twice as many people opposing as supporting him, especially given the state of the city."

"Yes, but the referendum is meaningless. The point is to excite a response. Look again."

I returned my gaze to the flyer and chastised myself for missing it the first time. Superimposed over the image, almost light enough to be a watermark, was a circular symbol whose lines created an illusion of funneling.

"A siphon sigil," I marveled.

"Yes, to capture the people's emotions. These sigils are everywhere now. On billboards, buildings, practically anyplace you look. The symbol will soak up that emotional energy like a sponge and direct it to where Persephone is storing it. The more intense the reaction, the better. And the process has already begun. I can feel it."

"Can we assume she's assembling an army of deities too?"

"She doesn't have to now, not with everything progressing apace. Her Iron Guard is sufficient."

My chest constricted as I recalled my encounter with her stone servants and their underworld magic. Exposure to the magic had felt like being crammed into a too-small coffin and buried. Something I never wanted to experience again.

"Not to mention her access to the underworld itself," Hermes continued. "Horrible beings down there, some of which she can summon by virtue of her powers alone. And once she siphons enough power from the city to free Cronus, every Titan imprisoned in Tartarus will be at their beck and call."

I stood and paced the room on unsteady legs.

Hermes took a slow sip of brandy as though giving me space to process the information.

"If it comes to war," I said, "I'm not sure the misfit crew you've assembled is the answer. I mean, a junior Amazon, a drunken centaur, a pair of nymphs who look all of ten, a god of stupidity, another god who's borderline suicidal, and a deity with a permanent hard-on, which also happens to be his weapon of choice?"

"Not yet, no," Hermes admitted. "But with training, I believe we can forge them into a capable force."

At that moment, glass shattered in the common room. A cheer or battle cry went up, I couldn't tell which. I leveled my gaze at him. "Capable force? They're behaving like they're in an episode of *Big Brother*."

"Then let's avoid war."

"Great, I'm all ears."

"Persephone's scepter is the source of her power."

"Yes? And you just said she's fortified her position at City Hall."

"What if I discovered a blind spot?" His eyes twinkled. "A way in?"

I tensed my jaw, tired of his little teases. "Well, have you?"

"Straight to the point," he sighed. "Yes, I have. And I know

Persephone well enough to know where she keeps her scepter. I have a plan to steal it, destroy it. A brilliant plan. This could all be over by tomorrow."

More crashes sounded in the common room, and the beings broke into drunken song.

He glanced over, then back at me. "But I can't do it without you."

8

_____

"Sorry I'm late," I called, hanging my coat and satchel on the door-side rack and dropping my cane in the umbrella holder.

At the dining room table, Ricki and her eight-year-old son, Tony, looked to be finishing dinner, while Bree-yark and his fiancée, Mae Johnson, carried dishes to the kitchen. The couple had picked up Tony from soccer camp, and Ricki invited them to stay for dinner. A dinner I was supposed to have partaken in.

"Everson!" Bree-yark barked. "Was starting to think you'd ditched us for your cooler friends."

Mae swatted the goblin's bottom as she passed him. "Stop giving him a hard time. Can't you see he's dog tired?"

"Aww, he knows I'm just busting his hump. Right, Prof?"

"Just keeping me honest," I agreed.

"Go on and have a seat, hon," Mae said to me. "I'll heat you up a plate." The large, cherub-faced woman, who'd become like a surrogate grandmother, disappeared before I had the chance to respond.

"Thanks for the offer," I called after her, "but I had a late lunch."

I'd made the mistake of sampling what was left from Hermes's feast. The pastrami sandwich had tasted as divine as it appeared, but like the brandy, it was intended for mythic beings, not a human digestive tract. It sat like a stone in my stomach and was only now beginning to break down.

"Are you sure?" Mae asked. "You look fit for the bean patch."

"Easier to launch myself onto buildings," I said, only half-joking.

"Well, I hope you saved some room for dessert," she said. "Bree-yark and I picked up a pumpkin cheesecake from Magnolias."

I patted my stomach. "I'm afraid I'm going to have to settle for coffee."

"Nonsense. I'll cut you a sliver."

Ricki came over and searched my face. "Long day, huh?" She wrapped her arms around my waist. As an NYPD homicide detective, not to mention Hoffman's partner, she knew all about long days.

I kissed her forehead and hugged her close. "It was interesting, at least. How's Tabitha doing?"

She followed my gaze to the divan, where Tabitha remained propped on her side. "No movement. Well, except for tipping over a couple times. I found that shoes work better than books for wedging her in place."

That explained the assortment of high heels. I frowned as I walked over to examine her. Tabitha's essence was still in there, hard and compressed, but I wasn't sure what concerned me more—that her forty pounds had remained inert all day or the idea of my pregnant wife maneuvering her.

"The magic can take a while," I said, "especially with a strong self-preservation response. I'll get some more potion into her before bed."

"Well, let me get your coffee." Ricki lowered her voice. "Mae makes it a little weak."

At the table, I scrubbed Tony's head and sat down heavily. "How you doing, champ?"

"Scored three goals in the afternoon scrimmage," he said, barely pausing between his final bites of mashed potatoes and meatloaf.

"Save some for your teammates next time." I winked.

He smiled as he finished. "Can I go play with Buster?" he called into the kitchen.

At mention of his name, Mae's pet appeared from behind a planter. The lobster-like creature chirped and wriggled his lip tentacles.

"He'd enjoy that," Mae said. "Just watch your fingers."

"*After* you bring your plate in here," Ricki called back.

Tony complied by assembling his dishware into a teetering stack. He somehow managed not to drop anything, even with Buster running circles around his legs and snapping his claws excitedly.

While Ricki helped Mae with coffee and dessert, and Tony led Buster to his room, Bree-yark updated me on our entertainment room in the basement. He was stoked about a cable deal he'd negotiated with a vendor out of Jersey City. It sounded super shady, but I nodded, only half listening.

Ricki and Mae returned with plates of cheesecake and a round of coffees, all decaf save mine. After so many late-night pots, I'd developed an immunity to caffeine.

"So why *are* you looking so run down?" Mae asked me.

"That's actually something I wanted to talk to you about. All of you. I need some opinions."

My wife's opinion would matter the most, of course, but I didn't want to put this entirely on her. Bree-yark, who had already devoured his slice and slugged his coffee, swiped an arm across his mouth.

"Of course, Everson," he said. "We're all ears."

Mae propped her fork on her plate and folded her hands to give me her full attention. "What's on your mind, baby?"

I smiled. Though wizarding hadn't gotten any easier since becoming friends with them, it somehow *felt* easier.

"You know the situation with Hermes and Persephone," I began. "Well, things are moving fast in the shadow realm, and Hermes is having a hard time keeping up. I met his so-called 'army' today. Don't get me wrong, they're fascinating beings, but as far as a fighting force..." I shook my head. "Not great."

Bree-yark grunted knowingly. "During my first years in the goblin army, I got stuck in more than one shoddy unit. Did I ever tell you about that time we tried to take a valley from a den of flower gnomes?"

Mae patted his hand. "Shush now, honey. Let Everson talk."

"Oh, sorry. I'll tell you another time. Go on with what you were saying."

"Well, Hermes thinks he's found a way to strike first and end this. It involves stealing Persephone's scepter. More specifically, *me* stealing her scepter. He says Persephone is too attuned to his energy for him to attempt it. Though it could also be that he's in love with her and doesn't trust himself."

Mae made a sound of interest.

"We spent most of the day rehearsing his plan," I continued. "For every question I threw at him, he had an answer. Every potential shortcoming I pointed out, he'd already accounted for. If his intel is good, it's a solid plan, one I can execute. And one that could end this god business once and for all."

"So, what's the problem?" Bree-yark asked.

"It would mean going back to the shadow realm. Not just the shadow realm, but City Hall, where Persephone and her guards are fortressed." I met Ricki's gaze. She'd known my going back was a possibility, just not straight into the dragon's den. "It's obviously not without its risks."

She nodded. "Let's hear them."

"Well, I could be caught. Or something could happen to Hermes, in which case I'd be stuck over there. At least until the Order figured out a way to recover me, which could be never."

"Why can't Hermes do it?" she asked. "Pop in, grab the scepter, and pop out again."

"Persephone has apparently cast some sort of defensive field around City Hall. If he attempted to transport inside, he claims the field would redirect him to an underworld prison. He can't even fashion a disguise without her knowing—she's that attuned to his energy, apparently. That's why he needs me."

"I've got your solution," Bree-yark announced. "Take me with you!"

"Both of us," Mae said. "It may not look it, but I've still got some boogie in this old body."

Ricki brought up her cup to conceal the smile curling the edges of her mouth.

"I would if I could," I said. "But the only reason I can go is because I'm peppered with Hermes's essence. It grants me a few abilities, including allowing him to transport me to and from the shadow realm."

"Then have him spray some of that stuff on us," Bree-yark insisted.

"Well, it has more to do with my bloodline. I'm descended from Michael, a First Saint. For a brief time during the Holy Roman Empire, Hermes was associated with him. Their energies overlapped. That's how he was able to bond with Alec and me. It won't work on just anyone, unfortunately."

Bree-yark crossed his arms with a grumble.

"What happens if you don't go?" Ricki asked.

"Persephone calls up Cronus, and then the Titans and all manner of monstrosities mop the floor with Hermes and his army. That's in the shadow realm, but at some point Cronus will grow powerful enough to come here. The Order might be able to stop him, but the battle would be a literal hell on earth, untold lives lost." Beginning with New York and its powerful intersection of ley lines, I thought anxiously. "Arianna placed me in charge of this with the understanding I'd nip it in the bud."

Mae and Bree-yark fell quiet, as though this had grown beyond their expertise.

I took a bite of the cheesecake "sliver" Mae had cut me—a generous wedge—and sipped my coffee without tasting either.

"The potential end of the world notwithstanding," I said, "I keep thinking how nice it would be to have all this behind us. For the arrival of our daughter, for you guys' wedding. For Alec, too. He may be a shadow, a probability, but he's no less real. And Hermes promised to release him when this was over."

"Where is the little pipsqueak?" Bree-yark asked, looking around.

"He said he needed to put some finishing touches on his plan. Well, Hermes did," I amended. "Through Alec. I'm supposed to give him my decision later tonight."

"Can you trust him?" Ricki asked.

It was a question I'd asked myself untold times already. And every time, it went back to a debate I'd had with Alec when he first appeared in my mythology class under the alias "Sven Roe." He claimed tricksters were often confused with cultural heroes, and vice versa. Tricksters were amoral beings with no concern for human life, he'd argued, while cultural heroes, though often prankish, acted on behalf of humans, usually in defiance of the ruling gods. It's what made them heroic.

Where did Hermes fall? Particularly *this* version of Hermes, patron of a thieves guild? Was he all trickster? Or was there just enough cultural hero in there to place my trust?

"I think so," I said at last.

I could see by the taut line of Ricki's mouth it wasn't the reassurance she'd wanted, but I didn't want to blow smoke, either.

"The last time I spoke with Arianna, she said my best resource for stopping Cronus would be the Tablet of Hermes," I said. "So he seems to have the Order's backing. I've also consulted my magic, and it's yet to return a hard no."

"What about the people who want you dead?" Ricki asked.

"Which ones?" I started to smile and stopped. "Sorry, bad joke."

She shot me a warning look, which was warranted. This

was serious. She meant the motorcycle-riding Street Keepers led by Red Beard, the one who'd cracked me with the whip and nearly ended me.

You're not supposed to exist.

"Now that I've captured the whip's essence, I'll get to work on a cloaking spell."

Ricki sighed, scattering the steam coming off her coffee. "Well, if you believe Hermes is trustworthy," she said at last, "*and* you can create a working spell, you have my blessing."

"Really?"

I read the frank concern in her eyes as a yes.

Mae patted my arm. "We believe in you, honey."

"Yeah, I've seen you up close in action," Bree-yark added. "If anyone can pull something like this off, it's you."

"I appreciate your confidence in me," I said. "It means a lot."

I just hoped it was warranted.

———————

9

I woke up that night at the Gowdie sisters'.

A few weeks earlier, Bree-yark and I had visited the trio of swamp hags, where they'd offered me a reading in exchange for a year of my youth. Foolishly, I'd accepted. Now I was back, perched on a stool in their cramped kitchen at the rear of their antique store. Before me, foul steam rose from a bubbling cauldron. I was dreaming, but I was conscious, lucid, the smell of the place inducing actual nausea.

Cackles echoed around me.

"Grizela?" I called, rising from the stool. "Elspeth? Minna?"

Lucid dreams were often my magic trying to tell me something, though sometimes I had to go searching for the meaning.

"Couldn't get enough of us, eh, Everson?" came Grizela's voice from behind me.

I spun, expecting to find the oldest of the gray-haired hags taunting me with a gnarled finger, but she wasn't there. Now

Elspeth's voice took up to my right. I turned, squinting for her wart-riddled face.

"He just *pretends* he can't stand us," she said.

"But we're clearly the women of his *dreams*," Minna chimed in.

"Clever," I deadpanned.

The sisters joined her in a taunting fit of laughter that seemed to come from all sides now. I gave up trying to find them.

"Was there something you wanted to tell me?" I asked.

Grizela snorted. "Tell you? *You* came to *us*, you cretin. And why would we tell you anything? Unless, of course," she teased, "you'd like to make another deal?"

"Oh, please say yes," Elspeth said. "Your youth was sooo scrumptious."

Minna made a lip-smacking sound. "*I* could certainly go for another four-month portion."

I recalled the sight of them guzzling the lumpy brown stew that held my essence and almost vomited in my mouth.

"Yeah, no, thanks," I muttered, but the sisters were quarreling now.

"You took *more* than a four-month share, you skank," Elspeth snapped at Minna.

"No, I didn't!"

"Then how did I end up with only three?"

"Ask Grizela!" Minna said. "She's the one with the fat mouth!"

"You're one to talk," Grizela snarled. "Have you seen your nose lately?"

I wasn't sure how much more of these three I could take. I picked my way around the kitchen, stepping over a bucket of plucked rabbit ears, bloody roots and all. My shoe squished into a puddle that felt like gelatin. I jerked my leg up, heart pounding, as the puddle screamed and squelched off into the shadows.

If you have something to show me, I urged my magic, *please do it quickly.*

The sisters were shrieking over one another now, their growing volume seeming to anger the cauldron. It spat and frothed. Before long, their voices combined into a single voice that sounded like none of theirs. I stepped back to find a monstrous being taking shape in the steam above the cauldron.

Holy crap.

The muttering being looked ancient, with a cadaverous face and a riot of frizzy hair knotted with bones. Murderous eyes glowed from deep in her sockets. This was the entity who had delivered my prophecy the last time, an ancestral spirit known as a Doideag.

"*Why have you summoned me?*" she seethed.

Steam jetted from between her pointed teeth, enveloping me in sickening fumes. I drew back, but the space was so crowded I only succeeded in upsetting a glass jar. It shattered, sending a ball of centipedes slithering off in all directions.

"I-I didn't," I stammered, dancing to keep the centipedes from crawling up my pant legs. "I'm dreaming—or nightmaring. I had no idea I'd end up here."

She leaned forward with a severe squint. "It's *you.*"

"Right, you did a reading for me a few weeks ago? Thanks for that. I left the sisters a nice review, by the way."

"Cursed wenches," she spat.

"I won't argue with you there, but I believe I'll wake up now."

A blistering hand shot out and seized my arm. When she yanked, I braced for a skin-sloughing plunge into the cauldron—she'd complained about not getting to share in my life blood the last time—but she held me at the bubbling verge. She stared into my face with eyes that appeared strangely vacant now.

"*If ye should fail and war should come...*"

I recognized the words immediately. She was repeating a line from the prophecy she'd delivered the last time.

"*If seas should boil and lands should run,*" she continued, "*allies gather, eleven and one, and be not afraid of thine own blood.*"

I'd scribbled the prophecy into my notepad, but after thwarting Cronus's return at the explorers club, I'd gotten caught up in other things. Rescuing Alec's mother, helping shadow Vega leave the city, hunting down a sea monster... Plus, I had a new notepad. It had been weeks since I'd read the words. But was this what my magic was trying to tell me? That the prophecy still mattered?

The Doideag's hand trembled now, shaking me.

"*Wage, young mage, till your final breath,*" she cried, enveloping me in another cloud of noxious vapor. "*And come night's fall... accept your death!*"

I kicked awake, a gag lodged in my throat, the Doideag's prophecy pounding in my head.

> *If ye should fail and war should come,*
> *If seas should boil and lands should run,*
> *Allies gather, eleven and one,*

And be not afraid of thine own blood.

A warning? A set of instructions?

Wage, young mage, till your final breath,
And come night's fall, accept your death.

My death? I tried to calm my breathing, tried to recall something Arianna had told me, until I realized a figure was standing in the room. Not Ricki—I could feel her behind me, drawing deep, sleeping breaths.

"Everson?" a familiar voice whispered.

I sat up, squinting at the slender, hooded silhouette. "Hermes?"

"No, it's me."

I released my breath. Alec. He retreated as I pushed myself up and followed him from the bedroom, closing the door gently behind me. In the living room, I snapped on a light. Alec had taken a seat at the edge of the couch to accommodate his backpack, hands grasped between his knees.

"Sorry to wake you like that," he said.

"No worries." A glance at my watch showed that it was after two a.m. "What's up?"

"You wanted me to tell you if Hermes has been acting through me. Well, I think it's been happening."

"What makes you say that?"

"My memories. If you asked what I did yesterday, I'd tell you I checked on my mom, came back here, went to a couple of bookstores, and then hung out around Washington Square Park. But it's like..."

As he examined the ceiling for the right words, I studied

his face. Dark crescents bruised the dusky skin under his eyes. I didn't have to shift to my wizard's senses to know that the threads bonding him to the tablet were drawing tighter.

"They're not reliable memories," Alec decided. "When I think hard about them, they dissolve, sort of like clouds. My other memories don't do that. Does that make sense?"

I nodded. Instead of displacing Alec's consciousness into a void, Hermes was filling those hours with mundane memories. It seemed benevolent, but only if I ignored the fact Hermes was possessing a fifteen-year-old kid.

"He was here yesterday," I said.

Alec straightened. "Hermes? Where?"

"He showed up at Dewitt Clinton Park. I spent the day with him. And, yes, he admitted to... using you this week." God, that felt awful to say. Helplessly, frustratingly awful. "So the cloudy memories you're describing make perfect sense because they're not real. He's been busy over in your realm."

"Doing what?"

"Getting your mother somewhere safer, for one."

Alec's brow furrowed, then smoothed again. "That's weird. I had no idea she'd moved, and then her location just popped into my head." He nodded, as though to himself. "Yeah, she'll be safer there."

I shared his relief. "He's also been making arrangements to head off all-out war with Persephone. It looks like I'll be getting involved."

"I still can't believe they're fighting. It defies every myth I've read."

"Well, according to Hermes, this version of Persephone was worshipped as a wronged and vengeful god. She hates that Zeus conspired with Hades to make her his queen in the underworld. She's determined to overthrow the Olympic order, which Hermes happens to be part of. He wants to preserve it."

Alec pondered that before asking, "What can I do to help?"

"You've helped a lot already."

"I knew you'd say that," he muttered.

"And I'm not just talking about helping me. You've given Hermes a major boost. After you acquired the tablet, he began channeling his powers through yours. That's how your abilities grew, but so have his. He has that advantage over Persephone: a magic-using... partner." I'd nearly said *host*. "We wouldn't be one-and-oh against Cronus, otherwise."

As I spoke, a sense of importance illuminated Alec's face, but it soon dimmed. "What happens when this is over?"

"Hermes will release you."

During our meeting, I'd made Hermes repeat the promise. Once his work was done, he assured me that he would have me open the box that safeguarded his tablet. The act would erase him from our existence and free Alec. "It's more important to preserve humankind," he'd claimed, "than myself."

When Alec spoke again, I expected him to ask whether I trusted Hermes, but he went in another direction. "I'll lose my abilities."

"But not your native magic. It's in your blood, a part of you."

"Minor runic magic," he said gloomily. "I won't be able to transport here anymore." He became momentarily distracted by Tabitha, who remained propped stiffly on her side, before refocusing on me. "To this version of the city, I mean." But he dropped his gaze from mine too quickly.

I'd been considering that, as well. The end of Hermes would mean not being able to see Alec anymore.

I took the seat beside him on the couch. "Bonding with a powerful being like Hermes, even if he's benign... It's not healthy. Our bodies weren't built to channel forces like that. It's better this way."

"Being stuck over there?"

"Your mother needs you."

"Yeah, but who'll teach me?"

Now it was my turn to glance down.

"You said it yourself," he pressed. "There are no magic-users over there, no one left of the Order."

"That I know of," I amended.

"And what about the Street Keepers? If they're hunting you because you're a magic-user, then I'm fair game too, right?"

"I'm working on that."

Seeming to realize his voice had been escalating, Alec paused to take a breath. "I'm sorry," he said. "You've got a lot going on, and my drama isn't helping."

From the start, that had been his concern about revealing his identity to me. He hadn't wanted to intrude on my life, become an encumbrance. I squeezed the back of his neck, then pulled him into a side hug.

"We'll figure it out, buddy."

When he hugged me back, I could feel the weight of his fatigue. I was going to miss this kid. Man, was I going to miss him. But I didn't want him bearing the trickster god's burden anymore.

After a moment, Alec said, "This could be nothing, but there's probably something else I should tell you."

I clapped his shoulder and released him. "What's that?"

He regarded me with his dark, serious eyes. But as he opened his mouth, green light glimmered from the depths of his pupils. His face morphed, setting in a way that heralded the arrival of Hermes.

The god grinned. "Have you come to a decision?"

10

I drew back slightly, bothered by the god's arrival. Had he wanted to keep Alec from revealing whatever he'd been about to say? Or was the timing purely coincidental? I searched his still-illuminating eyes, but they were hard to read.

"Well?" he pressed.

Something told me to keep a poker face. "Yes. I got the go ahead."

"Excellent," he whispered. "Shall we, then?" He gestured to my nightshirt.

I drew it up as he unshouldered the pack and swung it around to his front. From the small compartment, he produced Alec's silver-flecked grease pencil. Tongue tucked in the corner of his mouth, he began rendering a design on my stomach. We'd discussed this earlier, but the timing of his arrival continued to bug me. I watched the design take form —an elegant circle for concentrating energy.

Is this smart? I wondered. *Is there even an alternative?*

"There," Hermes said, sitting back to examine his work. "And now..."

He touched the tip of a finger to the design. I jerked as though I'd brushed a hot stove. The design glowed briefly before fading to a color a shade lighter than my skin tone. I already carried Hermes's energy inside me, but it was diluted. Good for staying under Persephone's radar, but bad when I needed to call on it, which was going to be crucial to the mission's success. The temporary tattoo would fix that.

Hermes nodded. "Go on, give it a try."

I concentrated into the symbol, restoring it to glowing life. A low hum took up. The dusting of Hermes magic inside me drew toward my core. I felt the crackling potential of new spells and invocations.

"It works," I said, releasing the energy and lowering my shirt.

"I've also collected the ingredients for your potions," Hermes said.

From the backpack's main compartment, he pulled out a plastic bag. As he handed it to me, my gaze lingered on the pillowcase in the bottom of his pack. The pillowcase held a box. Crafted by the ancient thieves guild who'd worshipped him, the box preserved the Tablet of Hermes, the impetus for everything.

Attracting ancient objects to the shadow realm, including Persephone's scepter... Compelling Alec to steal the tablet, which bound him to Hermes... Enabling Alec, and Hermes, to find me...

"By this time tomorrow, my friend," he said, "we'll be feasting."

"Thanks, but I think I'll forgo the celebration. We'll have a box to open."

He chuckled. "I'm starting to get the feeling I've outstayed my welcome here."

How perceptive, I thought. "It's nothing personal. I just don't want any loose ends."

"That's what I admire about you." His gaze turned keen with knowing. "This concern for your son. He'll be fine, I've told you this."

"Then how about offering something more than lip service?"

Hermes squinted as though trying to decide whether I'd insulted him. "What do you mean?"

"Yesterday you made a binding deal with your supernatural draftees. Let's make a similar deal. Let's *formalize* what you're promising. If I destroy Persephone's scepter, you agree to release him."

"Very well. And if you don't destroy the scepter?"

I hesitated. "Then we have bigger problems, right?"

"But what are *you* offering?"

"Isn't going after the scepter enough?"

"No, no, no, that's not how these agreements work. It must be something unfavorable to yourself that you give freely. Yesterday, for example, my draftees lost the contest and so pledged themselves to my cause. But had *I* lost, I would have released them from my service. Poof. All my reserve forces gone like that. Now, what are you willing to risk that is worth your son's freedom?"

I knew how binding deals worked, but I'd been hoping he'd just say yes and we'd move on.

"Of course, you needn't offer *anything*," Hermes continued. "You can choose to take me at my 'lip service,' as you call it."

"But if you're so trustworthy, why not make it binding?"

"I could ask the same of you. You're saying you'll recover Persephone's scepter, but how do I know you won't get cold feet at the last moment? Or, Father forbid, strike a bargain with *her*? They've already appealed to you once to go after my tablet. The answer is I *don't* know. I'm choosing to trust you."

I massaged the corners of my eyes. Did I really want to enter into a bargain with Olympus's craftiest god?

He scooted closer. "Everson, I've told you, I've no desire to remain here beyond undoing what's been done, what my box has brought about. The ones who worshipped me are gone. The magic of the box sustains me, yes, but that too will fade. By having you open the box, I'll become absorbed in my greater identity. My *archetype*, according to you scholarly sorts. I'll join my family on Olympus... along with Persephone." His eyes went hazy. "From there, we'll gaze from our cosmic perch on a world we once lorded over. Too distant now to interfere in, too abstract for us to care. I don't know how else to convince you that I *want* this, Everson."

Would a cultural hero say that, or just a trickster pretending to be one?

"But once again," he said, showing his hands, "the choice regarding an agreement is entirely yours."

After a moment, I stood and lifted the shopping bag of ingredients.

"I should get started on the potions."

11

F rom the driver's seat, Ricki looked over my shopping bag and the loaded pockets of my trench coat.

"I took inventory five times before leaving and twice since we pulled out," I assured her while gesturing to suggest she might want to keep her eyes on the road. "I have everything I need. I promise."

"How are you feeling?"

"Anxious, but it's the good kind of anxiousness. Stimulating. Like my neurons are in the team huddle and can't wait to run out onto the field."

She frowned at my clumsy analogy. "You barely slept."

"True, but I added an invigoration potion to my coffee"—I held up my New York Mets travel mug—"and it's working."

Though her face remained troubled, she laced her fingers through mine above the emergency brake.

It was the following morning, not quite eight, and she was driving me to the rendezvous point with Hermes. While I'd spent the rest of the night preparing potions and rehearsing the plan, Hermes had left to make final preparations. Our jumping-off point would be downtown near the government buildings. In the shadow realm that area was cordoned off with barricades and official checkpoints. No such obstructions here. When Ricki shot past Canal Street, I began tracking street signs. I released her hand and pointed.

"It's over there."

She rolled to a stop in front of a building covered in scaffolding, her tires grinding against the curb. I leaned over to kiss her, but she kept it to a peck. "This isn't goodbye yet. I'm going in with you."

I thought I knew why. "You sure?"

She answered by cutting off the engine. I finished the rest of my coffee in one tilt, then hustled around to open her door and help her from the low seat.

"Thanks," she said, leaning back to accommodate our child.

The building was in the throes of a massive renovation. At the third rolldown steel door, I grabbed the handle and raised it enough for Ricki and me to duck under. Morning light streamed through gated windows. Amid the building materials, I spotted Hermes sitting cross-legged atop a stack of pallets.

"Ahh, the missus came to see you off?" He jumped down. "How lovely."

"Yes, and to give you a parting warning," she said. "Anything happens to him, and I'll personally kick your ass."

And there it was.

Hermes's eyes twinkled as they shifted to me. "You married well, my friend."

"Yes, I did." I turned to Ricki. "I'll be alright." I kissed her frown, which soon molded to my mouth in a firm plea: *be safe.*

I caressed her cheek as we parted and turned to Hermes. "Ready?"

The sooner we did this, the sooner I could return home to my family.

Seeing my resolve, perhaps, Hermes spared me any more commentary as we gripped one another's arms. Construction dust kicked up around us. Then, in a stomach-dipping flash, we were crossing over.

With my next breath, it felt as though I were inhaling a gray grit that stuck to the soul. It cast everything in a shade of hopelessness—smell, taste, the very urge to live. I was definitely back in the shadow present. I found some consolation in knowing this would be my last visit, but then I thought of Alec having to live out his life here.

"Here we are," Hermes said almost cheerily as he released my arms.

He cast up a ball of green-tinged light, illuminating a space similar to the one we'd just left. An unfinished street-level business, though this project appeared to have been abandoned years before. I turned to where Ricki had been standing in the actual present. In her place was a shadowy emptiness.

I sighed and shook out my arms.

"Do you have everything?" Hermes asked.

"Here," I said, handing him the shopping bag, which contained what we would need to destroy the scepter. "You're absolutely sure we're safe here?"

"Not only straight to the point," Hermes said as though making a note to himself about the human species, "but incurable worriers. Yes, yes, I told you. The moment we arrived, I created a negative space to hide me from Persephone. That said, she'll eventually sense the void and send her goons to investigate, so enough talk." He produced a duffel bag from behind the pallets. "Go on, start changing. Chop, chop."

"Wait, first things first."

I drew a potion from a trench coat pocket and activated it. Designed to conceal me from the energy I'd extracted from the whip, the potion was a feat of advanced potion-making, one I was rather proud of. I drank it down hot, and braced myself as pinpricks spread throughout my system before nodding.

Hermes handed me the duffel bag, and I probed its contents. Gray military pants, an armored vest, a helmet, and what looked like a tactical rod. He'd also included a hand mirror, something I hadn't considered.

"How are we doing for time?" I asked.

"Plenty, plenty. You have about ten minutes."

"Ten minutes?" A charge went off in my chest. "You call that *plenty*?"

"Forgive me, I'm a poor judge of mortal time. I *am* a god of speed, after all."

With fresh urgency, I shucked my coat and stripped down to my boxers. The rune Hermes had drawn the night before showed pale on my stomach. I strained to pull on the tight-fitting military pants. Same with the armored vest. I had to suck in my stomach while Hermes fastened it.

Though both articles smelled like a musty locker room, I was more bothered by the lack of footwear. But that was the official uniform. At my hung coat, I transferred my potions to my pants pockets.

"Three minutes," Hermes said.

Nodding quickly, I produced and activated another potion. With the tube bubbling near my lips, I hesitated. "You're sure I can get there inside of twenty minutes? Because that's all the potion's going to give me."

"Follow the plan, and you'll be fine."

"You did just say you're a poor judge of time."

He smiled in concession. "Yes, well, if I'm estimating off the cuff. In this case, I've calibrated everything down to the seconds. Just remember the prompts, and all will go splendidly."

I rehearsed the prompts in my head, then tipped back the copycat potion. The last potion had gone down easily. This one was like trying to swallow liquid clay. I'd only managed to stop gagging when Hermes spoke again.

"You'll need to leave that."

I followed his nod to a construction pillar and swore. I'd meant to leave my cane in the car for Ricki to take home, but I'd slipped it through my belt without thinking, not even noticing it was there when we transported to the shadow realm. Just as automatically, I'd leaned the cane against the pillar before changing. I could have blamed it on my lack of sleep, but the cane had become such an integral part of me, I did that a lot. Just last week, I'd taken it with me into the shower.

Hermes opened a hand now and held out the tactical rod, as if offering a trade. I passed my cane to him reluctantly and accepted the rod.

"I'll take good care of it," he promised.

"Please do. It's irreplaceable." Besides being the most powerful item I owned, the cane was comprised of a staff that had belonged to my grandfather, while the sword it concealed was a very special gift from my late father. But as with my ring and amulet, which I'd left at home, the cane was too conspicuous to carry with me.

"The changes are starting," Hermes said.

The words were barely out of his mouth when I grunted. My flesh was compacting in on itself, hardening around my bones. I winced as a sudden pressure seized my head. Like being squeezed in a vice, it felt as though my skull was narrowing vertically. I focused past the pain, fixating on my feet as my toes turned square and rock-like.

Before long, the throbbing eased and the fossilization process ceased. I grabbed the mirror from the bag with a gray hand, nearly fumbling it before correcting my grip. A stone golem stared back at me.

Thanks to the biological material Hermes had scored— and I'd cooked into my copycat potion—I was now a soldier of the Iron Guard, Persephone's soulless force. The only difference was my eyes. While theirs swirled with under-world magic, the eyes that peered back from beneath a deep shelf of brow were my own.

"One minute to go," Hermes said.

I swapped the mirror for the helmet and secured it over my head. Its thick visor dimmed my view to near darkness, but it would hide my eyes. Hermes took my arm and guided me toward the door.

"Are you certain you're ready?" he asked.

"Are you certain you'll be at the meeting spot?"

"I promise it."

"Then I'm ready."

His eyes cut to the side and he thrust a finger against my lips. Outside, the engine of a large vehicle was approaching. Heavy tires rolled over glass and chewed-up asphalt. A second vehicle was followed by a synchronic pattern of foot-falls. Persephone's force coming to investigate, or a routine patrol?

When they passed, my nerves let out slightly before tight-ening again. The passing patrol was my first prompt to act. Hermes raised the steel door.

"*Go,*" he whispered, and shoved me outside.

12

Rain streaked my visor as I stumbled into the street.

"*I believe in you,*" Hermes whispered before the door banged closed.

Disoriented, I looked for the sentry that had just passed. Beyond the gray slant of rain, I spotted them: two armored vehicles and a short column of Iron Guard soldiers, already a block south on Church Street.

Swinging my stone-like limbs, I broke into a clumsy run after them.

The Iron Guard operated as a hive mind, according to Hermes. It was a two-tiered hierarchy: Persephone at the top and the Iron Guard underneath. "This is to our advantage," he'd said. "No supervisors or busybodies among the rank and file. They're little more than automatons that follow orders and alert the rest of their hive mind to anomalies. Do as they do, and they'll never notice you."

Easier said than done, I thought, struggling to balance my oblong head atop my emaciated body.

When I went to wipe my visor, my head tipped to the side,

pulling the rest of me after it. With a rude splash, my foot plunged into a pothole. It was a minor miracle I managed to retract it before face-planting.

Swearing softly, I corrected course and urged myself to do better.

Ahead, the column slowed to take a left onto Murray Street, allowing me a chance to catch up. I fell in behind the group of four soldiers trotting in lockstep. Like me, they wore visored helmets and went shirtless beneath their armored vests. Below the cuffs of their military pants, gray feet pounded asphalt. By depriving them of boots, Persephone seemed to be reinforcing their slave status.

I labored to match the soldiers' footfalls and swing my weapon in time to theirs. Two carried rifles, the other two rods like mine. But while red energy squirmed around the ends of their instruments—energy that recalled feelings of being buried alive—my own weapon was inert. Hermes had assured me they wouldn't notice.

"Just be as they are," he kept repeating. "Do as they do."

To my surprise, I was getting the hang of it. Enough that I could begin to take in our surroundings. We were in the civic center, beyond the formidable cement barricades and official checkpoints that ringed the entire government sector. Posters for the mayor's referendum plastered the sides of buildings, and on every one, the energy-gathering sigil lurked around Budge's grinning face.

At the end of a canyon of low-rises, a wall of cement barricades fortified City Hall Park. Guards flanked the entrance. I took extra care mimicking the soldiers in front of me, step for step, swing for swing. The guards watched us approach, their visors all seeming to aim at me, the odd number.

But I was more concerned with what was happening ahead. Each entering vehicle bent slightly, as though I was viewing them through a faulty monitor. The same effect happened with the lead soldiers.

Persephone's defensive field.

When it was my turn, I braced myself. A brief sensation of dipping, like when a high-speed elevator starts down, and then I was through. More disorienting was the environment in which I found myself.

In the actual present, the public park featured large shade trees, a handsome fountain, and plenty of benches where people ate their lunches or chatted idly over iced lattes. Here, everything had been uprooted and covered in ugly cement constructions that crowded the city hall building.

While the vehicles turned left, the foot soldiers continued straight and onto the grounds of the former park. Lines of soldiers entered from every direction, while fresh columns headed back out in some form of shift change. The rain and incessant marching had turned the grounds to mud. It was all I could do to keep from slipping as we advanced on an oblong building to one side of City Hall.

We filed through a narrow opening and into a dank darkness that smelled like a boy's locker room in need of bleach and a fire hose. I was tempted to cock my helmet back enough to peer from beneath the visor, but then I would look out of place. With my next step, I collided into the soldier in front of me.

Crap!

I staggered backward, my vision adapting enough now that, amid the squirming knots of red energy, I could make out stony silhouettes. The soldier's head swiveled. I held perfectly still, waiting for him to raise his weapon or broadcast an alarm to the hive mind. But in the next moment, he straightened and turned left.

I released my breath and took quick stock. Hermes had called this a barracks, but it looked more like a charging station. Soldiers slotted weapons into ports along the walls, then stood atop rows of blocks. I sensed magic in the blocks and ports, terminal outlets in some mystical grid.

Instead of joining the soldiers on the blocks, I resumed my robotic trot toward the back of the barracks. There, I fell in behind another line of soldiers who were freshly charged up and ready to patrol again. As Hermes promised, none of the soldiers coming or going gave me a second look.

As my new unit squelched through the mud toward Broadway, I broke off to take a position at the corner of the building, out of view of the guards stationed across the grounds.

"The guards are more sensitive to anomalies than the foot soldiers," Hermes had cautioned. "And though your potion *should* be enough to escape their notice, there's no penalty for treading carefully."

So far, so good, I thought.

Though City Hall's columned entrance was presently outside my view, I'd noted the heavy security. According to one of Hermes's informants, the clearance process could take thirty minutes. That spelled *no go*, even with a stealth potion.

"Fortunately, there's a hidden entrance," Hermes had said with gleaming eyes.

From where I stood, I could see the courthouse behind City Hall—at least its upper stories. The large historic building was ringed by cranes and construction fencing. Big vehicles trundled in and out along a muddy track. Persephone was repurposing the courthouse into a temple to

Cronus. The hidden entrance, according to Hermes, was an underground tunnel that connected the two buildings.

"Cunning, no?" he'd said.

Sure, Danny Ocean, but where the hell's my next prompt?

It was all I could do to keep from shifting my stone feet. Only they weren't so stony anymore, I saw in alarm. The skin was paling, the toenails starting to show color. The same was true of my arms, my hands. My head throbbed inside my helmet as my skull began to expand out again, returning to form.

Are you freaking kidding me? No, no, no!

The copycat potion was petering out.

13

I cast my eyes around in a desperate search for a departing column of soldiers. One I could join and then make my way to the meeting point, ideally before the copycat potion expired. But the columns were gone now and only guards remained. I couldn't risk running back out through the gate. Not while I was morphing.

Do I pull the ripcord and activate Hermes's magic?

It would get me out of there, but it would also alert Persephone that we'd breached her inner defenses. We'd never get this good of a shot again. I licked my stony teeth with a tongue that felt alarmingly human.

I only had a few seconds to decide.

A loud horn spanked the air, making me jump. A second horn answered. Ahead, two construction vehicles rumbled toward one another, one leaving the site, one entering, and neither one yielding.

I drew a steadying breath. *Okay. That's gotta be the prompt.*

"I've planted some subtle enchantments," Hermes had told me. "But that's all I'm willing to risk. Anything bolder, and I'll out myself. Be alert for a standoff. A spirited standoff that will seem natural, given the participants. It will attract just the right amount of attention, and that's when you'll move."

The two vehicles—a dump truck and a cement mixer—arrived nose-to-nose, the drivers laying full on their horns now.

I stepped from my post and walked toward them.

The drivers jumped down from their vehicles, a bearded man, sleeves rolled up to his burly shoulders, and a much shorter man who managed to appear the more menacing. They stalked forward bellowing, their fingers jabbing at the vehicles, the makeshift roadway, and increasingly at one another.

By the time I reached the far side of the idling trucks, the men were grappling in the mud. Shouts rose from the site, and workers spilled out, possibly to break up the fight, but more likely to cheer it on. I used the distraction to edge past the dump truck's rear tire and enter the construction zone.

With a row of porta-potties for cover, I made my way toward the office trailers, eyes trained on the second to the last one. I arrived behind it, heart thudding in my softening chest. At a window, I peeked inside, then ducked back, cursing silently. A figure had been facing me. But as my mind processed the image, I saw the glow of a screen on the man's face. He'd been looking at a monitor.

The operation seemed a helluva lot easier in the planning, I thought, catching my breath.

As I reached into a pocket for a potion, twin bolts bored into my temples, doubling me over. *Son of a bitch!* With my head returning to form, the helmet was threatening to become a permanent fixture.

I pried it off with a low grunt, ripping out some hair. Even so, the relief came instantly. And without the visor screening my vision, the shadow realm suddenly appeared vibrant. That wouldn't last.

I listened toward the brawl. Still a lot of shouting, but it was being punctuated now by calls to get back to work.

Speed it up, man.

I pulled the potion from my pocket and activated it. As it began to bubble, I slipped around to the front corner of the trailer, held my breath, and poured the sleeping potion across the doorway in a line. A curtain of pink mist drifted up. I capped the potion, rapped on the door, and returned to the back.

"Yeah?" an irritated voice called from inside.

The trailer creaked with shifting weight. At the window, I watched the project manager hitch his pants to the top of his crack and amble toward the door. He opened it, stuck his head directly into the potion's mist, looked around for several seconds, and closed the door again. I drew back and listened.

The trailer creaked some more, and then came the expected thud. And not a moment too soon. My pale arms told me I was ninety percent Everson Croft again.

I slid the window open and wriggled my way over a window-facing desk. Folders and papers spilled in my wake. I managed to grab a thick cable before the computer it powered crashed to the floor. I arranged everything back in its place before approaching the manager, who was slumped against the wall, fast asleep. I took a second to size him up. Larger than me, but the proportions were close enough.

The process of removing my clothes and then shucking and donning his took a good fifteen minutes. The movies always made it look easy. At last, I knotted the boot laces, then stood and shook out my legs. His jeans hung baggy on me, and his work boots bobbled on my feet, but as long as I looked the part...

I dragged the man into the trailer's bathroom, propped him beside the toilet, and locked the door. The Iron Guard disguise went behind a filing cabinet. All except for the rod.

I released a small clasp, and the rod opened vertically on a hidden hinge to reveal a hollow space. Nested inside was a slender tube like the kind architects carried. I removed it, took a hardhat from a shelf, and turned the ID badge on the pocket of my flannel shirt around so the man's photo and name—Jake Reilly—were hidden.

Pockets clinking with potions, I ventured outside. The fight had since broken up, and workers were ambling back to the site. I turned away from them and hastened toward the courthouse building.

"Given the pace of construction, there will be people everywhere," Hermes had said. "Different companies, different teams. Just look like you're in too much of a hurry to be bothered and proceed directly to the tunnel."

I nodded to myself. He'd gotten me this far.

I circled construction equipment, ducked under scaffolding, and entered the courthouse through a back door. Shouting and jackhammering reverberated from all sides. I proceeded down a corridor hung with sheets of industrial plastic, consulting my mental map of the courthouse as Hermes had sketched it.

At the building's rotunda area, which was being dramatically expanded, I peered into a fresh pit that cored out the basement levels. Brown water pooled at the very bottom. High overhead, an octagonal skylight allowed in gray light, but that wasn't all. The metal framing had been configured into a casting symbol, not unlike the one on the "Budge Train" posters, and it was channeling a column of raw energy into the pool below. This was the energy Persephone was siphoning from the city.

I resisted the urge to stare. None of the workers had given this wizard in disguise a closer look yet, and I wanted to keep it that way. My chest clenched now as I approached a ladder to the lower levels. I'd thought having a basement-level lab would relax my underground phobia some, but not yet.

Relax, I coached myself. *You'll be out of here before you know it.*

While waiting on a pair of workers to ascend the ladder, I forced several deep breaths. Too soon, the workers were moving past me, and I took their place on the ladder. I climbed down two levels and hurried along a catwalk to a ploughed-out room that ended at a metal door. A posted sign read: RESTRICTED ACCESS. Then, in a smaller font, TRESPASSING PUNISHABLE BY DEATH.

Wow, that's all?

I tested the door handle to find it locked. I pressed my ear to the damp metal. Nothing sounded from beyond. I began looking around for the key. Hermes had claimed it would be within "easy reach."

"Jake!" a man shouted above the noise.

Crap, that was me—or rather the person whose clothes I was wearing.

Without turning, I pretended to survey the wooden beams supporting the room, even pressing on one several times. In my peripheral vision, a figure hustled down the catwalk, a keychain jangling at his belt.

"Jake!" the man repeated. "What the hell are you doing down here?"

I turned toward him with a surly face. "You got a problem, buddy?"

He stopped suddenly, his mouth faltering. "Oh. Sorry. I thought you were someone else." He turned, then stopped as though something had just occurred to him. "Who *are* you?"

"What the fuck is it to you?" I snarled in my best Hoffman voice.

But it was the wrong tactic. Instead of cowing him, my verbal challenge set the man's chest heaving and his nostrils flaring like a bull's. He wasn't a small man, either.

"I'm the site manager down here, you little turd." He stalked forward. "And I wanna know what you're doing in my pit."

When he lunged, I raised an arm thinking he was preparing to take a swing. Instead, he seized my ID tag and yanked it from my shirt. I watched, stunned, as the man brought the card toward his screwed up face.

Before he could turn it around, I thundered, "Stop!"

According to Hermes, my potions would be safe if used sparingly. They released magic in a measured manner over time, not rising to a threshold that would alert Persephone. The same couldn't be said of invocations, though, which emerged as noisy blasts. And in my panic, I'd just set off a cherry bomb.

The man blinked at me slowly.

"Give it back," I said, drawing down my wizard's voice but not abandoning it.

I didn't see an alternative. If he learned I was impersonating Jake, he'd sound the alarm. And if I splashed him with sleeping potion, he'd collapse in plain view of a dozen workers. As it was, our standoff was already drawing some looks.

The ID was inches from the man's face, but his gaze remained on mine.

"Give it *back*," I repeated, compressing my power into a tight, forceful current.

At last, he extended his arm. It took two tugs for me to remove the ID from his grip. I returned it to my shirt and was about to send the man on his way when I connected his credentials to the keys at his belt.

"There are a few ways to access the tunnel," Hermes had said, "but the safest will be the most straightforward. Don't worry. When you arrive, I'll place a key within easy reach."

I gave a bitter inward laugh. Like with the obstinate truck drivers, Hermes had hit the man with a subtle enchantment, probably the night before, to ensure he would keep a suspicious eye on his pit. Hermes had trusted me to do the rest. Maybe I should have been flattered, but the god was also amusing himself.

I snapped my fingers at the man and pointed at the door. "I need that opened for inspection."

The man nodded as though he'd been shot full of Sodium Pentothal and fumbled through his keys. The one he finally produced was black and crusty, and I picked up a thin skin of magic along its length. The bolt released, and the man withdrew. But he remained standing there, staring at me dimly.

Oh, for the love of...

"Let's get back to work, huh?" I suggested.

He stared for several more moments before nodding slowly. At last, he turned and ambled away.

With no idea how long he would remain under the thrall of my voice, I opened the door and slipped inside. Cold blackness pressed around me. I pawed my helmet until I found the switch for the small headlamp seated in the hard plastic. The tunnel it illuminated had been drilled straight through the bedrock. Dark gray walls, buttressed every several feet by wooden beams, glistened with moisture.

I listened for a moment, rotating the cardboard tube in my sweaty palms. Hearing nothing, I started down the tunnel, boots splashing through puddles. Within ten steps my headlamp dimmed to a series of concentric rings.

Are you kidding me?

Jake had allowed the batteries to run down. Swearing, I sped my pace, but it was a losing race. The light was fading too fast. Before long, it was a single tan ring, so faint against the tunnel floor I might as well have imagined it. And then the light extinguished altogether. I stared into the darkness ahead, ears ringing.

From the deep void, a low growl sounded.

14

T he growl that followed was lower in pitch and a little closer.

Two of them... at least.

As I felt for the plastic cap on my cardboard tube, I recalled what Hermes had said. "I don't know what Persephone keeps down there, if anything. According to an informant, noises have been heard, but only on the days no tunnel work is scheduled. I would listen before you enter. If it's quiet, you're likely clear."

The growls were accompanied now by the scrape and patter of approaching footfalls. At last I located the plastic cap. Digging my fingernails underneath the rim, I pried it open, nearly fumbling the tube in the process.

"But I'll pack extra help," Hermes had finished, "should you need it."

Something fell to the ground with a metallic clang. The noise set off the growlers. In explosions of barking, they broke into a run.

I stooped for the fallen object, a small wand that glowed

softly. A pair of metal serpents twined its length, arriving at a pair of wings. The wand, known as a caduceus, belonged to Hermes. I grabbed it just before my would-be attackers arrived. Silvery green light swelled out, illuminating a pair of snapping snouts.

Holy ugly.

The creatures looked like canine versions of the Iron Guard. Built like German Shepherds, they were nearly as tall as me, lips wrinkled from teeth too large for their chiseled muzzles. I thrust the caduceus toward them. The beasts withdrew to the edge of the light, their barks shrinking to whimpers.

Okay, good, I thought with a shaky breath.

But their large bodies were still blocking the tunnel. I chanced another look at the wand. It wasn't Hermes's actual caduceus, but a weaker object that held the slimmest amount of his magic, lest Persephone sense him. He'd designed it as a channel for me to push my own power through.

"*Attivare,*" I whispered.

The wand glowed more brightly, forcing the stone dogs back further. When I stepped forward, they retreated some more. We proceeded in this manner, but it was a game of inches, and it was going much too slowly. I could feel the seconds ticking down, and there was still a good fifty feet of tunnel ahead.

"Go home," I tried.

That used to work on a neighbor's dog who would come bounding into my grandparents' garden to dig holes. But these dogs hunkered down, stone tongues lolling, tails scraping back and forth across the floor.

The caduceus was commonly mistaken for a symbol of medicine. That was actually the Rod of Asclepius, belonging to a Greek deity of healing. Hermes's rod held various charms, which the dogs were clearly susceptible to, but they were still blocking the way.

"Move," I ordered, turning sideways for them to pass.

They set their head between their paws. I stepped toward them now, watching for the least sign of aggression. The dogs' empty eye sockets remained fixed on the caduceus, even as I set it on the ground.

Magic, if I'm about to do something really stupid, please tell me.

No response came, and the caduceus would be fading soon. I crept up to the closer dog and, very gingerly, stepped on its forearm. When the dog didn't react, I parked my other foot on the knob of its shoulder and heaved myself onto its back. The dog shifted. I teetered in place, half expecting its jaw to snap around and remove my foot at the ankle, but it only seemed to be adjusting itself to my weight.

Like a tight-rope walker, I negotiated the ridge of its back, then crossed the small chasm to the other dog's back. The moment I had my balance, I jumped down. The two remained fixated on the caduceus.

Okay, I never *want to do that again.*

I broke into a jog. Ahead, the dim reach of the caduceus's light picked up the bars of a metal gate. I arrived, panting, to find it secured by a draw bolt, though easy enough for me to reach from the inside.

"Persephone is concerned with someone breaching City Hall from the courthouse," Hermes had said. "Not vice versa. But now isn't the time to get comfortable. You're about to enter her inner sanctum."

I drew the bolt back, stepped through the gate, and secured it behind me.

The sublevel I arrived in was heaped with old cabinets and file boxes, most of them mold-covered. Weak light entered from a staircase ahead. Conscious that the dogs could snap from their trances at any moment and erupt into more barking, I hurried toward the steps, extremely ready to be above ground again.

The steps led to another basement space. Light from a dangling bulb showed chairs and cabinets thrown atop desks and tables. I aimed for a large wooden cabinet not far from the staircase.

"This is the final enchantment I'm willing to risk," Hermes had told me. "They're all simple behavior modifications, none of them directly threatening Persephone, so they shouldn't alert her. But I don't want to press my luck. Now, a young up-and-comer has an important presentation tomorrow. I'll put it in his head that he's at risk of spilling coffee all over his suit. Better stash a backup, yes?"

Let's see if he delivered...

I opened the cabinet, amazed to discover a garment bag folded over once. A pair of buffed shoes sat beside it, as well as a spare briefcase. I swapped Jake's clothes for the suit—a decent fit this time. There was even a toiletries bag with a comb and styling gel, which I applied liberally, dragging my hair straight back.

From the cardboard tube I'd been carrying, I shook out a glove threaded with silver filaments and stuffed it into a pocket. Finally, I removed the briefcase from the cabinet, a slender leather number of Italian provenance.

Hopefully, I looked douchey enough not to stand out.

I ascended the next flight up and pushed open a door that led onto a corridor between conference rooms. Only then did my phobia release my chest, allowing me full breaths once more. Though I clenched the briefcase with purpose, my hands felt naked. I had no cane, no caduceus. Just Hermes's assurances that for these final steps—the most dangerous steps—I would have what I needed.

You're almost there, I told myself. *Almost done with this god crap.*

The corridor led onto the building's rotunda area. In the actual present, sunlight would flood the open space, enriching its architectural marvels: a ring of Corinthian columns, an elegant omega-shaped staircase that appeared to float, a regal dome high above. But here the gritty gray light made the space look like a mausoleum.

I peered around. No Iron Guard to suggest that my earlier invocation or encounter with the dogs had tipped off Persephone. Just officials and civil servants either trudging around in a soulless march or trotting in a just as soulless race. And none of them appeared remotely interested in me.

"Hey, feeling better than you look!" a boisterous voice called.

Damn, I knew that voice. I started to retreat back into the corridor, but I was too slow.

Leading an entourage of officials, Mayor Budge Lowder appeared across the rotunda and turned straight toward me. Unlike the Budge in my reality, a clumsy waddler, this one speed-walked with authority. He called out compliments as he went, mostly to women, and friendly digs, mostly to the men.

Amazing. Even in this hellish reality Budge managed to remain upbeat.

I prayed he'd veer off, but he kept coming. *Act natural, act natural, act natural.*

I parked my briefcase on a raised knee and pretended to

search through it. The only time that shadow Budge and I had met face-to-face, I'd just navigated two miles of ghoul-infested subway lines. My hair was in disarray, and grime had streaked just about every inch of my exposed skin. I looked nothing like that now. Still, the actual Budge swore he never forgot a face. Bluster or genuine skill?

The entourage stopped in front of me.

"Hey, pal," Budge snarled.

15

I raised my eyes from the briefcase slowly to find the shadow mayor pointing a finger at me. The lines of his face deepened around a scowl.

"Who do you think you're fooling?"

"I-I'm sorry?" I stammered.

"No one cops my style. Maybe try a combover next time?" And then, as though a switch had been thrown, a humorous smile broke over his face. He was talking about my hair, which mirrored his own slicked-back job.

In my relief, I laughed a little too loudly. He was already moving on, calling out final compliments and digs, and then he and his entourage disappeared into a conference room.

Thanking my lucky stars, I took the rotunda's floating staircase two steps at a time until I arrived at the second level. Directly opposite me stood the wooden door that concealed a stairwell to City Hall's little known third floor: a rectangular penthouse at the front of the building. Persephone's chambers. Even from my distance, I picked up protective magic squirming around the doorframe.

I activated and downed a stealth potion, then circled toward the door. When I'd come as close as I dared, I propped my briefcase on the stone railing that ran around the rotunda and pretended to search through it again. A few functionaries came and went, disappearing into doorways or down the stairs. Despite all the obstacles, I'd managed to arrive early, allowing the potion time to take effect.

"Don't be intimidated by the door," Hermes had said. "It won't remain closed. Like most goddesses, Persephone requires attendants for her morning bath."

I didn't have long to wait. A group of four women entered the rotunda below and ascended the stairs. They were all young and fresh-faced with ponytails that swished along the shoulders of their matching robes. According to Hermes, only virginal females attended to the goddess. They reminded her of the Oceanids, water nymphs with whom she used to gather flowers. There were also stories of her nude form driving mortals to madness. I didn't plan to test them, but good to know.

Within moments, the attendants were at the top of the stairs and moving past me.

"The trick will be in the timing," Hermes had said. "As they gather at the door, you must insert yourself among them. The door will recognize them and open. You will enter as well, but keep count! More than ten seconds, and the door will detect even subtle magic. Alarms will sound, and the game will be up!"

I left the briefcase on the railing and hurried into the young women's fragrant wake, my body tingling with my potion's magic. When they arrived at the door, I concentrated, pushing a little more power into the potion, coaxing it toward its peak. It wouldn't render me invisible, just very unnoticeable.

I joined the back of their line and started my countdown.

The frontmost attendant placed her hand on the doorknob. The door stayed closed.

When I reached four seconds, I began to sweat. What in the hell was it waiting for?

Five... six...

Then, as though it had been pressure locked, the door released and swung inward. As the attendants filed through, I pressed forward, coming so close to the final woman that I could smell the skin beneath her floral perfume. Pleasant though it may have been, it was all I could do to keep from shoving her forward.

Eight... Nine...

And then I was through, mouthing out a dispersion.

As the door slammed closed, the energy in the potion left me. I held my breath, expecting klaxons and flashing red lights, but neither one followed. The magic sealing the door eddied calmly. Once more, my potion had done its job. A monumental relief, but I was fully visible now.

I snapped my gaze back to the attendants. They had only to turn their heads to see me, but they were proceeding purposefully up the flight of steps.

With their footsteps covering mine, I followed. The stairwell ended at a regal corridor of polished wainscotting. The attendants turned left, and I broke right, placing myself behind a wooden column built into the wall. From my concealment, I watched them enter a room at the corridor's far end. Minutes later, they emerged again. I drew back. They were escorting Persephone across the hall to her bath chamber.

I didn't get a good look at the goddess—Hermes had cautioned me against it, even if she were robed—but I could feel her presence. A collision of bone-chilling decay and sun-drenched life, strangely intoxicating. The corridor rotated slightly in my vision. And then a door closed and taps turned on.

My final prompt.

I made my way toward the sound. Opposite the bath chamber, where water continued to cascade, the door to Persephone's room stood ajar. Heart pounding, I eased it open further and slipped inside.

The candle flames that illuminated the bedchamber looked slender and fragile against the darkness. Heavy drapery and defensive magic covered the windows, but the darkness was a feature of the room itself, of dread Persephone's presence.

For a moment, I stood perfectly still, not quite believing I was here, but wanting to make sure I was here alone.

An enormous bed canopied in airy silk curtains stood to one side of the room. Opposite was a breakfast table and sitting area, lavishly decorated, as though for a princess. Dried petals lay everywhere, but like with the candles and décor, the pleasantness they exuded was dominated by a darker, weightier force.

Innocence lost, I thought. *That's what Persephone represents, even this vengeful version of her. Innocence lost.*

In that moment, I understood Hermes's sympathies toward her, felt them viscerally. But her vengeance, however justified, would result in catastrophic destruction and death, something I couldn't allow.

I refocused, my gaze narrowing toward the paneled wall opposite me. One of the panels was open a crack, releasing a slipstream of pungent air. I crossed the room and peered into the cavern-like space. Shelving with oddly shaped bottles and tied-off pouches crowded a work area to one side: a lab where Persephone must have prepared her potions. A marble pool the size of a large well occupied the other.

I shifted to my wizard's senses in search of astral traps or alarms before slipping inside.

"Once you arrive at the pool, the scepter will be within your reach," Hermes had said excitedly. "Provided you have the ability to seize it."

I removed his silver-threaded glove from my pocket and pulled it over my hand. "*Attivare,*" I whispered.

Pale light encompassed the glove, cinching my wrist and warming my hand. I eased the gloved hand into the water, then circled the pool, my fingers combing the clear water like a dragnet. According to Hermes, the pool was similar to my interplanar cubbyhole—a place for Persephone to stash her things.

I'd gone halfway around when I encountered something slender and hard. Closing my hand around the invisible object, I pulled. It wasn't until it broke the water's surface that an ornate rod shimmered into view. I was gripping its twisted neck, right beneath a crown studded with beguiling black stones.

The enchanted glove buffered me from the object's magic, but I could feel the thrum of its power. I was holding Persephone's scepter. It was precious, but not pristine. Deep in the seams of the twisted handle, I noticed some rock and mineral deposits, as though the scepter had been excavated.

From the bath chamber, a fearsome scream sounded.

Shit.

I snapped to and concentrated into the symbol Hermes

had rendered on my stomach. As the searing power gathered, the pool waters churned and turned black with mud. A host of rotten arms lunged out. I staggered back. Hands seized the pool's marble edge and pulled, heaving decomposing heads and torsos from the water.

Zombies.

The lead one thrust a leg over the pool's side, streaming muddy water and rags of flesh. I slapped my stomach. *C'mon, dammit, power up!*

The zombie was out now and shambling toward me. Others followed. I'd backed up as far as the lab when the symbol finally glowed brightly through my shirt.

"*Viajare!*" I shouted.

The panel to the bedchamber flew open. I caught the briefest glimpse of the goddess's glistening form.

And then I was gone.

16

"We may not be able to transport *into* City Hall," Hermes had told me the day before. "But there's nothing stopping us from transporting *out.*"

"Back here?" I'd asked, meaning the actual present.

"That would be ideal, but it's impractical for two reasons. First, you can't manage it alone. You can, however, transport to another location in the shadow realm, one a safe distance from City Hall. I've already picked out the site, in fact. I need only mark it. That's where we'll destroy the scepter."

"Why not in the actual present?"

"That's the second impracticality. Her scepter has yet to cross the boundary from there to here, and it's better we keep it that way. Hers is a powerful object, and all manner of distortions could result, none of them healthy to your reality."

I considered the past three weeks and nodded. "We'll do it there, then."

"Just watch the landing."

"What landing?"

I came to a sudden, bruising rest against concrete. With much wincing and groaning, I pushed myself into a sitting position.

"Oh," I grunted. "That landing."

My head spun, whether from the jarring arrival or my brief glimpse of the open-robed goddess. I looked down, almost surprised to find I was still clutching the scepter in my gloved hand. But Persephone's inner chamber, with its pool portal, charging zombies, and the goddess herself, had disappeared, replaced by sooty brick walls and the slender arching windows of an industrial loft space.

Our meeting site. I made it.

Gray light fell over torn paintings that leaned several deep against walls and rusty metal beams. I was in the Chelsea neighborhood, in someone's former art studio. Not close to City Hall, but not distant enough for my liking, either.

I peered around, surprised Hermes wasn't already lifting me up and swinging me into a celebratory dance. But there was no trickster god, just a deep and unsettling stillness. I labored to my feet with the heavy scepter. A destination symbol had been drawn on the floor where I'd landed, indicating he'd been here at some point.

"Hermes?" I called.

When he didn't answer or appear, my disquiet deepened. Not only did he have my cane, but the spell implements I would need to destroy the scepter. He was also my ride back to the actual present.

I began a limping circuit around the dust-covered space.

"*Hermes,*" I whispered harshly. "*I'm here, dammit. I've got it.*"

The paintings depicted closeups of crazed and leering

faces that seemed to mock me as I passed. Was this Hermes's idea of a joke? Or was he just being negligent, like with the gods he'd stashed in the storage space and forgotten? I leaned my head back, half expecting to spot him perched on one of the exposed beams, an impish gleam in his eyes, but he wasn't there either. A sour taste filled my mouth.

The scepter was far too important for him to play tricks or flake out like this. Had something happened to him?

I returned to the wall I'd just walked along, recalling a peculiarity I'd noted. On one of the leaning canvases, a line of dust had been thumbed away, exposing the model's crazy green eyes.

A message?

I tipped the canvas forward. Sure enough, tucked between the canvas and frame was a folded piece of paper I recognized as having come from Alec's sketchpad. I opened it to find a single printed word:

Park

"Is he freaking kidding me?"

After everything I'd gone through to steal the scepter, my nerves were shot. And now he was tacking on an extra step? But there was a reason he'd changed venues as well as why he couldn't carry me there himself.

I drew several steadying breaths.

By "Park" he meant Dewitt Clinton Park, his preferred transport point. Did he plan on taking us back to the actual present after all? I'd find out when I got there, but it was thirty blocks uptown—a mission unto itself, especially without my casting implements. Then I remembered the stomach rune.

Wait a sec, I can transport there...

But that was assuming Hermes had drawn me another destination symbol. If not, I could end up in limbo. Worse, I could get caught up in Persephone's distortion field and be thrown down to Hades. My hope deflated like a leaky tire. I'd trusted him to this point, and he'd delivered, but we hadn't discussed a backup plan. Transporting now would require a very large, very blind leap of faith.

Need to consult my magic.

Closing my eyes, I exhaled and sank into myself. Deep tides eddied around me before seeming to resolve into a back and forth motion: *no.* That was a first when it came to Hermes, and as I emerged again, the entire enterprise felt shakier than ever.

If transporting was out, I'd have to leg it. I downed a stealth potion and chased it with one for cloaking, a booster to keep me hidden from the whip's essence. I then took Hermes's note and tucked it into my jacket's inside pocket.

As a hazy field spread over me for the second time that morning, I found a staircase that led to a back exit. Rain continued to fall in a ruthless slant. I shed my tie, popped up my jacket collar, and, using the surrounding buildings for reference, set off north along the alleyway, Persephone's scepter clenched in my swinging grip.

As rain matted my hair and soaked through my shirt, I recalled the goddess's scream from the bath chamber, her wrathful appearance in the doorway. She would deploy everyone and everything in her command to get this back. With helicopters sounding in the distance, I shook my head bitterly.

What in the hell happened, Hermes? We were almost—

The crack and flash registered a moment after I was

down, my pursed lips burbling in a puddle of water. The heat that skewered my chest arrived an instant later. Sputtering, I tried to turn my head.

The blunt toe of an engineer-style boot stepped into view. I squinted up a pair of thick denim-clad legs to where wrap-around shades framed a busted nose. A burly red beard dripped rainwater. The leader of the Street Keepers curled his lip as he smacked a tactical whip against his gloved hand.

"Welcome back, Everson."

17

R ed Beard advanced until he was standing directly over me. "Told you we'd hunt you down."

I squinted to where more of his motorcycle gang were rolling in. It didn't take rotating my head to know the rest were blocking the other end of the alleyway. Dammit. The cloaking potion I'd prepared from the whip's essence clearly wasn't as effective as I'd thought.

The only bright spot, if you could call it that, was that these weren't Persephone's people. They answered to another authority.

Red Beard grabbed the scruff of my jacket and lifted me until I was dangling in front of him.

Through the bulging shoulder of his black shirt, a skull wreathed in angel wings shimmered with protective power. His Street Keeper tattoo.

Maybe it was time to tap into my own tattoo, the Hermes symbol, and take that leap of faith. The only problem was I'd lost my grip on the scepter when I'd eaten asphalt. I couldn't see the scepter, had no idea where it had landed, but surely

Hermes could speed over and recover it now that it was out of City Hall.

Not that we had a choice. It was either leap now or die shortly. Assuming I had the power.

As Red Beard regarded me coldly, I concentrated past my lingering pain. To my surprise, energy began crowding my mental prism. The whip had put me down, hard, but the effects weren't as enduring as the last time. My cloaking potion may not have been a total dud after all.

My stomach burned now, but not from the channeled energy gathering around the symbol. It was the sting of road rash. I'd been running when Red Beard cracked me, and I must have skidded when I fell, the friction of alley on skin chewing away enough symbol to render it inoperable. I angled my eyes down to find blood soaking through the front of my shirt in pink camo-like patterns.

It just keeps getting better.

"First we've got some business to settle," Red Beard grunted. "This is for my nose..."

His knuckles smashed into the center of my face, throwing me back to two weeks earlier when I'd swung my cane into him with a shouted force invocation. The blow had cracked him between the eyes and sent him flying from the back of his motorcycle. My own collision with the asphalt shocked me back to the present.

"This is for my bike..."

He lifted me under my shoulders and legs as if I were a large sack of garden mulch. I went airborne for a moment and then his knee rammed into the center of my back. As I splashed to the alley, my mind flashed back to his motorcycle veering riderless over the seawall and into the East River.

I gripped my low back—possibly cracked—and held my

throbbing nose—definitely broken—and struggled to get up. But my legs only locked in a sharp spasm.

"And this," Red Beard finished, "is for being a general pain in the ass."

He gripped my foot at the ankle and swung me. I went flying into a graffiti-smeared wall and landed in a heap of soggy cardboard boxes. More things hurt, but I was too battered to say what and where exactly.

I squinted at where a very blurry looking Red Beard was drawing the tactical whip from the back of his pants. The rest of the Street Keepers sat astride their idling bikes to both sides. It struck me now that none of them had whooped or cheered during my beatdown. Their brooding silence boded worse, somehow.

"I wish you wouldn't have made this personal," Red Beard said.

I spit out a ribbon of blood and found a garbled ghost of my voice. "Pardon me for not wanting to be killed."

"We're just upholding our oaths."

I released a painful snort. "Oh, in that case…"

"You shouldn't exist, Everson. You're an aberration."

"I've been called worse."

There was something about dire situations that brought out my inner smartass, but I was also jockeying for time. As I spoke, I was silently calling to the collective: the Order's repository of raw magic. Assistance was never guaranteed. It required a degree of surrender I hadn't fully mastered. And even if the magic arrived, it would be on its own terms. This wasn't streaming on demand.

"We have a mandate," Red Beard said importantly.

"By whom?"

"It doesn't matter."

"I just thought we could sort this out over brunch."

He responded by curling his lip and lashing the whip. The cord branched into a lightning-like configuration, just as it had in my lab. I braced for the brutal crack, but the tendrils wrapped me like barbed wire and clenched. Sizzling white energy seized every nerve, sending me into a jumping, writhing fit.

As Red Beard looked on with the grim visage of an executioner, I dipped in and out of consciousness. Somewhere beyond my wrecked body and the fragments of my panicked, pain-torn thoughts, a detached part of me mused that this could be the end. The accompanying sadness was overpowering, more so because I wasn't fighting. How would I explain that to Ricki...? Our daughter...?

And then the tendrils retracted.

I looked over blearily. Beyond the smoke drifting from my body, Red Beard was regarding his whip in confusion. The attack should have finished me, but it hadn't. My cloaking potion? It was suddenly sprinting laps throughout my system.

Though maybe that extra kick was coming from the power of the collective, because fresh energy was pouring into me like God's breath itself. In my near death, I must have surrendered.

Red Beard cocked the whip back, but I'd already raised a hand. "*Vigore!*" I rasped.

Energy branched from my outstretched fingers, battering his halo of protection and sending him into a drunken dance. He tripped and became entangled in a destroyed shopping cart. With another Word, I twisted my hand and crushed the cart around him, trapping him.

Could I stand?

With wincing effort, I gained a knee and wobbled to my

feet. The collective was not only supercharging my cloaking potion but repairing my broken parts. I stumbled forward as the rain fell harder. The tide had turned so fast, the Street Keepers struggled to engage kickstands and bring firearms into position.

Surprise, lugnuts.

I shoved my palms to both sides. My force blasts were typically just that—blasts. But what followed my next shouted Word was flash-flood strength. Twin forces slammed into the alleyway, tearing up chunks of asphalt and plowing through the Street Keepers. They disappeared from my sides in a tumbling torrent. The invocation rolled out, leaving behind a scatter of bikes and groaning bodies.

Opposite me, Red Beard had managed to break free from the cart. With a grunt, he brought his whip down.

I crouched and crossed my wrists overhead. *"Protezione!"*

The energy shield that crackled into being was predictably messy. It shattered beneath the whip's strike, but it also sent the branching cords wide. I stumbled back and sent another force blast into Red Beard. But with the flick of his wrist, the whip's tendrils leapt up and scattered the invocation.

Can't keep going back and forth like this.

The collective had restored me, but its power was leaving now, going back out to sea.

Need an object to cast through...

Something winked darkly from the storm drain opposite me. The scepter! It had rolled partway down and gotten stuck behind a sodden lump of garbage. When I stepped toward it, Red Beard readied another whip strike, but his angle was bad and I was too near. Dropping the whip, he charged into my path.

I extended a hand and shouted, *"Recuperare!"*

The scepter jiggled and launched toward me. I grabbed it from the air and swung it as Red Beard arrived. The scepter's crown cracked off his temple and sent him staggering. For a transfixing moment, the skin above his ear blackened and began rotting away, revealing pale skull underneath. But it was already healing over, the protective power from his shoulder tattoo running white currents into the wound.

He pressed his palm to the temple like someone suffering brain freeze and raised his other hand to keep me at bay.

But I had stopped to study the scepter. I'd lost the buffering glove Hermes had given me, and the scepter's raw power coursed through me like a potent drug. I wielded Death. Terrifying, tantalizing Death.

As I fixed my grip on the twisted staff, I stared into the crown's gems that had winked from the storm drain, calling to me. Red Beard was regarding the scepter from his defensive stoop, though much more warily.

I grinned. "Aberrant enough for you?"

He glanced over at his scattered crew. Only a few had managed to stagger upright. "You can't keep running from your sentence, Everson."

"I'm not planning on it."

I drew the scepter back, poised to bring it down on his head, when red bursts stitched the alley between us. I staggered back as though I'd been shoved. But Red Beard stood defiantly, face tilted to the pounding rain.

"Stop!" he roared, shaking a fist. "He's mine, goddammit!"

A helicopter had swept into view between the buildings, a shooter perched in the bay door. It was a soldier of the Iron Guard. More soldiers were arriving down the alleyway, cutting around the bikers.

Persephone's forces had found me.

Shots cracked from weapons, sending preternatural rounds snapping past my head. I channeled energy through the scepter, and a dark, shimmering shield spread in front of me, reducing the arriving rounds to blood-red spatters. But I could still feel rain on my back. The scepter, however powerful, was not the natural fit of my grandfather's cane. No matter how much power I pushed, I couldn't seem to make the shield bigger. I wheeled to find more Iron Guard pouring into the alley's other end.

I would need to go on the offensive, an idea I suddenly relished.

But as I readied the scepter, a round struck me in the shoulder, enveloping my head in a cloud of toxic red mist.

The scepter clanged to the ground. A moment later, I followed.

18

I came to with a start and struck out at the darkness, certain I'd been buried.

When my hand didn't encounter an enclosure, I pressed it to my thudding chest. Not underground. Neither was I in an alleyway in the rain. I was on my back, breathing hard, my face damp with sweat.

And I was alive.

Swallowing, I thought back. It didn't take long for the memory fragments to conjoin. The Iron Guard had shot me with an underworld round, explaining the claustrophobic nightmares. It also suggested my location.

As my vision rendered the darkness dim, I brought my head up. Dammit. Not only was I in City Hall, but I was in the room off Persephone's bedchamber. Opposite me was the marble pool from which the zombies had emerged. The waters were still now, but too close for comfort.

I struggled until I was sitting up on the edge of what turned out to be a dainty couch. I listened, picking up a faint whistle of wind as though through a crack somewhere. I started when a voice spoke.

"I healed you."

The feminine voice belonged to a figure standing in the shadows near the lab area. She was holding a white flower to her chin. The radiant petals illuminated a large pair of eyes and pomegranate-colored lips.

I stammered mutely, struck dumb by the goddess's presence.

But I no longer hurt, I realized. Not in my low back or my face or where the whip had ravaged me, which was everywhere. When I touched my nose, the contours felt straight. When I inhaled, my shirt and slacks smelled fresh.

"Thank you," I managed quietly.

Already in enough trouble, I couldn't risk insulting her.

She set the flower off to the side and stepped forward. The room glowed with pale light from a large symbol on the floor around my couch. A circle trap? I summoned a quantum of power as a test. Sure enough, nothing happened. The trap isolated me from all forms of energy, killing my magic.

"Everson Croft," she said softly, as though testing the syllables.

The light of my enclosure illuminated her approach. Burnt chestnut hair spilled past the shoulders of a pale gown, long-sleeved with delicate floral patterns. Questioning eyes dominated a startlingly soft face. Not the face of a calculating antagonist. And though she was beautiful—inconceivably beautiful—she didn't wield it as a weapon, using fatal stares or haughty postures.

Even so, I remained on my guard.

She stopped outside the circle trap and stared at me with

the frankness of a child, as though waiting for me to explain myself. But the innocence in her eyes spanned a chilling abyss. I lowered my gaze. From a fold in her gown, she raised the scepter.

"Why did you take this?"

"Because you're about to make a terrible mistake," I replied carefully.

"Oh?" She seemed genuinely curious.

Had anyone actually tried reasoning with her?

"If you summon Cronus, war will follow. And if he wins, the Olympic order will fall, yes, but think about the destruction. The unimaginable loss of life. *Innocent* life. I've read the poems honoring you, good Persephone. I know you cherish life, its essential beauty. You can't want this."

"So you know my story?"

When I'd had time this past week, I'd read up on Persephone. Now I recited from a hymn by Homer: "'She stretched out both hands to pick the charming bloom, and a chasm opened. Out sprang Lord Hades on his immortal horses. Snatching the unwilling girl, he carried her off in his golden chariot as she cried and screamed, calling to her father, Zeus, son of Cronus, highest and best.'"

"And do you know my father's response?"

"Silence."

"Worse than silence." She turned away. "He knew Hades had taken me, he'd allowed it. But though my mother searched and searched, exhausted with grief, he lied to her. Said he knew nothing of my whereabouts. 'Highest and best,'" she repeated bitterly. "He isn't worthy of either name."

"I'm truly sorry." I waited the appropriate beat. "But there must be another way to put this right."

Her back stiffened. "Another way?" When she wheeled to

face me, her eyes blazed beneath her slanting brows, and the whistling of the hidden wind grew in pitch. "There is no other way. This is how it must be done!"

I showed my hands. "I'm sorry."

"What do you know? You're just a stupid mortal! A thief!"

I shuffled back. Though her tantrum sounded childish, the raw power coming off her shook my insides. And the power was growing. She raised the scepter, sending chaotic bands of energy from the gems. They circled the room in a growing storm, thrashing her hair and darkening her visage. Even her gown seemed to shift to something resembling a funeral dress, the flower patterns shriveling away.

Fair Persephone, goddess of spring, was becoming dread Persephone, queen of the Underworld.

When the water in the pool bubbled and blackened with mud, I made a break for the panel to her bedchamber. I was met by a full-body slap that sent me sprawling back onto the couch. The damned circle trap. Persephone stared down at me, eyes smoldering with wrath and the promise of death.

"I-I apologize," I stammered. "I didn't mean to offend you."

I cut my gaze to the pool, where the gurgling moans of the undead were growing. At any moment a zombie horde was going to explode from the muddy water, and I had nothing with which to defend myself.

"Persephone, hon?" someone called.

A short figure materialized from the shadows near the paneled doorway and hurried toward her. It was the mayor. With a nervous laugh, he arrived beside Persephone and rested a hand on her low back.

"You've had a long morning," he said. "Why don't you go to your bedroom, huh? Let me deal with him."

She remained staring at me as though willing my insides to combust. Then her gaze saddened suddenly. The arm holding the scepter sagged to her side, and the storm ended. The water stilled and cleared. Her features softened until she was fair Persephone once more. Wordlessly, she separated from Budge and sulked from the room. He watched her go, then smiled at me apologetically.

"What's with these gods, huh? The smallest thing and they go flying right off the handle." He shook his head. But beneath the nonchalance, I picked up an edge of nerves. "Anyway, how you been, buddy?"

I double-checked to ensure no zombies were climbing from the pool before standing again. "A lot better if I wasn't trapped in here."

Seeing a familiar face, even if it didn't belong to the Budge I knew, calmed me slightly.

"We'll see what we can do about that in a sec, but first I gotta tell you..." He lowered his voice. "I agree with every word you just said. This whole thing is nuts, right? Cooler heads need to prevail, and that's yours and mine, champ. You really wanna end this thing? Persephone's scepter isn't the answer. Neither is appealing to her *sweet* nature." He made an aggrieved face. "Believe me, I've tried."

Like the night I'd first met him, I marveled at how adeptly he finessed his way into my trust centers. The skill surpassed the actual Budge's by a mile, which was saying something. It also cued me to be extremely wary.

"What does that leave?" I asked.

"C'mon, Everson. You're too young to claim senility. We talked about this a couple weeks ago."

"The Tablet of Hermes."

"Right, 'cause it's ground zero. It's what's bringing all this stuff to my city, including you-know-who." He bounced his eyes toward the panel the goddess had disappeared through. "I mean, I enjoyed the Greek myths when I was a kid, ate them up, but this is ridiculous. And I'll tell you right now, her Iron Guard is freaking me the hell out. She couldn't give them even a little personality? Make them smile now and again? And you should see these mutts she keeps around for security."

I remembered my earlier encounter in the tunnel while affecting a questioning look.

"Anyway, his tablet is the glue that's holding this whole dog-and-pony show together. We get rid of that, and it all falls apart."

He edged closer until I could smell his bracing cologne. "Look, I don't know what Hermes is telling you, but I can guess. He's going on about the scepter, right? I mean, obviously, 'cause you just tried to steal it. But if you had managed to destroy it, then what? You think Hermes is gonna go quietly into that good night?" He laughed. "Sure, and I'm gonna run five miles before breakfast and cut out carbs."

I was listening cautiously, skeptically, but damn if he wasn't making sense.

"He has power ambitions of his own. I can't say what they are exactly, but I *can* tell you that he tried to join forces with her."

A fist landed in my gut. "Hermes? When?"

"This past week. Yeah, we had a summit right here in City Hall."

Did that explain Hermes's absence? His elusiveness?

"Well, I'm going to need more than your say-so."

"Fine." He pulled a folded square of paper from his pocket, flapped it open, and held it up to reveal a flyer for the referendum vote. With a finger, he jabbed the siphon sigil beyond his grinning mug.

"Who do you think designed that?"

For the first time, I studied the elements up close. Not a slam dunk, but a little too close to Hermes's style for comfort.

"Persephone came up with the idea for the referendum to capture public support," Budge continued, "turn it into worship for Cronus. But that meant I had to be popular. In this city?" He made an aggrieved face. "But then Hermes designed it so that *any* reaction would work, good or bad."

"Then why'd he send me after her scepter?"

"Why else?" He returned the flyer to his pocket. "He didn't get what he wanted."

"And what was that?"

He held up his left hand. "A ring on her finger."

"Marriage?" I knew about Hermes's infatuation with Persephone, but would he really have gone so far as to propose to her? Align with her?

"Hey, can you blame him? There's a reason every god and his father's fallen for Persephone, and if you can't see it, you're either blind or missing a pair. But she's already pledged her hand to Cronus."

I squinted at that. Not only was Cronus her grandfather, which wasn't so unusual in the ancient myths, but he'd once swallowed her mother. I couldn't see where Zeus lying to her mother was the greater offense.

"Yeah, part of some power-sharing arrangement they worked out," he continued. "Persephone wouldn't budge an inch on that, even after Hermes designed the symbol, so he went back to wanting her out of his way."

"Then why didn't he finish the job?" I challenged. "We had her scepter."

Budge shrugged. "I'm not privy to everything around here, but I have a theory. The second her scepter went missing, I think he contacted her. Told her he could return it in exchange for," he circled his hand, "some concession. She must have agreed, because the Iron Guard dropped on you like flies on stink, and she got her scepter back."

I sat heavily on the couch and studied the floor between my shoes. Had I been gullible to trust a mercurial god like Hermes? I remembered how Alec had been preparing to tell me something the night before when Hermes showed up. Or was I being gullible now, allowing this ridiculously charming version of Budge to seed doubts.

"Hey, don't beat yourself up," he said, hunkering so we were eye level. "Dealing with a god who's wearing your son as a skin suit can't be easy. No disrespect, but that's the long and short of it, right? By using him, Hermes is using you, too."

"How do you know his tablet holds everything together?"

Budge didn't miss a beat. "He said so himself, during the meeting."

"And you believed him?"

"Hey, I'm in the position I'm in 'cause I can read people like a book."

"He's not exactly a person," I pointed out. "And why would Persephone go along with this tablet-destroying ruse if it means her demise?"

He peered over a shoulder. "Well, she's not exactly in the know. Powerful goddess—damned powerful—but all kinds of naïve. She thinks we're after the tablet so she can lock it away in the underworld, get Hermes out of her hair." His expression turned grave. "And the tablet would still be attached to your boy."

I thought of Alec spending eternity in that hellish limbo and stood again.

"But that's only if she gets her way," Budge hastened to add, joining me upright. "Destroy the tablet, and your son's safe."

"What if you're wrong?"

"I won't lie to you, Everson. That very question has kept me up at night. But I figure if I'm right, this all goes away, and I get back to running my city. Before Persephone showed up and turned this place into frigging Mordor, I was this close to signing a bailout package." He brought his thumb and first finger together. "I had monster-clearing operations planned, large-scale redevelopment projects in the works... I was gonna put New York City back on the map, baby!"

It may have sounded like a pipe dream, but the actual Budge had succeeded in bringing about those very changes in the actual present.

"And if I'm wrong..." He shrugged. "It was worth a shot. Because either Hermes or Persephone is gonna take over, and neither one of 'em gives a rat's ass about us. I mean, they'll use us as long as it suits them and then"—he released a sharp whistle and hooked his thumb—"out like yesterday's garbage."

I massaged my temples. It was too much to process. I needed space to think, and Budge's gabbing wasn't helping. Neither was his overpowering cologne, which was starting to make me nauseous.

"Well, I can't do anything from in here," I said.

"Of course not. That's why we're sending you back."

I looked up at him carefully. "Back where?"

"To your reality, but not without some insurance." He

turned toward the bedchamber and called, "Persephone? Sephassa? Can you grab those ashes?"

She appeared moments later, no hint of wrath or malice in her eyes. She glanced from Budge to me inquisitively, then strode to her laboratory. Until today, I'd assumed she was manipulating the mayor, but he appeared to have flipped the script. Or had he? I caught his tongue dart out to dry his stiff smile, as though he knew he was playing a dangerous game. One he might not pull off.

"Can you tell Everson what you have?" he asked her.

She caressed what I recognized as a marble urn.

"His remains," she replied simply.

19

M y face prickled with heat. "My *what*?"

"Yes, your wife had your cremated remains interred at Green-Wood Cemetery in Brooklyn." He meant the wife of my shadow, Jennifer DeFazio. That version of me had died in Venice when Alec was three. "Not hard for someone like me to get my hands on. I'm sorry, Everson, I really am, but we've gotta keep you honest."

My gaze shifted to where Persephone had placed the urn on a counter. She removed the lid and from a bottle began pouring in a dark liquid. An unmistakable coldness spread throughout my body.

"What are you doing?" I demanded.

"That's a bonding potion, Everson," he said.

Persephone hummed a lyrical tune as she stirred the potion into my powdery remains.

My hand reflexively shot toward her, only for it to be struck down by the circle trap. "Hey!" I shouted. "Stop!"

Weeks earlier, the same potion had been used to bond several explorer club fellows to their shadow selves. One of

Persephone's minions, Eldred, had then extracted the victims' organs for the Cronus ritual. Their deaths in the shadow realm had resulted in their deaths in the actual present. By bonding me to my shadow's remains, Persephone was threatening me with the same fate.

I rubbed my arms, half expecting them to turn to ash and crumble.

"Relax," Budge said. "The potion is inert. For now. We're going to give you three days to deliver the tablet." He said the word *deliver* as though he were sharing a wink between us. He was telling me to destroy it. "After that, the potion stops being so inert. We'll say by Wednesday at midnight?"

"How do you know I'll even see Hermes again?" I asked, not moving my eyes from Persephone.

"Oh, you'll see him," Budge assured me. "He'll want to know what happened."

"Won't he be suspicious that I'm back?"

"No question. Tell him whatever you want, you just need to convince him that you're still on his side. Shouldn't be hard. Guy has an ego the size of Jersey. Probably working on another scheme to extract another concession. I know the way these jokers operate. Just go along. That'll be your best chance to get your hands on the tablet. Look, I'm sorry about this, but the tablet is non-negotiable. It's too important."

He turned to Persephone. "He's ready."

"Wait," I said, then lowered my voice. "I want something in return."

"Is your hearing going? I just said this is non-negotiable."

"Not about the tablet—I'll take care of that—it's the Street Keepers."

"Oh, those guys." He rolled his eyes as if they were a chronic nuisance. "What about 'em?"

"When this is over, I don't want them making trouble for my son."

"Yeah, sure." He gave a flippant wave. "I'll see what I can do."

"No, I need better than that."

He appeared to gauge the seriousness etched in my face before nodding. "We have an agreement that lets them patrol the city, help out with citizen safety. Nothing official, but it keeps the NYPD out of their hair. I'll make it crystal clear that if they bother your boy, the agreement's off, and the NYPD can deal with them however they see fit. It won't be gently. There's bad blood between them."

I'd seen the bad blood up close, so I believed that much of what he was telling me.

"Where did they come from?" I asked, still wanting to know. "Who sponsors them?"

"They're part of some extreme law-and-order group that started God knows where. Have offices all around the world. They're listed as a religious nonprofit—my people looked into them. That's about all I can tell you."

I didn't trust shadow Budge any farther than I could throw the actual Budge, but I didn't have much choice. "Okay, but if you don't follow through, and something happens to Alec, I'll find you."

His cheerful eyes assumed a hardness that told me he didn't care for the threat. He grinned tightly before turning to Persephone.

"Everson's ready to go," he called.

I watched apprehensively as she tapped the stirrer against the rim of my urn, signaling that my ashes were prepped. If I didn't destroy the tablet by Wednesday night, I'd crumble wherever I happened to be standing.

Persephone crossed the room to the pool and reached into the water, smiling as though fascinated by the tiny ripples. When she withdrew her arm, she was holding a sickle-shaped blade.

A charge jagged through me. I'd destroyed an identical blade at the explorers club.

They're objects, powerful objects, Arianna had told me, *but they came from Forms that still exist in their original realms.* They could reappear, in other words, and I was now looking at the proof.

The Scythe of Cronus swam with blue time-bending power.

Budge nudged me, and I turned to find his hand extended into the circle trap. I gripped it automatically. The shake he gave me was almost as hard as his stare. "I'm counting on you, Everson."

And then the room shifted.

I squinted around a dusty office being taken over by storage and released a shaky breath. The Scythe of Cronus had yanked me to the shadow present before, and Persephone had just used it to send me back to the actual present. I was on the top floor of City Hall.

Alive, yes, but I had a lot of work to do if I was going to stay that way.

I hurried toward the wall that had divided Persephone's sanctum from her bedchambers. Here there was an actual door, but halfway to it, I caught a soft moan. The sound sent my hand to where my cane would have been had I not handed it off to Hermes. The moan morphed into a panicked whisper, answered by another whisper, the exchange coming from behind a line of filing cabinets in the office's far corner.

A moment later, a young couple emerged, tucking in their shirttails. They rushed past where I stood, eyes avoiding mine, the woman hooking a pair of heels. As they disappeared through the door, I shook my head.

Office romances.

I followed at a distance, using them now as my sentry. We were all somewhere we weren't supposed to be.

With the third floor clear, they left "Persephone's bedroom"—another old office—and disappeared into the stairwell leading down. I arrived there just as the couple passed through the door leading onto the rotunda. By the time I emerged through the same door, the two were blending into the light-suffused bustle of civil servants.

In my clean suit, courtesy of Persephone, I looked the part enough to blend in, too. I hustled down the rotunda steps, already planning my next moves—a return to the apartment, for starters. Would Hermes be there?

I desperately needed my cane back, but I also needed to think up an explanation for how I'd returned to the actual present. Beyond that, I just needed to *think*.

Trust Hermes? Trust Budge? Or trust neither and figure out a third way?

With the main entrance of City Hall in my sights, a door opened and I nearly ran into the actual Mayor Lowder.

We both drew back and stared at the other. My brain was struggling to reconcile this dumpier version of him with his slimmed-down, slicked-back counterpart. He was likely recalling the stern note on which our last meeting had ended. His assistants emerged from the conference room and looked back and forth between us.

At last he wiped the cowlick from his pudgy brow and broke into his aw-shucks smile. "Everson, buddy. How ya been?" He clapped my shoulder. "I've been meaning to jaw with you. Hey, Janet, can you clear my schedule for the next twenty?"

"That won't be necessary," I told Janet.

I stepped around Budge, but he hustled to catch up.

"Hey," he said, arresting my arm. "I get that you're still sore at me, but I was hoping we could bury the hatchet."

The month before, he'd crippled our task force on missing persons, manipulating data to divert our attention from the rivers, all so he could promote a major waterfront concert for the following spring. As a result, we didn't stop the threat—an ancient sea creature—before it devoured more victims. But I had too much going on to relitigate that shitshow. I just wanted to go home.

"Keep up your end of the deal," I said, "and we'll consider it buried."

The terms of the deal were that he would not punish the detective he'd pressured into fudging the data; that he would never, ever pull a stunt like that again; and that he would tell me if he started experiencing losses of consciousness, an indication Persephone was sending shadow Budge into our reality.

I'd started to pull from his grip, but stopped suddenly.

"How's your health?" I asked him. "Any blackouts?"

He snuck a glance around, but we were beyond the earshot of his assistants, who'd hung back. It didn't seem to occur to him to ask what I was doing in City Hall. He was too desperate to placate me.

"No, none. I swear it."

I searched his eyes. He appeared to be telling the truth.

"Call me if you do. Like I said, your life depends on it."

He let out a nervous laugh and took another swipe at his cowlick. "Hey, I'd really love to know what that means." As I started walking again, he fell behind. "You sure you don't have twenty minutes? How about ten? Let me help you, Everson."

"I don't have any," I said, which was the grim truth.

In three days I would be bonded to my ashes.

20

With no money for a taxi, I hopped a turnstile at the City Hall subway station and came up for air twenty minutes later in the West Village. I'd deliberately left my keys and phone at home before setting out that morning. I called Ricki collect from a payphone to ask her to meet me at the front of our apartment building.

"Hello?" someone answered.

I hesitated. "Who's this?" I said coldly.

The voice wasn't Ricki's. It wasn't even a woman's.

"Well, I just happened to be... That is, I was standing closer to the..."

"Claudius," I said, releasing my pent-up breath. "What are you doing? Is everything all right?"

"Well, there's a little bit of a, ah, a situation, I suppose you could call it."

I stiffened. "Is Ricki all right?"

"Who's he?"

Claudius suffered from a badly perforated memory, but

with Ricki and our future child in potential danger, my adrenaline took over. "*She's* my wife. Is she there?"

"Oh, yes, yes. I'm looking right at her. A picture of loveliness, if I haven't said it before. Why, when I was younger—"

"And she's all right?" I interrupted.

"She's signaling something... What's that? Oh, she wants you to come."

"I'm two minutes away. Meet me at the front door. I don't have a key."

I sprinted the three blocks to our Tenth Street apartment. When I arrived, I was surprised to find that the senior member of my Order had actually heeded my directive. He was pacing the steps between the front door and sidewalk, carrying on a conversation with himself.

When he saw me approaching at a run, he parted his curtains of black hair, eyes blinking beyond his blue-tinted glasses. His confused face took on a look of alarm, and his fingers leapt into a casting position. In the space between us, a portal began to yawn open. Deep inside, lava sloshed and belched.

"Claudius, it's me!" I shouted. "Everson!"

As he looked again, the wrinkles around his eyes smoothed.

"Ah, Everson," he said, lowering his hands. "What brings you here?"

"I live here," I said, waving away the acrid smoke as I sidestepped the closing portal. "I just talked to you on the phone."

Fortunately, the door hadn't closed all the way behind him, or we both would have been locked out. He hustled inside after me on his sandaled feet. But when I headed for the stairs leading up, I noticed he was going down.

"Wrong way," I said.

"No, no, everyone's down here."

"Everyone?"

As I stepped through the doorway of the basement unit, I saw it was just my wife and Tabitha, but it took me another moment to make sense of the scene.

Tabitha, who still looked as if she'd been to the taxidermist's, lay stiffly on my casting table. Ricki stood over her. She'd changed into black leggings and a gray tank top after dropping me off that morning, and her right hand was inside Tabitha's mouth.

"What in the hell's going on?" I asked.

Relief welled up inside my wife's eyes at the sight of me, but her expression quickly turned stern again. "I made the mistake of calling *him*," she said, jutting her chin at Claudius, who had shuffled in behind me. He blinked from her to Tabitha, as though trying to recall exactly what he was doing here.

"Hmm, you did call me, didn't you?" he murmured.

Ricki tensed her lips and addressed herself to me. "Tabitha still wasn't showing any signs of life, and I wanted to give you one less thing to worry about when you got back. I also needed something to take my mind off your mission. When he said he could use an extra pair of hands, I didn't realize he meant literally."

As she spoke, I hugged her to my side.

"Everything went all right with you?" she asked, her expression softening. "You're okay?"

"I'll tell you about it in a minute." I kissed her. "But first, why *is* your hand in her mouth?"

She was wearing a yellow dishwashing glove, but the

sight of Tabitha's sharp teeth ringing her wrist made me uneasy.

"Oh, ah, I can explain that," Claudius said, seeming to have recovered his orientation. "Your wife, that is, ah, *Ricki*..." His eyes lit up at having remembered. "Yes, Ricki filled me in on your cat's condition. You're quite correct, she did withdraw into herself as a defense mechanism. However, she's not in stasis."

"She's not?"

"No, she's locked in a battle for her very life."

"Really? A battle against whom?" I asked.

"Well, that part isn't clear, but the signs are all there. Your stimulant helped, gave her some extra kick. Without it, she would surely have succumbed. But she needs something stronger, and it has to be applied directly to her core. So I prepared some... well, I forget the name, but it's essentially a mortar of *whoop ass*." He chuckled at his own turn of phrase. "I didn't think you'd mind me borrowing a few of your ingredients."

I looked over the mess on the far side of my casting table. Various herbs and tinctures were scattered around open jars and upended bottles. In the center was my mortar and pestle, which held the remnants of a purple paste.

"Not at all."

"The thing is, to really have an effect, the salve needs to be massaged into her stomach with a polished stone, preferably topaz. But I couldn't fit my own hand down far enough for the topaz stick to reach. Luckily, your wife, with her very lovely fingers, agreed to assist." Claudius's eyes swam with affection as he looked at her.

"How much longer do I need to massage?" she asked thinly.

"Oh!" He blinked. "It only requires three minutes, give or take."

"I've been doing this for *thirty*," she informed him through a clenched jaw.

"Yes, yes, then by all means..." He mimed retracting his arm.

"Careful," I said, bracing Tabitha's body while my wife worked her hand and the topaz stick back out. She peeled the glove off inside out and tossed it into the wastebasket. At the kitchenette, she scrubbed her hands vigorously.

"I hope she appreciates this," she said.

"She won't," I replied, "but I do. A lot. What happens now?" I asked Claudius.

"Well, we'll have to see whether it was enough. The rest will depend on her and how badly she wants to live."

As we peered down at Tabitha, my concern for her grew around my very real problems. Whatever I'd released from the whip was now attacking her. Correction, was *continuing* to attack her, since yesterday. Nuggets of guilt crab-crawled around my gut for having put her in this situation.

"Where did you go off to earlier?" Claudius asked.

"Hmm?" It only took a moment for the urgency of my situation to come surging back to the fore. "I was in the shadow realm. I called to tell you that this morning, remember? Regardless, I'm glad you're here. What I'm about to share needs to be communicated to the senior members of the Order."

Ricki returned, drying her hands on a dishtowel. "I'd like to hear this, too."

I scooted the room's two chairs together, helped my wife into one and gestured for Claudius to take the other. I then slid Tabitha's stiff body over before hiking myself onto the corner of the casting table.

"I captured Persephone's scepter," I said, "but Hermes never showed up to transport me back here."

Ricki's eyebrows drew together. "I warned that little jerk."

"It may not have been his fault," I continued. "He left me a—"

"Ah, can you hold that thought?" Claudius interrupted. From a pocket in his cardigan, he produced a piece of hard candy wrapped in green foil. "Ginseng," he explained, popping the candy into his mouth. "It makes me a little sharper." He suckled on it loudly for several moments before signaling that I was free to continue.

"Hermes left a note for me to meet him at the park, but en route I was intercepted by the Street Keepers. The bike gang with the whip. Persephone's forces intervened, recovered the scepter, and hauled me to City Hall. Intact," I assured Ricki. "In fact, the goddess healed me. She even freshened up my clothes."

Ricki looked at me in a way that suggested I could have left out that last detail.

"But then shadow Budge started into a full court press, trying to convince me Hermes was the actual root of the problem."

I recounted for them everything he had said, including his claim that Hermes had attempted to align with Persephone—that he'd even gone so far as to create the energy-capturing design that would open Tartarus.

"So who do you believe?" Ricki asked. "Team Hermes or Team Persephone?"

I massaged my forehead, suddenly very tired, and dragged the hand down my cheek. "Both sides could be trying to get the other out of the way for their own power aims. I've been siding with Hermes, but how much of that is because I *want* to believe he'll release Alec and leave our world for good when this is over?"

"Is there a way to know?" she asked.

"I've been chewing on it." I was also growing very worried about Alec.

But whatever his intentions, Hermes had been leading me around by the nose. Volunteering me to battle Koalemos to make his draftees behave, sending me on the mission for Persephone's scepter, then inexplicably disappearing. Now Persephone was doing the same, releasing me to obtain the tablet under threat of death. And shadow Budge was doing her one better, demanding I destroy the tablet.

"What I do know is that I'm tired of being yanked around." I looked up with fresh resolve. "I keep saying that these are *versions* of the gods in question, not the gods themselves. But to know these versions, to truly know them, I need to think less like a wizard and more like a professor—namely a professor in the field. I need to go to the sites where they were worshipped."

"Okay, and where's that?" Ricki asked warily.

"For Hermes, it would be Athens, Greece. The box holding his tablet came from an Attican thieves guild. As for Persephone, Hermes never told me her place of origin, only that she was worshipped as a wronged and vengeful god. But back at City Hall, I caught something. At one point Budge called her 'Sephassa,' likely short for 'Persephassa.' That was the name of a pre-Hellenistic goddess whom the Greeks adopted into their mythology as 'Persephone.' And the only cults to Persephassa resided in central Sicily."

"Athens and Sicily," Ricki repeated in a way that told me

she was not keen on me traveling to either one. "Can't the Order help you?"

"Well, ah, they're really tied up in the interdimensional planes at the moment," Claudius interjected. "I think they understate the gravity of the tears sometimes. But last I spoke to them, they reiterated their full confidence in Everson here." He smiled brightly, which did nothing to reassure my wife.

"What about Gretchen?" she asked.

"My teacher?" I snorted. "After embarrassing herself with that *boyfriend* stunt, she fled back to Faerie." Gretchen had enchanted a bugbear, dressed him in tailored suits, and called him "Enzo" as part of a wacky plan to make Bree-yark jealous. "No one's seen or heard from her since. Probably just as well."

"So no Order," Ricki recounted, "no teacher, and what happened to your cane?"

"I gave it to Hermes," I said dismally.

Though I'd tried several times, I'd been unable to connect with its energy, meaning it was still in the shadow realm. The thought that I might never recover my sword and staff roiled my insides, but I forced it aside.

"Great," she said. "Well, I can't let you go alone."

"I'm not." I turned to Claudius. "He's giving me a ride."

When Claudius realized I was referring to him, he sat up suddenly, nearly choking on his ginseng candy. "To where again?" he asked when he'd stopped coughing long enough to find his voice.

"Athens, Greece and Enna, Sicily."

He squinted off to the side and moved a finger around as though trying to recall old roads and byways.

"Yes, yes," he said at last. "I believe I know a good route to both."

I doubted the "good" part very much, but it was unavoidable. A commercial flight would take too long. I pictured my ashes in the urn on Persephone's counter, soaked through with the bonding potion. One more ingredient, or perhaps just a spoken word by the goddess, and I would crumble to dust.

I studied my fidgeting hands for a moment, debating whether to tell Ricki that part—Lord knew, I'd already piled enough on her for one day—before deciding that, yes, I couldn't keep this from her. When I raised my head, though, I found her looking toward the door, where a figure now stood.

Alec cleared his throat. "Can I come in?"

21

"Alec!" I jumped up from the table and rushed toward him. "Are you all right, buddy? What happened to you?"

The fatigue under his eyes had spread, and his slender body seemed to slump under the weight of his pack. Otherwise, he looked okay. It took me a moment to notice his quizzical expression.

"I'm... fine," he said, looking between me and Ricki, who had risen and was watching with maternal concern. Claudius was regarding him too, though I could tell he was having trouble placing him.

"I went over to the college to browse the bookstore," Alec said. "I ended up getting a used book on symbols, and I took it to a coffee shop to read. I didn't realize you guys were waiting for me."

"Solid or cloudy?" I asked.

His brow bunched up before he understood that I was referring back to our conversation from the night before regarding his memories. "Cloudy," he decided quietly. "So none of that was real, huh? Hermes made it up. Explains why I don't have the book anymore. Thought I left it on the bus. Were you with him?"

"He took me to the shadow present this morning, but he wasn't there to bring me back. I thought something might have happened to him—to you. Well, to both of you. Do you remember being over there?"

He shook his head in dismay.

I squeezed his bony shoulders. "It's all right." I searched his eyes for any glimmer of the god. "Hermes," I called in my wizard's voice.

Alec looked uneasily to one side. "It's... still me."

"You didn't happen to have my cane at any point today, did you?"

"Your cane? No."

It was worth a shot, but at the moment I was too relieved to have him back here, safe, to give it more thought.

As Alec adjusted his pack—not removing it, I noticed—I revisited the shadow mayor's claim. If I destroyed the tablet, all of the gods would fall, normalcy would be restored, and Alec would be freed. I wanted to believe that, but it was just as likely Budge was hoodwinking me, making it seem as though we were on the same team when, in fact, he was just a very persuasive pawn in Persephone's game.

"Hey, you wanted to tell me something last night," I said.

Alec angled his head in question. "I did? What about?"

"You shared your concerns about your memories, and then you said there was something else that could be important."

I was beginning to suspect Hermes had erased the memory when Alec nodded slowly. "It had to do with my runes. I'm always sketching new ones. Usually I have some idea what they are, or at least what they'll do. But I started working on a new one last week and..." He blew the air from his puffed cheeks and shrugged. "I have absolutely no idea what it was for. I thought maybe Hermes was up to something."

"Do you have the sketch with you?"

"Yeah." He brought the pack around to his front. But as he searched through the small pocket for his sketchpad, panic spread over his face. He unzipped the main compartment and dug around the box.

"It's—it's gone," he said.

Hermes may not have erased Alec's memory, but had he hidden the evidence of the rune he'd designed for Persephone? I remembered the note Hermes had left me in the loft and patted the inside pocket of my jacket to ensure it was still there.

"Do you have a pencil I can borrow?" I asked.

Still looking distressed, Alec nodded and handed me one. At my casting table I spread the note face up so the word "PARK" was showing. Ricki and Claudius came over. Giving up on his sketchpad, Alec donned his zipped-up pack and joined us.

"This could be nothing," I said, bringing the edge of the pencil to the paper.

I began shading over it very lightly, hoping to pick up something from the page that had been sitting on top of it. At first it looked like an artist's impression of a rainy day in London—a gray wash—and then faintly, very faintly, a network of lines began to stand out. When I finished, I tilted it toward the light.

Claudius let out a low "ooh."

"That's it!" Alec exclaimed. "That's the one I was drawing."

My heart sank into my stomach. It was the siphon sigil that Persephone was using to call up Cronus. The shadow mayor had been telling the truth, at least as far as that went. Did I need to believe the rest of what he'd said? Ricki, who had an uncanny gift for reading me, cocked an eyebrow as though to ask, *Is that bad?*

I gave a slight nod and turned to Alec. "You asked if you could help me last night."

The boy already looked up to me, and now watching his expression illuminate beneath the dullness of his exhaustion killed me. I searched his eyes again for any hint of Hermes before continuing.

"I'm going to level with you. I'm in a tough position, and there's some important work I need to do, but I don't want Hermes taking off with you again while I'm away. I warded this space to hold a minor god. Probably not enough to hold Hermes, but with an obfuscation sigil we should be able to keep him at bay, at least until I get back."

Understanding sank into his eyes. "You're asking me to stay down here? That's how I'm supposed to help?"

"That's what I'm asking, yes."

"Well, where are you going?"

Not knowing whether Hermes was hunkered in the tablet, listening to every word, I didn't want to tip him off that I was planning a deep dive into his origins. Meaning I had to keep Alec in the dark for now.

"I'm just going to check on some things."

"Why can't I go with you?"

"Because Hermes is unpredictable. I'm trying to help him, but he makes that really hard sometimes. I'm trying to help you, too." With my emotions threatening, I forged on. "We'll bring you plenty to eat, a bed, whatever books you'd like to read. All I can promise is that I'll come back as soon as I can."

His slumping posture suggested reluctant assent. "Well, is there anything I can do in here?"

I considered the question and nodded. I signed into the air, opening a small portal. Reaching inside my interplanar cubbyhole, I felt around and pulled out a thick tome. "Remember when you were going to be my graduate assistant?"

That drew a thin smile. "Feels like forever ago."

"Well, here you go." I placed the book in his hands.

He turned it around and read the title in confusion. "Numerology?"

"I want you to research the meaning behind the numbers one, eleven, and twelve."

"Why?"

I recalled the Doideag's verses from my dream:

> *If ye should fail and war should come,*
> *If seas should boil and lands should run,*
> *Allies gather eleven and one,*
> *And be not afraid of thine own blood.*

"Because they might mean something," I said. "Something we may end up needing."

22

It was late afternoon by the time Claudius and I finished modifying the wards in the basement efficiency and Alec had settled in. I assured him I wouldn't be gone long, but he seemed to have warmed to his assignment, especially now that it involved some research. I kept expecting Hermes to appear through him, eyes glimmering, to give me some song-and-dance about why he had bailed, but he never did.

As Claudius and I climbed upstairs, I asked, "How does the bonding look?"

"Between Alec and the tablet?" He'd been popping ginseng candies much of the day, which did seem to be aiding his memory. "Not good, I'm afraid. It has him wrapped tight. I don't think he can stray from the backpack even if he wanted to."

I nodded grimly. I'd considered taking the pack from him in the event I needed to destroy the tablet but opted against it out of concern for Alec. Plus, the box protecting the tablet had spawned energy guardians in the past and I didn't need them rampaging through the building while I was away.

"I didn't want to say anything in front of him," Claudius whispered, "but I don't think Hermes is planning to release him."

A cold fury gripped me. "Based on what?"

"Well, the bonds are fusing to him. Before long they'll become inseparable from the fabric of his soul." Claudius was an expert at complex bindings, and borderline senility or not, I placed high value on his assessment.

"How much time do we have?"

"If it continues at the current pace?" He sucked on his candy in thought. "A few days, give or take."

Another deadline, not to mention another strike against Hermes's credibility.

Back upstairs, I used the dining room table to organize spell items I'd selected from my basement unit and loft space. Without my cane, I chose a pair of wands, one for offense and one for defense, even though I didn't consider myself a wand person. That was more James Wesson's style, my wizard friend out West. Wands were precise, but I'd grown used to wielding implements with more heft.

Ricki prepared a plate of finger food so I could eat while I prepped for the trip.

"Think you'll find what you're looking for?" she asked as I crunched on a carrot stick.

"I have a good idea where to look in both cases."

"How long will it take you?"

"I plan to be back by Tuesday night, at the latest."

That would leave me one day until my Wednesday-at-midnight deadline. I straightened, preparing to tell Ricki about my shadow's ashes and the bonding potion when our front door opened.

"We're back!" Mae called.

Tony hustled ahead of her in his practice jersey, headed for the kitchen.

"Cleats off," Ricki called after him. He somehow managed to remove them mid-run, sending them flipping away in both directions. At the fridge, he pulled out a jug of apple juice and tilted it to his mouth.

"Hey, heard of a cup?" Ricki said, striding toward him. "You know better."

Bree-yark sauntered in behind Mae, but when he saw me packing my casting items, he stopped. "Where do you think you're off to?"

"Greece and Italy on a research trip. Very last minute," I was sure to add.

"Well, give me the flight numbers, and I'll see if they've got any last minute deals for me to jump on."

Claudius emerged from the bathroom. "About ready?" he asked.

"Why does he get to go?" Bree-yark challenged.

"Because he's my ride."

Claudius started to say something, but when he caught sight of Mae, he hurried over to take her coat and lavish her with compliments. She giggled and waved her hand. "You are *too* much, Claudius."

Bree-yark, who usually grumbled at the old wizard's affections for his fiancée, was too busy looking up at me with his hopeful "please let me come" expression. He'd even begun to bounce on the toes of his boots. Geez, what could I say?

"You know you're always welcome."

He thrust a fist toward the ceiling. "Yes!"

"But don't expect any action," I warned. "I'm going to be doing professor stuff, visiting museums, talking to experts, that sort of thing. The biggest challenge you're going to have is staying awake."

He barked a laugh. "Yeah, you say that, but it's always an adventure with you."

"I'd offer to come, too," Mae said as Claudius left to hang her coat. "But I managed maybe two winks of sleep last night, I was so worried about your trip this morning. How did that go, baby?"

"Not as well as I was hoping. Hence *this* trip."

"Well, you won't have to worry about leaving your wife this time, because I'm staying right here with her."

"No argument from me," Ricki said as she returned from the kitchen with Tony, who was gulping from a glass now.

"Me neither, Mae," I said. "Thank you very much." Her staying was a huge relief, especially with Ricki being so close to her due date. I turned to Bree-yark. "How soon can you be ready, buddy?"

"Hey, I'm *always* ready. I keep a bugout kit in the Humvee for just in case. Let me go grab it."

As he left, Mae came up and swallowed me in her thick, grandmotherly arms, which rivaled my best healing potions. "You're always working so hard, hun. Is there anything we can do while you're away?"

As she rocked me, I explained the situation with Alec and asked if she could periodically coax his bonds loose. Thanks to the bond's nether qualities, and Mae's innate understanding of nether energies, she had that power.

"It'll be my honor to tend to your handsome young man."

"Otherwise," I said as we separated, "I'll just ask you both to keep an eye on her."

I walked over to the divan, where Tabitha lay in a stiff mound. I scratched her around the ears and stroked her voluminous side. We'd managed to work her eyelids closed, but her teeth remained bared in a scowl.

"That's no problem either," Mae said from behind me. "Just concentrate on whatever it is you have to do and let us worry about the rest."

"Again, thank you."

I leaned toward Tabitha's ear, remembering the ominous figure when I'd opened the whip's defenses.

"You're a fighter, Tabby," I whispered. "Keep fighting."

Ten minutes later, Claudius, Bree-yark, and I stood in the center of the living room in a circle, arms clasped. My coat and satchel held everything I needed, while Bree-yark wore an oversized trekking pack ornamented with pots, pans, and a grubby pair of camp shoes. We'd already said our goodbyes to Ricki and Mae. Tony watched from between them, keen for the moment when we'd disappear.

"We'll be back Tuesday," I reiterated.

"Do I need to call Professor Snodgrass?" Ricki asked.

Shoot, I was going to miss at least three days of summer term classes. "If you don't mind. But since it's last minute, you better call his wife. She'll be more understanding." Professor Snodgrass was also afraid of her. "Tell her to tell him to have the students finish the week's reading. We'll get back up to speed on Friday."

Ricki gave me the okay sign. I blew her a final kiss.

"Hold tight, everyone," Claudius said. "Next stop, Athens, Georgia!"

"Whoa, whoa, whoa," I interjected. "*Greece.* Athens, *Greece.*"

"Ah, yes..." He muttered toward his sandals as though working out a new route before looking up again. "Next stop, Athens, Greece!"

"Bye, Dad!" Tony called, very ready for us to vanish now.

A moment later, he got his wish.

I braced for a wild ride, but no sooner than my feet had lifted from the rug, they were setting down again into something much softer. The living room was gone, replaced by wan light and a mossy smell that was thick and unpleasant. A purplish duff covered my shoes, while an ominous mist drifted all around us.

"This doesn't look like Athens," I remarked.

"No, this is just a transit point," Claudius whispered, releasing my arm. "We need to hurry, though."

"Why?" I asked, trotting after him. Bree-yark adjusted his pack and joined us.

"Because when the mist thins, the trees will awaken, and we don't have their permission to be here. I'd forgotten that last part. But since we're here, we might as well forge on. The transit point isn't far."

Massive trunks loomed redwood-like through the mist. If what Claudius said was true, their size alone was cause for concern. Bree-yark picked up on that, too. He clutched the pots and pans hanging from his pack to keep them from clanging. I held onto one he couldn't reach and ran clumsily beside him.

"Ooof!" Claudius exclaimed, pulling up suddenly.

Bree-yark and I nearly collided into his back as an object

the size of a small safe plummeted into the duff in front of him.

"Darn it, they're starting to awaken," he said. "This way!"

High above, branches clacked, and more objects—seeds, I surmised—impacted around us. I followed Claudius's chaotic course, swearing at myself for having believed he could deliver us without drama. I drew one of my wands from a coat pocket and circled it overhead with a "*Protezione!*"

Bluish light swam from the wand's end. I fashioned it into a circle, then coaxed the edges down into an umbrella-shaped protection. A moment later, an especially large seed bounced from it and tumbled away.

"How much farther?" I shouted.

"Oh, just ahead, just ahead," Claudius said in a way that told me he had no real idea.

He ran the length of a football field, doubled back, and veered right, then left, so that our actual progress in that span was only about five yards. Meanwhile, the clacking was growing angrier and the seed storm heavier. I grunted as another one landed on my protection, driving my planted foot into the duff.

"Hey, Everson?" Bree-yark said.

I followed his talon to where the last seed had cracked against a tree trunk and split open. A host of spider-like legs explored the seed's jagged edge before fluttering into the mist on giant moth wings. Not seeds, but eggs.

"Ahh, here it is," Claudius said, slowing as we entered a clearing. "Huddle up, arms together."

I did as he said while angling my wand awkwardly to grow our protection around us. The arriving spider-moths batted against its sides, hairy legs scrabbling for purchase. Bree-yark shrank from a fleshy mouth with hooks for teeth.

Claudius didn't seem to notice the creatures. A moment later, the trees faded out.

Powerful centrifugal forces sent my legs flailing. I lost my grip on Claudius and Bree-yark, and the three of us went crashing off in different directions. I rolled to a stop on my stomach, waving at the air around my head to ward off any spider-moths, but it seemed none had followed us.

We were in a house now. A table lay in ruins beside me, and the tiled floor was strewn with crockery, some of it still rattling to a rest.

Claudius, where in the ever-loving hell did you land us this time?

I peered up to find a woman leveling a glowing blade at my face.

23

"*T*i *sto diáolo káneis edó?*" she demanded.

That she spoke Greek suggested Claudius had at least landed us in the right neighborhood this time. She was asking what in the hell I was doing there. A reasonable question under the circumstances.

A colorful headscarf drew the woman's thick black hair from a freckled, sun-weathered complexion, while severe brown eyes bore into mine. But I was more preoccupied with the blade she thrust toward my face. Though it crackled with flames, it didn't give off the heat of fire, but magic.

A sorceress?

"*I'm sorry,*" I replied in Greek, bringing my hands up. "*We were trying to get to Athens, and we must have...*"

I struggled for how to complete the explanation, but she was no longer listening. Her eyes had cut to my right hand, where my wand was braced between thumb and finger. It was so light, I'd nearly forgotten I was holding it—another reason I preferred heftier implements.

She drew back. "*Who in the hell are you?*" Another reasonable question.

But before I could even attempt to answer that one, Bree-yark appeared like a cannonball. With a barking cry, he rammed his stout two-hundred pounds into her side and seized her around the waist.

"Teach you to point that at someone's face," he grunted.

"Bree-yark, no!" I shouted.

The two went rolling across the kitchen floor, but within three revolutions, she was on top, her blade raised to strike.

"*Protezione!*" I shouted from my stomach, thrusting the wand.

Her descending blade collided into my swirling blue plate of protection. The meeting of magics catalyzed into an explosion that threw her from Bree-yark and shoved me back against a wall. As shelf ornaments spilled over me, Claudius hopped into view on one foot while securing his sandal over the other. He peered around at the mayhem, his tinted glasses eventually stopping on the woman.

"Oh, hello, Loukia!" he said, parting his hair from his face.

The woman, who had landed in a three-point stance and been poised to spring, narrowed her eyes at him. "Claudius? How dare you show up here unannounced!" The thick accent underscored her scolding tone.

I looked between them. "You two know each other?"

"Why, of course!" Claudius said. "She's a magic-user of the Order, like you."

"Wait," I said, pushing myself to my feet. "A magic-user of the Order?" Even as I asked, I felt a familiarity in the ambient magic and sensed the portal Claudius had installed here for his visits. I was looking at the Athens version of me.

"You two haven't met?" Claudius asked.

"No, we haven't," I replied, not taking my eyes off her.

Though she'd yet to lower her blade, and her expression suggested she'd skewer the three of us in a heartbeat, I stared as though she were both a rare specimen and a long-lost sister. She looked to be in her mid-thirties, about my age. Fascination and a kind of sibling affection swirled inside me. I'd met so few of my counterparts, only two to be exact: James Wesson and Pierce Dalton, and we'd lost Pierce.

"Ah, yes, well, the Order has been busy," Claudius said. "They were planning a conference for all of you, a meet-and-greet of sorts, but then there was the business with the Harkless Rift and the rips, and, well... I'm sure it will happen eventually. I do hope so. There was talk of me emceeing."

"This is incredible," I said, still staring at the woman. "I'm Everson Croft."

I stepped toward her, passing Bree-yark, who was backing away to put a safe distance between them.

"Loukia Kouris," she muttered, giving my hand a cursory shake. Apparently, the feeling of sibling affection wasn't mutual, but she sheathed her blade at her waist as she looked between us.

"What do you want here?" she demanded.

"I'm really sorry about just showing up like this," I said, gesturing lamely to the mess we'd made. I foolishly thought Claudius would deliver us to a remote cul-de-sac or forgotten ruin, not the middle of someone's kitchen on a cyclone. "I'm working a case in New York City, and it involves the god Hermes. Or a version of him, a patron to an Attican thieves guild. I came here to research the guild."

"What do you want to know?"

"Namely, who they were and how they worshipped him."

Which would tell me a lot about who Hermes was. "I've jotted down the names of museums that should have that info, if not in the main collections, then in their archives."

"There are no museums open this late," she said.

I checked my watch and added seven hours. Indeed, it was after midnight here.

"Well, it doesn't have to be an *official* visit," I said. "My time is sort of tight."

A thoughtful line formed between her thick eyebrows. "If you want this information, I have a better source for you."

"Oh, yeah? Where?"

"*Who.* She is a contact of mine. She knows everything there is to know about Athens. She can tell you about your thieves guild and Hermes."

"That's excellent." I pushed my clasped hands toward her. "Thank you."

"Yes, I will take you to her, but I was leaving for a job when you... arrived." She looked around her kitchen. As though in penitence for attacking her earlier, Bree-yark had begun straightening up the mess.

"Is there any way you could take us to her on the way?" I ventured.

"My time is *tight* too, so we will help each other," she declared.

"What kind of a job are we talking about?"

"Vampire job."

Wonderful. "And how long will that take?"

"Until they are all dead."

I turned to Claudius. "What do you think?"

"Hmm, it's been a long while since I've had to deal with vampires."

Before we could discuss it further, Bree-yark hustled over

and elbowed me in the side. "Ha! What'd I tell you? Always an adventure." He looked up at her, his eyes blazing yellow. "Count us in!"

For the first time, the corners of Loukia's mouth turned up. "Very good."

———

24

A n hour later, we were careening through a warren of narrow streets in a battered Peugeot minivan. The driver, a large man who had to stoop to see through the windshield, carried out a rapid exchange with Loukia. Because the van's rear was piled with junk, Claudius, Bree-yark, and I got to sit three across on the middle bench seat, shoulders jammed together. The faulty seat rocked back as the van climbed.

I nudged Bree-yark and nodded out my window.

"Holy thunder!" he exclaimed, leaning to peer past me. Above the red-tiled rooftops, the Acropolis had thrust into view, a full moon glowing over the stately Parthenon building. "I've seen pictures of the thing, but... holy thunder," he repeated, lost for words.

"According to the myths, Athena and Poseidon competed for patronage of the city on that very hill," I said. "Poseidon struck the Acropolis with his trident, creating an upwell of seawater. That was his offering, a crappy one if you ask me. Athena planted a seed, which sprang into a bountiful olive tree. Not surprisingly, the king declared her the winner and named his city after her. The original Parthenon was a temple built in her honor."

As he stared at it, I could see his engineering cogs turning. "Marble, right? Boy, that's nice."

If there had been time, I would have loved to wander its ruins. I thought about bringing Alec here someday before catching myself.

"Hey, you all right?" Bree-yark asked.

I cleared my throat. "Yeah. Just thinking about how much Alec would have enjoyed this. He loves the Greek myths."

"Listen to me, Everson," he said sternly. "That kid's gonna be alright, and you wanna know why? 'Cause he's got a village looking out for him. There's you and me, Ricki and Mae, Claudius—heck, most the bigshots in your Order from the sounds of it." He craned his neck around. "Ain't that right, Claudius?"

But Claudius had fallen asleep, his chin bobbing against his chest.

"The point is," Bree-yark continued, "we're not gonna let anything happen to him."

I smiled warmly, appreciatively, but even if we somehow managed to extricate Alec from Hermes's grip, I would be condemning him to the shadow realm. A place I couldn't even think about without becoming immediately depressed. I peered out at where the Acropolis was disappearing from view.

"I just want a good life for him," I said.

"Course you do. You're his pops!" He slapped my knee. "And I see a lot of you in him, too. Means well, good head on his shoulders, resourceful. The way he faked like he was your student?" He barked a laugh. "Boy, that was gold. One way or another, he's gonna find his way. I mean, look how it all turned out for you."

He was right. Other than some early training from Lazlo, I'd negotiated those early years of wizarding on my own. Was that what it was going to take? Learning to let go of him? But I was getting ahead of myself. First, I needed the scoop on Hermes, patron of a thieves guild, which meant helping Loukia with her vampire job.

"Thanks, Bree-yark," I said. "I mean it."

Minutes later, the van heaved to a stop. I didn't know Athens well, but we were clearly in one of its night districts. The city streets had gone from empty, save for the occasional stray animal, to crowded with young men and women in slinky, club-hopping attire. The sudden transformation was jarring.

"I will let you out here," the driver said, switching from Greek to broken English for our sakes. "I will park behind building."

"Don't get lost this time," Loukia snapped.

From what I'd picked up of their conversation on the ride, I guessed the driver worked for her (poorly, judging from her list of criticisms), so it surprised me when she leaned over and kissed him on the lips.

"*Be careful,*" the driver told her in Greek. "*These are Contili.*"

"*They do not scare me,*" she shot back, then to us: "Let's go."

Bree-yark had to elbow Claudius, who was still sleeping. "Hey, time to roll out."

"Mmphm?" Claudius snorted, then blinked around. "Oh, are we here already?" He slid out after us, then sidled up to me on the sidewalk and whispered, "Remind me again what we're doing?"

"That favor for Loukia?" Seeing he needed more, I added, "In Athens, Greece?"

"Oh, right, right," he muttered, still not sounding absolutely sure of himself, but he became distracted by a passing group of women in tight sequined pants.

As the van pulled away, Loukia faced us. She'd changed into a black shirt and a pair of nylon leggings. A ribbed duster concealed the two enchanted blades she carried in her belt. For a magic-user, she looked pretty badass.

"Our targets are inside." She cocked her head toward the club at her back. "I can handle them. One of you will watch my back. The other two will keep the crowd out of harm's way."

"Your friend mentioned these were *Contili*," I said. "What does that mean?"

"It is the clan from which they became vampires. The most powerful clan in all of Greece."

"And you're not worried about retribution?"

"Grigoris is the head of the Contili clan. He is the one who hired me."

"Hold on a second," I said, making a back-it-up motion. "You're contracting out to a vampire clan?"

"What does it matter why I kill them," she snapped, "as long as they are killed. This is not New York. Yes, I know all about the *great* work you do in your city, how you work with the mayor to clean out the vampires and other monsters." She said it as though I were the goody two-shoes in the family.

"You know about that?" I asked in confusion. I'd never heard a peep about her.

"But my city is different," she continued, "and I must deal with it as it is, not how I wish it to be. And, yes, the Order knows what I do. Grigoris's time will come, but for now I must chip away at the edges. The vampires inside are a group that is becoming too bold for his liking. Too independent."

I turned to Claudius who shrugged as if to say, *Her turf*.

"All right," I allowed. "How powerful a group are we talking?"

"Powerful enough," she said. "But their power has made them weak. You will see what I mean."

With that, she led the way toward the club's entrance. A bouncer with arms as big as my thighs manned a velvet rope that blocked a line extending down the block. When I spotted his detection wand, I was nervous about Loukia's concealed blades, not to mention our own weapons, but she produced a card from a coat pocket and handed it to him. The bouncer took his time studying it before he spoke into a headset. A moment later, he nodded and opened a side rope, allowing us to enter.

"What was that?" I asked her.

"An official pass from Grigoris. He owns all the clubs on this strip."

That explained why this particular street was so active—Grigoris could afford his clientele special protections that no mortal establishment could match, and he no doubt profited handsomely as a result. But it raised another question.

"Why can't he take care of these guys himself?"

"He does not like to get his teeth bloody on his own kind," she said.

There was so much I wanted to unpack, colleague to colleague. What kinds of threats she faced in Athens, her methods of detection and elimination, who her allies were, but this wasn't the time nor place.

The club's strobe-lit floor throbbed with techno music

and bouncing bodies. We edged single file between the dance floor and a bar that ran the club's length, every lacquered stool occupied and the gaps stacked three patrons deep.

I could think of few worse places for a vampire fight.

I opened my wizard's senses, but the energy of Athens was still foreign to me. Amid the vibrant layers, I picked up several icy threads that suggested an undead presence. Nothing I could follow, though. I peered back to ensure Claudius hadn't wandered off, relieved to find Bree-yark prodding him from behind.

Loukia stopped and nodded. "There they are."

I raised my eyes to an elevated VIP section that over-looked the dance floor. Three young men lounged across a red leather banquette, the table in front of them littered with shot glasses and half-empty bottles of liquor. They wore black suits, shirts open to reveal toned torsos and strings of gold jewelry. They laughed loudly as they spoke, but when they swept or shook back their manes of dark hair to survey the floor, which was often, there was no humor in their obsidian eyes. Only predation.

I peered around the crowded venue again. "We can't do this outside?"

"They are more vulnerable in here," she replied without elaborating. "Who is coming with me?"

I raised my hand and nodded at Bree-yark and Claudius to hang back. She climbed the steps, leading me past other small groups in their own roped-off sections, until she'd arrived beside the vampires.

The nearest one's nostrils flared slightly.

"*Is that Loukia I smell?*" he asked in Greek, not looking over. "*Climb in and join us, my pet. I can promise you that after three drinks, you won't ever want to leave again.*" He grinned lasciviously, and the others snickered. He was referring to her blood. The three drinks in question would be for the three vampires.

"*I don't share drinks with Eurotrash,*" she replied.

"*And we normally don't care for Roma dogs,*" he said, "*but we'll make an exception for the right bitch.*"

Bristling with protective anger, I stepped up beside her.

"*Oh, look,*" he said, his black eyes sliding over. "*Loukia's brought a little friend.*"

Though the vampires appeared to be the same age, he was clearly the senior. His two juniors leaned over to size me up.

"*Do you play with magic, too, little friend?*" the middle one asked with a leering smirk.

I smiled tightly, my grandfather's ring, the one holding the power of the Brasov Pact, throbbing around my finger. If the vampires detected its power, they exhibited zero concern. That must have been what Loukia meant about their strength making them weak. They'd gone unchallenged for too long. Even as the vampires taunted us, their eyes roved the club hungrily. Probably why this Grigoris wanted them gone. Disappearances leading back to the club would be bad for business.

"*I've come to deliver a message,*" Loukia said.

The senior vampire threw back a shot and thumbed the moisture from his lips. "*Unless it involves a strip tease, we're not interested.*"

"*Even then, we're not interested,*" the farthest vampire put in. "*Do you see all that taut flesh down there. Next to them, you're an old whore.*" Once more, I bristled at their laughter, but Loukia stared at them, unperturbed.

"*It is from Grigoris,*" she said.

Their eyes snapped toward her in sync. That had gotten their attention. But while the junior vampires appeared bothered, their leader grinned viciously.

"*You're wasting your tongue on words, Loukia. We already know Grigoris doesn't want us here anymore.*" A blade of anger flashed in his eyes. "*But maybe we have a message for him, too.*"

He lunged with terrifying speed. Too slowly, I drew my fist from my pocket, but the vampire hadn't gone for Loukia. Instead, he seized the wrist of a passing waitress. She screamed as she left her feet and drinks splashed and crashed from her tray. In the next instant, she was splayed across his lap.

"*Tell Grigoris we don't care,*" the vampire finished.

His fangs dove toward the waitress's throat.

———

25

With the vampire's teeth sinking into the waitress's pale skin, I aimed my ring, but Loukia beat me to the punch.

"*Attivare!*" she shouted.

In bursts of searing light, the liquor bottles shattered, sending fire spilling across the table. The lead vampire shrieked and reared his head back, releasing the woman's neck. His two juniors broke into spastic fits.

What in the hell?

When they began slapping their torsos, sending smoke billowing from their shirts, I understood. Loukia had seen to it that the vampires' alcohol was spiked with latent liquid sunlight. Very crafty.

A blade flashed from under Loukia's coat, its length crackling with fiery magic. But though the senior vampire was thrashing, out of his head with pain, the waitress remained across his body and in Loukia's way. She seized the waitress by the back of her cocktail dress and yanked her from the banquette.

"Take her," Loukia said without looking.

I stepped in as the woman fell backward, catching her like a length of timber and standing her upright. Clear now, Loukia hammer-stroked her knife toward the vampire's chest, but one of his juniors lunged in. A battle of blade thrusts and spastic parries ensued.

"*Are you all right?*" I asked the waitress in Greek.

Punctures showed where the vampire had bitten down, but he hadn't breached a major vessel. The young woman nodded slightly, her eyes large with shock. I turned her toward the club, where our battle royale was just beginning to make waves. Several club goers were already pushing toward the exits.

"Go," I said to her.

She stumbled down the steps on wobbly fawn legs, where Bree-yark received her.

I turned back to the fight just as Loukia thrust her blade up and under the junior vampire's sternum. A loud crunch sounded as she twisted and jerked the blade free, depositing the vampire on the flaming table. He arched onto his head and the backs of his heels in a C shape, contortive snaps sounding throughout his stiffening body. His flesh shriveled to the bone, then grayed to powder.

Loukia wheeled toward the senior vampire, intent on finishing him. But the other junior, who had fallen from the far side of the banquette, pounced toward her back.

"*Balaur!*" I shouted, redirecting my ring.

The power of the Brasov Pact gathered in the silver ingot and released with a club-shaking *whoomp*, sending the vampire in a new trajectory. Flames burst as he met the rear wall and plummeted. Already weakened from the liquid sunlight, he succumbed to the fire in a fading death cry.

But the edge of my blast had caught Loukia, sending her stumbling into a neighboring section.

The senior vampire used the opportunity to scramble up a set of stage drapes and perch among the steel girders where lights were mounted. As he watched us with hunted eyes, he ripped away his jacket and shirt, revealing a muscled torso covered in smoldering sores. He appeared more animal than aristocratic playboy now. But even from my distance I could see that the sores were healing.

"*Balaur!*" I shouted again.

This time, the summoned power of the Brasov Pact took longer to gather and its discharge wasn't as forceful. The vampire bounded across the girders, staying ahead of my attack and out of harm's way.

"Everson!" Bree-yark shouted.

I looked over to find the goblin and Claudius planted in the middle of the emptying club. The lights had come on, the music had cut out, and the crowd was surging for the exits like a receding surf. But several people were fighting the tide, shoving patrons aside in improbable feats of strength. Blood slaves, I realized, coming to defend their master. That was what Bree-yark was alerting me to.

"Take them down, but don't kill them!" I shouted.

The slaves had been human once, a status that could be restored upon their master's demise. Bree-yark nodded and hefted a metal barstool while Claudius brought his fingers into a conjuring posture.

"*You have nowhere to run,*" Loukia shouted at the senior vampire.

She'd invoked shields over all the windows he could conceivably escape through. Now she thrust her blade. A fiery bolt shot out with an air-frying sizzle and bent toward him. Though he leapt away in time, the impact sent out a flash of light that had him screaming and clawing his eyes.

"*You Roma piece of shit!*" he shrieked. "*I'm going to rip out your bowels and feed them to the swine!*"

I readied my wands to defend Loukia, but despite the vampire's tough talk, he was hurt and on the run. The challenge was going to be finishing him. I turned to Claudius as he opened a portal ahead of a charging blood slave. The slave disappeared inside a grasping tangle of weeds, and Claudius signed it closed again.

"Hey!" I called. "Remember that portal you almost sent me through earlier today?"

Claudius tottered around, oblivious to another blood slave incoming. Fortunately, Bree-yark was there to meet him with a barstool to the face. Claudius shuffled away from the melee, mostly to hear me better.

"Um, yes, I think so," he replied.

"I need another one. *Just like it,*" I emphasized.

He looked from me to the vampire in the girders and nodded in what I hoped was understanding. Loukia, meanwhile, was sending up more bolts. The vampire managed to evade them, still hurt, but healing.

Loukia blew a strand of hair from her eyes in frustration.

"Can you drive him over there?" I asked her, pointing between the two sets of girders.

She nodded and sent another bolt into the vampire's fleeing wake, missing intentionally this time. I adjusted my grip on the wands. Between the sets of girders, a channel extended down the center of the ceiling. The vampire had already crossed it once, and as he prepared to leap it again, I was ready.

"*Protezione!*"

With nothing to obstruct my invocation, it crackled through the air, hardening into a barrier. The vampire rammed into it, talons scrabbling for purchase. I grew the hardened air into a long chute and tilted it toward the club floor. When the vampire attempted to bound up it, I thrust my other wand, directing a force down the enclosure. Down to where Claudius's portal had begun to yawn open.

Inside, lava belched and spat toxic smoke.

The vampire brought his legs around and kicked, as though trying to brake against the air itself. He then rolled into a swimming stroke, his cries growing more guttural and insane. They ended with a thick kerplunk into the lava.

Claudius signed the portal closed.

Our gazes turned to the half dozen blood slaves who'd shoved their way into the club. One by one, they crumpled to the ground, including the young man Bree-yark was poised to hammer with the barstool.

The influence of the senior vampire thinned from their bodies, and mortality rushed into its place. There was a chance not all of them would make it. But though several aged, some significantly, they were all alive and gasping.

I turned to Loukia as she arrived beside me. "Nicely done," I said.

"Yes, that is three fewer vampires in my city now." She accepted my fist bump. "Just a hundred more to go." Though she spoke like a fatalist, I noted a slight warmth in her eyes that hadn't been there earlier.

Bree-yark and Claudius joined us, the latter dusting off his hands.

"Great job, guys," I said. "But that blood slave you portaled?" I prompted Claudius.

He started, eyes wide with alarm, and signed into the air.

A hole reopened onto the tangle of weeds. He issued a stern command, and the weeds shoved the blood slave back onto the club's dance floor.

This one, a young woman-turned-middled aged, looked as though she was going to make it, too. My healing magic was of little help in cases of reversion. What the victims needed was time. I used my wand to squelch out the small fires that had sprung up around the club, reducing them to smoke.

"Come," Loukia said, putting her phone away. "I've called for ambulances, and Yiorgos is waiting out back."

"To take us to your contact, right?" I said.

"Do not worry, Everson. You've earned your meeting."

But as I followed her, a sliver of my own fatalism took hold. Would her contact have the information I was after? I looked up at where the junior vampire remained arched across the table in a C, stiff as a sculpture, flesh gone to dust. A good reminder of what would become of me if I failed here.

26

————

Yiorgos rattled us down backroads until the club was well behind us and the streets empty again. He'd been chain-smoking while he waited—the van reeked of it—but who could blame him? Every time he looked over at Loukia, his deep care for her showed in his Saint Bernard eyes. He spoke to her in snatches, expressions of concern from what I could pick up, but she gave him little back beside tired nods.

At last, he sighed and focused on the road.

"So, Loukia?" I ventured. "Does your contact have a name?"

"Yes." For a moment, I thought she was going to leave it at that. "Olidia."

"Is Olidia a scholar of some kind?"

"An observer," she answered mysteriously.

"Anything else I should know about her?"

"She will talk as long as you are interesting to her."

"And if I'm not?"

Loukia shrugged. "She will leave."

"How old is she, seven?" I asked in frustration.

In the rearview mirror, I caught Loukia's lips turn up. "You will understand when you meet her."

Before long we arrived in a neighborhood of old homes near the base of the Acropolis. As Yiorgos navigated the narrow streets, floral branches arced from beyond stone walls and brushed the van's rooftop. Yiorgos pulled onto a gravel drive and came to a stop in front of an old metal gate. The van's one functioning headlight showed the drive curving into the trees beyond.

"Olidia does not like motor traffic," Loukia said. "We walk from here."

"I will wait," Yiorgos said morosely, already pawing for the cigarette pack in his shirt pocket.

Loukia kissed him and got out. Claudius, Bree-yark, and I followed her to the gate. As she produced a key, Bree-yark tugged the sleeve of my coat. I looked down to find his goblin ears, lumps beneath his wool hat, angling toward the gate.

"Don't know about this place," he whispered. "I'm picking up some weird sounds."

"This is one of the safest places in Athens," Loukia said sternly, having overheard him.

She unlocked the gate and pushed it open on creaking hinges. Claudius sauntered through, whistling a jovial tune, while Bree-yark remained planted, regarding me with wary eyes. I nodded that we could trust her, which I truly believed. She was a fellow magic-user of the Order. As I filed through the gate, though, I picked up something, too. An unmistakable sensation of magic. Fae magic.

Crap.

Loukia locked the gate behind us. "Follow me."

I still trusted her, but I tried not to make a habit of dealing with the fae any more than I had to. They rarely, if ever, gave selflessly, and I was in no mood to bargain. But neither was I in a position to be picky.

I hustled after Loukia, who'd taken lead up the drive. The way soon narrowed to a winding path that topped out at a grove of olive trees. A pleasant scent, like blossoms and dried fruit, filled the air. Loukia whispered to one side of the path and the other in a sing-song voice, as though calling to a kitten.

As we crested the hill, I expected the lights of a home to glow into view, but there was no house. Only a clearing in the grove featuring an especially large olive tree. It all clicked for me now.

"She's a dryad?" I asked.

"Yes, now go ahead," Loukia said, stopping at the verge of the clearing. "She's agreed to meet you."

"Want me to come, Everson?" Bree-yark asked, gripping the hilt of his sheathed blade.

I looked to Claudius for council, but he was too busy trying to pick a pebble from the tread of his sandal. I shook my head to tell Bree-yark I would be all right and proceeded toward the old tree.

"Just remember to be interesting," Loukia whispered.

"Short of singing and dancing, I'll do my best," I whispered back.

"And don't piss her off," she added.

As the olive tree loomed nearer, its leaves glowing with moonlight and winks of magic, I reviewed what I knew about dryads. They were nature spirits from the fae realm who coexisted with trees, usually many trees of the same species, allowing them to survive over the generations by shifting between them. They were incredible stores of knowledge. Like the water their hosts drank into their roots, dryads absorbed the information of a region—all of its politics and beliefs, its alliances, betrayals, and accords, from the highest halls of power down to the filthiest alleys and hovels—and could recite them back like scribes. But dryads were also notoriously fickle and easily bored.

I had to hand it to Loukia, though. Earning a dryad's trust took careful and persistent effort over a long time, and she had somehow managed to pull it off. There were no dryads in Manhattan to my knowledge, just my regional informants such as Effie the ghost and Mr. Han in Chinatown.

Several feet from the tree, I stopped and peered up the twisted cords of its trunk into its thick branches. Though the air was still, the dark leaves rustled gently.

"Olidia?" I tried.

"Everson Croft?" a girl's voice said back.

"Yes, that's me."

I waited, half expecting a lithe spirit to separate from the trunk, but the dryad remained ensconced in the tree. I sensed both curiosity and caution.

"Loukia said you may be able to help me with something?" I said. "I'm looking for information on a thieves guild that would have been active in Athens around four hundred B.C. Hermes was their patron god."

"Thieves were common in Athens at that time," Olidia said, a touch impatiently.

"This guild practiced magic," I hurriedly added. "They developed the ability to transfer to a parallel realm."

As the dryad fell silent, the tree seemed to stare down at me. Its leaves fluttered and went still. After several seconds I was all but certain I'd managed to bore her into leaving when she spoke again.

"The Kleftians. I know of them."

I pumped a mental fist. If I got nothing else from her, at least I had a name now.

"Do you know how Hermes helped them?"

"With stealing, of course," she all but snapped. "He gifted them fast fingers, fleet feet, and shadows to conceal their deeds. They took from everyone, the privileged and the deprived. The Kleftians robbed gold and rustled cattle. When a wealthy landowner deeded his wealth to the city's first orphanage, they stole that, too."

"They stole from an orphanage?"

"There was a saying at the time," she said in a hushed voice. "'If it hasn't a lock and guard, it belongs to the Kleftians.'" Though she sounded more engaged now, this was not looking good for Hermes.

"And what did Hermes get in exchange?" I asked.

"The normal tribute—half of their spoils. They also constructed a box at his behest, one that would preserve him 'beyond the days of his worship,'" she said, as though reciting something else she'd overheard.

"That's right!" I said. "I have a photo on my phone here..."

But as I flipped open my primitive device, the leaves shook and the boughs drew back. "Squelch that horrid light!" the dryad cried.

"O-Oh, I'm sorry."

No motor traffic, no screen light, I noted.

As I returned the phone to my coat pocket, I pictured the rune-lined box I'd first discovered in a landfill and that now protected the tablet in Alec's pack. I'd assumed the guild had built the box out of self-interest, to protect the tablet that had made them master thieves and preserve it for future generations. But it now sounded as if Hermes had demanded the box in exchange for aiding and abetting them.

"He wanted immortality," I murmured to myself.

"But the Kleftians were stupid," she said, "for once they completed the box, Hermes had no more need for them."

That jolted me from my musings. "Hermes killed them?"

"Had them killed," the dryad amended. "Who do you think betrayed them to Pericles's soldiers?"

As I shuddered, a riffle passed through the leaves—in mimicry or sympathy, I couldn't tell. Dryads were strange beings. But is that what this version of Hermes amounted to? A god whose sole aim was to ascend the ladder of power and immortality, using humans as his disposable rungs? That jibed with shadow Budge's account and boded really badly for us. Though the night was cool, sweat broke out across my back.

"The box," I said. "Can it be opened?"

"Only with Hermes's consent. His word binds it."

"There's no other way?" I asked bleakly.

"Certain magics can open it, but not without destroying opener and bearer."

That would mean me and Alec. When I went quiet, the leaves rustled impatiently.

After another moment, Olidia yawned. "I am tired, Everson Croft. I will depart now."

Without ceremony or farewell, the dryad's magic thinned from the olive tree and its leaves fell still.

27

Loukia invited us back to her home for a late dinner, where she and Yiorgos prepared a platter of Greek staples and set out a couple wine bottles. I'd said little since my meeting with the dryad, and after picking at a wedge of moussaka, I excused myself to call home.

"Hey!" Ricki answered. "How's it going?"

"Well, I learned some things tonight. How's Alec doing?"

"Seems fine. I went down with Mae earlier when she loosened his bonds. He was snacking on a bag of nuts and reading that book you left him. Said he was comfortable, had everything he needed. And it was Alec, not Hermes," she assured me, as though reading my thoughts. "I know Hermes's smug little face."

"Okay, good," I breathed. "Don't go down there again until I get back."

"Why? What did you find out?"

"I don't think Hermes is on our side."

"Hmm. What does that mean for Alec?"

"I'm not sure yet. I'm working on it."

She fell silent for a moment. "What about for you?"

"I'm not sure about that, either. I—" I was preparing to tell her about the bonding potion and my ashes, but that needed to be done in person. "I'm working on that, too. There's still the Sicily half of the trip."

When we finished the call, I accessed my phone's photos and the shots I'd taken of the Kleftians' box weeks earlier. Back at the table, I asked if there was a way to print them.

Yiorgos wiped his mouth and stood. "I can help you."

Through a series of steps I didn't entirely understand, he mailed the photos to his account and printed them on glossy paper in a back office. I learned he was a welder, but with jobs hard to come by—"the corruption," he explained—he mostly contracted out as a driver, which was how he'd met Loukia.

He nodded at my ring finger. "You have wife. How does she..." He circled a hand in search of the word. "How does she *survive* when you are working?"

"You mean emotionally?" He nodded. "Well, she works in law enforcement, so she understands what I do. And I'm just as worried for her when she's out on a case. It goes both ways for us."

He expelled a troubled breath and shook his head. "Everything is new for me. Very new."

"I can't promise it will get easier, but I can promise that Loukia appreciates having someone caring in her life."

He gave me a dubious look, then broke into a laugh that shook his large body. "Yes, she is hard, but I know this."

Back at the table, Claudius had used Yiorgos's absence to scoot his chair closer to our host. He was telling her about a promising remedy he'd concocted for his portal-induced constipation. Loukia appeared to have tuned him out, while

Bree-yark grunted in disgust and slid his rolls of stuffed grape leaves back onto the main platter.

"I hate to interrupt," I said, "but can you take a look at something, Claudius?"

He glanced over with a distracted face, but when he saw Yiorgos with me, it quickly brightened. "Oh, yes, yes, of course," he said, scooting his chair back to where it was. "What can I help you with, Everson?"

"You're an expert on complex bindings." I arrayed the images in front of him. They showed the box and its glyphs from every side. "You've seen the box's magic up close. There has to be a way it can be opened safely."

"What d'ya need to open it for?" Bree-yark asked, pausing to wipe away his wine mustache. "Why not just throw it into one of Claudius's lava portals like you did with the vampire?"

"Because it would take Alec with it," I said.

"Oh, crap. Yeah, forget I said anything."

Plus, there was no telling what a release of energy like that would do and no guarantee that it would remain confined to the dimension in question. It could very well blow open an avenue between our world and the Deep Down, which was a whole new level of "oh crap" we could do without.

Claudius removed his glasses and squinted over the images. I wedged a thumbnail between my front teeth and watched. With Hermes's credibility blown to shit, I needed to know there was an alternative to destroying the tablet without harming Alec.

"I don't know, Everson..." Claudius said at last. "This is powerful magic that's had a lot of time to—"

"Just tell me you'll try," I interrupted sharply. "Keep the photos, study them, and tell me you'll try. Is that so hard?"

He blinked at me as he replaced his glasses, his face creased with confusion and hurt. Silence fell over the table. I had gotten aggravated with Claudius in the past, but I'd never spoken to him like that. I dragged my hands past my throbbing temples, through my hair, and then let them fall to my sides.

"Just... please try," I said quietly.

He cleared his throat. "Why, of course, Everson." He gathered the images into a stack, folded them over, and placed them in a jacket pocket. But when he glanced back at me, he looked like a dog in fear of being swatted.

Dammit. As if I couldn't have felt any worse.

I patted his back in weak apology. "We should probably get going soon."

"No, you're staying," Loukia declared. "You are tired, and it is still the middle of the night in Sicily. There are no members of the Order to help you there. Sleep here, I will make your beds, and then you leave in the morning."

"I think that's a good idea," Bree-yark said to me.

Though I was anxious to research Persephassa and return home, all of Loukia's arguments had landed solidly—especially the one about being tired. I'd managed four hours in the last forty-eight, been in several battles, faced near death and future death, and learned that Hermes was a two-faced dick. No wonder I'd snapped at Claudius.

"Are you all right with staying?" I asked him.

"Does she have a shower cap I can borrow?"

I yielded the queen bed in the spare bedroom to Bree-yark and Claudius, volunteering to take the living room couch.

Loukia brought in pillows and some mismatched sheets that I helped her tuck around the couch cushions.

"Thanks for your help tonight," I told her.

"And for yours. You are not as horrible as I'd thought you'd be."

I gave a startled laugh and straightened from the couch. "What's that supposed to mean?"

"I thought you were going to be a big know-it-all. I hear so much about you all the time."

She'd alluded to that earlier, and now my curiosity was truly piqued. "From whom?"

"Well, there is Claudius."

The guilt I felt for raising my voice at him earlier returned with a vengeance. "Oh. Well, we've spent a lot of time together in the last year, collaborated on a lot of unusual cases. He's like family now."

"And Arianna," she continued.

"Arianna? What did she say?"

"When I've had problems, you are the example she uses."

"That's hardly fair. Did she happen to mention my luck quotient?"

"She says you listen to your magic."

"Oh, that spiel," I gave a knowing grunt. "Believe me, I'm no poster child. I've heeded my magic, but only after I've exhausted every other avenue and am staring death in the nose hairs. That seems to be the only way I can let go enough to listen. I'm definitely still more professor than wizard."

She paused with a pillow at her stomach, eyes keen with understanding. "I act from instinct mostly," she said, "but according to her, it is not the same as listening. I set aside the time to practice, but my magic usually does nothing, says nothing. It just drifts around like a dreamer with his head in the clouds."

I pointed at her. "Right? It's like, can you make up your frigging mind? I swear, there are times I could strangle it."

"Let me know," Loukia said deviously, "and I will join you."

That got us both laughing. Despite everything, I still carried a childlike excitement at having met a fellow magic-user of the Order, a feeling that, like our magic, seemed to be shared now. There was so much I wanted to ask her—about her background, her practice, if she'd had any dealings with Chicory, my early mentor who'd turned out to be a corrupted First Saint, whether she had a real teacher now, what other magic-users she was in contact with, if any—but I really did need to get my sleep.

As our laughter wound down, I said, "Hey, we should exchange contact information. You know, so we can compare notes, bounce ideas off each other, that sort of thing."

"Of course. I will give you my number before you leave tomorrow." She fluffed the final pillow and dropped it in place. "But now you must sleep." She gave me a hug. "It is very good to know you, Everson."

"You too, Loukia. And I enjoyed meeting Yiorgos. Seems like a solid guy."

"He can be," she agreed. As we separated, she looked at me thoughtfully. "Arianna does not say it, but I think you are special to the Order in another way."

"What do you mean?"

She shrugged. "It is just an impression I have. Not from what you do, maybe, but from what you are."

28

I slept solidly until, sometime before dawn, I found myself back in the hags' kitchen as the Doideag spoke above the cauldron.

I awakened with a start, the verses she'd hissed ringing in my head. I sat up on the side of the couch, sheets wadded up in my lap, and stared into the darkness. That was the same two lucid dreams in the last two nights, as though my magic were whacking me over the head with the prophecy:

> *If ye should fail and war should come,*
> *If seas should boil and lands should run,*
> *Allies gather, eleven and one,*
> *And be not afraid of thine own blood.*

I had Alec working on the possible significance of the numbers, but "be not afraid of thine own blood"? Mine? Or was it referring to Alec, who was of my bloodline? And then there were the final, chilling lines:

Wage, young mage, till your final breath,
And come night's fall, accept your death.

The words seemed to resonate with something I'd told Loukia when we were preparing the couch last night. I listened to my magic best when I was in that fuzzy realm between consciousness and unconsciousness, life and death. Only then could I truly surrender. But was my magic suggesting I'd need to take it one step further and accept my *actual* death? Or was it being figurative?

Not questions I'd wanted to wake up to.

Arianna had said the prophecy could never come to pass, but that was before the shitshow with Hermes and Persephone had escalated to toilet-clogging proportions. And my findings in Athens only seemed to have plunged things deeper. In Sicily, I would need to find something I could leverage. Something I could use to flush the gods out to sea for good.

Following breakfast, our hosts took us to a secluded brick courtyard in the back of the building.

"You can transport here," Loukia said, side-eyeing Claudius. After our calamitous arrival yesterday, she didn't want us breaking anything else of hers. But Claudius was back to his usual self, cheerfully oblivious as he circled his arms out to the sides, then scissored them back and forth across his body.

"Yes, the fresh air will be nice for travel," he grunted as he leaned into a side bend.

"Do you have a direct route to Sicily?" I asked. "Enna,

specifically?" I reminded him.

"Well, hrmm, let's see. Yes! I believe I do."

Still feeling bad for how I'd spoken to him last night, I didn't press him on the specifics. I also let him use my shoulder for balance while he pulled his foot up behind him for a thigh stretch. But Bree-yark, who complained that Claudius had kept him up half the night with his kicking, wasn't feeling so charitable.

"How about a route that doesn't involve us being attacked by trees?" he barked.

"Yes, of course, of course," Claudius replied, as if he'd never think of putting us in harm's way.

I clapped my hands once. "Well, I guess we're ready then. Thanks again for your help and hospitality," I told our hosts. Loukia and I had already exchanged numbers. "Be sure to keep in touch."

She nodded warmly and clasped Yiorgos's thick hand, which wrapped her shoulder.

Following a final round of farewells, and the several minutes it took for Claudius to complete his stretching routine, the three of us joined arms in the middle of the courtyard. A moment later we were being sucked into a portal I could only hope was bound for Sicily.

We fell a short distance, breaking apart upon landing in what felt like a dewy field. Not knowing whether we were in Italy or one of Claudius's alternate planes, I dug into a pocket for a wand, grasping it just as Bree-yark shouted what I'd feared:

"Creatures!"

I rolled onto my stomach, wand humming with blue

energy, while Bree-yark released his blade with a sharp *zing*. In the dimness, a semicircle of wooly silhouettes peered back at us. Then bells jangled, and the sheep returned to their grazing. I lowered my wand, and Bree-yark dipped his face in embarrassment.

"Guess I'm a little jumpy," he said.

"You and me both," I chuckled, recalling the power from my wand. "But it's too early for roast lamb."

Bree-yark barked a laugh. "Speak for yourself, buddy."

"Well, I didn't land us *in* Enna," Claudius announced, pushing himself up and straightening his glasses. "But I believe we're close."

He peered off to the east, where the sky was just paling above the hilly pastures. He then tilted his face skyward and began pointing out the final stars, muttering as he tried to connect them to constellations that might give him a location.

"I used to be much better at this," he said.

"No worries." Bree-yark set his heavy pack in front of him, dug inside, and drew out a small bag. "I keep a GPS navigator in my kit. Learned to store it in a lead liner, though." He unzipped the bag. "Never told you this, Everson, but your magic fried my last one." He waved away my apology as he powered up the device.

"Let's see..." he murmured.

I came around to peer at the small screen, careful to keep my distance.

"Hey, we're not far from Enna at all!" he said. "It's just a few miles that way."

I turned to Claudius and gave him a thumbs-up. "Well done."

He straightened proudly.

Bree-yark donned his pack, clipped the GPS device to a

shoulder strap, and led the way toward the nearest road into Enna. "Where we heading first?" he asked as several sheep galloped from our path.

"Enna was founded over three thousand years ago by an indigenous group called the Siculi," I said, slipping into professor mode. "This area was an important agricultural hub—still is—so it's no surprise that the Siculi worshipped a powerful goddess of agriculture. That goddess later became Demeter, Persephone's mother. The story of Persephone's abduction originated with the Siculi to explain the seasons. In fact, the site of the abduction is a lake just south of Enna called Pergusa. Anyway, the town has an archeological museum with artifacts from that era, and the director is an expert on local mythology. I left a couple messages yesterday, but he never called back. I'm hoping he has info on the ancient cults to Persephone, specifically the one that crafted her scepter."

"So that's it?" Bree-yark said. "We came all this way to look at dusty relics and talk to some pencil neck?"

"Hey, I warned you this would be dry. Besides, you got plenty of action in Athens."

"Wait a sec," he said, squinting up at me. "I know that sneaky look. You've got something else planned."

"I believe he wants to steal a relic," Claudius said.

I looked over at him in surprise. Sucking on a fresh ginseng candy, he winked and shot me a finger pistol.

"Well, not steal," I stammered. "I mean, not exactly."

"Ooh, yeah." Bree-yark rubbed his hands together. "I could be down for something like that."

"Look, it's not what you think. I don't even know what's in their collection. But, yes, if there's an object that still holds the old worship for Demeter, I'm thinking it could be useful for dissuading Persephone. She loves her mother. She revealed that much when I was in the shadow realm. And her mother is—"

"An Olympian," Claudius cut in, his eyes bright behind his lenses. "And if Persephone's aim is to overthrow the Olympic order, you're going to make her face the fact she'll be overthrowing her mother, too."

"That's... right," I said, surprised once more by Claudius's sudden acuity. "One thing that struck me about Persephone is her youth. She's vengeful, but she doesn't seem completely sure of herself. I'm hoping her mother will be able to pull her back from the abyss."

Or maybe just distract her long enough for me to destroy the scepter. Because more and more it was looking as if I was going to have to annihilate the objects that gave both Persephone and Hermes their power. Take out the two warring gods, or allied gods, or whatever the hell they were to each other. Of course, that was going to be in addition to preventing Cronus from entering the shadow realm.

I inhaled the country air to calm myself and turned back to Claudius.

"Hey, have you had a chance to study the photos of the box?" I asked carefully.

"Not yet, I'm afraid. I can go over them in a café while you're at the museum. I always think better with an espresso in hand."

"That espresso's on me," I assured him. "As many as you need."

The sun was cresting the hills now. As we turned a corner, the isolated town of Enna glowed into view atop a craggy hilltop. This was going to be it. My last real chance to find that leverage over the gods.

29

I t was mid-morning by the time we walked into Enna by way of a steep, winding road. My first stop was an ATM, where I withdrew a small sheaf of Euros. At a corner café, Claudius claimed a small outdoor table, onto which I placed more than enough money for his espressos.

"This must be what they call 'remote work.'" He smiled at his expansive view of the countryside—a definite improvement over his dungeon-like office—before pulling out the folded images of the box. "I'll be waiting here when you get back. And, yes, I promise not to wander anywhere."

With that assurance, Bree-yark and I departed for the museum.

As we navigated the cobblestone streets, Bree-yark peered up at the historic stone buildings. "Nice place," he remarked. "Reminds me a little of Scriber's Cross—that's a walled town in the south of Faerie." He chuckled. "Hey, did I ever tell you about the time we overnighted in their countryside on a long march?"

It had been a while since Bree-yark had gotten to share

one of his goblin army stories, so I gestured for him to proceed.

"Well, to keep up morale, our captain ordered some casks of the homegrown ale. But instead of casks, this lanky guy shows up in our camp wearing a blouse and a cap with a blue feather. 'Who the hell's this joker?' we were all asking. The dialect down there is screwy, you see. Turns out his name was close enough to the ale that the town thought we were asking for *him*. He was the local poet!"

I snorted a laugh, but the sound caught in my sinuses and my smile straightened.

Misunderstanding me, Bree-yark said, "Oh, hey, we didn't hurt the guy or anything. He ended up being a great story-teller. We begged the captain to let us stay another night so we could hear some more."

"It's not that," I whispered. "I just picked up something."

"Where?" Bree-yark asked, digging under his shirttail for the hilt of his blade.

But the electrical sensation that had rippled through me like an explosion of hot pins was already fading.

"Not sure," I said. "A warning, maybe."

"What, like we're being watched or something?"

"It felt more... diffuse than that." I closed my eyes, tapping into my deeper magical currents. Though they had returned to their slow, eddying rhythms, they carried an edge now. "Let's just get to the museum," I said, opening my eyes again. "But be on the lookout for anything that seems off."

"Like no one being out in the streets?"

He was right. Even though Enna wasn't a major tourist destination—and even less of one in the years following the Crash—where were the locals? We'd seen a couple passing cars on our way up, but despite it being a pleasant morning, there were no pedestrians.

Enna's archeology museum was a two-story building that stood opposite a church in an empty plaza. I tested the museum's main entrance, a stout wooden door set in a stone archway, but it didn't budge.

"Closed?" Bree-yark asked.

"Man, I hope not." I rapped the door hard with my knuckles.

When no one answered, I stepped back. The first-floor windows were gated, but the second-story windows, each with an ornate balcony, were unencumbered. No one was visible beyond any of them, though. I took another look around the door. A faded square with empty screw holes showed where the sign for the museum, including its days and hours of operation, must have been posted.

"Maybe they moved," Bree-yark suggested.

"Maybe. Let's ask one of the neighbors."

At an adjoining building with dead flowers on the upper-story sills, I knocked and waited. Shortly, several bolts withdrew and the door cracked open. A dark eye set in a pale, wrinkled face blinked out.

"*Si?*" the old woman asked.

"*I'm sorry to bother you,*" I said in Italian. "*We want to visit the museum, but it seems to be closed. Do you know when it will open?*"

She shook her head. "*Don't know, don't know.*"

"*Is it still over here, next door to you?*" I pointed.

"*Don't know, don't know.*"

"*Did they move?*"

"*No, not move.*"

"*Well, do you know where I can find Franco Cortese?*"

He was the museum director and expert on local mythology. This time she simply shook her head and closed the door.

Before I could stop him, Bree-yark rushed up and pounded the door with a fist. "How the devil can you not know any of this stuff?" he shouted.

"Hey, whoa, whoa. We'll just ask someone else."

"Old bag," he muttered. "Want me to kick her door down?"

"Um, better you don't. Did she seem scared to you?"

"Hmm. Now that you mention it..." He unballed his fists and stepped back.

"Just my impression, but it seemed less like she didn't know and more like she didn't want to get involved." I was about to search for someone else to ask when Bree-yark seized my arm.

"What?" I asked, peering around.

"I say we make our move."

"What move?"

He lowered his voice. "The heist. Your time's tight, right? Well, let's take advantage of the museum being closed and the fact no one's around." He cocked his head at the old woman's door. "Or wants to get involved,"

I surprised myself by considering his idea, then surprised myself even more by nodding. My time *was* tight. Just how tight, I hadn't shared with Bree-yark—or anyone, for that matter. I needed to tell Ricki first.

"All right, but the front's too exposed," I said. "Let's check out the back."

We left the square at what we hoped looked like a casual stroll, ducked around the side of the museum, and soon found ourselves in a dirt lot with an outbuilding and some cast-off building materials. The most important feature, though, was the back door. Also locked.

"Should I kick it in?" Bree-yark asked.

"You're really anxious to put your shoe through something. No, I have a better idea."

I drew out a wand and inserted the tip into the keyhole— one of the few advantages of carrying a smaller casting implement. With a whispered Word, I sent a concentrated force from the wand's end into the locking mechanism. Light flashed from the keyhole, and metal snapped. I pulled the handle. The door opened, dropping the fractured bolt to the ground and releasing a dusty, shut-in odor.

Eyes glowing yellow, Bree-yark drew his blade. I almost told him to put it away when a ghost of the feeling from outside prickled through me again. I nodded at him and kept my own wand at the ready.

We entered a small storage area, crossing a floor littered with open boxes, crates, and packing foam. Another door led into the museum, but like the boxes and crates, the large rooms were empty. No artifacts or archeological finds. Just dusty outlines where the display cases must have stood.

"Mind checking upstairs?" I whispered to Bree-yark. "Just... don't stab anyone."

As he took the stairs, I circled the empty rooms, opening my wizard's senses. Objects of worship held a particular energy, like harmonizing voices, and I picked up a few remnants now. Though I couldn't identify the deities being worshipped, chances were good they'd been Demeter and Persephone, the mother and daughter duo so important to this region. But where had the objects gone? And why?

"No one up there," Bree-yark said as he returned. "Two

empty rooms, one looks like an old office. It's been cleared out 'cept for a big desk."

I followed him back upstairs, and he showed me the office. The desk was a mahogany number. The main drawers were empty, but the small one contained an organizer with several paperclips and an old pen. I lifted the organizer, and found a business card underneath. I fished it out and studied the information.

"This is him," I said.

"The director guy?" Bree-yark asked.

"Yeah, Franco Cortese. There's a cell number on here, too."

I drew out my phone and punched in the number. The call went to a voicemail with instructions in both Italian and English.

"Hi, this is Everson Croft again," I said. "The professor of mythology at Midtown College in New York City? I'm currently in Enna, and I'm only going to be here for the day. I'd like very much to meet with you to discuss Enna's history. Please call me at this number as soon as you can."

"Think he'll call back?" Bree-yark asked as I pocketed the phone and card.

"Let's hope so." I circled the room in thought. "But maybe we won't have to wait."

I went to my hands and knees and pulled out something I'd spotted under the desk: an empty thermos with the initials F.C. I unscrewed the top and showed Bree-yark the dried rings of coffee in the grooves.

"If there's enough saliva or skin cells in here, we can track him."

From my satchel, I removed my polyethylene sheet with the premade casting circle. I spread it over the desk and stood the thermos in the circle's center. Drawing my wand, I began to incant. As the circle glowed to life, I moved the wand in slow figure-eights, my incantation becoming the words for a hunting spell. Shortly, a pale brown mist drifted from the grooves and entered the wand.

"Got him?" Bree-yark asked.

I waited for the wand to jiggle.

"Got him," I replied with a smile.

But Bree-yark's eyes and ears were angled toward the window. A clamor of voices outside, coming from below. I sidled up to the window frame and peered down. Crap. I couldn't make out the people in the doorway, just a few of their backs. But the old woman I'd spoken to earlier was standing behind them on a cane, gesturing urgently. Had she seen us enter the museum through one of her back windows?

I withdrew from view just as she looked up.

"We need to get out of here," I said, refolding my casting sheet and stuffing it inside my satchel.

"We're not gonna stay and fight?" Bree-yark asked.

I shook my head as I waved him from the room. The prickling sensation had returned, suggesting danger. We were nearly to the stairs when a bolt released, and the museum's front door opened.

30

W ith the stairs coming up, I braked hard and backpedaled into Bree-yark. The pots on his pack swung and clanged together.

"*Ciao?*" a deep male voice called.

Shit. We crept back into the office and closed the door.

"If we're not going to fight 'em," Bree-yark whispered, "what does that leave?"

I pulled a premade potion from my coat pocket, whispered a Word, and unstoppered it while it was still activating. "Stealth potion," I whispered. "Drink half."

His nostrils wrinkled from the steam, but he did as I said and passed the tube back. I took down the rest, then hurried to the window. There was no one outside anymore, including the old woman. They'd all entered the museum.

"Aw, c'mon," Bree-yark said, "we can take 'em."

"They could all be in their eighties for all we know."

"My point exactly. We can *take* them."

"Sorry, but I'm not ready to start swinging on someone's grandparents."

Plus, my magic was still urging me to get out of there. I swung the window open, and waved Bree-yark over. He took a final, disappointed look at the closed door as I gave him a boost onto the iron balcony. I squeezed out beside him and his hefty pack, closing the window behind us.

"Watch how I do this," I said.

With an invocation and some wand maneuvering, I climbed over the edge of the balcony and dropped three feet onto a shelf of hardened air. I then dropped onto another one three feet below the first. Finally, I hopped the short distance to the sidewalk, the stealth potion quieting my landing.

The coast looked clear, but when I leaned back to peer into the doorway, I was dismayed to see that the old woman had hung back. *Thought you didn't know anything about this place, you liar.* Still, I was confident that my stealth potion would give Bree-yark and me enough cover to leave the scene.

Reinforcing the invocations, I waved for Bree-yark to join me.

He made the drop to the first shelf fine, then to the second. I signaled for him to stay put—I could lower the shelf the rest of the way to the sidewalk. But not seeing me, he jumped from that one, too, landing awkwardly. Before I could steady him, the weight of his pack toppled him onto his side.

He kicked his short arms and legs, swearing as he struggled to right himself.

The old woman appeared from the doorway, squinting up and down the street. Bree-yark's sphere of stealth muted his racket, but not entirely. I signaled for him to go still, then froze beside him. The old woman tapped up the sidewalk, away from us, pausing to peer around. Carefully, I pulled Bree-yark to his feet. But the woman was turning now, preparing to double back and explore our end of the sidewalk.

"*Vigore,*" I whispered, my wand pointed at her cane.

The force kicked her walking aid out from under her, sending it clattering away. She stumbled sideways and caught herself against the wall of the museum, hands splayed in a frantic effort to keep herself upright.

"*Aiutami!*" she shouted: *Help me!*

As running footsteps sounded from the museum, Bree-yark and I used the opportunity to hurry from the plaza. When we were several streets away, we slowed to a walk and peered back. No one had followed.

"For the record, I'm not proud of that," I said.

"What, tripping up that busybody?" He waved a hand. "She had it coming."

"I'm not sure why I was so anxious to get us out of there unseen," I said, thinking aloud. "My magic did flash another warning, but the way the people here seem to be hiding, the museum being empty... I don't know. I might not have given any of those a lot of thought, but taken together, something's off."

From the dryness in my mouth to the tension in my shoulders, my instincts agreed.

"Right?" Bree-yark put in. "And that old woman claiming not to know anything about the place, then suddenly she's calling in the cavalry? Maybe this Franco can shed some light on what's going on."

"Just what I was thinking," I said, tapping into the hunting spell.

My wand pivoted several degrees and urged us east. By the time we arrived at the outskirts of town, our half-doses of stealth potion had worn off. A row of houses ended at the edge of the bluff before the street dropped toward the fields below.

"It's that last one," I told Bree-yark, muting the hunting spell and returning my wand to my coat pocket.

I eyed the home, a pale stone and plaster affair with a green door and matching shutters on the windows. On the walk here, the town had felt more sinister, as if it were watching our every move, cloaked or not. At that thought, a shadow receded from an upper story window in the neighboring home.

"All right, listen," I whispered to Bree-yark. "I don't know what's going on, but there's a reason Franco isn't answering his phone or returning my calls. So we need to handle him very delicately."

"Say no more. I'll behave."

"Right, so no shouting or pounding on the door," I added to be perfectly clear.

He clasped his hands behind his back as if demonstrating his restraint and nodded for me to take lead. At the door, I knocked several times and listened. When no one answered, I knocked again.

"Franco?" I called. "It's Everson Croft. I phoned you earlier. I just want to ask you a few questions before I leave town. It won't take long." When that got nothing, I added, "I was really counting on your expertise."

Flattery sometimes worked with academics, but not this time, apparently. Or maybe he wasn't home. I'd never cast a hunting spell through my wands, which didn't have the same capacity as my opal-inset staff. If Franco was out of range, the magic may have led us to the nearest place where his energy imprint was strongest, in this case his domicile.

An impression came to me of Franco being cleaned out

along with the museum, but I quickly pushed the macabre thought aside. I was turning toward Bree-yark when, from inside the house, I heard a child's voice followed by an adult's harsh whisper. I stopped to listen, but the house fell quiet again.

"We hear you, you know!" Bree-yark shouted.

"*Hey,*" I hissed, patting my hand toward the ground.

"Oh, yeah." He reclasped his hands behind his back. "Sorry."

I cleared my throat and spoke into the doorframe. "If you're in trouble, we can help."

After another minute, I was convinced of two things: one, whoever was inside had heard me; and two, they weren't going to answer the door. Troubled, I pulled my head from the doorframe and nodded at Bree-yark that we could go.

"What now?" he asked, hitching up his pack.

Great question. One by one, my objectives were colliding into dead ends.

"Let's meet up with Claudius," I said. "I want to check out this Lake Pergusa. According to the stories, that's where Hades emerged from the underworld to abduct Persephone. The area is steeped in myth, and there may be some old shrines to the goddess. It's only a few miles south of here."

We arrived back at the café to find Claudius's table empty. Hands on my hips, I called his name several times, while Bree-yark went to look inside the café. He returned, shaking his head.

"Place is closed."

I checked my watch. "At eleven?"

"Does that really surprise you in this town?"

"Not anymore," I conceded.

Bree-yark stooped over until his squat nose was nearly

touching the cobblestones. "My sense of smell ain't what it was, but with the streets being so empty, I should be able to pick up his ginseng." He straightened and nodded in the opposite direction of the museum. "He went this way."

I followed as he navigated several twisting streets. Claudius had promised he wouldn't wander off, but judging by his meandering trail, that was exactly what he'd done. At last, Bree-yark reached a small cul-de-sac.

"Trail stops here."

I looked around and sighed. "He must have portaled."

I pulled out my phone and called him. Claudius surprised me by picking up on the third ring. "Ah, yes, hello? Hello?"

"Where are you?" I asked.

"I'm sorry, who is this?"

"Everson Croft," I said thinly. "I'm in Enna, Sicily? You were supposed to wait for us at that café?"

"Ah, hello, Everson. Oh, yes, yes, sorry about that. Shortly after you left, I realized there was no one there to wait on me. Very peculiar. Anyway, I hurried to catch up with you, and I must have, erm, well, I guess I lost my way."

"Where are you now?"

"I jumped back to my place here in..." He paused to think. "Annapolis? Or am I in Peoria? I can never seem to nail that down."

"You're back in the States?" I asked, incredulous.

"Well, yes, I thought I better check my messages. And a good thing because something has come up that requires my immediate attention."

"You're coming back, right?"

"Of course, of course, as soon as I tie this up."

"Okay," I breathed. "Bree-yark and I are heading to Lake Pergusa, just south of here."

"Pergusa," he repeated slowly, as though writing it down. "Got it. I'll meet you there, then. Should I pack a swimsuit?"

"Please don't."

"Oh, I'm, ah, I'm getting another call," he said anxiously.

I could hear the other phone ringing in the background. Before I could remind him where we'd be, he hung up.

"It might take a few more reminders, but he'll meet us there," I told Bree-yark.

"Then let's get going. According to my GPS, it's eight klicks away, and I doubt we'll be getting a ride."

We set off down Pergusa Via, a road that wound steeply downhill. Every time a vehicle approached from behind, we stuck a thumb out only for it to whoosh past. I was surprised, then, when a gray minivan pulled onto the scant shoulder ahead of us. I palmed my wand as I approached the driver's side.

"*Il lago?*" I said. *The lake?*

A thickset man stared back at me. "Yes, I can take you," he replied in accented English.

But I hesitated, not so sure anymore. There was a manic intensity in his eyes at odds with his jowly face.

"You are Everson Croft, yes?"

I stiffened. "And who are you?"

"Franco Cortese. Get in. You're in danger."

That explained the intensity. I hustled around the van to where the side door was sliding open. Once Bree-yark was inside, I slid the door closed, and Franco took off. A box occupied the front passenger seat, so we sat on the two-seat bench directly behind him. I kept a hold of my wand, though.

"It's good to finally meet you," I said, hoping this was the break I'd been after.

I waited for a response, but his gaze kept cutting between

the road and rearview mirror. Bree-yark and I exchanged uneasy looks.

"You said we were in danger?" I prompted.

"Yes, and the sooner you leave Enna, the better it will be."

"I have a lot of questions," I said. "First, can you tell me—"

"Not now," he interrupted. "I will answer your questions at the lake."

He drove in silence for the next several minutes. His window had gone back up, and the inside of the van was stifling. Sweat dribbled down the folds of his neck. At a fork in the road, Franco turned left.

Bree-yark nudged me in the side and angled his GPS device toward me. It took me a moment, but I saw what was happening. Franco was driving in the opposite direction of the lake. I was about to say something when a startling thought hit me. Still holding my wand, I tapped into the hunting spell I'd cast on the thermos. The wand gave a sharp tug, but not in the direction of the driver.

This wasn't Franco.

31

I stared at the back of the man pretending to be Franco Cortese. There were a dozen ways I could take him out, but not at sixty miles an hour. When his eyes met mine in the rearview mirror, I glanced away, pretending to become interested in the scenery zipping past.

Bree-yark nudged me again, his hand turned up: *What do you want to do?*

He was referring to the fact we were still traveling away from the lake. He had no idea this guy was an imposter, and I couldn't communicate that to him without being obvious.

"Hey, do you mind pulling over?" I asked the driver, then gave an embarrassed laugh. "I need to make water, as they say."

I had decided to start with the easiest tactic and go from there. He surprised me by slowing down. The van eased toward the shoulder of the road. We were in the country now, not a house in sight. But it felt more important than ever to get outside.

I looked at Bree-yark intently and shifted my eyes to the door. He nodded, seeming to understand the urgency.

The van rolled to a stop.

"Hey," Bree-yark said, tugging the door handle. "It's locked."

I looked back at the driver and recoiled at the sight of something alien in his place. He'd pulled one of those antiquated gasmasks over his face and was now reaching into the box on the passenger seat. My wand was in the casting position before I even heard the hissing release of compressed air

.

"*Protezione!*" I shouted.

The air hardened into spheres around Bree-yark's and my heads as a jet of mustard-colored gas spewed from the box. In the next instant, vapors flooded the van. The man watched us through the insectoid goggles of his mask, no doubt waiting for us to collapse.

Instead, Bree-yark launched his stout two-hundred pounds at the man. I couldn't hear what my friend was shouting, but his fists translated the message just fine as they pounded the man's head and torso.

I inserted the wand into the locking mechanism in the side door. With a Word, light flashed through the smoke, and the door released.

I pulled it the rest of the way open, then grabbed Bree-yark by the back of his shirt. I was on the verge of running out of air, and with him expending so much energy, he couldn't be far behind. Anyway, the man was slumped over now, his mask displaced, his face thoroughly pummeled. Bree-yark landed a final pair of thudding shots to his ribs before yielding. He grabbed his pack, and we cleared the van. Only when we were a safe distance upwind did I dispel the shields around our heads.

Bree-yark and I gasped for air, him bent over, me clutching my knees. Ahead of us, the vapor pouring from the van's open door started to thin.

"Son of a bitch tried to gas us!" Bree-yark panted.

"Yeah, he's not Franco," I wheezed. "Don't know who he is."

Holding my breath, I returned to the van and opened the driver door. I pulled the man's arm, and he collapsed onto the road in a dispersion of yellow vapors, his fractured mask hanging around his neck.

"Holy hell," I muttered, scuttling back.

Bree-yark arrived beside me and looked at the man grimly. He was bleeding from his nose, mouth, both staring eyes, and his ears. He was also dead.

"I roughed him up, but not *that* much," Bree-yark said.

I shook my head. "It's from the gas. Some kind of poison."

Bree-yark looked at me in disbelief. "These people don't want us in their town, so they go straight to murder?"

"Apparently so."

I threw out the box with the spent cannister of poison and, using a force blast, expelled the remaining fumes from the van. I then fumigated the interior as well as our clothes with a neutralizing potion. A quick search of the van turned up nothing of interest, but we had a set of wheels now.

"Some faction in the town obviously sees us as a threat," I said. "And I don't think it's an accident this guy intercepted us on the way to the lake. How do you feel about driving us there?"

Because of his short limbs, Bree-yark used hand controls in his own vehicle. He studied the van's standard controls.

"I'll make it work," he decided.

Ten minutes later, we were on a road that circled Lake Pergusa, a band of trees between us and the water. Bree-yark had slid the driver's seat back so he could stand, operating gas and brake pedals with his foot while still being able to see over the wheel. He looked from the road to his GPS device, which he'd clipped to a vent.

"Looks like there's a parking area at the north end," he said.

"Okay, good—whoa!" I braced against the dashboard as the van's tires slipped off the shoulder.

Bree-yark returned his attention to the road, popped his eyes wide, then righted the van, swerving into the other lane. It didn't matter; there was no oncoming traffic. In fact, there was no traffic, period. As the turnoff for the lot came up, the trees separated, revealing the lake's expanse—and deep redness.

"Holy thunder!" Bree-yark exclaimed.

"Some call Lake Pergusa the 'Lake of Blood,' but it's not actual blood," I said. "Apparently the sulfur content in the lake peaks in the summer months, attracting a sulfur-eating bacteria that turns the waters red."

I'd come across that fact in my research, but mundane or not, the redness brought back the image of the dead driver. We'd concealed his body behind a wall at the edge of a field. Done in by his own poison, but something told me he'd just been the messenger. Someone else had sent him.

"Sulfur, huh?" Bree-yark waved the air in front of his nose

with a grunt. "Explains the smell. I thought you were having an intestinal reaction to last night's moussaka."

He parked in the empty lot, and we got out of the van. Wand in hand, I scanned our surroundings. To the right, a trail entered the woods, aiming in the general direction of a rock outcropping that overlooked the lake.

"I'd like to check that out," I said. "I don't guess I need to tell you to be ready for anything."

With a nod, Bree-yark unbuttoned his shirt down the front, exposing his tattooed torso, then he patted the blades he'd sheathed at each hip. Next, he drew a pistol from his pack and shoved it down the front of his jeans, gangster style. By the time he'd donned his pack again, he looked like a diminutive action hero.

"Let's roll," he barked.

The well-trodden path circled the lake through the trees. Before long, a narrower path split off, climbing toward the outcropping. I led the way up that one while Bree-yark walked backward, covering our rear. At the rocks, the trail turned dusty, and I picked out a multitude of shoe prints. Advancing cautiously, we were soon facing a large opening in the rocks that went back a good fifty feet.

"Some sort of worship site?" Bree-yark asked.

"And still in use, from the looks of it," I said, ducking inside.

Partially melted candles covered the interior of the cave like mini stalagmites, hundreds of them. They converged toward a pair of clay urns in the back of the cave. I studied the floor. More prints, but these had been left by bare feet. I also picked out some patterns suggesting sweeps, from the skirts of a robe, maybe. The urns themselves were plain and the size of tree planters. Charcoal and grey ashes filled the insides, while something dark, blood possibly, spattered the ground between them.

"Can you tell what was burned here?" I asked Bree-yark.

He looked to either side of the entrance before joining me. Leaning forward, he sniffed over one urn, then the other. "Organs," he concluded darkly. "And they're human. Same with the blood down there."

I nodded. "Must be offerings."

I imagined a robed figure standing between the urns, facing the candle-lit cave, which could hold several dozen worshippers, easy. I saw the figure plunge a blade into the torso of a victim, much like what had happened to the explorer club fellows in Persephone's first bid to summon Cronus. Currents of what might have been magic lingered in the cave, but I needed to go deeper.

"Mind keeping watch outside?"

"Gladly," Bree-yark grunted. "This place gives me the creeps."

"You're not the only one."

As he assumed his post, I closed my eyes and opened my wizard's senses. The lingering energy was dark and chaotic, flashing around the space like wayward bats. It came from a magic I'd felt before. Someone was wielding a powerful artifact, using it to perform rites they had little to no control over.

Whether that made them less dangerous or more, I didn't know, but I needed to get my hands on the artifact.

"What's the verdict?" Bree-yark asked when I joined him outside the cave.

"Persephone worshippers," I said. "Dread Persephone to be exact, the version of her that's in the shadow realm. I know her magic, and it's all over the inside of the cave."

The folds of his brow bunched together. "How can she be there and here?"

"She's not, but an artifact to her is. You see, in the shadow version of New York, the Tablet of Hermes attracted several ancient objects to the city, a scepter to Persephone among them. But in the *actual* present, that scepter may not have gone anywhere. In fact, I'm betting it was in Enna's museum."

"So what changed?"

"That's what I'd like to know," I muttered. "I'm wondering if the two scepters are communicating somehow. If so, that could be really bad. Regardless, I want to come back here tonight."

He looked at me uneasily. "You do?"

"The scepter's dangerous in the wrong hands—hell, in *any* hands." I checked my satchel to ensure I'd packed enough neutralizing salt. "Judging from our encounter with the van driver, our presence here agitated the cult. I'm betting they'll meet again to consult the goddess. Let's find a good stakeout place."

"If we're gonna bivouac, I've got us covered." He patted the side of his pack, pleased with his preparation.

"Let me call Claudius first, give him an update." I flipped open my phone and frowned. "Damn, no signal."

"We can head back toward town until you get one. We'll stick to backroads. We should look for a place to stash the van, anyway."

I nodded at his idea. As we started down the path, the wind shifted, blowing the sulfurous stench into our faces. Bree-yark wiped his eyes with the open flap of his shirt and blew his nose. I glanced toward the lake and noticed a furrow through the trees, as though something had been dragged from the red water up to the cave or vice versa.

Back at the lot, I was relieved to find the van where we'd parked it and no other vehicles in sight. As Bree-yark pulled out, I kept my eyes on my phone's signal indicator. We'd gone about a mile when Bree-yark swore.

"What's up?" I asked, looking over.

"That car that just passed going the other way? The driver stared right at us, and now he's turning around."

As the van's engine strained for another octave, I craned my neck. Sure enough, a boxy white Fiat was performing a three-point turn in the middle of the road. The driver must have recognized the van and seen that his homicidal friend wasn't driving. With a squeal of tires, he completed the turn and quickly gained on us.

Bree-yark stomped the gas. "Damned thing's as slow as a bogwaddle in mud."

"Just hold her steady," I said, rolling down the passenger window. "I can handle this guy."

I lined up my wand with his front axle. But when the Fiat had come to within a few car lengths, the driver began flashing his headlights and jabbing a finger to the left. I glanced ahead to a turnoff in the middle distance.

Yeah, fat chance.

But before I flipped his car, I took a closer look at the man whose curly black hair matched a stylish stubble. Though the eyes beyond his glasses were animated, they appeared intelligent in a way the van driver's hadn't. He pointed up now. Between a pair of hills, I spotted a distant line of cars snaking down from Enna. I tapped into my hunting spell until my wand tugged.

With the turnoff rushing up, I blurted out, "Go left!"

"Huh?" Bree-yark looked over. "You serious?"

"This is the real Franco!"

32

Bree-yark stomped the brake and cranked the wheel. The van tipped for a moment before slewing onto the hard-packed road, gravel pelting the undercarriage. He managed to visit both grassy shoulders before regaining control.

"Now what?" he asked.

I pointed. "Pull over up there."

Bree-yark slowed and began to ease off the road. I expected Franco to stop beside us, but he only slowed long enough to wave urgently for us to follow him before pulling ahead. The line of cars was no longer in sight, but I felt their approach like a growing drumbeat. I nodded for Bree-yark to follow.

"You sure this is Franco?" he asked.

"Yeah," I said, but double-checked anyway. The wand, which had tugged behind us the last time, now tugged straight ahead, making the appropriate adjustment as the road banked to the right.

Franco went perhaps a mile farther before pulling over.

Bree-yark slowed to a stop behind him. Franco got out of his car and hustled toward us. Tossing his hair from his glasses, he looked from Bree-yark to me, then back at Bree-yark.

"You are Professor Croft?"

Bree-yark smirked. "I'm the sidekick. The brainiac's riding shotgun."

Franco nodded at me, then addressed both of us. "I'm Franco Cortese, but they are coming and we haven't much time."

"Who's coming?" I asked.

"I will explain, but now you must help me push the van off the edge."

He pointed to the left shoulder where the road gave way to a rocky precipice with no guardrail. Bree-yark looked at me uncertainly, but I nodded. With a shrug, he slotted the van into neutral and turned the front wheels so they were aimed toward the precipice. As we got out, Franco inserted his upper body through the open driver door to steer. Bree-yark and I moved behind the van to push. I could have force-blasted the thing off the edge, but I didn't want to show my hand before I knew Franco better.

"Okay, all together!" he called from the front.

We dug in our feet until the van began to roll. When it picked up enough momentum, Franco broke clear and Bree-yark and I gave it a final shove. The van plummeted through a wall of brush. Moments later, metal crunched and glass shattered. I could tell Bree-yark was eager to see the after-math, but Franco was waving us toward his car. Bree-yark climbed in back, throwing his pack across the seat, and I got in front.

"Okay, that is done," Franco breathed as we pulled away.

"Where are we headed?" I asked.

"Someplace safe."

He drove us deeper into the countryside, glancing into the rearview mirror every few seconds. After a couple miles, he relaxed enough to extend his hand toward me. "It is good to meet you," he said, giving me a firm shake. He reached back and repeated the greeting with Bree-yark. "I am sorry that it is like this."

"How did you know where to find us?" I asked.

"You went to my house in Enna, yes? It is just my wife and daughter there now." I remembered the child's voice I'd heard through the door followed by the adult's whisper. "My wife saw you leave for the road to the lake. She also saw Bruno follow you. He is the town butcher. He is the one they send to take care of the 'intruders,' so they are called. She contacted me on the satellite phone and gave me your description. I came to find you as fast as I could." He cocked his head back. "I saw the blood in the van."

"Bruno's," I said grimly.

"Yes, but better than yours."

"So, what the hell's going on in Enna?" Bree-yark barked.

"That is what I am trying to learn." He blew out his breath. "The trouble started early this year when an artifact disappeared from the museum. There was an investigation, the police were involved. But one investigator disappeared, then two, and the investigation stopped." He made a horizontal cut with his hand. "I thought maybe it was mafia, so I said nothing more. But the people in town started to change."

"Change how?" I asked.

"Many in Enna own businesses, but they stopped tending to them—stopped even opening them. One day we took my daughter to school only to be told the school was closed. Not enough teachers. Many of our friends stopped talking to us.

No one was going outside anymore, not during the day. But at night, I would hear their vehicles driving down to the lake. They would not return until early morning."

Bree-yark, who was leaning forward between our seats to hear better, muttered, "Explains why the place looked like a ghost town."

"I was still running the museum, but there were no more visitors," Franco continued. "Tourists would come, think Enna was closed, and they would leave again. There were others in town like me and my wife, confused why so much was changing. We started to talk, to share stories. Paolo said the mayor was leading rituals at the lake. Lucrezia claimed the entire town council was involved. Sergio planned to talk to them. He was last seen getting into Bruno's van." He cast me a knowing look.

"Do you know why some in the town changed while others, like you, didn't?" I asked.

"No. If you asked questions, you were not long for Enna. But if you stayed quiet, no one bothered you. And so that is what my wife and I did. We stayed quiet, drove to the next town for our supplies, and schooled our daughter at home."

He paused to make another turn.

"Then one day, the mayor came into the museum. Marta was looking ill, very pale and thin. 'We are closing the museum,' she told me. I was very surprised to hear this, very upset. The museum had been my life's work. 'How can you do this?' I asked her. A strange look came over her face like she was my master and I had just peed on her rug. 'Are you an ally, Franco,' she asked me. 'Or are you an intruder?' It was certainly a threat. 'Ally,' I told her, thinking of my family. 'Good,' she said. 'Do not come in tomorrow.' 'What will happen to the collection?' I asked her, thinking of the museum again. I had spent so much time acquiring the pieces. 'Ally or intruder?' she asked again, her voice even more threatening. 'Ally,' I repeated, and said nothing more."

Bree-yark grunted. "Smart move."

"But when she left, I looked at the bag on her shoulder. There was something inside, poking the fabric at both ends. It was the size of the piece that was stolen. When she turned to remind me that I was not to come back, she caught me staring at her bag. That afternoon, as I was locking the museum for the last time, Bruno drove up in his van. He offered me a ride home."

"Oh, crap," Bree-yark said.

"Yes, I knew what this meant, so I put him off. I told him I would walk, but that I would need a ride for a car part the following day. I had been preparing for this. That night, after everyone had left for the lake, I took the things I'd packed, kissed my wife and daughter good-bye, and I came here."

We were deep in the remote countryside now, and he turned down a lane toward an old farmhouse with an over-grown field. He parked the car inside a weathered shed, and we all got out.

"This belonged to a distant relative," he said. "No one knows about it. When Bruno arrived the next day, my wife told him I had left for France, an emergency matter with my family. My sister lives there, you see."

"Aren't you worried about leaving your wife and daughter in Enna?" I asked as he closed the big door to the shed.

"Yes, of course. But I also want to find out what happened to my beautiful town. I want to put it right again. My wife and I both. She is my eyes and ears in Enna, and I am the remote nerve center, I suppose."

We followed him to the house, where he unlocked the

front door and opened it wide for us to enter. The inside was basic. In the living room, a laptop and communication equipment were arrayed across a table that looked out onto the driveway and road. Spare battery packs lined the near wall, while a diesel-powered generator, presently off, was parked beside them, ready for recharging duty.

"Please, make yourselves comfortable," Franco said, gesturing to a small sitting area. "Can I bring you something to drink?"

"Just water," I said.

"Something stronger, if you've got it," Bree-yark put in.

"Who was in that line of cars back there?" I asked as Franco disappeared into a kitchen.

"The mayor's followers," he called back. "Marta was probably waiting for a call from Bruno that never came. Others say she now has odd powers of knowing. Were you at the lake?" When we confirmed that we had been, he said, "Yes, they go to an old cave where the cults once prayed to Persephassa. Under the Greeks she became Persephone, but my wife says you are a professor of mythology, so you probably know this already. Marta may have sensed your presence there. My scholarly mind is not inclined to agree with this, but I have seen too many strange things lately."

"You're not the only one," I said, reflecting on the past few weeks.

Franco returned shortly with a tray of bottled waters, crackers nested beside cured meats and olives, and a bottle of scotch.

"Please, help yourselves," he said, setting the tray down on the coffee table.

While Bree-yark dug into the hors d'oeuvres and downed two shots, I unscrewed the cap from one of the water bottles and took an exploratory sip. I trusted Franco, but not quite as much as Bree-yark.

"The artifact the mayor stole," I said. "Was it a scepter to Persephone?"

Franco, who was in the middle of taking his own sip, stopped and stared at me, water dribbling from his mouth. He blotted his chin with his sleeve.

"How do you know this?" he asked.

"An educated guess. Can you tell me more about it?"

"The scepter is a beautiful piece of craftsmanship," he said wistfully. "Bronze, gold, silver, pieces of black opal. It was discovered in a quarry in the foothills north of Catania. The scepter went to the local museum, but the museum closed during the financial trouble. We were able to acquire it along with several other pieces, thanks to a local benefactor who has since passed away."

"How did you know it was linked to Persephone?" I asked.

"Persephassa," he corrected me. "But, yes, we can call her Persephone. From descriptions in the early literature, dating technology, and the fact it was found here in Sicily. The scepter was probably commissioned by a chieftain to honor the goddess. It would have been used in ceremonies to ensure her return each spring."

"So she was worshipped primarily as an agricultural god?" When he nodded, I asked, "What about as a wronged or vengeful god? You know, kidnapped against her will, forced into queenship in the underworld?"

"This is possible. We do not know everything about the Siculi who worshipped her. Why do you ask this?"

"I'm, ah, I'm just thinking about the changes that came over Enna," I hedged. "Your mayor steals the scepter, and the whole town gets turned on its head. They're eliminating so called 'intruders.' They're performing sacrificial rituals down at the lake." No doubt the organs had come from the police investigators and those who'd asked too many questions. "Let's assume for a moment that the scepter holds the old worship for Persephone. Why the hostility and violence? Something doesn't add up."

"Yes, this is where I am stuck, too. After the museum was closed, my wife says there was smoke from the metalworks. I believe Marta had the remaining artifacts destroyed." He glanced away in obvious pain.

So much for acquiring an object of worship for Persephone's mother.

"Did you ever notice anything unusual about the scepter?" I asked. "Strange, even."

"Other than its state of preservation?" He shook his head and took another swallow of water. He was reaching for a cracker when his hand faltered and came back to his lap. "Well, now that you ask me, there *was* something strange that happened. For several days before the scepter disappeared, I would hear a sound, like the way the wind will sometimes whistle in a storm. *Whishhhhhh*. Very high."

I'd been sitting forward, forearms on my knees, but now I straightened. I'd heard the same sound in Persephone's chambers.

"After a while, it was driving me crazy. From what I could hear, it was coming from the case with the scepter. I checked the walls, I checked the windows, but I could not find an opening. The next Monday, the sound was gone, but so was the scepter. I never connected them until now. Do you think it is anything?"

"Possibly." But damned if I knew what.

When I said nothing more, he set his water down. "They

will be out searching for you today, but tonight, when they are at the lake, I will drive you to Catania. From there you can leave Sicily safely."

I refocused on him. "We're not going anywhere."

"That's right," Bree-yark put in through a mouthful of crackers.

He looked between us nervously. "What do you mean? It is too dangerous here."

"When I was at your house earlier, I said that if you were in trouble, we could help. Well, I meant that. We'll wait here until dark, but then Bree-yark and I are going back to the lake to retrieve the scepter. If it's doing what I think it's doing, we should be able to put your town right again."

33

Franco wheeled his car around so the headlights illuminated the span of a field that ended at a hill. "On the other side of the hill, there is the woods," he repeated for us. "The path will be old and overgrown, but it leads to the lake."

"Much appreciated, Franco," I said.

"Are you sure there is nothing more I can do?"

"Just be at the meeting spot in two hours," I said. "By then, everything should be back to normal."

He clutched my right hand in both of his. "If this is true, I will, I will..." His eyes glistened with moisture as he struggled for the words. "I will kiss you!" he decided. "I don't care, I will be so happy!"

I smirked. "I only do cheeks with anyone who isn't my wife. Just so you know."

Franco laughed and shook my hand. "I will be honored to kiss your cheek, my friend."

"Thanks for finding us earlier," I told him.

"Yeah, buddy," Bree-yark said, clapping Franco's shoulder from the backseat. "Sorry for cleaning out half your pantry."

We'd spent the remainder of the day at Franco's, eating, resting, and studying survey maps of the countryside. Franco said the roads to Lake Pergusa would be under surveillance, but he knew a back way, an overland route.

I also borrowed his sat phone. My first call went to Ricki. After I filled her in, she told me everything was quiet at the apartment, including Tabitha, though she thought she'd seen her twitch. A promising sign.

The rest of my calls were to Claudius, or rather his voice-mail. That he wasn't answering suggested he was still dealing with the other matter he'd mentioned. Either that or he was having brunch with one of his many lady friends. I left messages reminding him we were in Sicily and would need a ride home.

I also asked him to bring more neutralizing salt.

Late in the day, Bree-yark and I took a walk around the farm, discussing our strategy for recovering the scepter. When Franco pressed us for details, I told him we'd had experience in such things and that he could trust us. I could see he didn't like being kept in the dark, but that was much less complicated than having to explain magic.

"I will be at the meeting place in two hours," he promised now as we got out of his car.

Bree-yark and I gave him a thumbs-up. He waited until we'd crossed the field before circling away.

By the time we reached the back of the stone outcropping above Lake Pergusa, the full moon was high, illuminating the rocks and treetops and glistening over the blood-red lake. A murmur of voices rose on the breeze.

Bree-yark nudged me and pointed. "There's one of 'em."

A figure came into view, climbing around the side of the outcropping. With a whispered Word, I drew the shadows around us like a large cloak. The figure—a man, it turned out —surveyed the trees where we were crouched before resuming his patrol. Moonlight glowed along the barrel of his rifle.

I tracked him with my wand. "*Entrapolare.*"

The air around the man's head gleamed with light. He dropped his weapon onto its sling and pressed his hands to the airtight sphere. Then he began beating it with his fists.

Taking his cue, Bree-yark dropped his pack—slimmer for having left some of its contents at Franco's—and hustled toward the struggling figure. With a blow to the stomach, he doubled the man over. He then removed his weapon, patted him down, grabbed him by the scruff of his shirt, and dragged him back toward the trees. By the time Bree-yark reached me, the man was unconscious.

"Go on ahead," he grunted. "I'll get him trussed and gagged."

With a nod, I dispersed the invocation and crept toward the outcropping. I crawled up the rocks on hands and feet. At the top, I peered over the edge. I couldn't see inside the cave from my vantage, just the aura of candlelight and a large pile of shoes. The light was accompanied by low chants.

I also spotted two more armed sentries, one off to the left, at the head of the path Bree-yark and I had ascended earlier. The other sentry stood away to the right, watching a path that dropped back toward the lake.

I swirled my wand until I'd created two tubes of hardened

air in front of me. I then drew a sleeping potion from my pocket, poured half into an empty vial, activated both, and placed them inside the launcher-shaped tubes.

I aimed the tubes and, with an uttered Word, sent the vials off like shots. They shattered at the men's feet, releasing a pair of pink cloud swells. The men wavered in tandem and collapsed to the ground. The echoing chants from the cave continued. Moments later, Bree-yark joined me on the rock.

"Got my guy tied to a tree," he whispered. "Are those the last ones?"

"Up here, anyway," I whispered back. "But keep an eye out. I'm about to drop."

"I'll drop with you."

"Let's stick to the plan. You have a better vantage from up here."

With a reluctant nod, Bree-yark got into position. I activated and downed a neutralizing potion. I then scooted until I was sitting on the edge of the outcropping, a wand clenched in each fist.

"Careful, Everson," he said.

I shoved myself from the rock and plummeted. With the ground rushing up, I shouted a force invocation. It broke through my body and branched down the lengths of my down-pointed wands, blowing mini craters into the sandy ground and stalling my descent. I landed with flexed knees and spun.

The cave was packed with people in hooded cloaks There were a good fifty of them, more than I'd expected. With a Word, I activated two potions and drew them from my coat pocket.

The chanting broke apart, and heads began to turn. I

underhanded one of the potions into the left side of the cave and jabbed my wand at the airborne tube.

"*Vigore!*" I shouted.

The tube exploded, spraying glass and potion over the devotees. I repeated the act, tossing and exploding the other tube over the right half of the cave. Shouts sounded and several arms raised to point, but the encumbering magic was already taking effect, slowing the rpm's on both their sound and motion.

"Watch the path," I called up to Bree-yark.

If there were people posted in the parking lot, chances were good they'd be coming up now.

"Covered," Bree-yark called back. "Do your thing!"

Bringing both wands into casting positions, I ducked into the cave and shouldered my way through the devotees. My rough passage registered in their staring eyes, but their efforts to grab me were comically slow. A few fell over in my wake, their stiffening muscles unable to compensate for the loss of balance.

My reasons for not sleep-potioning them were twofold. One, I didn't know whether the potion would be effective on the bearer of the scepter; and two, I wanted to use the mass of devotees as cover until I reached her.

I edged between two more devotees, and there she stood, between the smoking urns, blood spattering the floor at her bare feet. Something told me the cult had found Bruno's body and harvested his organs for the night's offering.

The mayor's head was hooded, like the others, but instead of a cloak, she wore a long black robe. I glimpsed several purple-robed figures flanking her—probably the town commissioners—but my gaze was fixed on the mayor's right hand, which held the scepter of Persephone. Stiffly. The potion had encumbered her, too.

This may be even easier than I thought...

But when my shoulder brushed the final devotee, I quickly discovered the mayor *hadn't* been immobilized. She'd merely been watching, because as the devotee tipped forward, the opening of the mayor's hood snapped toward me. Long black hair spilled from either side of the void.

I shouted a force invocation and thrust my wand at her.

The bolt of force and light struck her—and disappeared, the scepter inhaling my magic.

"*Intruso!*" she screamed back, swinging the scepter in a clumsy arc. But there was nothing clumsy about the effect. A sweeping force slammed into me and her devotees, throwing us from the cave like bowling pins.

34

I landed on someone heavyset, cushioning my impact, but caught several sharp elbows and knees during my subsequent roll. Groggily, I pushed myself up, an ill feeling passing through me. Thankfully, the neutralizing potion had blunted the worst effects of the scepter's underworld magic.

As my wands crackled with fresh magic, the devotees around me moaned and rocked, still under the influence of my encumbering potion.

"Two incoming!" Bree-yark called from the top of the rock.

I turned to see a pair of men running up the path. Wild shots cracked from their weapons. *Dummies are going to hit their own people.* With a wand in the underhand position, I fashioned a blunt battering ram from thin air. This was no time to be gentle. Driving my second wand into the back of the first, I shouted, "*Impatto!*"

The air sizzled as my ram shot away. It met the men at face level, snapping their heads back with enough force to throw their feet into the air and send them crashing onto their backs.

"Pow!" Bree-yark barked. "I'm coming down!"

I didn't argue this time. I turned back to the cave, but the candles were out. Though I couldn't see into the deep recess, the mayor was back there. I sensed the dark power of Persephone's scepter around her.

The tips of my wands gleamed brighter. "*Entrapolare!*"

The invocation hardened the air over the entrance into a barrier, its light drawing the mayor and her commissioners from the shadows. Four of the commissioners were down, victims of the encumbering potion. But the two closest to the mayor had been spared by the scepter's magic-absorbing power. They stepped in front of her defensively, but she shoved them aside and stalked forward.

"*Intruso,*" she repeated, this time in a low, seething voice. *Intruder.*

As she aimed the scepter, I upped the power I channeled into the barrier. The scepter's magic sent it wobbling and filled me with a graveyard dread that cut to the marrow. Blue light arced from the barrier as I gritted my teeth and doubled down. The mayor may have been an amateur, but the power of the scepter was leveling the playing field. Fortunately, experience had taught me a few things.

"*Respingere!*" I called.

I released the barrier, channeling the prodigious output of light and force into the cave. It pancaked the commissioners into the rear wall, where they crumpled. But the mayor's scepter absorbed the brunt of the blast. She skidded back on her bare feet as her hood was blown from her face.

Sweet Mother of Mercy...

When Franco had said the mayor wasn't looking well,

that had only been the beginning, apparently. Her skin was now so bone-white and drawn so severely to the contours of her face that she had essentially become her skull. Her waves of dark hair, still lustrous, bracketed a living death mask.

Recovering myself, I drew out my bag of neutralizing salt and spiked it into the cave. It broke open in front of the mayor, scattering toward her feet.

With the spectral power of Persephone's scepter permeating the woman, she was susceptible to salt. A theory I confirmed a moment later when I hit the salt with a force blast, sending it into her ghastly face. The impact erupted into black flames. Hands to her eyes, the mayor screamed and angled the scepter out blindly, clumsily. A windy force whistled past my head, fluttering my hair.

Missed me.

I invoked another wall over the mouth of the cave. With one wand reinforcing the glimmering barrier, I stirred up the salt with the other, sending it around the inside of the cave in an expanding cyclone.

The mayor staggered as salt and dark flames whipped around her. I just needed to disrupt the magic possessing her long enough to secure the scepter.

Another scream sounded, but not the mayor's this time. It had come from the lake. And it wasn't human. Down the slope behind me, brush broke and trees shook. I remembered the furrow I'd seen through the growth earlier that day.

Shit.

Her last assault hadn't been intended for me. She'd cast toward Lake Pergusa. And with the lake being the mythic portal between the living world and the dead, there was no telling what she'd called up.

Bree-yark, who'd already descended to collect the

weapons from the downed gunmen, turned toward me, eyes glowing. The view from his perspective must have been insane. I was standing amid an avalanche of downed devotees, casting on a cave where a woman with a skull for a face was running in circles as black flames chased her.

"Um, do you need any help?" he asked.

Through gritted teeth, I said, "Might have company from the lake soon. You're gonna need salt rounds."

"You got it, buddy," he said, dropping his pack to switch out the ammo in his pistol.

Meanwhile, I labored to up the cyclone forces in the cave. I needed to hit my target with more salt, more frequently. I was getting there—the warping effect of the scepter was weakening—but whatever the mayor had summoned from the lake was still coming. A tree snapped behind me and crashed to the ground.

"Mother thunder!" Bree-yark exclaimed and opened fire.

Amid the ear-splitting cracks, I peered over a shoulder. A serpentine head with blood-red eyes had slithered up from the lake. It reared now as Bree-yark's shots blew chunks from its scaly hide. But like with my salt, it wasn't enough, not yet, and Bree-yark soon emptied his weapon into the thrashing creature.

"Dammit," he grunted as he slapped home a fresh magazine. "Should've packed my shotgun."

I refocused on the cave, shrinking the enclosure while willing more and more energy into the cyclone. As Bree-yark resumed shooting, I sensed movement, this time coming up the path. I swung a wand over, but the figure wasn't a gunman or another serpent.

"Oh, good!" He hustled toward me. "This is the third lake

I've visited tonight, and I was beginning to think I'd misheard you."

"Claudius!" I exclaimed in relief. "Please tell me you brought salt."

"Now *that* I heard clearly." He slung a large sack from his shoulder. "Will this be enough?"

I laughed in relief. "More than enough. Can you get it in there?" I asked, jutting my chin at the cave.

Claudius squinted toward the scene inside, then looked back at the thrashing serpent in puzzlement. "Goodness, that's loud," he said of Bree-yark's shooting. "How much salt do you need?"

"All of it," I replied.

He signed into the air, opening a horizontal portal. He upended the bag over it while signing with his other hand to create a second portal inside the cave, where the salt emptied onto the floor. The cyclone quickly swept it up. By the time Claudius finished pouring, the visibility inside the cave had been reduced to white-out conditions.

With a final scream, the mayor collapsed. I heard the scepter clang and roll. Behind me, the serpent released its own anguished cry and crashed back toward the lake. Bree-yark gave chase, firing after it.

I absorbed the barrier and maelstrom back into my wands, reshaping the forces so they piled the scattered salt over the scepter. Only when it was buried beneath a sizable mound of the neutralizing medium did I lower my wands, exhausted. For the second time in three days, I'd captured Persephone's scepter.

I limped to where the mayor had sprawled onto her stomach, dark smoke rising from her salt-coated robe. As I rolled her onto her back, I expected the worst. But with the scepter's magic leaving her, her face was filling out again. I checked to ensure she was breathing. Only then did I sit back on my heels, allowing the relief to pour in. Not only had we recovered the scepter, we'd managed to save its first victim.

Claudius ventured forward, and together we returned the salt to the sack and buried the scepter inside. As I hoisted the sack by its neck, Bree-yark returned, grinning with all his teeth.

"I reduced that slithering sucker to smoke before he could reach the water." He laughed. "I wish you could've seen it."

"Me too," I said, not having the heart to tell him that negating the scepter's magic had been key to the serpent's demise. But he had kept it at bay long enough for Claudius and me to do the deed, which was no small thing.

Bree-yark nodded at the sack. "That the scepter?"

"We got it." *Again*, I thought to myself. "Great going, everyone."

"Yes, yes, a delightful team effort," Claudius agreed, blinking at the dozens of still-encumbered devotees. He started to say something, hesitated, then said it anyway. "And what exactly was this all about?"

35

By the time Bree-yark met Franco at the pickup point, the encumbered devotees were able to stand under their own power, and the ones I'd put to sleep, whether by potion or force, were conscious. Several needed healing magic, but all were alive and just as perplexed as Claudius as to what had happened.

They had little to no memory of the past several months, which was unfortunate, especially when it came to the mayor. She might have answered some key questions, such as what compelled her to steal the scepter in the first place and how it had directed her. More and more, I suspected that the growing power of the shadow scepter had bled into this one.

But as I bathed the mayor in healing light, I thought mostly of Alec and how the Tablet of Hermes was fusing to him, controlling him, possessing him, much as the scepter had possessed this woman.

With that weighing on me, I looked over at Claudius. He was flirting with one of the devotees, an older woman. "Oh, and my pasta primavera was voted best dish at our last home-owners association potluck," I overheard him say.

I had yet to ask if he'd made any progress deciphering the magic sealing the Kleftians' box—or if he'd even remembered to begin. There would be time for that when we returned to New York. I hoped.

With medical services in Enna having more or less ceased, Franco arranged for an ambulance from the next town to pick up the mayor from Lake Pergusa. Given the extent of her possession, she would need to be checked out and monitored. Franco then recruited a number of healthy adults in Enna to help the former devotees return home. I took the opportunity to collect a jar of the smelly red water from Lake Pergusa.

It could prove useful if, God forbid, I ever had to return to the shadow realm.

Shortly before sunrise, Franco drove us back to his farm-house. In his living room, he went to us one by one, seized our hands, and delivered the promised kisses to our cheeks. Claudius let out a surprised chuckle. "Oh, that's nice," he said.

Franco finished and stood back with an enormous smile. "I am so happy you came. You will always be welcome in our beautiful town, where you will be forever celebrated." His eyebrows folded down. "But I still do not understand what you have done."

I cleared my throat. "Remember how you said your scholarly mind was having a hard time accepting some of the strange things you'd seen lately? Well, what happened tonight was one of those strange things."

"Ah, I see," he said, looking at us more curiously.

Before he could press for details, I said, "In any case, it

was our pleasure. I'm just sorry we weren't able to help Bruno." He was the driver who had attempted to gas us before choking on his own poison.

"Yes..." Franco said hesitantly. "But if it makes you feel better, Bruno was a bastard."

Bree-yark barked a laugh, which he quickly disguised as a cough. I spoke over his ensuing snorts until he excused himself. "There is work we'll need to do on the scepter," I explained. "To make it safe again. Is it all right if we—"

Franco showed both hands. "Take it. I trust you will return it when it is safe, and if it is not safe, then do with it what you must. My town is worth more to me than the scepter. What time is your flight home?"

"Oh, ah, we have another way of getting back," I said, gesturing to Claudius. "And it's probably best if we do it outside."

He raised an eyebrow. "May I see?"

"You can. But do you really want to?"

He considered my question before shaking his head. "You are right. I only want to go home to my wife and daughter. One day soon, I hope to begin collecting pieces for the museum again. These are my three loves. I need nothing more."

I swallowed the small knot in my throat and nodded. "You're a lucky man."

Following a final round of handshakes, Claudius, Bree-yark, and I took our leave of Franco and filed into the backyard.

"Well, then, back to your place?" Claudius asked me.

"Please, but before we do, I want to apologize for last night. I shouldn't have spoken to you that way."

Claudius scratched his nose. "Last night?"

"At Loukia's? Regarding those photos of the box?" When that didn't appear to register either, I hugged him, then looked him in the eyes. "I couldn't do this without you, Claudius. You're a good man."

He just wasn't good at faking actual confusion—his way of defusing the tension.

"Oh, well, erm..." He coughed into a fist as his cheeks brightened. "Thank you very much, Everson. Shall we go now?"

"A direct route, if possible," I suggested.

I knotted the salt-filled sack with the scepter around my wrist and then gripped it extra tight. A plan for the scepter had been taking shape in my mind, and I couldn't afford to lose it in another dimension.

"Yes, yes, I'll see what I can do about that," Claudius said.

Bree-yark gave me a skeptical look as we joined arms.

Claudius almost delivered. Following a brief passage through a realm populated by butterfly creatures with large, endearing eyes but sharp, nipping beaks, we landed on the floor of my old lab space. Bree-yark shook a packing box from his foot, but we'd all arrived upright, our arms still linked.

"Nicely done," I told Claudius, squeezing his shoulder.

I took a moment to inhale the comforting smells of home. But as the rushing sound of the transition faded from my ears, it was replaced by grunts and sharp chirps from downstairs. My reading lamp fell with a clang. I hurried down the ladder, the sack with the scepter in one hand, my other hand plunging into my pocket for a wand. When I arrived, I was greeted by an orange comet shooting past.

No way, I thought.

I peered over at the divan. Only a deep depression in the cushion, no Tabitha.

"Holy thunder!" Bree-yark exclaimed, arriving beside me. "I've never seen her move like that!"

"None of us have," I assured him. "Is everyone all right?" I called.

"We're in here!" my wife answered from the kitchen.

I rounded the corner to find Mae in a floral night gown, her broad body backing my wife toward the fridge while holding out a rolling pin in a defensive position. When Tabitha passed again, Mae grunted and struck out at the air. Buster, who'd crawled onto the kitchen counter, chirped and snapped his claws.

"What in the heck's happening?" I asked.

Ricki peered from behind Mae's shoulder with a perturbed face. "Tabitha was twitching on and off, then suddenly she jumped up and started doing this. She hasn't attacked us or anything. Mae's just being extra... careful."

"Darned right I'm being careful," she said, leaning forward to peer out. "In my thirty years as a veterinarian, I heard of a cat doing this twice, and both times the owner got torn to shreds—get away!" she shouted, stuffing Ricki back behind her and striking out with the rolling pin as Tabitha raced past again.

"Okay, hold tight," I said, suppressing a smile, then snorting a laugh. I was short on sleep, relieved to be home, and thrilled that Tabitha was alive and kicking. The perfect recipe for delirium. "Let me see what I can do."

I sidestepped into the living room, wand at the ready. Tabitha shot between my legs, her heft nearly forcing me into a split. She disappeared into our bedroom and blasted back out a moment later.

A glimpse of her face sobered me. Eyes wide and dilated, ears pinned back, hair poofed out as though she were running for her very life. She may have been recovering from whatever had attacked her, but her woefully unfit heart wasn't going to be able to handle much more of this panic and exertion.

"Whoa, Tabby!" I called. "It's Everson! Slow down!"

When she didn't respond, I uttered a Word and swirled the wand above a choke point formed by my fallen lamp and the kitchen counter. Blue light glimmered as the air hardened into a ramp.

On her next pass, Tabitha propelled herself up it. With a quick incantation, I grew the ramp out until it was a sphere. Tabitha raced around the inside of it like a motorcycle rider in a Globe of Death.

Bit by bit, I shrank the enclosure, depleting it of oxygen. Tabitha slowed by degrees. At last, she arrived at the top of the sphere and plummeted to the bottom, where she lay panting, eyes at half-mast.

Then she stopped breathing altogether.

"Tabitha!" I called, dispersing the sphere.

Without thinking, I closed my lips over her nose and mouth and began breathing for her. I went light at first, then heavier when I realized her lungs were struggling to inflate against the sheer amount of fat in her torso. I must have put a dozen breaths into her and was about to switch to compressions, when she wriggled her head.

I recoiled to find her eyes open and a scowl curling her lips.

"I always knew you had feelings for me, darling," she rasped. "But you're a *dreadful* kisser."

This was the Tabitha I knew and sort of loved, her barb removing any doubt. Her eyelids slid closed, but she was breathing on her own again. I picked her up, her body wonderfully pliant now, and carried her to the divan, where I arranged her back inside her depression. The others gathered behind me.

"Tabs gonna be all right?" Bree-yark asked.

"Yeah, I think she's out of the woods." I looked to Claudius for confirmation, and he nodded.

Mae checked Tabitha's pulse and took a closer look at her eyes and nose before seconding my opinion.

"Welcome home," Ricki said, slipping an arm around my waist as I straightened. "I'd kiss you, but..." Her eyes cut down to Tabitha.

"Yeah, let me swish some lye first," I chuckled. "Then I'll tell you about our trip."

She squinted up at me. "Is that optimism I hear?"

"Could be, but don't jinx it."

A quick glance at my watch straightened my smile. With the time difference it was late Tuesday in New York, which gave me about twenty-four hours until I was scheduled to meet my shadow's ashes.

36

Though it was after midnight, Mae insisted on making us pancakes. While Bree-yark and Claudius helped her, Ricki and I took turns plunging heated goat's milk into Tabitha's mouth. She swallowed on reflex and by the time we finished, she was purr-snoring soundly, her belly creeping over the divan's edge like a heap of warm dough.

As we sat down to our very late, or very early, breakfast, I started into an account of our trip.

I began with Sicily, explaining how Persephone's scepter had found a vessel in the mayor and driven most of the townspeople into a trancelike worship for the goddess. The parallels to the situation in the shadow version of our city weren't lost on me, only instead of possessing Mayor Lowder, Persephone had assumed her own form and insinuated her way into his halls of power.

Bree-yark interrupted to tell everyone about the giant serpent he'd gunned down.

Not to be outdone, Claudius said, "Yes, and I brought the salt, oh, and then I met the loveliest woman," referring to the elderly devotee he'd been chatting up. He popped his eyebrows up and down. "A real *belladonna.*"

In their defense, neither one knew the dire nature of my time crunch.

"The important thing is that we have Persephone's scepter now." I nodded at the sack I'd placed at the end of the table. I was watching it like a hawk, but buried in five pounds of neutralizing salt, its magic couldn't so much as gasp. "The *actual* scepter. I believe I can use it to destroy its shadow."

"How?" Ricki asked.

She was sitting beside me, holding my hand while she carved her pancake with a fork.

"Remember how Persephone used a potion to bind the explorer club fellows to their shadows and then extracted their organs for ritual use?" She nodded darkly. "Well, I was able to isolate the bonding potion from that bottle of scotch. And by applying the potion to the scepter, that should bond it to the one in the shadow realm. When I destroy this one, we can kiss that one goodbye as well."

Hence, the optimism she'd picked up earlier.

"Will it work on objects, though?" she asked.

"Inert objects, probably not. But I'm betting that the worship has instilled enough life force, enough *god* force, into the scepter to make this work."

"Hmm, I believe you're right," Claudius said.

"And I don't think hers is the only god force in there," I continued. "I think worship to Cronus infiltrated the scepter somehow." That would have explained the sacrifices in Enna —the literature was rife with stories of human offerings to Cronus, devourer of his children. "But that's beside the point. Destroying the scepter will take care of her as well as any malevolent energies that are compelling her to free Cronus."

Ricki squeezed my hand twice. "Then why do you sound hesitant now?"

"Well, that brings me to the Greece part of our trip," I sighed. "Based on what I learned from the resident dryad, Hermes appears to be operating entirely from self-interest. The box that preserves his tablet? He tricked the thieves guild into building it for him and then had them executed."

"Goodness!" Mae exclaimed.

Bree-yark licked the syrup off his empty plate, then gestured toward mine. I nodded that I was done and slid my remaining pancakes his way.

"But not before the guild stashed the box in the shadow realm," I continued. "I'm not sure if Hermes intended for that to happen, but with the box assuring his longevity, he only had to wait for the right vessel. Eventually, the box made its way to New York. And Alec."

I felt our collective concern for the boy draw taut around the table. Like Bree-yark had said, we were his village. Even Claudius appeared anxious as he massaged his chin and mumbled to himself.

"In the interim, the worship for the gods of Olympus waned," I said, "and Hermes became the most powerful one by default. I think his plan was to coerce a new generation of mortals into worshipping him—not to destroy the old Olympic order, necessarily, but to rearrange it, putting himself at the pinnacle. He knew the power of his tablet would attract some old objects, jolt them back to life, but he didn't count on Persephone coming in so hot. Right now, she's the only thing stopping him."

Ricki nodded knowingly. "And you're afraid that if you destroy the scepter, you remove that impediment to Hermes's power grab."

"Exactly. Right now, she has the upper hand. She's made a deal with Cronus, and together they're preparing to battle the remnants of the Olympic order, namely Hermes, and it won't even be close. Hermes knows this—he's been trying to bargain with her—but she doesn't need him, not in the grand scheme of things, and I think he knows that too. If I destroy the scepter, he'll run unopposed, so to speak. He'll assert his authority there *and* here to prevent another 'Persephone' from happening."

I remembered how the box had spontaneously jumped from my upstairs lab several weeks ago back to the shadow realm, despite being packed in salt and stored in a casting circle. I wasn't confident enough in the obfuscation sigil to believe it would keep the trickster god at bay for much longer.

"Is there a way to destroy the tablet without hurting Alec?" Mae asked, seeming to read my face.

"That's the hope. Then I would be able to take care of Persephone's scepter." Shadow Budge had claimed that Hermes's tablet supported Persephone, but now that I had a way to destroy her scepter, I wouldn't have to take his word for anything. "With both objects gone, the support for the minor gods and beings will collapse. Everything should go back to the way it was."

I hated to put Claudius on the spot, but this was his department. "Anything yet?"

He wiped his mouth and cleared his throat. "Yes, in fact."

From a jacket pocket, he pulled out the folded images of the box. When he spread them across the table, I was shocked to find numbers, writing, and sketches in the margins—lots of them, like someone's graduate thesis on advanced mathematics. He peered up at me as though the arcane equations spoke for themselves and he was awaiting my assessment.

I couldn't help but laugh. "When did you do all this?"

"Yesterday. That was why I was so late getting to the lake. After finishing up with some other business, I really sat down with these."

"Wow, way to go. And what did you find?"

"Well, ah…" He glanced from me to the images and back. "Maybe we should discuss this privately?"

I looked around the table. Mae and Bree-yark were angling their head at the images in puzzlement, but my wife was staring at me.

"Whatever you need to share," I told Claudius, "you can share with the team."

"Well, okay." He gathered the images up again, leafing through them as though to refresh his memory. "You asked if there was a way to open the box safely. I've studied these from every angle possible and, well, I believe I've discovered a way to open it without harming Alec."

"Really?" I said excitedly.

"Yes, though it will require extremely precise magic."

"Magic within our means?"

"Oh, yes, yes, absolutely."

I talked my jubilant heart back down. His expression was anything but triumphant. "So what's the catch?" I asked carefully.

"It would destroy the one casting the opening magic."

When Ricki's hand tensed in mine, I massaged her knuckles with my thumb.

"Alternately," he continued, "we could spare the opener, but that wouldn't bode well for Alec. No, not well at all."

"There's no way to spare both?" I asked.

"I've looked and looked, I assure you. I ate an entire bag of my ginseng candies in the process." He grimaced as though only now remembering and scooted aside his half-eaten plate of pancakes, which Bree-yark quickly appropriated. "But no, Everson, it's in the nature of the bonding. It was designed to be released by Hermes's will and his alone. When another's hand or tongue attempts it, the destruction visited on them is absolute. Indeed, the box has claimed many lives over the centuries."

Both Hermes and Arianna had told me as much.

"The method I've discovered *channels* that destruction either outward or inward," he continued. "Through the opener or through the bearer. But it can't be neither." He leafed through the images as if in a last ditch effort to find a loophole that had escaped him, but he shook his head. "It just can't."

I fell silent, my mind chewing on the discouraging news.

"Do you mind if I talk to my husband alone for a moment?" Ricki asked.

With murmurs of "not at all," "of course not," and "you go right ahead, baby" rising from the table, Ricki and I excused ourselves and went to the bedroom.

She closed the door and sat on the side of our queen. I lowered myself next to her and hugged her to my side. Her head nestled wearily against my neck. I closed my eyes until I felt her and our daughter's energies moving through mine.

At last she said, "I would never ask or expect you to harm Alec, shadow or not. You'll find another way."

I kissed the crown of her head. "There's something I need to tell you."

She straightened, her dark eyes searching mine with a look somewhere between concern and resolve.

"When I was in Persephone's chambers," I said, "Budge revealed that they'd acquired the remains of my shadow. They were in an urn, and I watched Persephone stir a bonding potion into them, a precursor anyway. He said that unless I destroyed the Tablet of Hermes, they would activate the potion."

"How long do you have?"

"Until tomorrow night, at midnight."

"Do you think he's bluffing? Do you know for a fact they were your ashes?"

She was still Detective Vega. Under different circumstances I might have smiled. "I don't, but I'm not ready to find out."

"Me neither, but if time runs out, you can destroy the scepter, right?"

"And roll the dice with Hermes," I said, completing her thought. "Yes."

I wouldn't have a choice, and that's what really bothered me. I'd gone to Greece and Italy to take control of my destiny. But without the ability to destroy Hermes's tablet, it felt like I was right back to being putty in his hands. Unless, of course, I was willing to blow myself up, and that was a nonstarter.

"Do what you need to do," she said. "I trust you."

"That's going to mean consulting my magic."

She released a long, pensive sigh through her nose. "I know. But if it tells you to sacrifice yourself, your magic and I are gonna fight. I'm serious. Before you do anything, I want you to tell me."

Wage, young mage, till your final breath
And come night's fall, accept your death.

I pushed away the Doideag's prophetic verses and nodded.

"I will," I promised. "But first I want to check in with Alec."

"What are you going to tell him?"

"Everything. It's his life. He deserves to know."

A deep furrow formed between my wife's glistening eyes. "Even what Claudius said about the box?"

"That too," I decided.

"And what if he wants to sacrifice himself? What will you say to that?"

I pictured Hermes's demise, followed by Persephone's. An explosive one-two bang. The conclusion of the godly wars, the end of the threats to our worlds. But I also thought of Alec. The son of my shadow. My flesh and blood. Because the question Ricki posed was a very real possibility.

37

I knocked on the basement door before cracking it open. Being after midnight, I was surprised to see a light on inside.

"Alec?" I called. "Are you awake?"

"Dad?" he said, then caught himself. "Is that Everson?"

I pushed the door the rest of the way open to find him propped up in bed, the thick numerology book against his knees, an open notepad beside him. I exhaled, relieved he was still here and that he was himself.

"How you doing, buddy?" I asked.

In his semi-reclined position, his hair slightly tousled, he looked more at ease, more rested. Being confined here rather than playing host to Hermes had no doubt helped. But when I shifted to my wizard's senses, I saw what Claudius had meant. While the obfuscation sigil may have been scrambling the signal between the tablet and Alec, the bonds were still biting into the corona of his soul.

"Not bad." Smiling, he rubbed an eye with the heel of his

palm, then stretched the arm overhead. "A little tired. How did your thing go?"

I wavered a hand. "So-so."

I'd carried down the salt-filled sack with Persephone's scepter, and now I placed it in my warded safe beside Red Beard's whip and a bottle of what remained of the energy I'd extracted from it.

"Anything you can share?" he asked.

God, where to begin? I thought as I sealed the safe.

"Let's hear about you first," I deflected. "Looks like you're pretty deep into that."

He followed my nod to the book on his lap. "Oh, yeah." He gave a tired chuckle. "Sort of got absorbed."

"It's a well-known Croft trait."

"Man, this is intense stuff. Eye-opening, too. I knew symbols and words could channel power, but I hadn't given a lot of thought to numbers. Makes sense, though. Runes are geometric symbols, and sound is vibrational energy, right?" His hands grew more animated as he sat up straighter. "And some runes and sounds are more powerful than others. Well, that can all be represented by numbers and formulas, suggesting they can act as a medium to achieve similar or even identical results."

I smiled proudly. "That's right. A practice known as numeromancy."

"As far as what you were looking for..." He swapped the thick tome for his notebook. It wasn't until he flipped back to the beginning that I realized he'd filled most of it with his drawings and insights. It wasn't Hermes's influence, either. This was all coming from Alec's head and our shared bloodline.

"You ready?" he asked.

I scooted up one of the chairs and took a seat. "Go ahead."

"Let's start with the number twelve, because there's a lot of info. But at its core, twelve represents entirety, wholeness. The number of months in the year, the signs of the zodiac." He pointed at me, eyebrows raised. "The principal gods in the Greek pantheon. There were also twelve major Titans."

I nodded. If we were to refight the Titanochamy, even some stripped-down version of it, a force of twelve made sense.

"Twelve represents a beginning and an end wrapped into one," he continued. "So it's robust. In fact, at the foundation of a lot of powerful spells you'll find some element of twelve. It's what holds the configuration together, keeps the energy from overwhelming it."

Damn, this kid was sharp.

"And check this out." He flipped back through his notebook. "I doodled some of my more powerful runes. Turns out that most of them feature twelve of something, usually major intersections. See?" He turned the notebook around to a runic drawing where he'd circled all of the intersections in question, twelve of them. In his eyes, I saw my own youthful excitement when I would make unexpected discoveries. I still experienced the odd joy, but nothing like in those early days.

"There it is," I said with a laugh. "It's fun, isn't it?"

"It's amazing. It's like seeing this new layer of reality that's been in front of my face the whole time."

"That's the essence of magic."

And you're going to grow up to be a powerful magic-user.

Though the thought came from nowhere, I held onto it. Seized it with both arms. No matter how dire things looked now, he was going to get the chance to grow up and become an advanced practitioner someday.

"Okay, let's take a look at the number eleven." He flipped back to his early notes. "There's some obscure mathematical significance, and some mystical traditions deem it powerful, but only much later. Most early societies regarded it negatively, believed it represented incompleteness. Stands to reason, one short of twelve. I went back over my runes again, and sure enough, I couldn't remove any of the major intersections without the power falling apart. Not even when I tried to reconfigure them."

"How about the number one?" I asked.

"That's the whole enchilada. One with a capital O. The source of all numbers, One *is* all numbers. No more duality or many. It's the ultimate, indivisible symbol of unity." He backhanded the book beside him. "That idea, or some version of it, comes up no matter what tradition or period you're talking about. In Greek mythology, it's Zeus, even though he also belongs to the twelve principal gods. I looked for it in my runes, but I guess it's the entirety of each one?"

"That's right," I said. "Something else that's hard to see until you realize it's right in front of your face. You can study it, but more often than not the revelation happens on its own, when you're not looking for it."

I took a moment to revisit the Doideag's prophecy: *Allies gather, eleven and one...*

Was that just a fancy way of saying *twelve*, or did it mean the imperfection of *eleven* plus some vital, missing *one* that represented unity?

And be not afraid of thine own blood...

"Does any of that help you?" Alec asked.

I blinked him back into focus. "It does. Thanks for doing this."

Now I'd have to take my own advice and let it sit, trust

that if and when the time came, the significance would reveal itself.

"And for doing this," I added, gesturing to his confinement.

Alec dropped the notepad on top of the numerology book and threw his legs over the side of the bed. "Your turn. I want to know where we are with everything." His backpack had been crammed between his far hip and the wall, and now he pulled it up beside him in what seemed an unconscious act.

"Would you mind if I took a look at that first?"

"The pack?" He hesitated, but only briefly. He held it toward me by the haul handle, the freeness of the offer surprising me a little.

"I just want to see something," I said.

Conscious of the bonds, I remained close to Alec as I took the pack and unzipped the main compartment. I dug a hand past his stuffed hoodie and reached into the pillowcase at the pack's bottom. A low hum buzzed in my bones as I drew out the metal box with the glyphs, the container holding Hermes's essence.

Alec looked between the Kleftians' box and me, his shoulders hunched as though coiled to reach forward if I dropped it or tried to yank it away.

I turned the box around carefully in my hands. A box crafted by a thieves guild so Hermes could outlive them and their worship. I examined each glyph as I considered the conundrum: open the box to destroy Hermes, but destroy myself or Alec in the process. One or the other. As Claudius had said, there wasn't a "neither" option.

How in the hell to put that into words for Alec? Should I even try?

A part of me was paranoid Hermes would hear, despite

the obfuscation sigil. But more than that, I was thinking about Ricki's question. What if after I explained everything, Alec volunteered to sacrifice himself?

I could see him looking up at me expectantly, trustingly.

Wordlessly, I replaced the box in the pillowcase, zipped the pack closed, and returned it to Alec's hands. "Here."

I couldn't put him in the position of feeling like he had to choose between my life or his own. I cared for him too much, and he was still a kid. This wasn't his choice to make. It was mine as his father, his mentor, and his protector. And that settled the matter in my mind. The box would claim me or no one.

"I'm stuck with it, aren't I?" Alec said.

Out of habit, he'd started threading his arm through the shoulder strap before stowing the pack beside him again.

"No," I said resolutely. "You're going to grow up to be your own person."

"Don't take this the wrong way, but you don't sound like you have a lot of answers right now."

"I don't," I admitted, taking a seat beside him. "But I'm asking a lot of questions. I'm gathering a lot of info." I gestured to him and the numerology book. "I've come to some conclusions, but I've also run face-first into some challenges. Big challenges. That's where being a magic-user comes in. It's not all spells and invocations. It's trusting that the work you've done—that effort and intention—that it's swimming in the collective magic and will emerge as the right solution at the right time. That's real magic."

"But... how do you know?"

"I've told you the story of our bloodline. We're descended from the First Saint Michael. In the battle against the nine elemental demons, he was the last one standing by dint of what he represented."

"Faith," Alec whispered.

"Faith," I repeated. "To answer your question."

His lips pursed in thought, then he nodded with what I hoped was at least a small sense of optimism.

"Oh, and there's one more thing," I said.

He looked over, his eyebrows drawing in.

"It's all right to call me 'Dad.' In fact, I'd prefer it. 'Everson' makes it sound like we're friends or something." I punched his shoulder, drawing a laugh.

My phone buzzed in my pocket, and I pulled it out.

"Hey, Hoffman," I answered, standing. "What's up?"

"We've got another shitshow spilling into the streets," the detective growled.

Crap. I'd all but forgotten about Hermes's draftees. So much for their *binding* agreement. "Dewitt Clinton Park?"

"City Hall Park. And they're not the same yahoos."

My heart dropped into a dull, foreboding beat. "No?"

"Zombies, and they're not staying down."

38

"What's going on?" Alec asked me.

"There's a situation at City Hall."

"Connected with the god stuff?"

"Possibly," I said, already thinking about the bleed-over between scepters. Was a similar bleed-over happening between the shadow City Hall complex, where Persephone was channeling energy, and the one in this reality? I began refilling my coat pockets with potions. "I need to check it out."

"Anything else I can do to help?"

"Yeah, get some rest. I have a feeling tomorrow's going to be a big day."

I expected pushback, but he set the numerology book and his notepad on the floor beside the bed and climbed under the sheets. As he settled in, I called Ricki upstairs and explained what was happening.

I finished by telling her that Hoffman was sending a police cruiser.

Bree-yark's sensitive ears picked that up. "Then it's gonna

be an escort," he barked in the background, "'cause I'm driving him. Tell him to meet me out front."

"Did you catch that?" Ricki asked.

"Loud and clear. Love you."

"You too. Be safe."

I replaced the phone and finished packing my pockets. I was still carrying the two wands but would have given two hundred of them to have my sword and staff back. At the safe, I removed the sack I'd just locked inside. I didn't relish the thought of wielding Persephone's scepter again, but if this *were* a bleed-over...

Might come in handy.

I turned to Alec, regretting I had to break away so abruptly. He'd just finished moving his shoulders around to bulk up his pillow, his pack nested back beside his hip. I walked over and held out my fist.

"All right, buddy," I said.

He bumped it with his own. "Give 'em hell."

———

I climbed into the front of Bree-yark's Hummer, surprised to find Mae and Claudius filling out the backseat. Before I could say anything, the escorting police officer blooped his siren and pulled ahead. Bree-yark took off after him, the acceleration pinning me to my seat. I managed to crane my neck around, but Mae was already holding up a hand.

"I know what you're going to say, Everson, but after your cat decided she was the Tasmanian Devil, I'm wide awake. You're not gonna keep this old lady at home in her gown and slippers."

Bree-yark gave me a look to suggest he'd lost that battle more than a few times and I'd be wise to concede.

"I'm happy to have you, Mae. You too, Claudius."

"Oh, yes, of course, it's always my pleasure," he said.

Though he smiled from me to Mae, I could see he had little idea where we were going. The truth was I had little idea what we were heading into and could use all the help being offered, knowingly or not.

Beyond a flashing police cordon at Broadway, our escort led us to a command and control center in Foley Square. Ahead, military-style vehicles trundled down the street, while personnel in Centurion tactical gear ran beside them.

"My, my, my, would you look at this?" Mae tsked. "Shouldn't we be going with them?"

"Not yet," Bree-yark replied as he pulled over. "We're gonna get the lay of this thing first, right Everson?"

"That's right," I said, putting my phone away.

I'd been talking to Hoffman on the short drive, and now he appeared outside the main tent and waved us over. We got out to the sounds of shouts and gunfire mere blocks away. With my wand ready to cover us, I had the others go first. Bree-yark threw his stubby arm over Mae's back as he hustled her toward the tent.

As we arrived, Hoffman cocked his head. "Trevor's inside."

Though he spoke with his usual roughness, he had the look of someone who'd seen more than his brain could process. As we approached the leader of the Sup Squad, Hoffman stepped away to take a call. Trevor stood at a table, one fist propped before the line of monitors he was staring at while talking into a headset.

"Numbers growing at the east side near Spruce," he said. "Red Two, pull down. Red Four, tighten up. You've got more coming your way."

I peered past him to the largest monitor. A drone feed showed a bird's-eye view of City Hall Park, but what the hell was I looking at? The entire park was undulating, as though the grounds themselves were coming to life. I squinted closer. They were erupting, in fact—with zombies. They spilled and shambled toward the bordering streets where they were met by the flashes of Sup Squad fire.

Trevor noticed me. "Hey, thanks for coming, Croft." He glanced over at Bree-yark, Mae, and Claudius with a questioning expression, but gave me the benefit of the doubt. "And for bringing help."

I gestured to the monitors. "When did all of this happen?"

"Started about an hour ago. Fortunately, we were close enough that we were able to get up a containment perimeter pretty quickly. Composite rounds are slowing them, but they keep coming. Can't seem to inflict lasting cranial destruction on these things. We've also tried flames, direct missile strikes, but they're just not behaving like your textbook zombies. At least not the ones in your manual."

I scanned the other monitors: another bird's-eye view as well as outdoor feeds from the city hall and courthouse buildings. Animated cadavers shambled past the latter, but the nighttime feeds were too grainy to pick out details.

With Trevor at the helm, the Sup Squad had been running like a well-oiled machine, only consulting me on cases that landed outside the norm. This was one of those cases, and I thought I knew why.

"Can a drone zoom in on a zombie?" I asked.

"Singer!" Trevor called across the tent. "Get us a closeup on a target."

The drone operator nodded, and one of the overhead feeds jostled before plummeting toward the ground. In the next moment, the gnashing, dirt-caked teeth of an emerging zombie filled the monitor.

Claudius flinched back. "Ooh, that's unsightly."

The operator adjusted, zooming out until the entire creature was framed. It was riding an upthrust of dark earth, half crawling and half ejecting from the ground. It had started out skeletal, but now flesh was growing over bone, then scraps of clothing over the flesh. My companions murmured.

"Where are they coming from?" Trevor asked.

Before I could answer, Mae said, "The poor house."

We turned toward her. She was looking at the monitor, but her eyes stared through the flickering image as though seeing something beyond it. She was tapping into her inner nether whisperer.

"But back then it was called an *almshouse*."

"That's right," I said. "There used to be an almshouse there, an institution for the sick, indigent, and criminal." I'd walked right past it during one of my trips into the time catches. "They buried their dead on the grounds. The records didn't survive, but when a utilities crew accidentally turned up some bodies a few years back, a historian guessed the total number of interred to be in the hundreds."

Bree-yark let out a low whistle.

The zombie was cascading down the mound now, thrusting himself upright before falling and landing at painful looking angles. When at last he found his legs, I switched my focus to his shambling outline.

What I was looking for would be faint, hard to see...

"There," I said, pointing. "See that slight distortion around his body? The same magic that's restoring their remains is also offering them protection, limiting the damage you're able to inflict on them."

At that moment, gunfire lit him up. He danced this way and that, like a marionette at the end of a spastic hand. Flesh and sinew blew from his form like spindrift until he fell again. But the dark magic was already restoring the damage, and he soon heaved himself upright and into a fresh shamble.

"So what's our move?" Trevor asked.

Claudius stepped forward. "I could open a portal in the ground, drop them all into another dimension. Of course, the whole park would have to go with them, including the buildings. And I wouldn't be able to guarantee the integrity of Lower Manhattan."

I pictured the resulting sinkhole, the inrush of water, and shook my head. "Let's save that as a last resort."

"Okey-dokey," he said brightly. "Just let me know."

Trevor held up a finger as he watched the big monitor and ordered several units to shift positions again. "Their numbers keep growing," he said to me. "We're gonna need something fast."

I nodded. "Can we center this feed on the courthouse real quick?"

Trevor gave the order, and the operator moved the drone into position. It only took me a moment to pick out what I was looking for. Like the effect of a waterfall into a pool, energy was spreading from the courthouse in faint, concentric waves. Made sense. In the shadow realm, that's where Persephone was concentrating the public's energy, channeling it into whatever had been beneath the brown water in the cored-out pit inside the courthouse. A receiver of some kind. Here, though, there *was* no receiver. Instead of opening Tartarus, that bleed-over was animating our dead.

"There's a tear inside the building," I said. "A rift between realities. Getting there shouldn't be a problem"—I glanced over at Claudius, who nodded—"but repairing it is going to take me some time. You'll need to keep the zombies contained, but you'll have help. Can you broadcast sound over the park?"

"We have speakers on the vehicles we can link up."

"Perfect." I brought Mae forward. "Trevor, I'd like to introduce you to my associate Mae Johnson."

She straightened proudly. "It's nice to meet you, young man."

He nodded and shook her offered hand, then looked at me as if to say, *And...?*

"Mic her up to those speakers, and I'll lay out the plan."

39

We landed on a mound of upturned earth and tumbled off in different directions. Claudius had said he wouldn't be able to portal us into the courthouse—too dangerous without a target—but by the time I'd skidded to a stop, I saw he'd come close. We were in a lawn on the building's east side, smoke covering the ground in a misty stratum.

Through the surrounding gunfire and gargling cries of zombies, I whistled for the others.

Bree-yark jogged into view, a tactical shotgun on loan from the Sup Squad hanging from a shoulder strap. He struck a flare. It ignited in a red hiss, and he waved it back and forth overhead to show our position to the drones. Trevor's job was to keep friendly fire off us. Meanwhile, Mae was already doing hers.

"*You people cut out this raggedy-ass nonsense right now!*" her voice echoed over the speakers. "*Attacking officers of the law? You ought to be ashamed of yourselves!*"

Because the magic animating the zombies held nether

qualities, Mae could influence them. And it wasn't my imagination: the volume of gunfire had lessened. She was shaming the creatures into submission.

"You with the straw hat! Back off this instant or I'll come down there and pop you myself!"

I whistled again. Claudius appeared around the mound a moment later, rubbing the side of his head and muttering, "I don't think I can do too many more of those. Ah, there you are. Is it that building or this one?"

He pointed between the courthouse and City Hall.

"Follow me," I said, drawing a wand as I slung the sack with Persephone's scepter over my shoulder and ducked low.

I led the way, circling mounds of torn-up earth and skirting a fallen tree. With the courthouse's east doorway in sight, the ground erupted. I stumbled back as a trio of skeletons emerged from the hillock, morphing into zombies in waistcoats and breeches. They turned and threw themselves down at us.

"Mother thunder!" Bree-yark exclaimed.

"Protezione!" I called, circling my wand overhead.

A blue-tinted dome glimmered above us. As the undead bodies crashed into it, I shouted a second invocation, detonating the dome in a burst of light and force. The zombies somersaulted off like rag dolls.

With the way clear, I resumed running, but the undead regained their feet. It was the damned magic protecting them: the emotional power of the shadow realm spun through Persephone's underworld mysticism. Bree-yark backpedaled, blasting shotgun shells into them. Even so, by the time we reached the door, they were already catching up to us again. I swung around and thrust my wand.

"Vigore!"

Though the force blast landed squarely in the lead zombie's chest, it did little more than throw him back a few feet.

Fed up with their immunity, Bree-yark lunged and drove his flare into the next one's face. The rod smashed through his teeth, met his swallowing reflex, and lodged halfway down his throat.

"Yeah, eat that," Bree-yark barked.

The creature clutched his gargling neck as he stumbled back, the flare spitting red sparks between his fingers. Bree-yark followed him, emptying another shell into his stomach.

"*Is that Thomas Allcock?*" came Mae's voice over the speakers.

The third incoming zombie paused and angled his decomposed head toward the sound.

"*Stealing horses from the livery wasn't bad enough, now you've gotta get all up in my friends' business?*"

He looked abashedly from side to side, eyes jiggling in their sockets.

"*And don't think I don't know about that house you set fire to on King Street,*" Mae added.

The other two undead backed away, as though no longer wanting to be associated with him, and shambled off in search of someone else to attack. The chastened zombie hung his head. I used the opportunity, and two different invocations, to slingshot him into the distance, something I'd always wanted to try.

Claudius, who had been working on the door behind us, threw it open. "Got it!"

Bree-yark and I rushed inside, and he closed the door, sealing it with his magic.

"If you know where you're going, I'll secure the rest of the doors and windows," he said. "Keep the spookies out." That was part of the original plan, but he'd apparently forgotten.

"Great idea." I clapped his shoulder. "C'mon," I said to Bree-yark.

With my wand lighting the way, we hurried through a vaulted room and down an iron staircase. The stairs deposited us onto a basement level crammed with boxes. I navigated a corridor between two towering piles until we were nearing the center of the courthouse.

In the shadow reality, this section of basement had been cored out beneath the rotunda. But here there was no open space, and the energy bleed was coming from another level down.

"Be on the lookout for a staircase," I told Bree-yark.

"How about a trapdoor?"

He hurried past me, his keen eyes picking out a wooden door beyond my light. Planting his feet on either side, he seized a metal ring and pulled, grunting and straining until something snapped and the door scraped open.

The steps beneath were rotten and slick. We ventured down, soon arriving inside an old boiler room. Rusted machinery loomed on all sides, sending bolted lengths of tubing into one another and the darkness overhead. While Bree-yark examined the antiquated system, I opened out my wizard's senses.

Colors and currents grew in my vision, but they were dominated by a dark cascade of energy. It washed past our feet like the surf, out through the walls, and beneath the grounds where it was animating the dead. I traced the flow back to an obvious tear that flapped and snapped like a sheet on a clothesline. It was smallish now, its effect limited to the surrounding area, but that wouldn't last.

"Watch my back," I said.

In my wizard's vision, Bree-yark was a compact constellation of colors. A gold hue—the color of loyalty—surged through them as he nodded and brought his shotgun into position. "You got it, buddy."

I waded toward the rift as though up a river, body inclined, coat flapping, legs thrusting to maintain my forward momentum.

I secured the sack with Persephone's scepter through my belt and drew my second wand. I was an expert at shallow holes—I'd been closing them my entire career—but lately I'd been studying more advanced closing techniques. In the event Arianna ever called me up to help with a larger rift, I didn't want to look like a complete rube.

I set my feet now and studied the tear.

The equivalent of a blanket stitch should close it.

I called power to my wands and set to work, threading energy through one loose end of reality, fording the gap, looping it through itself, and pulling taut. Thanks to the time I'd spent practicing, I was able to progress along the tear at a decent pace. And by God, it was working. Stitch by stitch, the inflow of energy thinned. And where the flaps of reality met, the seam was already starting to fuse.

"Everson!" Bree-yark shouted. "We've got company!"

I was so close to finishing, I considered going for it, but the urgency in his voice made me look. As my vision returned, I saw the problem. Zombies were spilling down the trapdoor. They must have sensed the threat to their animating source and overwhelmed a door or window Claudius had yet to seal.

Bree-yark blew a pair of shells into them. The lead ones fell, but there were plenty to take their place.

"Step aside!" I told him.

Bringing both wands up, I shaped a funnel back toward the trapdoor and attempted a negative pressure vacuum to suck them out. The invocation swept up the creeping cadavers, but thanks to the magic shielding them, the effect was far weaker than I'd been counting on. The zombies slammed into one another, but the exhausting invocation only succeeded in redistributing them around the boiler room.

And now more were dropping through the trapdoor.

"Everson?" Bree-yark looked back and forth between us.

I needed to finish sealing the rift, to pinch off their remaining lifeforce, but there were too many of them, coming in too quickly. Bolstered by dark magic, they would overwhelm any barrier I invoked.

"Get behind me," I told Bree-yark, pulling the sack from my belt.

As he scooted to my side, I gripped the twisted shaft, and in a burst of salt, drew out Persephone's scepter. Downing a neutralizing potion would have been smart, but there wasn't time. The scepter's potent energy filled me immediately. I aimed its crown at the undead horde.

"What life you have," I said in a cold voice that sounded little like my own, "I withdraw!"

I yanked the scepter back. The zombies jerked forward as though on ropes. When they hit the floor, their bodies scattered back into bones, the energy that had sustained them now swirling around the scepter in my grip.

Bree-yark barked a surprised laugh, then took another look at me. "Hey, you all right, Everson?"

The answer was no. Like the last time, I was transfixed by the scepter's power. It pounded through my pleasure centers, inflating me with a ridiculous sense of importance and purpose, of dominion over life and death.

Put the scepter away, I urged myself. *Stuff it in the sack and finish closing the damned rift!*

I was teetering on the precipice between control and impulse when a slender figure came wading through the bones. A pair of green eyes glimmered from the depths of his hood.

I brought the scepter forward, but Hermes beat me to the draw, hitting me with a brilliant burst of light. The force threw me from my feet and the scepter from my hand. I landed over a metal tube, grunting as my back cracked and the air left my lungs.

Bree-yark swung his shotgun around, but Hermes shoved him aside with an effortless invocation. Struggling to sit up, to breathe, I dug desperately inside my pockets as Hermes strode toward me.

But my wands were gone.

40

Hermes didn't speak. I couldn't see his face inside the gray hood, just the green points of his eyes. I struggled to sit up from the pipe, but pain gored my side and my weight slid me back until my head met the floor.

Pushing a hand toward him, I gasped, "*Vigore.*"

He waved away the branching invocation with whatever he was carrying.

I tracked the faint blue light of the room to its source, one of my fallen wands, and stretched a hand toward it. But Hermes was almost to me now, and from my inverted position I could see what he gripped in his hands.

A staff and a rune-lined sword. *My* staff and rune-lined sword.

Thanks to the fact Alec and I shared the same blood, Hermes could cast through both.

With a hissed word, he brought the sword down. Brilliant white light erupted from the blade, swallowing me. I thrashed from the anticipated pain, but none arrived. If anything, the goring in my side eased, and I felt the last of the influence of Persephone's scepter evaporate from my system.

I threw my legs to the side and pushed myself upright.

Hermes stood between me and my fallen wand, but he was peering along the length of the blade as the light faded from the first rune, the one for banishment. With a small noise of interest, he slotted the blade back inside the staff. Still not speaking, he set it on the ground beside me, and turned away.

Huh?

I stared, dumbfounded, as he walked over and retrieved Persephone's scepter from the floor. Bree-yark, who had regained his feet, circled back from him, shotgun aimed.

I took the opportunity to rush forward and grasp my cane. I didn't have to look at it closely to know it was mine. I knew the worn grip, the familiar weight and energy. I felt an urge to hug it to my chest, but now wasn't the time.

"You all right?" Bree-yark whispered, arriving beside me.

"Yeah," I said. "How about you?"

He nodded as we watched Hermes. He was regarding the scepter now. If he was aligned with Persephone, he'd be able to wield it, combining his powers with hers in an unholy trinity of speed, trickery, and death.

I released my sword from the staff, blade glimmering with light, a protection on the tip of my tongue. I readied myself for the moment Hermes would swing the scepter toward us, unleashing the weight of its power. But he only sighed.

He placed the scepter in the sack, giving it several jostles to bury the scepter deeper in the salt. Inexplicably, he set that down too and backed away. "Well?" he said, dusting off his hands and drawing his hood back.

I swallowed, adjusting my grip on sword and staff. "Well what?"

"Are you going to finish closing that, or do you want me to?"

I followed his nod to the tear, sealed save for the final needed stitches. Energy continued to seep in from the shadow present.

"If you don't hurry it up, I believe the dead will take matters into their own hands."

I dropped my gaze to the floor where several of the bones were starting to jitter. I even caught a moan.

"I'll cover you," Bree-yark said, not seeming to care if Hermes heard. Not that it was much of a threat. I nodded at him and approached the rift. Hermes backed away, as though to give me plenty of space.

I took a final look at him before returning to my wizard's senses. Using my sword and staff—the implements I'd practiced with—the remainder of the repair went quickly. As the inflow trickled to a stop, Hermes clapped and came forward.

"Well done!"

I leveled my blade at him, my fear and confusion replaced now by a seething anger. "Why weren't you at the meeting spot?" I demanded.

He grinned and patted his hands toward the floor. "Now, now. You have a right to be upset, but there's no need to threaten me. I'm going to explain everything."

"And make it sound completely above board, I'm sure," I growled.

He turned his hands out. "That will be entirely for you to decide."

"What are you even doing here?"

"Well, helping you, for one. Nothing good ever comes

from wielding that." He nodded at the sack holding the scepter. "I thought you would have learned your lesson, if not in the alleyway, then in Sicily."

How in the hell did he know about that?

His eyes danced mischievously. "I'm a part of you, remember?"

I'd known about the scattershot of Hermes's essence in my system, of course, but I hadn't thought it was fully conscious. Did that mean he knew everything I'd been doing, even my wish to destroy him?

I kept a poker face. "How did you get here?"

"Ahh, you mean how did I get around your obfuscation sigil? Your son figured it out, actually."

"Alec?"

"Your discussion on numbers tonight got him thinking. Your sigil oscillates, you see. He sensed this and designed a rune to measure its cycles. It appeared the sigil could be disrupted at the cycle's very bottom, when its power was weakest. Don't be cross with him. He wasn't trying to help me. He was merely curious, and, yes, I may have nudged him a little, but you can't keep a curious mind caged. Not one like his."

"I agree. Let him go."

"Now?" He assumed a look of surprise. "But war is coming, my friend."

"Really," I said skeptically.

At that moment, someone slipped down the steps and into the boiler room, scattering bones every which way. I pivoted my sword and staff slightly, and Bree-yark raised his shotgun to chest level.

"Ah, there they are!" Claudius called.

He was leading a group of Sup Squad members. I lowered

my arms and signaled for Bree-yark to do the same. As the group searched the room, their weapon-mounted lights flashing behind tanks and pipes, Trevor came forward.

"We saw the zombies infiltrate the building," he said. "Everything all right?"

"Yeah, for now." I slotted my sword. "We sealed the rift that was animating them, hence the ossuary. How's it looking out there?"

"No more zombies, but take a look at this."

He brought his forearm down so I could see the flex tablet mounted in his armor. It showed a drone feed of Lower Manhattan. My eye was immediately drawn to the flames licking across Upper Bay.

"Is that a fuel spill?" I asked.

"No, it's not. I was hoping you could tell *us*."

Persephone's connection to the underworld had me thinking of the Phlegethon, the fiery river in Hades. "Possibly a result of the bleed-through," I said, wondering what else may have imprinted on Lower Manhattan.

"It's going down now," Trevor said, "but it blazed up so hot, Harbor Patrol said dead fish actually came bubbling to the surface."

> *If ye should fail and war should come*
> *If seas should boil and lands should run…*

I glanced over at Hermes, who raised his eyebrows.

"Maybe it's time we talked," he said.

41

At The Metro, downtown's only twenty-four-hour diner, I sat impatiently across from Hermes at a back booth while he studied the menu.

"I'll have your twin beefburger, cooked rare, and a side of... let's see... how about the onion rings for a change? Oh, and a piece of your strawberry shortcake for dessert. What about you, Everson?"

"Coffee," I said brusquely.

Hermes chuckled. "Like father, like son. His boy hardly eats," he explained to the waitress, "so it falls on me to make up the difference." He patted his lean stomach, drawing a confused look as she took our menus.

"Lovely girl," Hermes remarked when she left.

It was just the two of us. Bree-yark was driving Mae back to the apartment, despite his insistence on coming. He only relented when I entrusted him with returning the scepter to my safe. Claudius had remained behind with the Sup Squad to ensure the integrity of the courthouse's sub-basement. If it had breached once, it could breach again, especially as Persephone continued gathering energy.

I leveled my gaze at Hermes. "Talk."

"I assume you want me to clear up the matter of our little operation."

"For starters."

He was seated casually, his back to the wall, a battered Converse Chuck on the bench seat. "I know you've already made up your mind about me. It's only fair. I failed to show, and it wasn't because I was in any danger. You were my coin flip."

"Coin flip?"

"If you'd found the note behind the painting and reached the park, heads: I would destroy the scepter. But if you failed to reach the park, tails, and I would take more time to consider the matter." He shrugged. "Tails it was."

That sealed it for me: human life meant nothing to him.

"You promised you'd be there," I fumed. "I got the scepter. I kept up my end."

"Yes, and I applaud your commitment. But the promise wasn't binding. Your decision." He affected a sad face. "And keeping my word isn't exactly something I'm known for, is it? There's a reason I'm referred to as *mercurial*." He chuckled at his own joke. "I knew you recovered her scepter, of course. Knew it the moment you seized it with my glove. And that's where my suspicion was confirmed."

"What suspicion?"

"That our opponent isn't Persephone. Not entirely."

I'd come to a similar conclusion, but I returned a straight face.

"Oh, come now, you felt it, too. I'm not privy to every little thought in your head, but I know when you feel something strongly. It hums in those little bits of me." He wriggled his fingers toward my chest, exciting the Hermes particles in my system.

"Stop it," I snapped.

He lowered his hand. "The point is you felt it both times you wielded her scepter. There was a malice at odds with Persephone's nature. It's a product of worship, yes, and that's what threw me. I believed the worship to be for *her*, but no. Worship for another being had penetrated the scepter, corrupting her. It stoked the aspect of Persephone that had been wronged, fanned it into a violent blaze and put her on a path of revenge. But not revenge of a sort that would benefit her. One that would benefit *him*."

Another way? I remembered Persephone seething at me. *There is no other way!*

I collected myself. "Oh, cut the crap. I know you tried to align with her. I know you drew the siphon sigil that's channeling the public's emotions into worship for Cronus. And it's already blowing goddamned holes in our reality."

He looked past me at the waitress, who was standing to one side with a tray. "You'll have to excuse my friend. He's under a great deal of stress, though I suppose I'm partly to blame. So do accept my apology as well."

She distributed our orders with a tight smile and left.

Straightening, Hermes took a large bite of his burger. "Mmm, that's good." He wiped his chin with a napkin and nodded. "I did design the sigil, yes. And I did propose we align. It was a gambit to get close to her, to earn her confidence. But she remained determined to marry Cronus and wage her war against the Olympic order."

That conformed with shadow Budge's version of events.

"It was then that I chose to proceed with the plan to

destroy her scepter," he continued. "But when the moment came, I had second thoughts. I turned it into a coin toss, and, well, you didn't turn up at the park."

Trickster or not, he was filling in all the holes, and that bothered me.

"Destroying the scepter would have taken care of both of them," I pointed out.

"Yes, and bound the two of them together for all time— my beloved Persephone and this... this monstrosity. Not to mention the discord it could seed, even in the cosmos. I couldn't allow that."

"What a saint," I scoffed.

I knew he'd had the Kleftians build his box to attain immortality. I knew he had them killed, as the dryad had told me. But I also knew he'd have an answer for every charge I leveled at him. I could already hear them:

Immortality? What god doesn't aspire to immortality? It's in our nature by our very nature.

Of course I had the Kleftians killed. Being their patron was fun at first, but they got greedy and did dishonorable things in my name. I could no longer allow it.

While the imagined conversation ping-ponged back and forth in my agitated mind, Hermes took another bite of burger. "Mmm, this is truly divine. Are you sure you don't want some? How about one of these?"

I slapped the offered onion ring from his hand.

He watched it fly away. "A simple 'no thank you' would have sufficed."

"Yeah, well, I'm a little goddamned short on etiquette right now. You went back on your word, you left me for dead, and you're using my son. You've given me no reason to believe you, none, much less treat you decently."

"Well, I've explained myself, and that's all I can do. I thought returning your cane would make you more reasonable."

Though I could feel my cane across my thighs, I touched it again to reassure myself. "You know Persephone wants me to destroy you, right?" I said, partly out of anger and partly to gauge his reaction.

"Persephone, no." He paused to lick his fingers. "The other being, yes."

"That doesn't bother you?"

"Why should it? You can't open the box without my consent, not without being destroyed in the process. And I fully intend to give that consent once we free Persephone and dispose of her tormentor."

"So this is a rescue mission now?"

He snapped his fingers and pointed at me. "I knew you'd come around, friend."

"I haven't 'come around' to anything, and I'm not your friend."

"Well, you haven't much time. Less than twenty-four hours by my count." His lips quirked up on the same side as his cocked eyebrow. He knew about my ashes and the bonding potion, making his playfulness all the more infuriating.

"Why did you let me get captured?" I demanded.

"That was rather fortuitous, actually. With all the attention on you, I was able to poke around undetected. And a good thing. When I stepped out to give your son a breather, you slapped that annoying sigil on us, made it so I couldn't use him adequately. Fortunately, he sprang us in the nick of time."

Every time he brought up Alec, I pictured the bonds

biting into his soul more deeply, causing my own hands to draw into fists.

"You haven't asked me who the being is yet," he said.

"I assume you're still talking about Cronus," I said dismissively.

"*Errnnnt.*" He crossed his forearms into an X as he made the buzzer sound. "Care to try again?" He regarded my dead stare and lowered his arms. "All right, I'll tell you. But I want you to check the answer against the evidence you've gathered —evidence I'm not privy to, mind you—and you'll not only see that I'm right, but that I gain nothing from aligning with this being."

I nodded grudgingly. "Go ahead."

He'd pushed the last of his burger into his mouth and held up a finger as he chewed. I sighed through my nose.

"Typhon," he said at last.

I repeated the name, recalling what I knew of him. Half-man, half-serpent, and all monster. By some accounts he sported a hundred serpent heads. By *all* accounts he was the deadliest monster in Greek mythology. When he attacked Mount Olympus, the major gods fled, terrified, until Zeus met him in battle and won—barely. Thanks in part to a thunderbolt delivery by none other than Hermes.

Depending on the author, Typhon was either imprisoned in Tartarus or buried beneath Mount Etna in Sicily. I slapped a hand against the table, causing some coffee to lap over the rim of my untouched mug.

Of course!

Franco had said the scepter was recovered from a quarry north of Catania, which would have been right in the shadow of Mount Etna. Cults to the monster must have sprung up around the mountain. In the millennia that followed, their objects had broken down and their worship for Typhon flowed into the mineral-rich layers of the volcanic mountain's slopes, eventually infiltrating the buried scepter to Persephone.

There were deposits in the scepter—I'd seen them. It explained the human sacrifices at Pergusa as well as the serpent summoned from the lake. It also explained the strange sounds Franco and I had both heard. Typhon was originally a wind god.

Hermes, who was already halfway through his cake watched me closely.

I nodded, the knowledge seeping into my gut like frigid water. Whatever reservations I still held toward Hermes were being replaced by the horror of having to confront a being of Typhon's stature and malice.

"But where does Cronus come in?" was all I could think to stammer.

"I believe there was a battle for dominion over Tartarus, and Typhon emerged victorious. But Persephone, even corrupted, would never have joined forces with him. Have you seen him?" He stuck his tongue out and made a face. "So Typhon put Cronus forward as his front man, a more palatable choice. And once Persephone releases Cronus, Typhon will slither out in his wake and consume him."

"Claiming all of his power," I said in grim understanding.

Meaning there would be no second Titanochamy. Cronus may have been a tyrannical ruler, but Typhon was a destroyer. He would simply wipe everyone and everything off the face of the earth.

"We have Persephone's actual scepter," I said urgently. "By applying the bonding potion, we can destroy them both in the next thirty minutes. I get your concern, but this is too damned important." If recent events at City Hall Park were any indication, the energy buildup in the shadow realm was approaching Typhon-freeing proportions.

But Hermes simply shook his head. "You have your future to worry about, and I have mine. If we destroy the scepter in such a way, that connection between Persephone and Typhon will persist and seep into the cosmos. Hardly the retirement I was looking forward to. But I have a plan." Taking a final bite of cake, he pushed his plate away and leveled his green eyes at me. "One I can't do without you."

"Where have I heard that before?"

"Join forces with me, one last time, and we'll both get what we want. Peace for ourselves and our loved ones."

As his gaze pressed into mine, I considered the Doideag's prophecy. Upper Bay, a tidal estuary of the Atlantic, *had* boiled. And when I'd first looked at the drone feed of City Hall Park, the erupting zombies had made it look as though the land was running. War seemed imminent, but could I trust him?

"Come, Everson," he urged. "What say you?"

42

Ever since confirming Hermes's true nature—an amoral trickster—I'd considered whether I could outmaneuver him. In the end, it was a fool's errand. After all, how did you outmaneuver a divine being who embodied the very essence of trickery? Answer: you couldn't.

But I could still strike a deal.

"I'll only consider joining you under a binding agreement."

"Oh, we're back to this?" He circled his hand playfully. "And what are the terms?"

"If I help you, we'll see the plan through to the end. No backing out this time, no playing me as a *coin flip*. And after we repel Typhon, you'll forfeit your immortality here. You'll allow me to open the box, freeing Alec. And then you, Persephone, and the other beings will head out to the *cosmos*, never to interfere in our world again."

"I've already said I would do as much."

"But keeping your word isn't exactly something you're known for, is it?" I said, throwing his own admission back in his face. "There's a reason you're referred to as *mercurial*. Ha ha," I added flatly.

He grinned. "Well played, Everson, but what are you prepared to give if you fail to carry out your part? And failure would include destroying Persephone's scepter without my say-so, which I don't intend on giving."

The scepter had been my ripcord for if things went sideways and I needed to take out Persephone before she did the same to me. I'd even assured my wife as much. But Hermes was yanking that off the table. On the other hand, he was giving me his guarantee that I could safely open the box when this was over.

"Oh, and remember," he added, "it must be a sacrifice in league with what you're asking of me. Nothing less will suffice."

I held his arrogant gaze. "My life."

He blinked. "You don't say?" He'd been expecting me to lowball him, but I had my reasons for overbidding. He drummed his fingers against his chin in thought, then nodded. "We have a deal, Everson Croft."

He extended his hand. When I shook it, I felt the agreement take hold between us. With each of us pledging our lives, the binding was especially powerful. There was no turning back now. For either of us.

"What's the plan?" I asked.

"Come, let's take a walk."

He sprang up, dropped several bills on the table, and mimed a chef's kiss to the waitress. I caught up to him as he hurried up Bowery. To the south, a halo of spotlights glowed over City Hall Park.

"There's a way to extract Typhon's influence from Persephone's scepter," Hermes said. "But not in the way you're thinking, in a laboratory with potions and unbinding magics. No, no, that would risk destroying her too, and then we're back to the problem of Persephone being stuck to Typhon for all time."

"What does that leave?"

"Convincing Persephone to exorcise him herself."

"I thought you already tried that. Isn't that what your summit at City Hall was about?"

"I tried to persuade her to call off her war against the Olympic order, but that was before I understood the dynamics at work. As I mentioned, I used your time in captivity as a diversion to poke around. Also, the siphon sigil I designed for Persephone wasn't an entirely selfless gift. It's given me some eavesdropping abilities among other things. You met the mayor over there, I understand?"

"Oh, yeah. Budge."

"Typhon is acting through him."

I pulled up in surprise. That explained a lot, including his preternatural ability to persuade. But it didn't explain his nervousness. "Are you sure? He acted like he was having to tiptoe around her."

"As he should." He motioned for me to keep walking. "Typhon's yet to emerge, so he's nowhere close to his full strength. Persephone can still overpower him—and that's exactly what we need her to do. The problem is that the mayor sticks close to her side, coaxing her with his multiplicity of forked tongues. He's charged you with destroying my tablet, not because of any number of lies he may have told you, but because he knows I'm his biggest threat. I delivered Persephone from the darkness once. I can do so again."

"How do you plan to get past her defensive field?"

"That's where you come in. You're friends with the mayor here, yes?"

"I wouldn't say 'friends.'" Especially after the crap he'd pulled with our missing persons task force. "But, yeah, I know him."

"Let's play that to our advantage."

I saw where he was going with this. "You mean send him over?"

"With your potions and my runes, I'll be able to anchor myself to him. And with a little coaching, he'll be able to create that opening I need, the one that will take me straight to Persephone's heart."

As I considered the proposal, Hermes squinted at a set of approaching headlights.

"Ahh, how fortuitous," he said. "I believe this is the good mayor now."

The headlights belonged to an SUV. If it *was* the mayor's, his security detail was probably taking him from his uptown mansion to City Hall to survey the aftermath of the attack. Hermes must have known this, explaining his hurry to bring me to this spot. But I needed no more convincing. I was on board.

Calling light to the opal inset in my cane, I stepped into the street and waved it overhead. The SUV braked hard and idled a half block away. I pictured Budge leaning forward for a better look.

A moment later, my phone buzzed.

"Hi, Mayor," I answered without looking.

"Everson? What the hell are you doing out in the street?"

"Remember that help you offered me the other day?"

He hesitated. "Yeah?"

"I'm calling it in."

43

"Okay, hold on a sec." Budge wiped his cowlick from his shiny brow as he paced another circle around my basement lab. "So what's gonna happen to me here?"

He'd removed his jacket and rolled up his shirt sleeves, but now that it was go time, he was stalling. Hermes and I had spent the last two hours going over everything with him. He knew what to do. I'd also promised that this would square us. He no longer had to worry about me telling the world how he'd fudged the missing persons data and cost his city lives. To his credit, this was still a big ask.

"You'll sleep," I repeated.

"And over there, I'll be me, just another version?"

"That's right."

He peered over at the closed door. His security detail was posted outside, and for a moment I thought he was going to shout for them to take him out of there. But with a final swipe at his cowlick, he nodded and extended a pudgy hand.

"All right," he said, "let's have it."

The tube I passed him held a bonding potion coupled

with a second potion that would buffer him from Typhon's influence. As he regarded the still-steaming tube, he licked his lips nervously. Once again, I thought he was going to back out.

"I'm putting a lot of faith in you, Everson." He downed the potion with a grimace. "God, that's horrible."

"Welcome to my world."

I then passed a stoppered tube to Hermes. It contained a neutralizing potion for him to soak my ashes in, negating the bonding potion. A little insurance in case things didn't go according to plan.

"As good as done," Hermes said, stuffing the tube into the pocket of Alec's gray hoodie.

I nodded, even though I knew how much his word was worth. But our binding agreement would hold him to what mattered most: freeing Alec and removing himself and the rest of the beings from our world.

With a grunt, Budge got down on the floor beside my lab table where I'd arranged a foam sleeping pad. Hermes sat behind him, legs crossed, and placed a rolled-up towel under his head. Budge lay his short arms along his sides, then laced his fingers across his belly before dropping them to his sides again.

"Comfortable?" Hermes asked.

Budge snorted dryly. "Not really, but if you say this is going to save a lot of lives, I'm okay with a little discomfort. Whether there or here, these are New Yorkers we're talking about. My people." But he couldn't stop himself from angling his head toward me. "And we'll be good on everything?"

I gave him a thumbs-up.

The plan was premised on something we'd learned about the actual and shadow realities. If you existed in one and not the other, you traveled back and forth as you were. That was Alec's and my situation. However, if you existed in both, you shifted from one form to the other, as Budge was preparing to do.

He was about to very literally become our inside man, arranging the pivotal meeting between Persephone and Hermes. Of course by agreeing to be bonded, he was accepting that whatever happened to him there would happen to him here, too. Getting killed, for example. Like I said, a big ask.

Budge adjusted his body and swallowed. "All right. I'm ready."

As much of a political animal as he may have been, he was showing some impressive brass. "Good luck, guys," I told them.

Hermes placed his hands on Budge's temples and closed his own eyes. "Be back shortly."

In a flash of green light, he disappeared. Budge went slack, his consciousness gone from my basement and transported to his slimmer, slicker self in the shadow present.

My contribution may have amounted to a couple potions, but I felt like a major stakeholder. By removing Typhon from Persephone's ear, Hermes was confident he could compel her to end the war. As I watched Budge, my original relief at not accompanying them was soon outweighed by the anxiety of not being able to follow what was happening. Everything depended on them getting this right.

A knock sounded at the door.

"Yeah?" I called over a shoulder.

"You have a visitor," one of Budge's bodyguards answered. "Someone named Bree... bark?"

"*Yark.*"

"He's safe," I said.

Before opening the door, I positioned myself to ensure the bodyguards wouldn't be able to see past me to Budge's unconscious body. I waved Bree-yark inside, who was carrying Tabitha over his shoulder for some reason. I nodded at the guard that we were good and quickly closed the door again.

"What's up?" I asked Bree-yark.

"I was tossing and turning," he panted. "Couldn't sleep, so I cooked up some eggs and sausages. The smell roused Tabby, and we got to talking. But the things she started telling me... Oh, boy. I told her to save it for you. I came down here so fast those goons nearly ventilated us."

"Yeah, now may not be the best time." I glanced over at the mayor.

"Nah, you'll wanna hear this." He set Tabitha on the lab table, where she promptly sagged into an orange pile, fast asleep. Bree-yark prodded her. "Tabs, wake up. Tell Everson what you were telling me."

"What?" she moaned irritably.

"Tell Everson what you just told me."

Eyes closed, she smacked her mouth. "Is he here? Oh, never mind, there's his body odor."

That she was well enough to pick up where she'd left off was a blessing, but I was far too preoccupied with Hermes and Budge's mission right now. "If now's not good for you, I can catch you upstairs later," I told her.

"Fine," she sighed. "I'll tell you."

Dangling information was no fun for her when I had no interest in leaping for it. She slitted her eyes open. Realizing she was in my lab, her expression turned to alarm and her gaze shot around the room.

"The whip's packed away," I assured her. "I'm sorry about that, by the way."

She relaxed slightly, but her lips drew into a spiteful scowl. "You mean that angel's sadistic toy?"

"Angel?" I repeated.

"Why do you think he was so obsessed with destroying me?"

"You've mentioned your bloodline a couple times," Bree-yark stepped in. "Being descended from a big time saint and all that, so I thought you'd wanna hear this. I mean, what would an angel be attacking *you* for? Tabs I can understand. No offense," he told her. "Being related to a demon and everything, you know?"

"Yes, Everson reminds me daily," she muttered.

"But saints and angels are supposed to be on the same team, right?" Bree-yark said over her. "What kind of an angel goes around attacking the descendant of a saint? Especially someone like you, doin' all this righteous stuff all the time?"

"Certain angels might," I said faintly. "But they no longer exist."

The Street Keeper tattoo was taking shape in my mind's eye: a skull wreathed in angel wings. Was that the answer? An Avenging Angel?

Had one returned to the shadow realm and regarded magic-use as an aberration on par with infernal activity? That would explain the absence of practitioners. An Avenging Angel was one of the few beings who could manage that kind of annihilation, even taking out Lich, the First Saint turned Death Mage.

With a chill I recalled the looming figure I'd seen upon opening the whip's protection.

But how would an Avenging Angel even have come into

the world over there? According to the stories, they were the Creator's first response to the nine elemental demons. But they proved too violent. Fearful the Angels would devolve into demons themselves, the Creator swapped them for the kinder and wiser First Saints, the antitheses of the demons' sins. But now that I thought about it, the stories never said exactly what became of the Angels.

"Can you describe him?" I asked Tabitha.

"Besides being a freakish zealot? I'm sorry, but I was too busy running for my life to pick out a more defining feature. I didn't realize I'd be sitting through a fucking interrogation when I got back."

And if it *was* an Avenging Angel, what would that mean for Alec?

"Well, how did you manage to get away?" I pressed. "Did you fight?"

"See what I mean?" she said to Bree-yark. "No, I'm not dumb enough to fight an angel. But I haven't forgotten how to mist. A power you denied me when you bonded me to this distended sac of hair. "

"It wasn't distended when I bonded you to it," I reminded her.

"So I ran," she said tiredly, "turned to mist, ran some more, turned to mist again, and so on and so forth. All the time he was chasing me through this horrific heaven-scape, trying to shock the literal hell out of me. And when I finally escaped, there *you* were, taking advantage of my defenseless body. I'm not sure which was worse."

"That was CPR," I said thinly.

She turned to Bree-yark. "You were there. What did it look like to you?"

"Well, ah, you know..." He gave an embarrassed chuckle. "I couldn't really see so well..."

Friends with Tabitha, Bree-yark didn't want to have to choose sides. I nodded at him that it was all right. The most important thing was that my stimulant, Claudius's salve, and Tabitha's survival instincts had done their jobs.

"I'm just glad you're back," I told her. "Why don't we talk about this some more later."

I was still monitoring the mayor, but my gaze was increasingly shifting toward my safe. If the whip was being powered by an Avenging Angel, it no longer felt secure in my reality, much less my lab space, warded or not. Twice now the whip had nearly killed me. The third time it could well succeed.

Bree-yark must have seen the growing anxiety on my face. "C'mon, Tabs, let me take you back upstairs. Everson needs to finish his work down here. How's it going, by the way?"

I blew out a shaky breath. "I should know soon. Thanks for telling me. Both of you."

Bree-yark clapped my arm as he lifted Tabitha over his shoulder. With his goblin strength, he made it look easy. Tabitha only peered at me blandly before perching her head on his thick neck and murmuring something about getting out of there before I set another one of my angels on her.

Locking the door behind them, I turned back to the mayor. His foot jerked.

I walked over and knelt beside him. Both his arms twitched and his head spasmed to the side.

"Budge?" I asked.

He murmured in a high, straining voice.

Heart galloping in my chest, I shook him, but this wasn't someone having a bad dream. He was reacting to whatever was happening to him in the shadow realm. I mentally cycled through my invocations, spells, and potions, but if I canceled out the bonding, he would become stuck over there.

He murmured again, more forcefully this time.

His arms and legs began to bounce. His head shook from side to side. I pressed my hands to his chest. His heart was going a mile a minute. And now blood began bubbling from the corner of his mouth.

"Budge!" I called, shaking him again.

The door rattled with pounding. "You all right in there, Mayor?" a bodyguard called.

"C'mon, goddammit," I whispered next to Budge's ear. "Don't you die on me, man. This is too important."

Plus, I didn't want to have to explain the mayor's lifeless body to his security.

Budge's head arced back and he began to choke, coughing out more blood. I stripped off my belt. Working it into his convulsing jaw, I pressed his tongue to the floor of his mouth, then stepped on the belt on either side of his head.

More hammering on the door. "Open up!"

Stretching a hand toward my cane, I called, "*Recuperare!*"

As it slapped into my palm, I brought the opal end around to his face, uttering words of healing. Blood was running down the belt now and puddling near my shoes. Behind his closed eyelids, his eyes beat madly.

But I remained focused on the healing incantation until a cocoon of gauzy light took shape around him. My magic wouldn't return him from the shadow present, but it could slow the damage—here as well as there.

Just need to keep him alive until he's out of danger.

Another burst of blood erupted around the belt.

"C'mon, Budge," I urged. "Stick with me, man."

What in the hell was going on over there? Kicks were landing against the door now.

Following his next convulsion, Budge let out a long, sputtering breath and slumped over onto his side.

Behind me, the door flew open.

44

The mayor's bodyguards burst into the basement. Leading with service pistols, the two men looked from me to Budge's laid out body. My belt still bisected the mayor's mouth while a ropey current of blood and saliva slid into a spreading pool on the floor. And I was still standing over him.

"Get back!" the lead guard shouted.

In shock, I stepped away, leaving a bloody trail of shoe prints, while the other guard rushed up to Budge. The first one held me at gunpoint.

"Drop the cane!"

"This isn't what it looks like."

"He's not breathing," the second guard said. He called into his earpiece for emergency services as he started into chest compressions.

"Drop it!" the first guard shouted, pistol at eye level. "Now!"

I brought the cane around slowly, uttering a Word for protection. But the moisture had been sucked from my mouth, replaced by the bitter taste of chalk. I smacked and tried again, but this wasn't the effect of adrenaline. My tongue simply wasn't responding. I had no way to shape the sounds.

I only realized I'd dropped my cane when it clattered to the floor. My fingers had contorted and gone numb, and my hand looked pallid, drained of blood.

"Now turn around!"

I tried to kneel for my cane, but my legs wouldn't respond. The guard angled his head in question, then withdrew it in revolt. Something was happening to my face, but like with my hands, I couldn't feel anything. My scalp suddenly itched like mad, though. I dragged a hand through my hair and looked at my fingers. Chunks of hair were snagged under the pale nails, their roots giant clots of ash.

No, no, no!

Ignoring the guard, I managed to get a hand on my cane.

"Hey! Back away!" he ordered, recovering from his revulsion.

Dust scattered as I worked the cane around, angling it toward my body. But when I attempted words of healing, only dry clicks emerged. When I tried again, I inhaled my own ashes and fell into a fit of hacking. I could barely even summon breaths now. My lungs felt as if they were dried out and fissuring.

The gig was clearly up in the shadow realm. I was being bonded to my cremated remains.

The guard continued to shout commands, jabbing his pistol for emphasis, but my hearing was muffled. In my right leg, something cracked like a chunk of cinder—felt more than heard—and I collapsed, dropping the cane and landing against the wall. A frightening amount of dust scattered around me upon impact.

Nothing hurt, though. That was because I no longer had nerve endings to feel with.

The guard stepped forward and swept the cane away with his foot. Beyond him, the second guard was still pumping the mayor's inert body with chest compressions. But now my vision was clouding over. And soon Budge, his two body-guards, and the entire room became a jumble of fading colors.

My thoughts deadened, my brain no longer able to wrap around what was happening.

I was in danger, mortal danger, but my panic had dulled, becoming something soft and scattered. I still had one card left to play, though. Closing my eyes, I called to the power of the collective.

Whatever you've got, give it to me...

Like a slowing reel, time seemed to crawl, then stop. And now it eased into reverse.

The room sharpened by degrees. My hearing returned. I watched my hand, which had begun to crack and dust over like an arid landscape, smooth and fill with color again. Pins and needles erupted throughout me as my nerves came back to life. Somehow, someway, the bonding potion was losing its grip, but not from the power of the collective. There hadn't been the energy dump I'd felt the last time.

I drew a shallow breath and coughed. I coughed again, clearing more of my lungs.

The guard was no longer jabbing his gun at my face. He'd joined his partner, and they were kneeling on either side of Budge—who was sitting up!

One of them pulled Alec's bed over so they could lean him against it.

"I'm all right," the mayor rasped, drawing a forearm across his mouth.

With a hand that worked now, I scratched my head. Only a few strands came away, no ash. When I struggled to stand, a sharp pain speared my thigh. I could feel again—hallelujah! —but I couldn't stand. With a grunt, I slid back down the wall to the floor. I felt along my thigh until the pain returned.

That crack earlier... Must've snapped my femur.

Able to shape sounds again, I retrieved my cane and uttered words of healing. As light swelled around my thigh and endorphins dumped into my system, I slumped, exhausted from my trip to near cremation and back.

A hand gripped my shoulder.

I looked over to find Alec peering down at me. No, Hermes, but his eyes were darker and more serious than I'd ever seen them.

"We hit a snag," he said.

The paramedics arrived within minutes and surrounded Budge. I was more of an afterthought. A young woman who appeared to be in training asked me a few questions while manhandling my leg. The fracture wasn't displaced, thankfully. But though my healing magic was dulling the pain and repairing the surrounding tissue, the fusion of bone would take longer. She left to retrieve a brace.

"What in the hell happened?" I whispered to Hermes.

He looked up, eyes sharpening through his brooding thoughts. "Oh, don't worry about them." He gestured to the paramedics and mayor's security detail. "I've cast an enchantment. Whatever they overhear will sound like idle conversation, entirely forgettable. And you're no longer under suspicion for the mayor's state of health."

"Guys, I'm all right," I heard him insisting, but his voice sounded hoarse and garbled.

Hermes glanced over at him. "Getting there was a cinch. Anchored to the mayor, I arrived in a suite he's been using to stay close to Persephone. Your mayor infused his counterpart's body, I materialized beside him, and everything was going to plan. Persephone sensed me, naturally. She came rushing in, but your mayor talked her down. He was exceptional in his role, in fact. And without Typhon to stoke her hate, I convinced sweet Persephone to meet cordially. The three of us adjourned to her back room, where she safeguards her portal to Hades. Your ashes, as well."

I automatically rubbed my arm to ensure it was no longer turning to dust.

"I made my pitch," he said. "I explained how Typhon was manipulating her. And she heard me, Everson! I could see it in those exquisite eyes you and I so love—I was getting through! But Typhon heard me, too, and he launched into a spectacular attack to reclaim his hold over the mayor."

With a wince, I remembered Budge's convulsing body, the blood pouring from his mouth.

"At the same time he ordered Persephone to bond you to your ashes. And just like that, the understanding I'd built up shattered in her eyes, revealing the depths of their emptiness. She became dread Persephone again, and I her enemy. I struggled with her for the urn, but the mayor was getting absolutely butchered. Typhon would have ensured the mayor's shadow survived, even if it meant resorting to necromancy, but to keep his vessel from being infiltrated, he intended to kill the mayor here."

"I thought he succeeded," I said shakily.

"Yes, I hit the mayor with a paralysis charm to halt the assault, but it meant relinquishing control of the urn. And within moments, you were joining your ashes. Following another pitched battle, I managed to douse your remains, undoing the bonding. But then her Iron Guard were at the door, undead creatures were pouring from her well, and Typhon was overcoming my charm. Using my speed, I drew a healing rune on the mayor's chest, seized his consciousness, and transported us both back here."

"Geez."

"It was no easy feat," he confirmed.

Across the room, the paramedics were still working on Budge. I shook my head. "I can't believe my potion for protecting him crapped out like that. I'm sorry. I feel like I let you both down."

"No, that falls on me. Typhon was much more powerful than I anticipated. He would have overcome any such magic eventually."

With my broken leg extended out in front of me, I looked over at Hermes with a sinking feeling. "Where does that leave us?"

"In a bind, my friend. Persephone remains under Typhon's thrall, and they've wrested away control of my siphon sigil. It's dumping energy into the courthouse temple like Edessa Falls, and the portal to Tartarus is creaking open. Meanwhile, Persephone has extended her defensive field well beyond their original boundaries. And she's sure to have secured the mayor as well. There will be no riding him in again."

"What's powering her field?" That was essential info if we were to take another crack, but Hermes only shrugged, his anguish too deep for logistics. With a sigh, he showed me his upturned hands.

"I had her, Everson. She was as near to me as I am to you. I could feel the moment of delivery. So closely did it resonate with our escape from Hades, I was trembling, I tell you. And then..." He balled his hands into helpless fists. "I failed. Failed to deliver her from that wretched darkness."

As tears ran down the god's face, I felt my own despair deepening.

So far, nothing had worked out as planned. Tartarus was opening. Typhon was nearing victory. And we were drawing ever closer to the point when Hermes would become inextricably fused to Alec.

The paramedic returned with my brace and secured it to my leg. It would keep the bone from shifting, she said, but I wouldn't be able to bend the knee. In fact, I was to keep my weight off the leg entirely until it had been X-rayed.

"Do you have a way to get to a hospital, or do you need an ambulance?" she asked.

I felt like laugh-crying. The leg was the absolute least of my worries. But as I looked at Hermes's distraught face, I caught a glimpse of my son. Just the night before, I'd told him that magic-using wasn't all spells and invocations. It was trusting that everything we'd done would sink into that magical collective and reemerge as the right solution at the right time. That was true magic.

And the key is our faith.

As I repeated the mantra, a charge caught in my bloodstream and spread throughout my system like electricity, making my hair stand on end. I wrapped an arm around Hermes's neck and kissed his temple firmly.

He looked back at me in confusion.

"We're not going to the hospital," I told the paramedic. "Here, help me up."

She was hesitant, but my wizard's voice compelled her. With her assisting me under one arm and Hermes the other, I rose to my feet. Leaning on my cane, I took a tentative hop-step. A fresh spear shot through my thigh, but I remained upright. I thanked the paramedic and assured her I was all right.

"We're going back to the shadow realm," I told Hermes.

He released a forlorn sigh. "To do what? They'll know we're coming."

"Your love for Persephone... It's understandable, and noble, but it's limiting you. Do you really want to deliver her? Then let me call the shots."

Even as I spoke, pieces were assembling themselves in my mind. There was a way to get Typhon out of the picture, close the portal to Tartarus, and rescue Persephone, and we had the necessary pieces.

Almost...

Across the room, the medics were loading Budge onto a gurney. The extendable legs came up, and they rolled him toward the door, his security detail in tow.

"Wait, hold up," I called, hop-stepping toward them.

Budge spied me through a gap in his entourage. His hair was mussed, and he still had blood smeared across both cheeks.

"Is that Everson?" He pulled down his oxygen mask.

"How are you feeling?" I asked as he rolled to a stop.

"Like I just went twelve rounds in the Garden with the heavyweight champ." He snuffled a laugh. "But these guys say I'm gonna be all right. Just need to spend a day or so in the hospital."

As I shouldered between the paramedics, they looked on dumbly, thanks to Hermes's enchantment.

"I understand you did really well over there," I said.

"Did the best I could. Hey, I was serious about wanting to help out."

"I need to ask you something. When you were in your counterpart's body, did you pick up any thoughts?"

"I was mostly impressed with how damned trim I felt. Boy, that was something. But, yeah, a few thoughts. Background noise, mostly."

"Think for a minute. Persephone has a mystical network of some kind that she uses to power her soldiers and defenses." I was recalling my visit to the barracks, picturing the blocks the Iron Guard stood on, the ports where they inserted their weapons. "There has to be a hub or central node, something to power it."

His exhausted face furrowed in thought, then he shook his head. "Gee, Everson, I'm sorry..." But then he squinted, a light seeming to flicker behind his eyes. "Wait a sec. There's an old bunker behind City Hall—we've got it here, too, for the emergency utilities. But during the construction of all the new buildings over there, they installed something in that bunker and fortified the crap out of it."

"A lodestone, most likely," Hermes said softly. "They're abundant in Hades."

"I remember, because we buried copper cables all over the place, and it wasn't easy procuring that copper." Budge gave me a knowing look, then hesitated. "Or I guess *he* remembers," he said of his shadow, suddenly confused.

But I nodded fervently. That had to be it.

The paramedics shifted now, anxious to get the mayor to the hospital.

"Real quick," I said. "Did you pick up anything else that could be important?"

Budge thought some more, then shook his head apologetically. "Only that the guy who was beating up my insides is scared shitless of Zeus."

That made sense. Zeus had been the one who'd reduced Typhon to "a maimed wreck" when he'd tried to claim Olympus. Unfortunately, we didn't have a version of Zeus at our beck and call. Still, something suggested the info could be important.

I gripped his hand. "Thank you, Mayor."

He squeezed mine back and clapped it with his other one. "I owed you, buddy. More than that, I owed my city."

"You're even on both counts."

That made him smile. I moved back as the team wheeled him out into the corridor. The basement unit fell silent again, but not for long. I hopped over to my lab area and began pulling down ingredients.

Hermes's drying eyes glimmered with interest. "So, what's this grand plan?"

"It involves a few steps, but we're definitely going to need your army."

45

Bree-yark drove Hermes and me to Rizo's Storage. We pulled up in front just as the sky was beginning to pale.

"Want me to wait out here?" Bree-yark asked.

"Actually, I have an important job for you inside," I said.

"Oh, yeah?" He drew the brake with gusto, and the three of us got out.

From the back of the Hummer, we unloaded several containers and duffel bags, Bree-yark having to carry the bulk of them on account of my leg. After completing my prep work in the wee hours, I'd gone upstairs to say goodbye to Ricki. It was a quiet goodbye, more holding than talking. I told her I'd be back soon.

Now I limped on my leg brace after Hermes. The bone had healed enough that I'd begun experimenting with a little weight on it. Still hurt like the dickens, though. Hermes led the way through the building's steel doors, up the ramp, and toward the storage unit he'd enchanted for his draftees.

As he released the door with a flick of his fingers, I prepared myself for the space to be trashed and empty. After all, my introduction to the beings was a knock-down, drag-out that had spilled into the city.

The suite *was* disorganized, but Phrixus the centaur was splayed across a couch, wine bottles scattered around him. Some snores sounded from the surrounding bedrooms, indicating the others were here as well.

"I'll rouse them," Hermes said.

"Wait, let's take care of the scepter first," I said, limping toward the library.

"Are you sure this magic won't harm her?" he asked for the tenth time as he followed anxiously.

"It's not magic," I reiterated. "Not the kind I normally practice, anyway."

From one of the containers I pulled out two cauldrons and set them on the library's walnut reading table. Into one, I poured the bonding potion I'd prepped back in my lab. *That* was magic. But the solvents I lined up beside the other cauldron were purely chemical.

Consulting a book I'd earmarked, I decanted the solvents into the cauldron in the appropriate amounts.

"The chemical combination will soften the minerals attached to the scepter while sparing the precious metals," I explained. "Collectors do it all the time. The worship for Typhon is in those minerals, the worship for Persephone in the metals. If we can weaken Typhon's influence, we'll have a much better shot at recovering her. It'll take time, though."

"I'm afraid there isn't much," Hermes lamented.

"Which is why we're going to multitask. But first things first."

I donned a rubber glove I'd enspelled and a pair of lab goggles. Hermes watched nervously as I drew out the scepter and placed it in the bonding potion, rotating it until it was thoroughly coated. Then, with a whispered incantation, I bonded the scepter to its shadow, the metal resonating slightly as the connection took hold.

"A little fire?" I prompted Hermes.

He cupped his hands together, and a brazier of green flames burst into the air above them. I passed the scepter through it, baking the bonding potion into the metal, making them inseparable for the next step.

But Hermes caught my wrist. "You're absolutely certain."

"I'm still bound to our agreement," I reminded him. "If this destroys the scepter, I forfeit my life."

As he considered that, I saw just how thoroughly his fixation on Persephone had limited him, limited us. Though he exceeded me in power, he was obligated to the stories that formed him, making him rigid, slow to adapt. Case in point, he'd lost Persephone to Hades, and now a part of him was resigned to losing her to Typhon. Or just losing her, period. It was up to my agency and faith to rewrite that script.

"This is your chance to deliver her," I urged.

At last he nodded and released my arm. "Just go carefully."

I slipped the scepter into the cauldron of solvents and stirred it several times.

"Bree-yark, I'm going to need you to do this every fifteen minutes. It will help slough off the minerals as they soften."

"I'd rather be fighting," he muttered. "But I'll just have to imagine punching Typhon in the mouth every time I stir this thing."

"Be sure to wear the glove. The solvents are corrosive. More importantly, it will protect you from the scepter's magic."

He made a surly face, as though neither one was a match

for his tough goblin constitution, but he donned the glove anyway. I transferred the goggles from my head to his. As he took over, Hermes watched closely, a knuckle pressed to his lips, as though the scepter might dissolve at any moment.

I squeezed his shoulder. "It's time to rally the troops."

He managed to drag his eyes from the cauldron. "Yes, I'll get them up."

Several minutes later, everyone was standing around the dining room table, where I'd placed my holographic model of the city. Phrixus looked hung over, Priapus, the dwarf-sized god with the tented pants, grumbled irritably, and Madge the Amazon had the worst case of bedhead I'd ever seen, but bound by their agreement with Hermes, no one complained. The two nymphs, Comet and Ivy, with their white and green pixie cuts, looked on with school-girl attentiveness. Koalemos, the god of stupidity, simply looked on.

Arimanius, aka Mr. Funny, took the spot beside me.

"How you doing?" I asked him. "Everything going alright?"

He let out a beleaguered sigh. "I'm here."

Hermes moved to the head of the table and clapped his hands sharply. "Everson is going to lay out the plan, and I want everyone to listen. I needn't remind you that you've pledged yourselves to the cause."

"I'll give you the overview first," I said, "and then we'll get into the specifics."

As I looked around, I was acutely aware that the Doideag's prophecy had called for allies "eleven and one." The One, I'd decided, was magic. That indivisible, unifying power that permeated and bonded all things. I would act as its channel by dint of my bloodline: "Be not afraid of thine own blood."

Zeus had been both a One and a member of the Twelve, and so it would be with us. Still, we were short three. And as these were all the beings Hermes had been able to gather, they were the only ones he could transport to the shadow realm. I would just need to lean that much harder into my faith.

We'll get our twelve, I told myself.

And the "accept your death" part? The true meaning would reveal itself if and when it mattered. I wasn't going to run from it.

"All right, the operation I've drawn up has four main objectives. First, taking out this power source." I zoomed the hologram onto the city hall building and the lid of the cement bunker that held the lodestone. "That will cripple Persephone's Iron Guard and kill her defensive field—essential for everything that follows. The challenge is that the power source is *inside* the defensive field, but more on that later."

I centered the hologram over the larger building just north of City Hall.

"The second objective is the courthouse. This rotunda, specifically. You can't see it here, but the pattern in the skylight has been configured to channel energy into twisting open a portal to Tartarus. Once the defensive field is down, Hermes will alter the design to reverse the twist, sealing the portal."

At mention of Tartarus, a few concerned mutters went around the table.

"While he's doing that, we'll pursue the third objective," I said over them. "Accessing Persephone's inner chamber. There, we'll neutralize the mayor and deny Persephone use of her portal to Hades."

Hopefully enough of Typhon's influence will have sloughed off the scepter by that point. Catching myself, I truncated the thought to simply: *Enough of Typhon's influence will have sloughed off by that point.*

"Once she's isolated, the final objective will fall back on Hermes. Delivering Persephone from her second stint in darkness."

Passion rekindled inside Hermes's eyes. The very reaction I'd been gunning for.

"And if we are successful," he said, "you will all be welcome to our home on Olympus!"

The gracious announcement drew loud cheers from Madge the Amazon, Phrixus the centaur, and both nymphs. Koalemos looked on stupidly and Mr. Funny stared glumly at the hologram, which was to be expected. Just so long as they carried out the roles I had in mind for them. Priapus peered around before raising a tentative hand.

"Um, even me?" he asked.

Hermes smiled at the god who'd been denied entrance to Olympus for his ugliness. "Even you, my friend."

Priapus grunted a laugh, then broke into a toothy grin.

"But listen to Everson now," Hermes said sharply. "If we're to get what we all desire, we must do exactly as he prescribes."

46

It was still early when a Sup Squad personnel carrier dropped us off at a brick building in SoHo. Using subtle magic, Hermes broke into the street-level clothing business. He waved for everyone to join him in the back beside a summer fashion display.

"Come, gather in quickly," he urged. "We haven't much time."

Moments later, we were flipping into the shadow realm, the same building now a burned-out shell.

Hermes wasted no time establishing a negative space to forestall detection. He then went to work drawing communication runes behind each being's ear. I pulled a clutch of amulets from my satchel and followed him, draping an amulet over each being's neck, additional protection against the Iron Guard's specialized weapons. When I finished, I leaned my head to the side for Hermes to render a rune behind my left ear.

"Your plan is brilliant," he whispered. "It's going to work."

"Let's just take it one step at a time," I cautioned, but I felt good about our prospects, too. Partly from the novel resources the mythic beings provided, but more from a growing confidence in my magic.

Hermes's completed rune hummed briefly, resonating in the hollows of my ear. He patted my back eagerly as he stepped away to address the group. "To use the communication runes, simply concentrate on a teammate and speak naturally. Your voice will sound in their ear. To speak to the group, think of everyone."

"*Like this?*" Priapus boomed.

I grimaced as his voice blasted my eardrum, complete with feedback. Priapus roared with laughter as the others complained loudly. Madge stalked toward him, threatening to punch his copper phallus out his backside, but Hermes stepped between them and leveled his gaze at Priapus.

"*Don't* do that again," he warned.

Realizing he was jeopardizing his invitation to Olympus, Priapus's smile staggered. "Oh, uh, sorry."

I turned to Arimanius. "Are you ready?"

"I suppose," he sighed, backing away from us.

He closed his eyes and raised his arms. Shadowy magic seemed to detonate from his core, ruffling his slovenly suit jacket and permeating the walls around us in a thin, pulsating wave. He was putting out a call.

We didn't have long to wait for the first squeaking answers.

Rats. Lots of them and arriving from every direction. Some were already in the building. They emerged from piles of cinders and blackened bricks, filthy whiskers twitching eagerly as they scampered up to the god of darkness and vermin.

Soon trickles and then rivers of them arrived from

outside, crawling through the empty windows. I winced. You always knew there were rats in the city, but you never wanted to see just how many. The ones here looked scrawnier than those in the actual present—sicker, too. Boils bulged from their sides, while fluid seeped from the corners of their eyes, matting their fur.

"Gnarly," Koalemos guffawed.

Before long, Arimanius was surrounded by hundreds of the rats, many of them perched on their hind legs, awaiting his command. It was as remarkable as it was revolting, and entirely my idea.

Activating a stealth potion, I emptied the tube into a rain puddle in the middle of the cement foundation.

Arimanius mouthed something, then waved his hands in a scattering motion. And scatter the rats did. I just managed to limp aside before they arrived at the puddle. They lapped the stealth potion with pale tongues, then poured out the back of the building like the Hudson River. More vermin arrived, all following the same protocol, as though Arimanius had inscribed the instructions into the air.

I kept the puddle spiked with potion, hobbling this way and that to prevent the rats from scrambling over my shoes. Finally, the new arrivals slowed to a thin but steady stream.

By that point thousands had passed through our staging area, and I imagined the first rats arriving at the Canal Street checkpoint. Cloaked by my stealth potion, they would wriggle between the cement barricades, the Iron Guard none the wiser, and continue their journey south.

I was betting that Persephone's defensive field wasn't cali-brated for rats. They were too small, too prevalent in the city —and thus the ideal candidates to infiltrate her stronghold and chew into the copper conduits Budge had seen in his shadow's thoughts.

"They're getting through," Arimanius announced in a faraway voice, his graveyard eyes partly rolled back.

Hermes arrived beside me. "No alarms raised, either. I should depart now."

"Be careful." I meant it as much for my son as the god. "Take care of him."

In the dim space, Hermes's eyes seemed to dance. "The lad will be fine. I'll meet you at City Hall, yes?"

"*I'll* be there," I said, unable to forget the last time we'd planned to meet somewhere.

Hermes seized my hand, the forceful contact humming with the power of our bargain, and drew himself close. "As will I."

I gave his hand a final warning squeeze before releasing it. "Good luck, then."

He left my side and leapt onto a windowsill. "Goodbye, all," he announced. "Though I'll see you soon enough. Wait for my word, then off to battle you go! Fight, fight, fight! For the glory of Olympus and your place among its temples and banquet halls!" He opened his hand in a sweeping farewell.

The beings cheered and pumped their fists, all save Arimanius and Koalemos, the latter chuckling in wonder at the sudden enthusiasm in the room. With a parting smile, Hermes jumped from the sill and out into the city, where he would soon become visible to Persephone. That was the point. With his superior speed, he would lead the Iron Guard on a chase that would at least thin the way for our assault.

Right now, though, everything depended on our rat army.

As the vermin neared City Hall, I reviewed the game plan with the others, going point by point so there could be no misunderstandings. I then turned to Koalemos, who understood absolutely none of what I'd just said. "Stick close to me," I told him.

"You've got it, bud."

Stupid though he may have been, he was powerful—a lesson I'd learned during our contest—and I had a specific job in mind for him.

But now came the waiting. I hobbled circles around the burned-out space, testing my leg and pushing more power into the healing. The sharpness had dulled to a throbbing ache, but my biggest problem was the brace. It was in my way. I tested it with the straps loose, then took it off altogether. More painful without the support, but I was more mobile. I just hoped it wouldn't come back to bite me.

While we waited, Madge performed pullups from an exposed beam while bicycling her massive legs. Phrixus kept pawing for his wineskin, which Hermes had denied him before we'd left. Priapus and Koalemos sat in a ring with the two nymphs, playing a rhyming game, while Arimanius remained standing, communicating with his rat horde. I was anxious to ask him about their progress, but I didn't dare break his concentration, not with his history of despondence and sobbing fits.

At last, a humming picked up in my ear followed by Hermes's voice.

"*The field is weakening,*" he proclaimed. "*Go now and take out the lodestone!*"

Madge dropped from the beam with a roar, but before she and Phrixus could lead the charge, I reminded the centaur that I needed a lift. He pulled up grudgingly and knelt for me to climb aboard. When I struggled with my leg, Madge hoisted me as though I were a three-year-old, placing me on his broad back. As Phrixus rose again, I wrapped a hand around his leather belt and adjusted my grip on my cane.

"Stay in formation," I reminded everyone.

Phrixus led the way out onto Grand Street, the motion of his back surprisingly smooth. Madge strode beside him, a spear ready in her grip. The nymphs flanked us in a hover, while the minor gods of darkness, fertility, and stupidity jogged in our wake. The morning was overcast, the sky a sooty gray. A few rats scurried past—latecomers to the show.

As we approached Broadway, I called power to my mental prism.

And then we were on the main thoroughfare. Phrixus took a sharp right and picked up his speed. Madge broke into a loping run. Ahead, several Iron Guard soldiers stood ready at a checkpoint, but we had the advantage of surprise. I aimed my cane past Phrixus's torso, steadying the jostling tip on the center of their pack.

"*Forza Dura!*" I shouted.

Hermes had rendered a fresh rune on my torso, one I could use to gather his magic, overcoming the limitation of the realm's shadowy energy. And, boy, did it ever overcome. The force that shot from my cane felt like a cannonball, knocking over a parked military vehicle and sending the five guards flying.

Above me, a long bow materialized in Phrixus's hand. From a quiver on his back, he nocked and released arrows in swift succession. Sober, the centaur's aim was exceptional. He porcupined two guards before they'd even landed.

Madge heaved a spear that caught a third guard in the stomach. It knocked him around in a spray of stony flesh, nearly cleaving him in half. Comet sent bright blasts from her tiny hands, igniting another guard in ethereal flames, while Ivy summoned a mass of leafy tendrils to swallow the final one.

Hermes's promise of Olympus had galvanized them, helping to vanquish any doubts I'd had about this team.

"Keep going!" I shouted as we approached the cleared checkpoint.

I invoked a glimmering shield around us and hunkered low as we barreled toward the opening between barricades. Had the rats weakened Persephone's expanded field enough? According to Hermes, the field had been calibrated for him and nothing short of its complete demise would allow him to pass.

But what about the rest of the beings? What about me?

As we passed into the government sector, I experienced a sick, stomach-folding sensation, worse than when I'd entered City Hall Park disguised as an Iron Guard soldier. That was because I wasn't disguised this time, and I was freely channeling Hermes's magic.

But Phrixus didn't break stride, and Madge and the nymphs appeared unaffected. Behind us, the gods were largely keeping up, though Priapus was having to yank the god of stupidity by the sleeve of his Baja hoodie to keep him on course. Soon enough, though, they were all through.

I nodded to myself. *Yes!*

That was why Hermes had stashed them in the actual present, I realized as my amulet mitigated the lingering effects of the field. He wasn't just playing keep-away—he'd made it so Persephone couldn't plan for them. Much as was the case with the beings themselves, I hadn't given Hermes enough credit.

But it was way too early to celebrate.

Though the street ahead was clear, it was still nine blocks

to City Hall. And though we'd gotten past Persephone's field unscathed, we were now on her radar. Hermes confirmed this a moment later.

"*I've been leading a grand and growing parade,*" he radioed through his rune, "*but they're starting to break away.*"

"How long before they reach us?" I asked.

"*Oh, you know I'm terrible with time. About ten minutes?*"

Damn, that was going to be cutting it close. But the more copper the rats chewed through, the longer it would take for the Iron Guard to recharge, if they'd be able to recharge at all —and it sounded as if Hermes had given the group a good workout.

"Arimanius," I called behind me. "Can you get the rats to work faster?"

The god shook his head with a sharp wince. "The holes must be giving them away. They're getting slaughtered." He winced again, his connection to the vermin—and their demise—registering somewhere inside him.

That meant *we* needed to pick up the pace.

I gave the order and redoubled my grip on Phrixus's belt. As we crossed Worth Street, I spotted a unit of soldiers and vehicles coming in from the east. I reinforced my shield as preternatural rounds arrived from blocks away, impacting my protection in thumping red bursts. We cut over to Church Street and paralleled Broadway, putting another row of buildings between us. At Murray Street, we cut left again and were soon closing in on the final barricade, the one around City Hall Park.

Beyond the entrance, the grounds were packed with Iron Guard. Far more than I'd anticipated.

47

"Keep straight!" I shouted to Phrixus.

The soldiers manning the entrance to the cement barricade had begun firing, their preternatural rounds thumping and splatting against my protection in a growing storm. But the soldiers beyond were sweeping the grounds, addressing the more imminent threat—the rat infestation.

As Phrixus picked up his gallop, I spoke to Arimanius through the rune. "Forget the cables," I told him. "Turn the rats on the soldiers."

He nodded wearily, and within moments the operation beyond the gate turned into mass confusion as soldiers struggled to knock the invisible vermin from their legs and bodies with rods and rifle barrels.

The more disorder we can sow, the better.

With the entrance drawing closer, I shaped my shield into a wedge. "Get ready to hit them with everything you've got," I told the team. "Here, Madge." I drew several lightning grenades from my pocket and tossed each one to the

Amazon, who caught them deftly and clutched them in her left hand.

Nearly to the entrance, I shouted, "*Respingere!*"

I shoved our wedge-shaped protection forward an instant before it detonated, blowing the Iron Guard soldiers off to both sides and even shifting the cement barricades several feet. With our shield dispersed, Phrixus resumed sending arrows through soldiers as he kicked and trampled over others.

And then we were inside. City Hall loomed ahead, while the larger courthouse building stood off to our left. The construction teams had cleared out, suggesting they'd completed at least the initial phase of work.

I could see the city's chaotic energy warping the air around the courthouse's skylight. A coagulating mass of anger, fear, righteousness, and indignation. It was being funneled through the rotunda and down to the receiving rune, where the portal to Tartarus was slowly turning open. And it felt considerably more powerful than the last time. A constant wind-like whistle permeated the air.

"Now, Madge!" I called through our communication.

She hurled the grenades in succession. I tapped into each one as they arced toward different parts of the grounds.

"*Attivare!*" I hollered.

Electricity rippled through the sooty sky then cracked in a series of blinding branches toward the still-tumbling grenades. By the time I squinted my eyes open again, masses of soldiers were down and scattered around the smoke-covered impact zones.

More disorder.

Madge switched to her spears, hurling them at anything that moved. Stony heads broke from bodies and limbs from torsos. When an armored vehicle rumbled across the grounds, she turned and sent a spear through its front quarter, dropping a section of body that ground the vehicle to a halt.

The nymphs joined in on the ranged assault with blasts and vine attacks that were mesmerizingly effective. Arimanius directed his surviving rats to swarm individual soldiers, the sheer weight of the vermin taking them to the ground.

Priapus, meanwhile, had broken away from us and was gripping the base of his phallus like a baseball bat, though he'd grown it to battering ram proportions.

"Get some!" he shouted, swinging it into a soldier's head, cracking his helmet.

He wheeled and batted away another's tactical rod before hammering him into the muddy ground. Priapus looked over at me with a triumphant smile. I returned a thumbs-up that I had very mixed feelings about.

As the soldiers returned sporadic fire, I finished shaping a form-fitting shield around myself. Priapus received a pair of shots to the torso, but with the added protection of the amulet, he grunted them off. The underworld magic may have induced horrors in mortals, but they were far less effective against mythic beings. Yet another one of Hermes's genius foresights that, in my exasperation, I'd missed.

Before Priapus could mete out more penile justice, I waved for him to corral Koalemos and follow us.

"Keep moving!" I called to everyone.

The surviving soldiers were retreating to the rear of the city hall building. I imagined them drawing around the lodestone that powered the recharging stations and what remained of Persephone's defensive field.

As we pursued them, I noticed that every barrack was

packed, filled with flagging soldiers who couldn't recharge. Similarly, small trench lines along the grounds were filled with dead rats—the real heroes of our first phase. With my stealth potion leaking from their blown-out bodies, I could see copper filaments glinting from several sets of incisors and gave silent thanks for the rats' service.

Our arrival in the park had been an adrenaline-fueled blur, but we were doing well.

At the back of the building, we were met with a fresh barrage of shooting. Dozens of soldiers formed a final bulwark around the bunker's cement lid. Some were already down, their power spent, weapons dead. Others appeared to be hanging on, thanks to the field radiating from the unit they guarded.

"They're where we want them," I radioed everyone. "Give me an opening."

Madge lifted me from Phrixus's back and set me on the ground, where I limp-ran to keep pace with our forward momentum. The same adrenaline blurring the action tempered my pain, but I was still hobbled.

Madge and Phrixus charged ahead, pummeling and trampling soldiers. I pulled a scroll of wax paper from my satchel. With Madge and Phrixus forcing the soldiers back, Comet blasted a path for me to the bunker.

The air above the bunker wavered with locking magic as I peeled a large sticker from the wax paper and slapped it down on the cement lid. The sticker featured a rune within a rune, an arrangement Hermes had designed.

"Clear out!" I called as the outer rune glowed to life.

I broke from the bunker. Madge soon overtook me, scooping me up and holding me to her side like a stack of books. As she set me down again, the others galloped, hovered, and staggered in. I waved them all behind me. With Hermes's rune pulsing green, I conjured a shield between us and the distant bunker. Much like the rune he'd designed to weaken my obfuscation sigil, Hermes had created one to challenge Persephone's locking magic at the lowest ebb of its cycle. And it was working.

The field around the bunker began to wobble.

Chopping sounded. I looked over to find a pair of helicopters swooping in above a large unit of arriving military vehicles and foot soldiers—the ones that had been pursuing Hermes. I grew our shield into a dome, pushing power into it as rounds arrived. Back at the bunker, Persephone's protective field fizzled apart.

The adhesive's central rune took over now, this one designed for sheer destruction.

Hurry it up, I thought, peering between the brightening rune and the arriving reinforcements.

Deep cracks sounded from the bunker, and the lid imploded, dropping the rune into the enclosure with the lodestone, the heart of Persephone's mystical network.

Okay, time to blow this mother—

The explosion was almost immediate, landing against my shield with enough force to push us back several feet. The ground tremored. Behind us, the incoming helicopters veered into steep dives, crashing into buildings and spilling as fiery wreckage to the streets. The ground vehicles simply rumbled to stops, while the foot soldiers collapsed facedown. Cheers erupted around me, and Madge chest-bumped Phrixus.

"It's down!" I radioed Hermes.

"*Yes, I just felt it,*" he replied excitedly. "*I'm on my way to the courthouse!*"

"And we're heading inside."

"Be careful with her," Hermes said, meaning Persephone.

I turned to my teammates. "All right, we're on to phases two and three."

That meant Hermes reconfiguring the energy-channeling skylight while the rest of us declawed Persephone. Hermes hadn't believed Typhon would send her out to fight—too risky for his prospects of escaping Tartarus. More likely, he would have her call up reinforcements from Hades to defend them. I had a solution for that, but we needed to reach her inner sanctum, like five minutes ago.

Comet and Ivy darted away to meet Hermes. Given Persephone's rapport with nymphs, we'd felt it would be safer to keep them from the goddess's proximity. Plus, they could act as Hermes's backup.

That left Madge, Phrixus, and the minor gods of darkness, fertility, and stupidity to escort me into City Hall. We were partway up the steps leading to the back entrance when a set of engines roared up behind us.

I knew who they were before I even turned.

Phrixus drew an arrow back on his bowstring, and Madge retracted a spear.

Red Beard roared up on his bike, flanked by two members of his Street Keepers. The tactical whip that dangled from Red Beard's right hand crackled with the energy of their benefactor, an Avenging Angel. Thick tires bumped over fallen Iron Guard soldiers as they coasted to a stop.

"Hello, again," he growled.

48

I'd known that the Street Keepers showing up was a good possibility. What I hadn't expected was for them to show up so damned quickly.

But there were only three this time, including Red Beard. Recalling how thoroughly I'd devastated their ranks with the power of the collective, I was tempted to call down, "What's the matter? Your numbers seem a little thin these days." But there wasn't time for smartassery. There wasn't time, period.

"What do you want?" I demanded.

"We need to talk."

Though I couldn't see Red Beard's eyes beyond his shades, I imagined them shifting between Phrixus and Madge and the projectiles aimed at his head. Priapus rocked his hips from side to side as though taking warm-up swings. Red Beard had to be wondering whether his angelic protection would stand up to mythic beings.

I barked a laugh. "Hell of a time to pick another fight. In case you haven't noticed, we're in the middle of a battle so your shitty city doesn't get a whole lot shittier."

"I'm not here to fight."

I nodded at the men flanking him. "Is that why they're pointing guns?"

He looked over at them and gave a subtle nod. The men lowered their weapons.

"I've been told to call a... truce," Red Beard said, seeming to have trouble with the word. "We're offering our help. Until this is settled."

I released another laugh, preparing to shoo him off, when I noticed the numbers. Three of them. That would complete the twelve. At the mere thought, my magic seemed to nod. With his offer came the potential for wholeness, the fulfill-ment of the prophecy: "allies gather eleven and one." But I didn't tip my hand.

"And you promise to leave my boy alone," I said.

With Budge's pledge off the table, I needed to secure new protection for Alec. That part was nonnegotiable.

"Not my call to make," Red Beard replied.

"*And you promise to leave my boy alone,*" I repeated over him. "Or we end this right here."

"Just give us the word," Madge growled.

Phrixus grunted his assent, adjusting his grip on his bow.

When Red Beard remained silent, I said, "Look, I have no problem sending your Avenging Angel three Street Keepers. Not with what's at stake. It's my boy or your bodies. You make the call or I will."

At last he nodded. "Okay."

And with that, I felt the energy around them shift from hostile to something less so.

I waved grudgingly for them to join us. As they parked their bikes, I filled them in on the attack plan. I then tossed down the remaining amulets in my satchel, more to bond us as twelve than to offer additional protection, though the amulets would do that, too. As the bikers draped them around their necks, I felt the balance and stability really take hold. Alec had been right—it was in the numbers.

"Let's go," I said.

As Red Beard hustled up the steps, Madge met him halfway with a hand to the chest. "Just so we're clear, you so much as touch him with that," she nodded at the tactical whip in his hand, "and I'll shove that thing so far up your ass you'll have sparklers for eyes."

Red Beard looked ready to push her hand away, but he wisely grunted his understanding.

"Stay together and keep moving," I reminded everyone as I hunkered beside the doors. "And no one attacks Persephone."

I blasted the doors wide with an invocation, and we surged inside. Several soldiers lay inert around the rotunda area, but a handful of human guards cracked off shots from behind stone columns. My shielding caught the assault, then sent back a concussive wave that sprawled the guards into submission.

I imagined the rest of the City Hall staff huddled in conference rooms and locked offices where I prayed they would stay.

I climbed onto Phrixus's back under my own power, and he led the charge up the rotunda's floating staircase. I was retracing the route I'd taken to steal Persephone's scepter just days earlier, only now stealth was out the window—and that felt good.

We arrived on the second floor and rounded toward the wooden door that concealed the final stairwell to Persephone's suite. Like before, its frame squirmed with locking magic straight from Hades. But I'd come equipped with rune stickers this time. As I pulled the wax sheet from my satchel, the door shot open and a host of rotting humanoids tumbled out before scrambling to their feet.

We may not have gotten to her pool fast enough to head off zombies, but I was anxious to arrive before she called up anything bigger.

As I activated my sword's banishment rune, Phrixus and Madge filled the doorway with arrows and spears. Red Beard's two henchmen fired shotguns, the enhanced ammo blowing through the undeads' protection in scatters of limbs and rotten flesh. Meanwhile, Red Beard lashed his whip with just as devastating an effect, each crack combusting a zombie's insides in bursts of white fire.

They lacked the same protection we'd seen in the actual present. Here, that power was being directed into opening the portal.

As their numbers thinned, I called a "hold fire" and had Phrixus take lead. He charged through the doorway, trampling rotten bodies, and surged up the stairwell. I hacked my sword down one side of us and the other, the light of banishment cleaving through the grasping creatures, splitting them apart like rotten fruit. The rest of the team cleaned up in our wake. Bolstered by the power of Twelve, our efforts were syncing strongly.

"We're inside," I radioed Hermes. "How are you doing?"

"*I'm at the skylight, but the design appears to be locked by some kind of a cipher. I'm working on it now.*"

A hiccup, but I trusted Hermes would get it done.

Phrixus summited into the corridor, his hooves skidding over zombie fluids and mud as he veered left and bore down on Persephone's chambers. A fresh wave of undead poured from her doorway, but we made quick, messy work of them. We arrived in her bedroom spattered with their sludge and gristle.

The panel to her back room slammed closed.

"Get me beside it," I told Phrixus, eyeing the magic sealing the doorway.

Phrixus brought himself around, and I placed the adhesive with Hermes's rune over the panel. He turned away as it began to glow. A moment later, the rune detonated, pelting my invoked shield with splinters and chunks of wood.

Not only had the rune taken down the locking magic, but much of the wall as well, exposing Persephone's inner sanctum. At first I saw only darkness, then light from my shield glimmered from the goddess's eyes. She had backed up to her pool, one hand holding her scepter's twisted shaft, the other palming its crown.

I pictured Bree-yark stirring its twin and wondered about the progress of the solvents. Had enough of the mineral component sloughed away that Typhon's influence was failing, restoring Persephone to herself?

The answer came a moment later when her eyes narrowed and she thrust the scepter.

The force blew apart my protection, shoving us back and sending a shockwave around her bedroom that whipped up flower petals and toppled furniture. We may have demolished her lodestone, but she remained plenty powerful.

When she trained her scepter on the water, it bubbled and smoked like a cauldron. She had been calling something to the surface, and it wasn't another host of zombies. What crawled forth was massive and vaguely humanoid with a vulture-like head and the glistening blue-black skin of a filth fly.

Damn, I recognized the thing. It was Eurynomos, a daemon of Hades and extraordinarily powerful.

Phrixus released several arrows, and Madge put her entire body into a spear-heave, but their projectiles disintegrated on contact with the being. Two of the Street Keepers unloaded shells, but the shots went up in wisps of black smoke. The daemon stared at us, the wings on its back chittering like a giant fly's.

"Hold fire," I said and spoke an invocation.

The air around the creature glistened and hardened into an enclosure. The light gave me a better look at Persephone. It wasn't the look I'd been hoping for. Her burnt chestnut hair had deepened to a shade somewhere between molten and midnight. The locks fell from a crown of dead flowers and over the shoulders of a funeral gown. There was no spring in her. She was one-hundred percent dread Persephone.

She stood back with her scepter, regarding the daemon with a stare that was both intense and empty. The shadow mayor was nowhere to be seen, and that bothered me. But that didn't change the calculus. I needed to seal the pool, denying her access to Hades. That would deplete the daemon, too.

From my satchel I drew out the jar of red water from Lake Pergusa.

The daemon's wings buzzed fiercely and cut out, buzzed fiercely and cut out. He was rotating his vulture head as though sizing us up, saliva dripping from a row of serrated teeth that hooked down over his beak.

"Move in," I whispered to Phrixus. "Slowly."

He stepped lightly through the failed wall. The others followed and spread into a semicircle a safe distance back from the creature, though I had Arimanius keep Koalemos even further behind me.

"Don't let him touch you," I warned. "Or you'll join the undead."

Indeed, mere contact with Eurynomos had turned both mortals and gods alike into zombies. Which meant attempting to banish him with my blade was out. Too risky. Fortunately, that wasn't going to be necessary. I adjusted the jar in my slick grip. Back at my lab, I'd cooked a barrier spell into the mythical lake water. Just needed to shove the daemon a few feet to the right for a clear shot at the pool.

But I didn't get the chance.

With an ear-splitting screech, Eurynomos swiped a taloned hand. I grunted as my enclosure around him exploded in sparks. A bright pain filled my head, turning into a deep, festering ache that took a long moment to subside.

Shotgun blasts sounded as the Street Keepers moved in.

"Stay back!" I managed, but the warning came too late.

The daemon lunged and slashed his talons down the front of one of the burly bikers, severing his gun barrel from the stock end in a scatter of shot. The amulet fell away, too, the daemon's attack overwhelming the protection. The biker staggered back and collapsed, ragged tears down his black leathers already seeping blood. When the daemon lowered his head to feed, he was met by a sharp crack.

Red Beard's whip caught the creature's face in a flash of white light.

The daemon didn't appear hurt so much as confused. With a forearm to his beak, Eurynomos stepped back. Red Beard brought the whip across him again, forcing the creature back another step. He was getting dangerously close to the daemon for my comfort, but he was also driving him from the pool.

I guided Phrixus the other way for a clearer shot.

At that moment, the biker who had gone down spasmed and coughed up a pitch black fount of bile. His hand shot out, catching Red Beard by the cuff of his pants. Red Beard struggled to shake him off while landing another whip crack, but the biker-turned-zombie tugged him back with abnormal strength.

I swung my cane, but a shotgun blast met the zombie-biker first. His other teammate had taken matters into his own hands, emptying a shell into his head. The hand clutching Red Beard's cuff fell open. I felt the power of the Twelve stagger back to eleven. But at the moment, I had the daemon to worry about.

"Watch out!" I called, switching my cane's aim to Red Beard.

I managed to shove him aside with an invocation as the daemon slashed again—and missed him by inches. With a gruff shout, Priapus charged forward, his phallus pulled back in striking position.

"No, dammit!" I called.

Madge lunged, grabbed Priapus by a wad of his wiry hair, and yanked him back.

"The hell do you think you're doing?" she shouted. "You saw what he just did to the other dude!"

Exactly. None of us wanted to battle a zombie version of *that*.

With the daemon focused on Priapus, the centaur veered around to give me a clear shot at the pool. The daemon pivoted to cut us off, but Red Beard met him with a sharp whipcrack. And just like that, I had my opening.

"*Vigore!*" I shouted, sending the jar from my hand.

It shattered in a burst of red water—but not against the far wall of the pool.

I stared in disbelief at where the liquid seemed to be running down the air itself.

The hell?

Familiar laughter sounded. "Boy, I wasn't sure that would work."

I turned to the lab area. For an instant, the doubting part of my mind saw Hermes—Lord knew, I'd been fooled before. But the figure who emerged, still chuckling, was the mayor's shadow. Budge strode over to Persephone and wrapped an arm around her waist. "But you suckers walked right into it."

When I looked down at the floor, I nearly choked at the sight of a large design glowing to life.

The eight of us were standing inside a circle trap.

49

Budge tsked. "Everson, Everson, Everson. And here I thought you and me had an understanding. Only for you to go running back to that winged-footed rapscallion."

I turned from him and lowered my voice. "Hey, Hermes? We've got a problem."

Budge laughed. "Oh, he can't hear you. You're cut off. The trap is drawing power from Tartarus itself. Can't you feel it?"

I winced as a sharp whistle sounded through the communication rune, the sound of the wind. The sound of Typhon.

"The chasm is opening," he continued, "and if you're waiting on Hermes to close it, you'll be waiting a long time. The cipher was installed by sweet Persephone, a powerful curse in a language of the underworld. One foreign to Hermes, and he'll have his hands full soon enough as it is."

I sensed the others looking to me for direction. But I was the one who'd led us into the trap. How could I have been so freaking stupid? I'd allowed my confidence in my magic to blind me, no more so than when we'd attained our army of twelve. I'd thought we were unstoppable, and now here we were—stopped cold.

"Persephone, listen to me," I said, climbing down from Phrixus's back. "You're not dealing with Cronus, but Typhon. He's the one you're releasing from Tartarus. He's the one who's been in your ear this whole time."

"Oh, don't listen to him, dear," Budge said over me. "This is the thief who stole your scepter, remember?"

Persephone, who'd been staring at me with a face haunting for its emptiness, flinched suddenly and drew her scepter close to her chest. The giant daemon, meanwhile, stalked the outside of the trap, watching us with hungry vulture eyes.

"He also aligned with Hermes," Budge continued, "who's made your life *so* unnecessarily difficult."

If I'd had any doubts as to the growing presence of Tartarus, I could see it now in Budge's posture and arrogance. This was no longer a vessel for Typhon, walking on eggshells and licking his nervous lips.

No, this was Typhon himself sensing victory.

Red Beard, who'd been watching us with growing impatience, grunted, "Screw this."

He lashed his whip against the wall of the trap, and his teammate opened fire. That spurred Phrixus and Madge to join in. But despite their deafening assault, our enclosure didn't budge. The trap was too complex. Indeed, it was using the energy from the attack to reinforce itself.

Persephone's eyes darkened, and she raised her scepter as though to strike back, but Budge lowered her arm gently.

"Now, now, they're no longer a threat," he said as the assault tapered off. "In fact, we'll allow Eurynomos inside to feed in a moment."

The daemon buzzed his fly wings, sending saliva spattering against the outer wall of the trap.

"But first, we had a deal with Everson, do you remember?" Budge asked her. "If he insisted on working against us, we were going to bond him to his ashes. Hermes bought him a stay of execution, but I've got news for him." He patted Persephone's bottom, a gesture as bold as it was crass, and ambled over to the lab. He bent down, and when he straightened, he was holding my urn.

"We've neutralized the neutralizer," he said with a superior grin.

As he set my urn on a counter, I thought of my original strategy for Koalemos. He was to have swapped his stupidity for Budge's intelligence, effectively suspending Typhon's control over Persephone.

But the damned trap wouldn't allow it now.

"Sephassa, would you do the honors?" Budge asked, gesturing to the urn.

"Hey, hold on," I said, recalling how terrifyingly close I'd come to crumbling to dust the last time. "What do you want?"

I was cycling madly through the prophecy—*allies gather eleven and one, and be not afraid of thine own blood. Wage, young mage, till your final breath, and come night's fall accept your death.* I refused to believe my magic had misled me. This couldn't be the "death" prophesized. It didn't make any sense.

"Oh, we're way past that, pal," Budge said.

I eyed Persephone's scepter. Time. I needed time.

"You're wrong about Hermes, you know," I heard myself say.

Budge laughed. "Is that right?"

"He used to guide souls to the underworld, or did you forget? That's the reason Zeus sent him to escort Persephone from Hades. Hermes knows the terrain. He knows the *languages*. He'll crack her cipher."

Budge's grin faltered by a degree. I was getting to him.

"Maybe it's time you met with him," I pressed. "If you're lucky, he may still be willing to bargain."

I was talking out of my ass, but if I could convince Typhon his portal was in jeopardy, I could buy us more time for the solvents to do their job. With a flick of his ringed fingers, though, Budge dismissed me.

"Go ahead, sweetie," he said to Persephone. "Everson's just blowing hot air."

Persephone hovered her scepter over the urn, dark magic gathering around its crown.

"Don't listen to him!" I shouted, pushing power into my wizard's voice. "That's Typhon talking to you! Typhon!"

"So long, Everson," he said, waggling his fingers. "It's been—"

Persephone's scepter cracked across his face.

Budge clamped a hand to his bleeding mouth, his slick hair fallen over his brow, and looked at her aghast. "Persephone, honey. What's—"

She struck him on the other side of his face. "Cease your poisonous talk," she snapped.

Budge looked wildly from her to us, blood dripping from his jaw. "What are you doing to her?"

I gave him my most innocent shrug, but I could see it happening. The minerals in the scepter that carried the old worship for Typhon were breaking away. The solvents—and Bree-yark—were doing their job.

"I see you, *serpent,*" she seethed. "You foul *snake.*"

Budge shrank as she stalked toward him. She still wielded the dark and terrifying power of the underworld, but in the depth of her midnight eyes, a just as powerful astuteness was climbing from the void.

He swiped his hair back with a blood-soaked hand. "What are you talking about, Princess?" he said, desperately trying to switch the charm back on. "I'm the Mayor of New York City. I've been helping you!"

"I see you, *Typhon*," she seethed, "son of *Gaia*, mate of *Echidna*, scourge of *Tartarus*."

"W-wait," Budge stammered. "Remember how your father conspired with Hades and—"

"Begone you beast!" she bellowed, thrusting the scepter. The power that detonated from the crown blasted out the last of Typhon's contaminants and landed against Budge's chest, driving him across the room.

He landed in a heap beside the ruined wall.

Persephone turned to the hulking daemon. She didn't need the scepter to subdue him, just her penetrating stare. Cowed, the daemon slumped his great shoulders and slipped back into the pool's muddy waters. He submerged with scarcely a sound. With a wave of her scepter, she rendered the waters clear again.

Then she turned to us, her power warping the space between us.

"Who are you?" she demanded. "What are you doing here?"

As everyone backed from her intensity, her frightening beauty, I held my ground and cleared my throat. "We're here with Hermes. He came to free you from Typhon's spell and to stop his arrival from Tartarus."

She looked over at Budge, who was still down. "Him?" she scoffed.

"Yes, but it's not over yet. Typhon compelled you to gather

energy from the city. That energy is opening a portal to Tartarus as we speak. Hermes is trying to reverse it, but the channel is locked by a cipher."

Her eyes turned misty, as though trying to recall pieces of a dream. "Portal," she said softly. "Cipher."

"Typhon said the cipher was a curse in a language of the underworld."

The mist suddenly thinned from her eyes. She stepped forward and drew her pristine foot across the perimeter of the circle, creating a breach. The trap's energy released with a powerful gust that stirred her lightening gown and hair.

"Hermes," she said. "I want to talk to him."

I nodded quickly. "Hermes?" I radioed. "Can you hear me?"

"*I can, but I've not made any more progress on the cipher.*"

Persephone spoke a guttural word I'd never heard a human voice speak before.

"Try this." I repeated the sound, articulating each syllable as carefully as I would have with one of my own invocations.

Silence for a moment, then: "*Yes, yes, it's working. And now just to...*" I heard a sound like glass crunching and metal snapping. "*There, I've reversed the rotation. The portal is... Yes, it's closing!*"

My legs went weak as I exhaled a sharp laugh.

"*How did you know the cipher?*" he asked.

"Persephone is standing right next to me."

"*Persephone?*" He released a lovelorn sigh. "*And she's herself?*"

I couldn't help but smile. "She's herself. And she wants to talk to you."

But at that moment, the entire building shook. I staggered for balance as water lapped from the pool and potions spilled from shelves. I looked over at Persephone, but the goddess appeared just as puzzled.

"Hey, is something happening over there?" I asked Hermes.

"*I'm not sure,*" he replied. "*The closing stopped suddenly. It's no longer responding to the energy's new orientation.*" He went silent. When he spoke again, his voice fell flat. "*Oh, no, Everson.*"

"What's wrong?" I asked, my heart pounding through the words.

Through the communication rune, the sharp sound of the wind picked up again. In the background, the nymphs shrieked.

"*Something's coming through,*" Hermes said.

50

Persephone led the charge from her inner sanctum. We fell in behind her—the five mythic beings, the two remaining Street Keepers, and me.

"What's going on?" Red Beard asked from beside me.

"That thing we were trying to stop from happening? I think it's happening."

But I couldn't quite get my mind to bend to the enormity of the possibility. Typhon emerging? When he'd threatened Olympus, the major gods fled. That's how ridiculously powerful this guy was. It wasn't until Zeus confronted him in a match for the ages that Typhon was ultimately put to pasture.

"And trust me," I said to Red Beard. "It's bad."

When we arrived in Persephone's bedchamber, I was surprised to find Budge up and staggering in befuddlement. The goddess glanced at him dismissively in passing. Just as Typhon's influence had been blown from her scepter, it had been blown from the mayor's body as well. He was himself again.

"I'll catch up," I called as I veered toward him.

Seizing Budge's arm, I said, "Listen, I need you to get everyone out of this building. And keep all emergency services the hell back. Police, fire, medical. I don't want them coming within ten blocks of the park. Do you understand?"

Budge stared vacantly before a spark of authority took hold in his eyes. He blinked and nodded his head. "Yeah, alright."

I left him and caught up to the others on the ground floor as they were pouring out the back of the building. Across from us, the courthouse was rocking on its foundation, cracks climbing the granite and marble walls. Every window facing us had already shattered.

Now the skylight above the rotunda burst in a spray of glass. The gathering energy from the city dispersed as a thicker, murkier energy erupted from the building and fountained up, spreading through the clouds like a toxic spill. The wind turned wild and cut around us, its pitch nearly deafening.

Hermes suddenly appeared with Comet and Ivy, terror written on the nymphs' faces. Hermes rushed to Persephone, and the two gods clutched arms. Their embrace was familiar, but this was no tender reunion. The contact was as urgent as their voices. I picked up pieces, but they spoke in the language of the gods.

At last Hermes broke away and approached me. "Persephone and I are going inside."

"To do what?" I demanded, sounding more like a father to Alec than an ally to Hermes.

"To push Typhon back down, or attempt to. This is the most vulnerable he's going to be." He clasped my hand and pulled me into a hug. It was strong and brief, and before I knew it, he'd departed.

"What can we do?" I shouted after him.

"Say a prayer that we might know the strength and courage of our father."

"Wait!" I shouted, fishing an amulet from my satchel. I threw it to him. "For Persephone!"

He snatched it from the air with a nod. Before I could say anything else, he followed Persephone and the two disappeared into the courthouse.

I waved everyone else back. We could only stand among the fallen Iron Guard and watch the building as more darkness spewed into the sky and fragments of stone fell to the ground. For the first time, Koalemos's jaw wasn't hanging open. Even the god of stupidity sensed something very bad was happening.

I cast a shield to keep the wind off us and the piercing whistle from our ears.

"Do they have a chance?" Red Beard asked from beside me in his gruff voice.

I clutched the amulet hanging around my neck. With the addition of Persephone, we were twelve again. "The numbers are right," I said, not bothering to elaborate. "We just have to pray they really mean something."

"You're a strange dude, Croft. If things were different, we might've gotten along."

He flicked his tactical whip back and forth as though anxious to use it on something. I knew the feeling. I released the amulet and drew my sword from its staff. As I gazed along the blade's runes, I noticed them dimming by degrees. It was the energy emptying into the sky, turning what passed for daytime in the shadow realm to an early twilight. I lowered my gaze back to my father's sword.

Be your magic, I thought, knowing it was the only thing I could do. The only thing I needed to be doing.

As I began to open myself, a distressing chain of cracks sounded, and a wall collapsed from the courthouse's west wing. The beings around me murmured worriedly, and I felt our cohesion wobble.

"Stand firm," I told them. "This isn't the end."

I refused to allow myself to consider it, breathe it, even think it for an instant. Instead, I sheathed my sword and closed my eyes. I concentrated wholly on the idea of faith in magic. I filled myself with it. I channeled it into our amulets. I asked that it hold together our twelve in the face of Typhon.

Shouts went up. My eyes opened to stone bursting from the base of the courthouse in a series of gunshot-like reports. And then the entire building imploded as though from a controlled demolition, landing in an outrush of dust and debris. The storm washed over my shield, slashing and swirling like a spectral attack.

"*Respingere!*" I shouted, fear displacing my faith. I might as well have shouted *Alec!*

My shield blew out, taking the dust storm with it. The force washed over the ruins of the courthouse, and what I saw stopped me in my tracks. Crouched in the debris was an enormous figure.

He unfurled slowly, head lifting from his lap, stones tumbling from his bare back.

By the time he straightened, he was much larger than the building that had once stood in his place. Streaming gray hair joined a thick beard that hung past his navel. Muscles flexed across his torso as he moved a giant scythe from his left to his right hand. This was Cronus, son of Heaven and Earth, father of Zeus, embodiment of Time, lord of the Titans.

The nymphs squealed in terror while the other mythic beings fell to the ground in submission before this eater of gods. Madge yanked Koalemos down beside her. Red Beard and the other biker backed away.

I remained frozen in place.

From his tremendous height, Cronus peered around. You couldn't possibly understand the power and scale of a major god until you stood before one. He looked grand, eminently divine, but when his gaze touched mine, I saw the frosty blue eyes of a killer. I'd thought my first meeting with Persephone was intimidating, but Cronus made her look like a Girl Scout. His gaze lifted again, surveying the lands he meant to rule.

It was then that I remembered Typhon.

And it was then that Cronus released a booming cry.

The ground shook as he peered down the lengths of his immense legs. Something wasn't so much devouring them as growing over them in a torrent of dark scales, spines, and serpent heads. Lots of serpent heads.

Cronus drew back his scythe, but the being was already spreading down his arms, encompassing and inhabiting them until they took possession of the scythe. More serpents sprang from his sides.

Cronus's face was the last to disappear, its look of pompous outrage twisting into sheer terror before becoming the visage of a demonic being so incomprehensible that I felt my sanity bending at the struts. But I couldn't avert my gaze. Cronus's beard fell away in a column of flames as the creature continued to grow.

It filled more and more of the darkening sky with scales and serpent heads and cruel gouts of fire. This was truly

Typhon—more awful than any account I'd ever read. The mere sight of him was going to send thousands jumping from windows, drowning themselves in bathtubs, chugging household chemicals. Anything to scrub the horror of his existence from their eyes and shattered minds.

And now it was Cronus who seemed like the Scout.

I ripped my gaze away and searched the park. Where were Hermes and Persephone?

The communication rune had become dead air—or maybe it was that the wind had grown so insanely loud that I couldn't hear anything else. As I tapped into my amulet, determined to bolster our twelve, the mythic beings behind me got up and fled, scattering whatever power the number still held.

When Red Beard turned to follow them, I surprised myself by grabbing his thick arm and yanking him toward me. Maybe it was that I couldn't bear the idea of facing Typhon alone, because face him I had to. As long as he wielded the scythe, he wielded power over time—including access to our present.

"We can't do a fucking thing against that!" Red Beard shouted, his voice verging on a scream. The sky was so dark now, he was little more than a wild impression. He tore off his shades, his enormous pupils staring past me.

I turned in time to see the scythe cutting toward us.

51

I released Red Beard and brought my cane around. "*Protezione!*" I shouted.

The scythe met my gleaming protection in a blinding explosion that slammed me from my feet. I flew with the remnants of my scattering shield, landing in a bruising roll. When I flopped to a stop, I peered around.

I was nearly to the city hall building, or what remained of it. The energy from the scythe had blown its top half away. I could hear masonry crashing for what seemed blocks as more buildings crumbled in succession. Back at the courthouse, Typhon's serpent heads lit up the darkness like hellish gas flares. The giant scythe glinted blue in his monstrous grip. To say I was outgunned was being kind.

The landscape reeled as I stood. I staggered forward, the side of my head warm with blood, my thoughts a foggy jumble.

I stopped when I reached Red Beard. He was on his back, mouth agape, torso ripped open, right arm missing. In my stunned state, it didn't seem real. I staggered past him and the other fallen Street Keeper. Parts of him, anyway. The single sweep of the scythe had torn him asunder, just as it had done to the lingering power connecting us.

Ahead, thick serpents lunged from Typhon's still growing body, spouting fire, promising devastation, annihilation. As though in exclamation, a giant pair of wings unfolded from Typhon's back.

Everson!

Someone was gripping my shoulder, shaking me. I turned to find Hermes looking at me with frantic eyes.

"Please tell me you've seen Persephone!"

It took me a moment to process his words. I started to shake my head slowly when I saw something on the ground ahead. I looked at it for a long moment, its contours finally connecting with something I'd seen and held and cast through. Persephone's scepter. Its dark gems glinted in the light of Red Beard's whip, which lay a short distance away, the cord giving off sparks of energy.

Wage, young mage, till your final breath...

The Doideag's prophecy, a scrap in my head, as though the wind had blown it apart and I was catching pieces.

"I did wage!" I shouted back. "I gave everything I had, dammit!"

And come night's fall, accept your death...

I was about to shout, "For what?" but I stopped myself. I was in shock, losing it. I couldn't fall apart, not now. The Twelve may have scattered and been cut down, but the One remained: my magic.

I steadied my thoughts and repeated the words, "'Come night's fall, accept your death.'" I peered from the blackened sky down to Persephone's scepter. "Death..."

Was that the answer? To take up Persephone's weapon, a

symbol of Death with a capital D? Use it to somehow repel Typhon?

When Hermes saw me staring at it, he sped forward and picked it up. I thought he was going to wield it himself, but the scepter's power appeared to have faded. He held it to his chest and cried Persephone's name into the wind-torn darkness, captive once more to his myth. I was about to demand the scepter from him when my gaze switched to Red Beard's whip, writhing and crackling on the ground.

Then it clicked.

If the stories of the Avenging Angels were to be believed, they and the First Saints were essentially siblings. They shared blood. Blood I'd inherited.

And come night's fall, accept your death...

Not Death with a capital D, but *my* death, which the whip had threatened me with several times. I remembered Red Beard's confusion in the alleyway when his attack had failed to end me. Given the angel-saint connection, maybe the whip *couldn't* end me—hence the "be not afraid" part. Not only that, I could wield it.

That was it. That *had* to be it.

"Hermes!" I called. "Bring me the whip!"

He looked over at me, then up at Typhon, who was slithering from the wreckage on a giant serpent's tail. When Red Beard's whip crackled in another writhing fit, I remembered what Budge had said about his time inside his shadow self: *The guy who was beating up my insides is scared shitless of Zeus.*

My magic, the symbol of ultimate unity, the One, was nodding fervently now.

"The whip!" I repeated, fresh clarity and courage bursting through me. "Bring me the whip!"

Hermes plucked it from the ground, and much as he had

delivered lightning to Zeus's hand, he sped the crackling weapon to mine.

"Get behind me!" I shouted as the magic of the collective began surging inside me.

With Typhon drawing the scythe back, I opened myself to the whip's power. Electrical energy fissured the sky, and in the next moment it was as though I'd been struck by a bolt and knocked from my body.

The landscape became a misty wash of gray. A massive, winged figure stood before me, but it wasn't Typhon. It was the same being I'd glimpsed when I'd opened the whip's defenses in my lab. No face, no distinct features, just an outline and an enormous pair of wings that seemed to merge with the mist itself. I sensed judgment and violence, but I also sensed the truce Red Beard had offered.

And then I was back in my body, the magic of the collective swaddling me, holding me together, while fierce angelic power pounded through me.

Typhon had stopped, the scythe down at his side. Scared shitless.

I lashed the whip forward. As it forded the distance separating us, the whip stretched into dozens of crackling cords, which stretched into dozens more. They cracked Typhon's serpent heads, causing them to shriek fire and rear back. When I stepped forward, I realized I was growing, rising to the stature of my opponent.

But there was no time to marvel.

Teeth gritted, I cracked the whip again. Typhon managed to swing the scythe around, the power of the blade sending my cords whistling wide. I dragged them back toward me, leaving smoking furrows of white fire in the ground.

With a flick, I brought the cords leaping up as if I'd been

commanding them my whole life, and I swung them at Typhon again. This time, they wrapped his scythe. Power sizzled and arced from the contact of our opposing energies as Typhon and I wrestled for control of the other's weapon.

He began to laugh, a deep, hissing sound that squirmed through my soul.

I could hear his taunts in my head: *You're not Zeus. You're nowhere close to his power. You're just a puny mortal playing dress up.*

Or maybe he was merely stirring up my own self-doubts.

He jerked me forward, and the serpent heads snapped at my face.

"*Respingere!*" I cried, directing the power to repel into the whip.

The building energy between our weapons burst in a ferocious explosion of light, fire, and force. The cords released the scythe's blade, and I staggered back until I was safely out of his range again.

Typhon resumed laughing.

I didn't like his confidence. I liked it even less that with every attack he felt stronger. I was setting up for another strike, when I noticed a figure wander between us. He looked up at me, then over at Typhon.

"Whoa," Koalemos guffawed. "You dudes are, like, ginormous."

With a grunt, Typhon flicked the scythe. My heart leapt as the blade severed Koalemos cleanly between his hoodie and surfer shorts. The god of stupidity disappeared in a fizzle of light, his chaplet rattling to the ground. I raised my eyes to Typhon, bracing myself. He had me on my back foot, and he knew it.

But his hundred serpent heads suddenly appeared limp

and listless. Then from Typhon's demonic jaw came a lazy staccato laugh.

Holy crap. By attacking Koalemos, he'd taken on the god's stupidity!

Seizing the opportunity, I channeled every last ounce of energy, angelic and magical, and poured it into the whip as I brought it singing around.

Typhon had no answer this time. Bright white cords branched into more cords that branched into more still until they cinched every one of the serpents' necks. Steam hissed up as angel-charged metal bit into scaly flesh. The final and longest cord wrapped Typhon's throat several times, cutting off his hissing laugh.

I staggered forward, temporarily off balance.

Typhon had an instant to realize what was happening before I set my feet again.

"Not Zeus," I grunted, yanking back with all my strength. "An Avenging Angel."

Serpent heads rained to the earth as the cords severed them completely. Typhon's head was the last to go, erupting in a fount of black blood. It bounced over the ground, the forked tongue hanging out in a crazed death leer. The rest of Typhon's body teetered back and then fell into the ruins of the courthouse.

But he didn't stop there. The energy that had opened Tartarus and drawn Cronus forth was collapsing back into itself. Typhon's taloned hands grasped furiously, carving trenches into the ground as they were pulled after the rest of him. They disappeared along with the tonnage of stones, debris, and rolling serpent heads, all plummeting back into that deep and mythical abyss.

Though I leaned back, I held my stance, even as the potent vacuum drew the murkiness from the sky.

Before long, night returned to day, and the ruins of the courthouse settled. I waited several moments in the smoky stillness, not quite believing it was done.

At last, I picked my way forward and peered down.

Typhon was gone, the portal already sealing over.

Only then did I relax my hold on the whip. White fire had erupted over the cords, and they withered to ash now, like strands of incense rope. At last, only the handle remained. Light glinted from the sweaty imprint of my fingers. I peered skyward. Beyond the drifting smoke, the sun peeked through the clouds.

Then the scene wavered, and I collapsed onto my back.

52

When I came to, I was myself again. Wobbling to my feet, I squinted through the smoke and dust. I didn't seem to have been out long. In the middle distance, Hermes was picking his way through the debris, the scepter still in his grip. It was only when he stopped and knelt that I realized he'd been approaching Persephone.

The goddess lay on the ground, the locks of her hair blowing across her pale face. Hermes placed the scepter in the hand that rested across her stomach. He then pressed her grip around it with his own hands, head bowed. He was speaking, but I couldn't hear the words. A plea? A prayer?

His head jerked suddenly.

A long, thick torrent of smoke passed between us. When it cleared, Hermes was helping Persephone to her feet!

He stood with her for a time. Then together, they made their way toward me.

I took the opportunity to dust off my coat and comb my fingers through my blood-matted hair. For all I knew, I was cleaning off particles of my own shadow's remains, scattered to the winds with the destruction of City Hall.

I was still a mess by the time the gods arrived. Hermes was grinning from ear to ear, tears standing in his eyes. Persephone was smiling as well. Tiredly, but she was smiling, her lips turned up softly at the corners. Power moved through her scepter once more, a scepter that now featured sun-infused gems alongside the darker ones, reflecting her true nature. And her eyes appeared tender now, as though she didn't so much wield death as nurture it, much as she'd coax the world back to life each spring.

Hermes looked around. "We've done it."

In the enormity of my relief, I couldn't resist a joke. "Was it ever in doubt?"

Hermes chuckled before gathering himself. "Persephone, let me introduce you to my friend, Everson Croft. He puts his loved ones before himself, and he never gives up. He is a hero among mortals. Indeed, it was he who felled Typhon."

She extended her arm. "Thank you, Everson."

I took the goddess's gentle hand and bowed slightly. "It was my honor."

She returned my bow and stepped back again, the brief contact leaving me rejuvenated.

"She's agreed to return with me," Hermes said, hardly able to contain his excitement. "And, well..." He removed his backpack and placed it at my feet. "A deal's a deal." He stared at it for a moment. "I must confess, there was a time in all of this when I considered remaining in the box. Do you know what changed my mind?"

I shook my head, still dazed from the goddess's touch. "No."

"When I told you to hold onto your care for your son, it

was because I needed to see that care up close, to feel it. I had been too long from my own father. And when your son responded to your care in kind?" He sighed. "I learned something, Everson. For all my rebellious acts, Zeus remained and shall remain my father, despite his faults. And now we will reunite in the cosmos, and there I will become whole again."

I swallowed back my emotions, at a loss for words. "I'm... I'm glad we could help."

He looked around at the mythic beings who'd fled Typhon. They had ventured back and were now watching from amid the debris.

"Come!" he called. "Say farewell to Everson! Soon we depart for Olympus!"

Phrixus trotted up first and bent to one knee before Persephone with a soft "M'lady" before addressing me.

"Well fought, Everson," he said, returning to his gruff voice. "If there was more time, I would invite you to the vineyards of Thasos where we would drink the finest vintage and hunt the hills and dales."

"And I would gladly accept," I said, a little disappointed that it would never happen. "Thank you, Phrixus."

I clapped his equine shoulder. As he rounded behind Hermes and Persephone, Madge came striding in on her powerful Amazonian legs. Unlike Phrixus, she only gave cursory nods to Persephone and Hermes before holding out her fist to me. I raised mine for the expected bump, but she met it with a punch.

A pulled punch, but still. It freaking hurt.

"That battle was pretty kick ass," she said as I shook out my hand. "Sorry we bolted on you."

"Hey, you got me here, and that was no small thing." I

flexed my fingers to ensure they still worked. "Be well, Madge."

"You too, Everson."

Next came the nymphs, Ivy and Comet. They kept their farewell to simple curtsies, and I commended them for their battlefield prowess. I wasn't just being polite. They would have been my top picks for teammates, and not just for their white and green hair. Their powers were too cool.

Priapus waddled in behind them. Though he would have bottomed out my picks, I greeted him with a firm handshake. His fighting style was a little too unconventional for my tastes, but you couldn't argue with the results.

"Way to, you know, bat around out there," I said. "Take care of yourself, huh?"

"Yeah, goodbye, Everson," he replied, but I could see his mind was elsewhere.

He looked from me to Persephone, adjusting his legs in a way that made his tented pants a little less prominent. His wiry eyebrows rose in question. She smiled and nodded, confirmation that he would indeed be joining them in Olympus. With a chortling laugh, he hustled around to the rest of the beings.

As I scanned the ruined landscape for any others, a hillock of debris shifted and a figure emerged. He shook out his scruffy hair, then squinted around as though he'd just woken up from an afternoon nap.

"Koalemos!" I shouted.

He shuffled in the wrong direction before spotting us. He tripped several times as he hustled in on his canvas shoes, his mouth breaking into a sleepy smile. I was tempted to run up and tackle the god of stupidity in a full-body hug, but there was the issue of transference—something Typhon had learned too late.

But what was he even doing here? I'd watched Typhon cut him in half. I glanced over at Persephone. Magic haloed her scepter, while a mysterious smile played across her lips. It paid having an underworld goddess on your team.

Koalemos shuffled to a stop in front of me. I pointed at his heart and crossed my arms over my own. "Huge, man," I told him, emotions rising in my chest. "I couldn't have done that without you."

"Righteous," he guffawed. "But done what?"

"Come, Koalemos," Hermes called. "We're off to Olympus soon."

"Oh, yeah?" He guffawed some more. "Guess I'm outta here, hombre."

Smiling, I watched him join the others. I was about to ask if anyone had seen Arimanius when I felt a brooding presence beside me. I turned with a start to find him fixing me with his graveyard stare.

"Goodbye, Everson," he said.

I gripped his shoulder. "Mr. Funny!"

His face creased up as though he were about to start weeping, but it smoothed again. "I think I'll go by my real name from now on. To be 'Mr. Funny,' it seems you have to be funny first."

I chortled at that. "I guess you're right."

His head tilted in sudden interest. "You laughed."

"Yes, I did," I realized. "That was good."

His face began to glow. "Yeah? You know that reminds me of this woman I met at a bar once. She introduced herself as 'Anita Bang.' All I said was 'How badly?' and she threw her drink in my face."

I laughed harder. Not so much from the material but from seeing it finally click for him.

His voice grew more animated. "And then I turned to my other side, and the fellow sitting there introduces himself as 'Hugh Jassol.' So I lowered my voice and said, 'Maybe you should try being nicer.' Next thing I know, wham-o!"

This time it was the physical humor that landed as he mimed a fist being driven into his face. He crossed his eyes, tongue jutting from his mouth, as he wavered back and forth like a jack-in-the-box.

That got the nymphs giggling and Priapus roaring.

Straightening, Arimanius seized my hand and gave it several vigorous pumps. "Thank you, Everson, you've been great!"

He joined his cohorts, who welcomed him into their huddle with kudos and claps on the back. He may have been a god of darkness, but for that moment, anyway, his face beamed like a sun god's.

Hermes stepped forward. "Yes, I do believe we're all a little better for having known you, Everson. You'll find that I've returned Alec's sketchpad. It's in the small pocket. Please take a look at it together." He regarded me meaningfully. "As for your return, I noticed something about your sword."

He held out a hand for it, much as he had the morning I was preparing to steal Persephone's scepter. Since that moment, he'd used me as a coin flip, saved me from the scepter's influence, saved my *life*, and deferred to my lead when it mattered most. In other words, he'd gained my trust.

I released the blade from the staff and offered it to him hilt out.

"These runes your father designed, they're not predetermined. They conform to energies introduced to them, so long as they align with your path." He touched the first one. "He created this one for banishment." He then moved to the next one. "But it appears someone else installed fire here, yes?" I nodded, recalling the efreet. When his finger came to a rest on the third rune, green light flashed. "There."

He returned the sword to me, his magic lingering in the rune. A rune that appeared to carry sharper angles than it had just a moment before.

"You only need concentrate into the rune, and the bits of me that still move in your blood will carry you home. You may even find additional uses for it," he added mysteriously. "Please wish your spirited wife well for me."

"I will."

He lowered his twinkling eyes to the backpack. "It's ready to be opened."

I unzipped the pack, removed the Kleftians' box from the pillowcase, and set it on the ground between us. As I knelt before it, light shone along the seam between box and lid making the glyphs glisten.

Above me, Hermes took Persephone's arm, gently, reverentially.

"Go on," he told me, eager to deliver the goddess back to her mother on Olympus.

I placed my thumbs under the lid and lifted, something that many had attempted over the centuries, but none had accomplished.

I expected resistance so was surprised when the magic broke with a small but satisfying snap.

In the wool-lined interior, there rested a glowing green tablet—or rather a fragment of one. The Tablet of Hermes. Writing was etched in the stone: the universal knowledge he'd stolen from his aunts and uncles. I angled my head, but the tablet was already fading, crumbling to rubble, and then to dust. The wind lifted it from the box, whipping it past where the deities and beings had been gathered.

Hermes and Persephone were gone, along with the seven others. All that remained were their objects, fallen to the ground, stripped of their old worship. And Alec. He stood in Hermes's spot, peering around the ruined scene in confusion. His eyes took in his open pack and then the open box, understanding sharpening his gaze.

As I straightened, his dark eyes met mine and his face filled with relief. We embraced, sharing that relief.

He was alright. He was himself. He was free.

When at last we separated, I caught an aching in his expression, no doubt reflected in my own. This was going to be the hardest goodbye of all. To delay it, I lifted his backpack from the ground and opened the small pocket.

"Hermes said he put your sketchpad back," I explained. "He wants us to look through it together."

I pulled out the familiar pad and handed it to him. I looked on as he flipped past notes and designs old and new, including versions of the siphon sigil Hermes had drawn for Persephone.

At last, he arrived at a full page of neat writing. It was addressed to us. Alec read it aloud:

"'Dear Everson and Alec, It has occurred to me that while I will be reuniting with my father, and he, his son, I have denied you the same. How cruel that I brought you together only for you to remain apart. I haven't the power to change that—it goes with me to Olympus. But I believe I have a solution. On the fifteenth day of each May, a festival known as the Hermaea is held in my honor. The worship should be enough, Everson, to carry you here and back on this day.'" I glanced at the third rune on my sword—what I would henceforth call the Hermes rune. "'I'm sorry I cannot give you more,'" Alec continued to read, "'especially after you both have given so much to me. Ever in your debt, Hermes.'"

Alec lowered the sketchpad. "Every May fifteenth," he repeated.

"How does seven a.m. at Dewitt Clinton Park sound?" I asked. "That way we can get in a full day."

Alec nodded, then chuckled in disbelief. "Sounds too good to be true. But I have a question. In your academic opinion does this make Hermes a cultural hero, or is he still an amoral trickster?"

He was revisiting our first debate, but though he tried, he couldn't keep a serious face.

I laughed loudly. "It makes him very confusing. I think we can both agree on that."

Alec smiled in accession and looked over the beings' fallen objects. "Do we need to do anything with these?"

"They're clean now. In fact, they're collectibles. Here."

Together, we gathered them up and placed them in his backpack.

When we finished, our eyes fell to the empty metal box. The way it rested atop the debris reminded me of how I'd discovered it in the landfill weeks earlier. The main difference being that nothing powered the box now. Alec loaded it into his pack last. Though he didn't say it, I suspected he would return it to the home Hermes had compelled him to steal it from months earlier. He'd carried the burden long enough.

He straightened, peering toward a growing chorus of sirens in the distance. "Guess I should get going."

"Let me walk with you," I said, helping him don his loaded pack.

"That's all right. You're limping, and I've got my vagueness rune." He slapped the thigh where it was tattooed.

My urge to insist was strong, but the Street Keepers were no longer a threat, and I seemed to have reached a ceasefire with their Avenging Angel. Plus, this was part of letting go, allowing Alec to become his own man in this shadow reality. Thanks to Hermes, he wouldn't have to navigate it entirely on his own now.

"All right, buddy." I pulled him into a final, fierce hug. The goodbye hug. "I'll see you in May."

He snuffled once against my chest, then gathered himself. I clapped his shoulder and stood back.

"Sure you're going to be all right here?"

He wiped his eyes and nodded resolutely. "It's home."

"Hey... I love you."

"Love you too, Dad. Say goodbye to everyone for me. And tell them thanks."

"I will. Remember what you learned and keep practicing. We'll pick up where we left off."

I was having a hell of a time keeping it together, but I had a family to return to. So did Alec. He hadn't seen his mother in days.

With a final nod, I raised the blade between us and focused on the third rune. Green light glimmered around the angular design. I felt the Hermes particles gathering inside me, charging up. Before I was ready, a flash swallowed me, and I caught a final image of Alec as a shadowy silhouette, waving goodbye.

For now.

53

By the time I arrived back at Rizo's Storage, the space Hermes had enchanted into a grand suite was a cement unit once more. Where the library had been was simply part of the back wall now. No bookshelves or walnut reading table. Just Bree-yark kneeling in front of the cauldron, smoking puddles of solvent around him as he dutifully stirred the scepter.

I cleared my throat. "You can stop anytime."

He turned with a start and wiped the condensation from his goggles. "Everson!" he exclaimed.

He leapt up, stripped off the glove, and play-boxed me in the stomach a few times before throwing his arms around my waist. I hugged him back, the other hero in our Greek drama. He'd broken down Typhon's influence over Persephone when we'd needed it the most. When *I* had needed it the most.

I filled him in as we loaded duffel bags and containers into his Hummer and drove back to my West Village apartment. His eyes glowed with amazement at the unfolding saga, though I also picked up hints of envy that he hadn't been there to duke it out with the Iron Guard himself.

"Alec wanted me to tell you goodbye and to thank you," I finished.

"Yeah, too bad I couldn't see the pipsqueak off myself. How are you doing with that?"

My chest hitched when I sighed. "Better than I thought I would. Your pep talk in Athens helped. And being able to visit him each year is about the best parting gift Hermes could have given us."

I'd already called home, of course, and Bree-yark and I arrived in the apartment to a celebration in waiting. Following a hot shower and a much needed change of clothes, I sat down to a huge spread of comfort foods that Mae had spent the morning preparing. She'd never had any doubt I would come back.

Bree-yark, Ricki, Tony, and I wasted no time digging in. For her part, Tabitha found something to complain about with every dish, but I noticed she had no trouble putting away sizable portions of each.

After we'd eaten and I'd retold the epic saga of our triumph over Typhon, Tony put on his favorite funk mix. I may or may not have danced on one leg to "Jungle Boogie." I only wished Alec could have been there, too.

As the music wound down, Ricki announced that it was time for the guest of honor to hit the sack. She was right. For three days, I'd been running on little but coffee and invigoration potions. My exhaustion was verging on delirium. After a round of hugs, and an extended kiss with my wife, I fell headlong into sleep.

I awoke to a sunlight-flooded room, feeling as though I'd slept a solid twenty-four. A glance at the bedside clock showed me I'd come close. There was a note from Ricki saying she and Tony had gone with Mae to do some last-minute shopping for the baby.

"There he is," Tabitha muttered after I'd freshened up and emerged into the living room. "The conjurer of sadistic angels."

"At your service," I said, flapping my hands like wings.

"It's *not* funny."

"No," I agreed. "But the memory of you bolting around the apartment will *never* fail to cheer me up."

"Then you'll be overjoyed to know I pulled a groin."

"Well, maybe if you'd warmed up properly..."

Though we were back to our old dance, Tabitha's role in the saga had proven unexpectedly pivotal. If the Avenging Angel had never terrorized her, I may never have made the connection back to my bloodline. And I would have seized Persephone's scepter instead of the whip, dooming us all.

I almost shared that before deciding against it. We were on speaking terms again, and it wouldn't help for her to associate me with a violent angelic being any more than she already did.

"Hey, how about some goat's milk?" I offered.

"Oh, I suppose, darling. If you can heat it evenly this time. The cold pockets hurt my teeth."

As I warmed up her milk in the kitchen, I thought more about the implications of the angelic connection. The whip I'd wielded had burned up, but the first one I'd procured from Red Beard remained in my basement lab, along with what was left of the energy I'd extracted. My concern harkened back to something Hermes said about not wanting to destroy Persephone's shadow scepter in the actual present:

"Her scepter has yet to cross the boundary from there to here, and it's better we keep it that way. Hers is a powerful object, and all manner of distortions could result, none of them healthy to your reality."

A part of me feared the same was true of the whip.

I'd left a message with Claudius the day before, explaining what the whip was and asking for the Order's counsel on how to handle it. I was making a mental note to call him again when a knock sounded at the front door.

I set Tabitha's bowl of steaming milk beside the divan, and I hustled to answer it. "You're going to make me climb *all* the way down there?" she asked, offended.

A look through the peephole had me scrambling to open the locks. A casual observer wouldn't have known it, but the older woman in slacks and a sky-blue blouse was one of the most powerful magic-users in existence.

"Arianna!" I exclaimed.

She smiled. "Hello, Everson. May I come in?"

"Of course, of course." I showed her into the living room and motioned for her to take the couch. "Can I get you anything?"

"No, I'm fine," she said as she lowered herself, moving her long, white braid to her other shoulder. "First, congratulations on your success with the Greek crisis. You conducted your magic very well." She meant it in the literal sense that I had acted as a *conductor* for my magic rather than micromanaging it.

"It's still a work in progress, but thanks."

"But you've discovered the most important component."

I nodded, settling into my reading chair. "Faith. I just have to get in the practice of, you know, practicing it. I still feel obligated to do the busy work first, and I'm always questioning whether I've done enough."

"The work remains important, but finding the balance will come. That's part of the reason I wanted to talk to you. How do you feel about Gretchen?"

Caught off guard, I stammered, hesitant to throw my mentor under the bus. She had taught me some important lessons, such as learning not to depend on my luck quotient (black luck, anyone?), how to fashion interplanar cubbyholes, tricks for strengthening my neutralizing potions, as well as how to cook several new ones, including one of my faves, the "many-many." But she wasn't exactly consistent, reliable, or, let's face it, sane. And that was saying nothing of her grotesque noises and odors.

"Well, you know..." I said at last.

Arianna nodded. "It's all right. We've been short of advanced magic-users, and she was the best fit for you at the time. But we feel she's taught you all she can. We're arranging another mentor for you."

From her milk bowl, Tabitha muttered, "Thank God."

"You're coming to understand the true relationship between practitioner and magic," Arianna continued. "You're starting to live it. As such, you're ready to take more advanced steps in your development."

I nodded, relieved I would no longer have to suffer Gretchen's abuses, but also a little nervous for what was to come.

"I'll let you know when you're to begin," she said. "Now, about the whip."

"You got my message?" I asked in surprise.

"Yes, and I've been discussing it with the other members of the Order."

"I thought everyone was tied up with the tears... Wait, you're not actually here, are you?" So potent was her magic, I hadn't realized I was engaging with a projection this whole time.

"I would have come myself, but this is too important to wait."

I scooted to the edge of my chair as she folded her projected hands.

"Your encounter with the Avenging Angel alters what we thought we knew about them. They existed so long ago, and for so fleeting a time, they're hazy to us, their energy little more than background static. We accepted that they were no more, but the fact one exists in a probable reality changes things."

When she paused, I swallowed, not sure where this was going.

"You've always been a little different, Everson. Even from the Refuge we saw this. That you were able to channel angelic energy yesterday, that your magic *guided* you to channel this energy, may explain why."

"Okay," I said, not knowing how else to respond. But I recalled what Loukia had told me in Athens: *I think you are special to the Order in another way... Not from what you do, maybe, but from what you are.*

"You have angelic blood," Arianna finished.

"Because of their kinship to the First Saints, right?"

She shook her head. "It seems the Avenging Angels were here longer than previously believed. One began his own tree. Not nearly as robust as Saint Michael's—most branches would have died off. But not all."

"And somewhere along the line a descendant of Saint Michael's and this Avenging Angel's... cross pollinated?"

"We believe so, yes. We're still looking into it."

Concern tightened my brow. "Would that change anything?"

"Regarding your membership in the Order? No, Everson, not at all."

That was a relief, but another anxiety grew in its place. "What about the whip in my basement? The energy I extracted?"

She showed a hand. "It will be safe there for now. The reason I'm sharing this is because soon we may ask you to assume work of a different nature, and I didn't want it to come out of the blue. This new information regarding the angels presents many questions, but possibly some new opportunities as well."

"Anything you can elaborate on?"

"Again, we have more to look into."

I couldn't help myself. "Why was the angel hunting magic-users in the shadow realm?"

In the moment I'd chosen the whip, my magic had under-scored the angel-saint connection. But only because I had angel blood from an actual angelic line. Something the other magic-users must have lacked.

Though Arianna's face didn't show it, I sensed that the question unsettled her. "That can wait until later," she said simply, then smiled as she stood. "Your personal life is about to become very busy. We'll talk again soon."

She disappeared before I could follow up, or even say goodbye, but my phone was buzzing. "Hello?" I answered distractedly.

"Hi, Everson, it's Mae—"

"Is everything all right?" I blurted, remembering she was with Ricki.

"Everything's fine, hon. Your wife's water just broke, and we're on our way to General..."

She was still talking, but I didn't hear most of it. I was already slinging Ricki's hospital bag over a shoulder and running for the door.

54

Abigail Eve Croft Vega entered our world a little after nine o'clock on a warm July night, tipping the scales at a healthy seven pounds, two ounces.

Her first and middle names were in honor of Ricki's and my mothers. She had a pinched red face, a tuft of midnight hair, a mewling cry, and she was the most beautiful thing I'd ever seen. Indeed, the love I felt as Ricki lifted her tiny, wrapped body into my arms that first time nearly knocked me over.

The sense of responsibility, too.

Ricki often said that a girl's relationship with her father could be the most special one in her life. She talked fondly of her own father, how he'd always been there for her and her brothers, from their years in the Ferguson Towers housing project to their eventual home in the Bronx, where he died mediating a gang dispute. He was the reason she'd gone into law enforcement and public safety.

As I watched Abigail sleep that night, I resolved to be there for her, too, and to never make a promise I couldn't keep. I'd managed to keep my first one: clearing the board for her arrival. It was a matter of lining up the rest and sticking each one, starting with whatever came of the Avenging Angel business.

Did I mention how perfect she was?

I kissed her wrinkled forehead and nuzzled her cheek. As I did, that immense sense of responsibility morphed into a new power, one I would carry with me into every case, every negotiation, and every battle, because failure would mean not keeping my most important promise: making my daughter's world as bright as possible.

"We've got this, Abi," I whispered.

THE END

But the series continues. Join Prof Croft in his next spell-crackling adventure, Angel Doom!

ANGEL DOOM

PROF CROFT BOOK 12

Is this the end?

If there's one enduring tragedy in my line of work, it's amateur casters falling prey to their own conjurings.

But when I catch a fire druid lurking around the latest victim, the deaths don't seem so innocent. Add a kidnapping case involving Manhattan's most hallowed cathedral, and I'm seeing dangerous parallels to my first major outing as a wizard. The one that landed me face-to-face with a demon lord.

I'm a stronger, more practiced magic-user now, bolstered by powerful allies. But I also have a lot to lose—not least my family. And the threat is more imminent than I ever imagined. Indeed, it's already here.

As demonic forces besiege the city, my spells and studies may not be enough. Do I dare turn to my angelic blood, even if it risks conjuring a violent, vengeful being intent on annihilating magic-users?

When the alternative is Hell on Earth, do I have a choice?

AUTHOR'S NOTES

And so ends the godly wars: with victory, farewells, and a precious new introduction.

Going forward, we'll be exploring Everson's angelic makeup and what it means for the magic-using community. That is, of course, when he isn't changing diapers, on bath duty, or cleaning pureed blueberries from his hair.

I also see some more teaming up, this time with fellow wizards Loukia, whom we met in Athens, and James Wesson of *Croft & Wesson* infamy. And we never did find out how Everson's shadow died in Venice, did we? Hmm...

For location research, I leaned heavily on Google maps and YouTube vids, taking several lovely trips to Greece and Sicily (I have no idea what desk-bound writers did before Google Street View). I also learned that Lake Pergusa turns red each year, which I couldn't *not* include. Now whether it's an actual portal to Hades, I can't say and have little interest in finding out.

Thank you to the team at Damonza.com for designing yet another in a long line of excellent covers.

Kudos to my beta and advanced readers, including Beverly Collie, Mark Denman, Bob Singer, Linda Ash, Erin Halbmaier, Fiona Harford, and Larissa, who all provided valuable feedback during the writing process. And thanks to Sharlene Magnarella and Donna Rich for taking on the painstaking task of final proofing. Naturally, any errors that remain are this author's alone.

I also want to commend James Patrick Cronin, who brings all the books to life through his gifted narration on the audio editions. Those can be found at Audible.com. We also feature a catalogue of our shorter works on YouTube.

Writing on Prof Croft 11 began in Asheville, North Carolina and finished in Gainesville, Florida. No international locations for this installment, but that will change with Prof Croft 12, when I'm headed to... (cue cliffhanger). Thanks to the Bagel Bakery and Coffee Culture in Gainesville, where I did much of my remote work and rediscovered my love for Americanos.

The Croftverse wouldn't be possible without the Strange Brigade, my dedicated fan group whose enthusiasm serves as motivation jet fuel, book after book. Thanks, guys.

And thank you, dear reader, for taking another ride with the Prof.

Till the next one...

Best wishes,
Brad Magnarella

P.S. Be sure to check out my website to learn more about the Croftverse, download a pair of free prequels, and find out what's coming! That's all at bradmagnarella.com

CROFTVERSE CATALOGUE

PROF CROFT PREQUELS

Book of Souls

Siren Call

MAIN SERIES

Demon Moon

Blood Deal

Purge City

Death Mage

Black Luck

Power Game

Druid Bond

Night Rune

Shadow Duel

Shadow Deep

Godly Wars

Angel Doom

SPIN-OFFS

Croft & Tabby

Croft & Wesson

BLUE WOLF

Blue Curse

Blue Shadow

Blue Howl

Blue Venom

Blue Blood

Blue Storm

SPIN-OFF

Legion Files

For the entire chronology go to

bradmagnarella.com/chronology

ABOUT THE AUTHOR

Brad Magnarella writes urban fantasy for the same reason most read it...

To explore worlds where magic crackles from fingertips, vampires and shifters walk city streets, cats talk (some excessively), and good prevails against all odds. It's shamelessly fun.

His two main series, Prof Croft and Blue Wolf, make up the growing Croftverse, with over a quarter-million books sold to date and an Independent Audiobook Award nomination.

Hopelessly nomadic, Brad can be found in a rented room overseas or hiking America's backcountry.

Or just go to www.bradmagnarella.com

Printed in Great Britain
by Amazon

44968526R00223